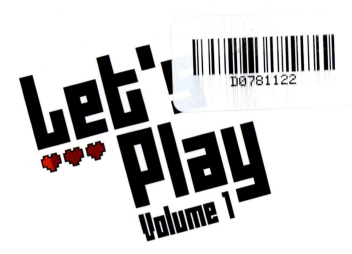

Let's Play
Volume 1

D0781122

Leeanne M. Krecic

Layout assists by **Nicholas Hogge**

"Bowser's Big Day"

Color assists by **Danielle Conti**
Color assists by **MeliZbeauty**

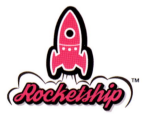

Rocketship Entertainment, LLC

Tom Akel, CEO & Publisher
Rob Feldman, CTO
Jeanmarie McNeely, CFO
Brandon Freeberg, Dir. of Campaign Mgmt.
Jed Keith, Social Media

rocketshipent.com

LET'S PLAY originally published digitally at WEBTOON

LET'S PLAY VOLUME 1
ISBN: 978-1-952126-02-4
First printing. October 2020.

↑ ↑ ↓ ↓ ← → ← →   start   ← → ← → ↓ ↓ ↑ ↑

WHEN
I WAS LITTLE
I FELL IN LOVE
WITH GAMING.

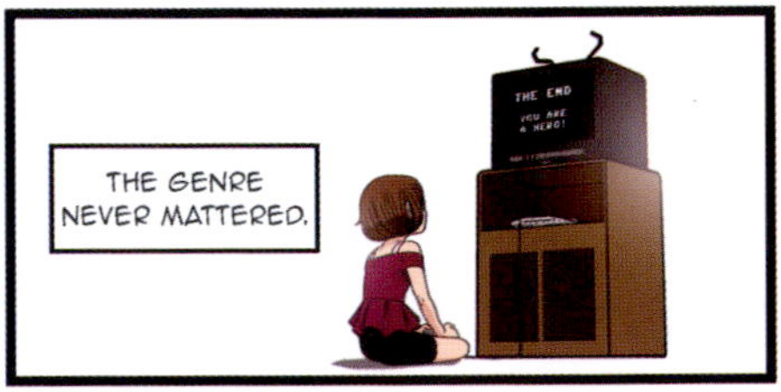
THE END
YOU ARE A HERO!
THE GENRE NEVER MATTERED.

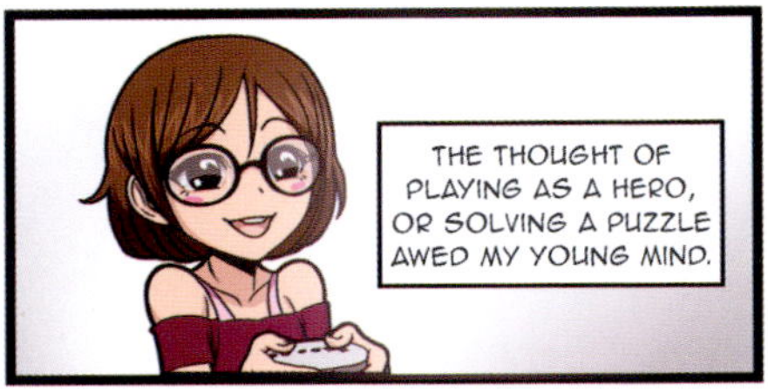
THE THOUGHT OF PLAYING AS A HERO, OR SOLVING A PUZZLE AWED MY YOUNG MIND.

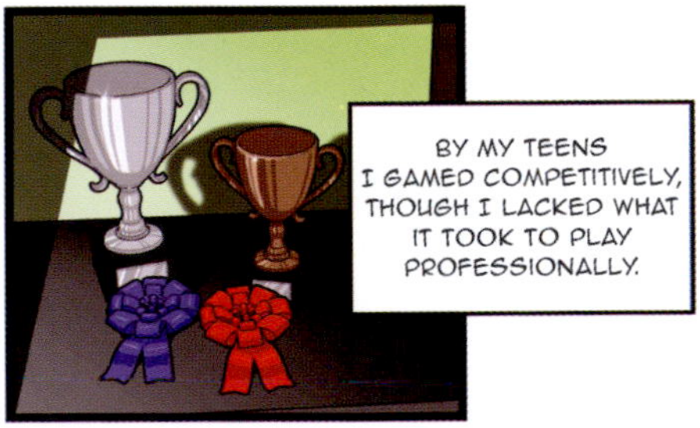
BY MY TEENS I GAMED COMPETITIVELY, THOUGH I LACKED WHAT IT TOOK TO PLAY PROFESSIONALLY.

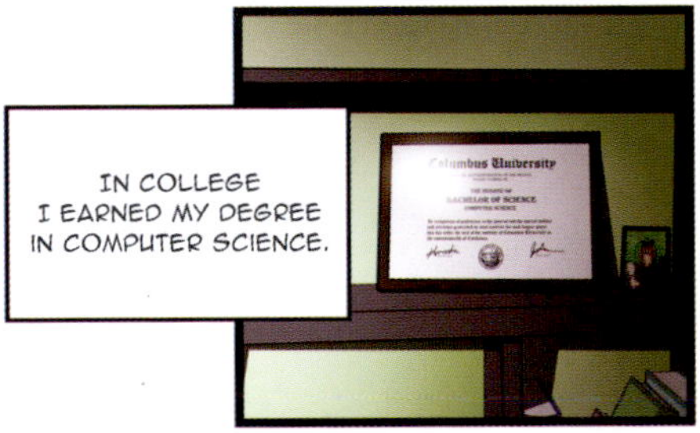
IN COLLEGE I EARNED MY DEGREE IN COMPUTER SCIENCE.
Columbus University
BACHELOR OF SCIENCE

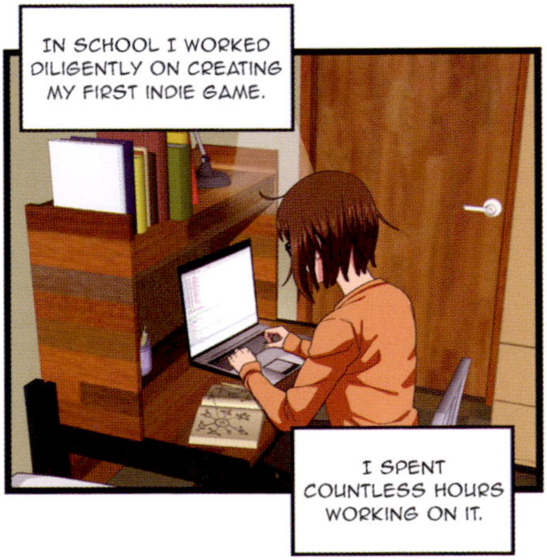
IN SCHOOL I WORKED DILIGENTLY ON CREATING MY FIRST INDIE GAME.
I SPENT COUNTLESS HOURS WORKING ON IT.

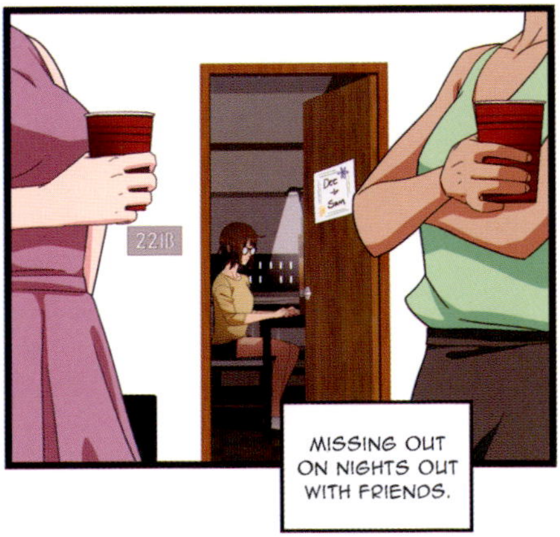
221B
Dee + Sam
MISSING OUT ON NIGHTS OUT WITH FRIENDS.

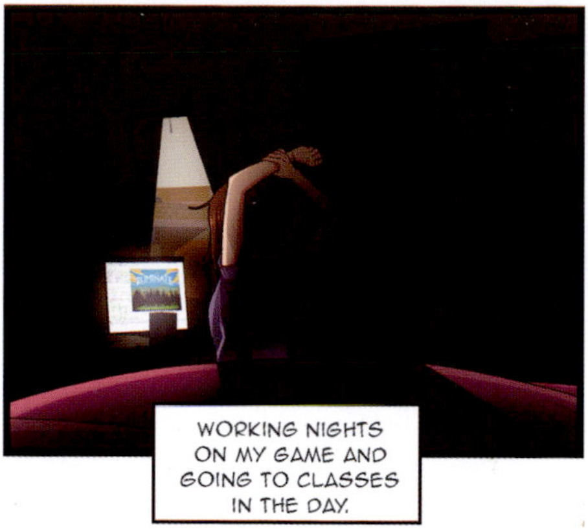
WORKING NIGHTS ON MY GAME AND GOING TO CLASSES IN THE DAY.

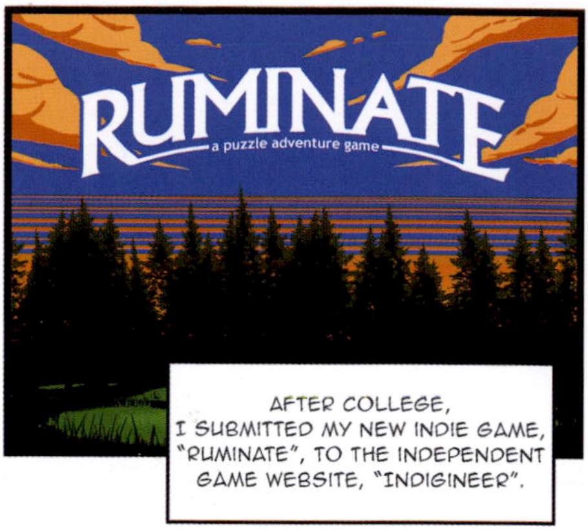
RUMINATE
a puzzle adventure game
AFTER COLLEGE, I SUBMITTED MY NEW INDIE GAME, "RUMINATE", TO THE INDEPENDENT GAME WEBSITE, "INDIGINEER".

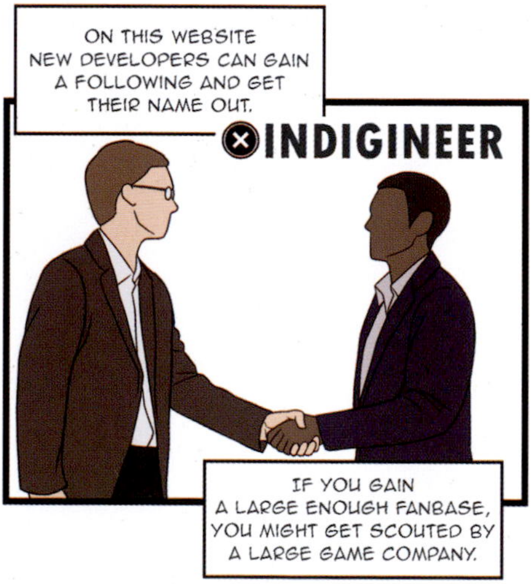
ON THIS WEBSITE NEW DEVELOPERS CAN GAIN A FOLLOWING AND GET THEIR NAME OUT.
INDIGINEER
IF YOU GAIN A LARGE ENOUGH FANBASE, YOU MIGHT GET SCOUTED BY A LARGE GAME COMPANY.

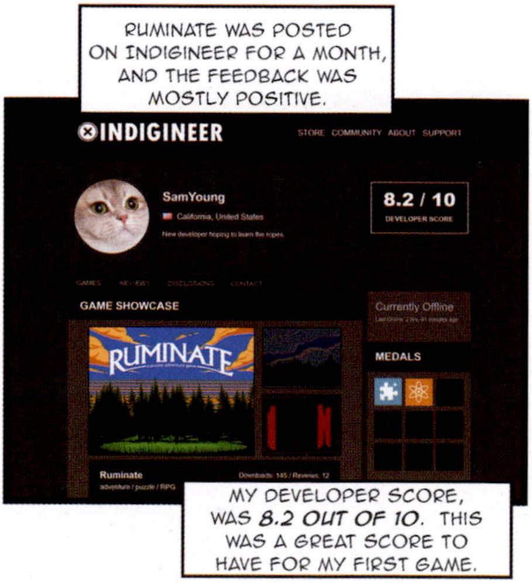
RUMINATE WAS POSTED ON INDIGINEER FOR A MONTH, AND THE FEEDBACK WAS MOSTLY POSITIVE.
INDIGINEER
STORE COMMUNITY ABOUT SUPPORT
SamYoung
California, United States
8.2 / 10
DEVELOPER SCORE
GAME SHOWCASE
Currently Offline
MEDALS
RUMINATE
Ruminate
adventure / puzzle / RPG
Downloads: 145 / Reviews: 12
MY DEVELOPER SCORE, WAS ***8.2 OUT OF 10***. THIS WAS A GREAT SCORE TO HAVE FOR MY FIRST GAME.

BZZT
BZZT

I HAD HOPED THAT BY BEING ON INDIGINEER, A GAME COMPANY MIGHT OFFER ME A JOB IN GAME DEVELOPMENT.

BZZT
BZZT

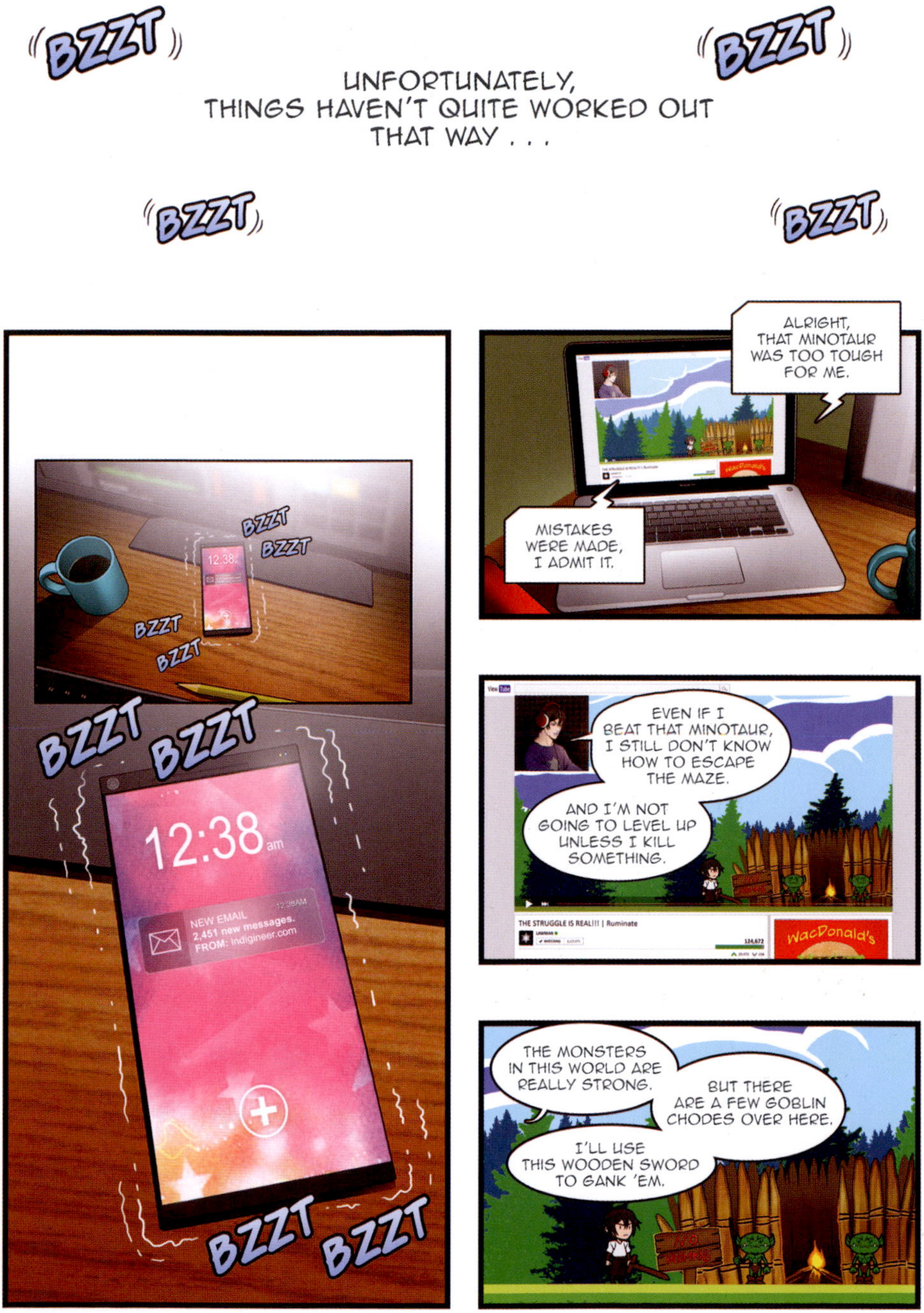
BZZT
BZZT
UNFORTUNATELY, THINGS HAVEN'T QUITE WORKED OUT THAT WAY . . .
BZZT
BZZT
BZZT
BZZT
BZZT
BZZT
BZZT
BZZT
12:38am
NEW EMAIL 12:38AM
2,451 new messages.
FROM: Indigineer.com
BZZT
BZZT
ALRIGHT, THAT MINOTAUR WAS TOO TOUGH FOR ME.
MISTAKES WERE MADE, I ADMIT IT.
ViewTube
EVEN IF I BEAT THAT MINOTAUR, I STILL DON'T KNOW HOW TO ESCAPE THE MAZE.
AND I'M NOT GOING TO LEVEL UP UNLESS I KILL SOMETHING.
THE STRUGGLE IS REAL!!! | Ruminate
124,672
WacDonald's
THE MONSTERS IN THIS WORLD ARE REALLY STRONG.
BUT THERE ARE A FEW GOBLIN CHODES OVER HERE.
I'LL USE THIS WOODEN SWORD TO GANK 'EM.

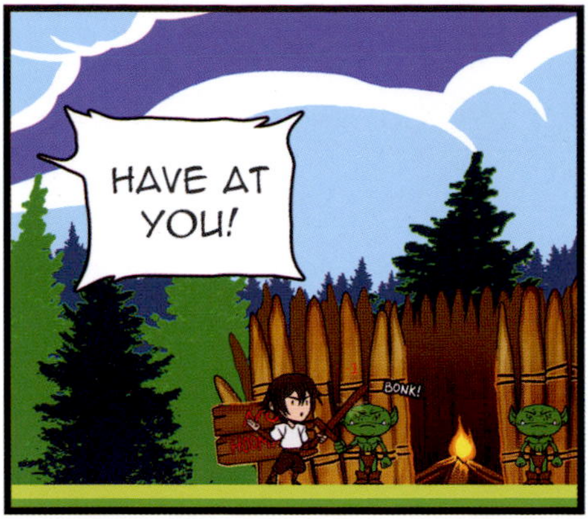
HAVE AT YOU!
BONK!

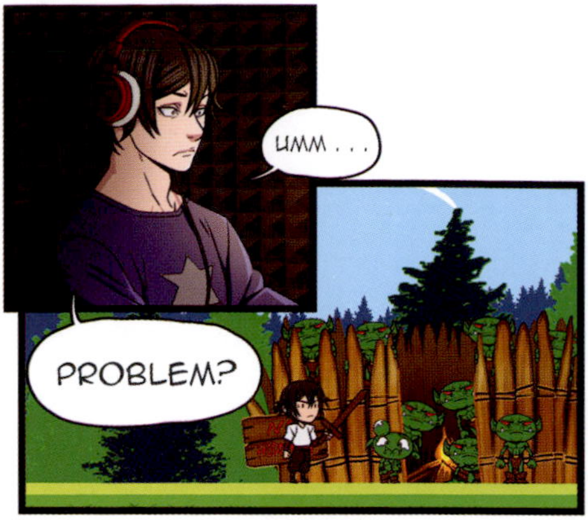
UMM . . .
PROBLEM?

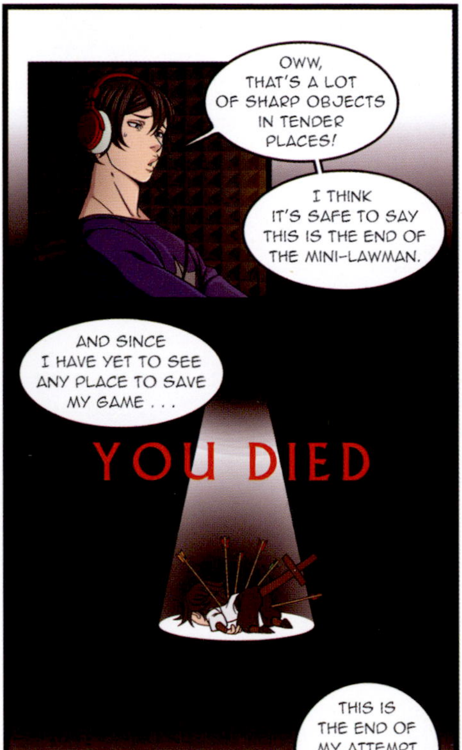
OWW, THAT'S A LOT OF SHARP OBJECTS IN TENDER PLACES!
I THINK IT'S SAFE TO SAY THIS IS THE END OF THE MINI-LAWMAN.
AND SINCE I HAVE YET TO SEE ANY PLACE TO SAVE MY GAME . . .
YOU DIED
THIS IS THE END OF MY ATTEMPT AT PLAYING, "RUMINATE".

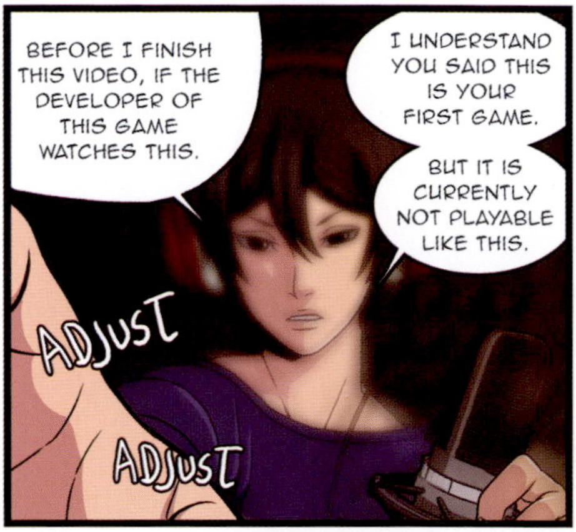
BEFORE I FINISH THIS VIDEO, IF THE DEVELOPER OF THIS GAME WATCHES THIS.
I UNDERSTAND YOU SAID THIS IS YOUR FIRST GAME.
BUT IT IS CURRENTLY NOT PLAYABLE LIKE THIS.
ADJUST
ADJUST

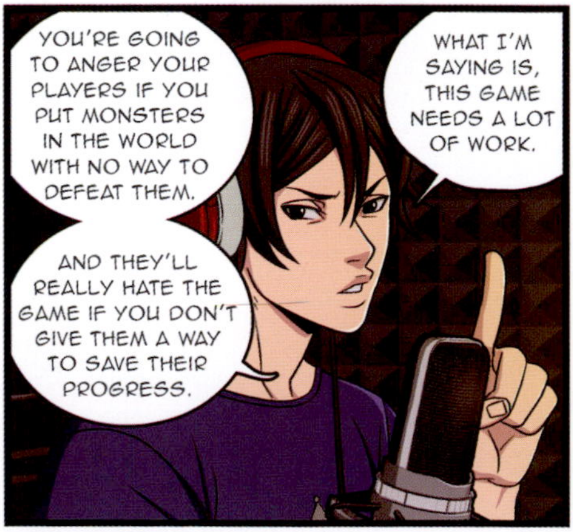
YOU'RE GOING TO ANGER YOUR PLAYERS IF YOU PUT MONSTERS IN THE WORLD WITH NO WAY TO DEFEAT THEM.
WHAT I'M SAYING IS, THIS GAME NEEDS A LOT OF WORK.
AND THEY'LL REALLY HATE THE GAME IF YOU DON'T GIVE THEM A WAY TO SAVE THEIR PROGRESS.

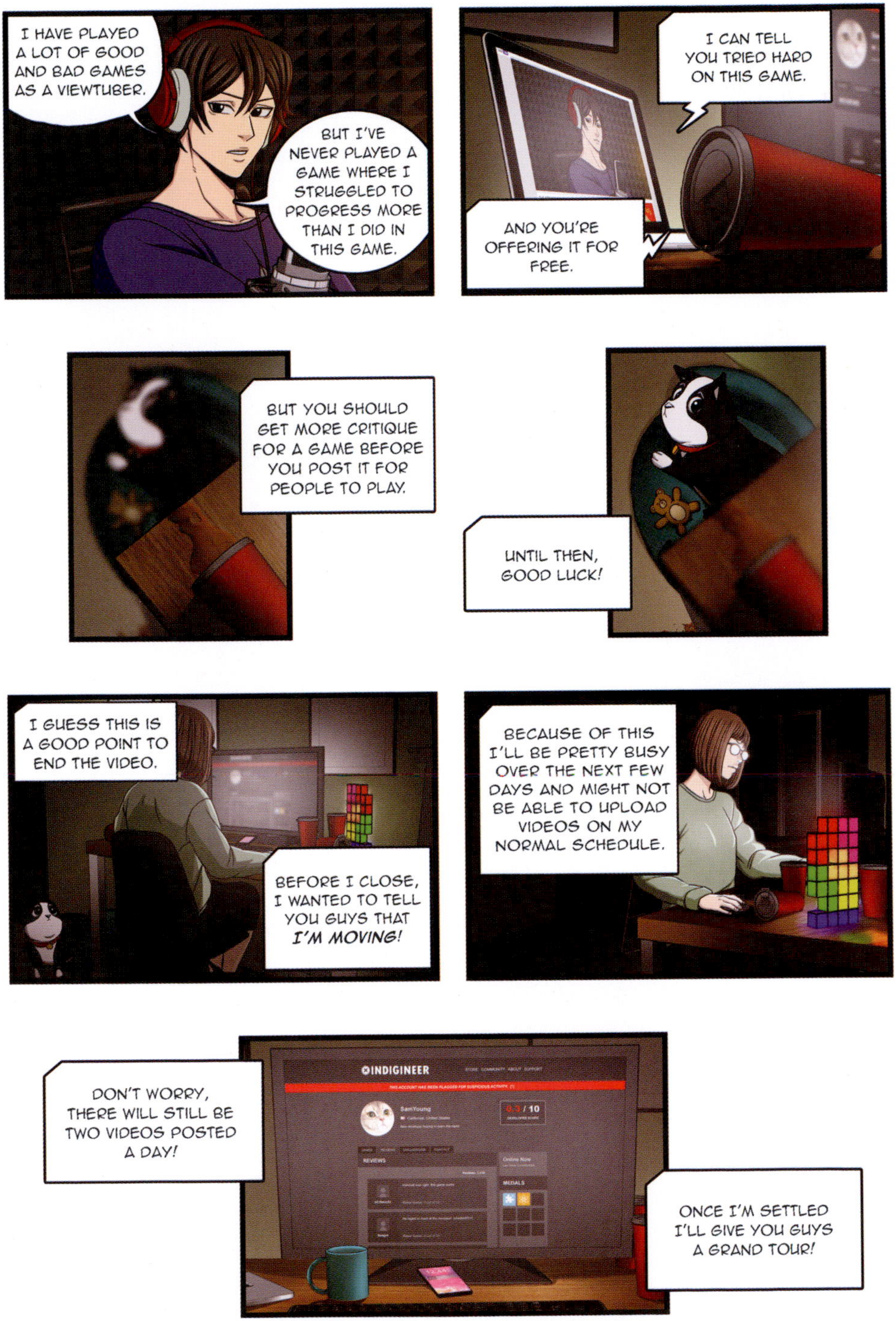
I HAVE PLAYED A LOT OF GOOD AND BAD GAMES AS A VIEWTUBER.
BUT I'VE NEVER PLAYED A GAME WHERE I STRUGGLED TO PROGRESS MORE THAN I DID IN THIS GAME.
I CAN TELL YOU TRIED HARD ON THIS GAME.
AND YOU'RE OFFERING IT FOR FREE.
BUT YOU SHOULD GET MORE CRITIQUE FOR A GAME BEFORE YOU POST IT FOR PEOPLE TO PLAY.
UNTIL THEN, GOOD LUCK!
I GUESS THIS IS A GOOD POINT TO END THE VIDEO.
BEFORE I CLOSE, I WANTED TO TELL YOU GUYS THAT *I'M MOVING!*
BECAUSE OF THIS I'LL BE PRETTY BUSY OVER THE NEXT FEW DAYS AND MIGHT NOT BE ABLE TO UPLOAD VIDEOS ON MY NORMAL SCHEDULE.
DON'T WORRY, THERE WILL STILL BE TWO VIDEOS POSTED A DAY!
INDIGINEER
ONCE I'M SETTLED I'LL GIVE YOU GUYS A GRAND TOUR!

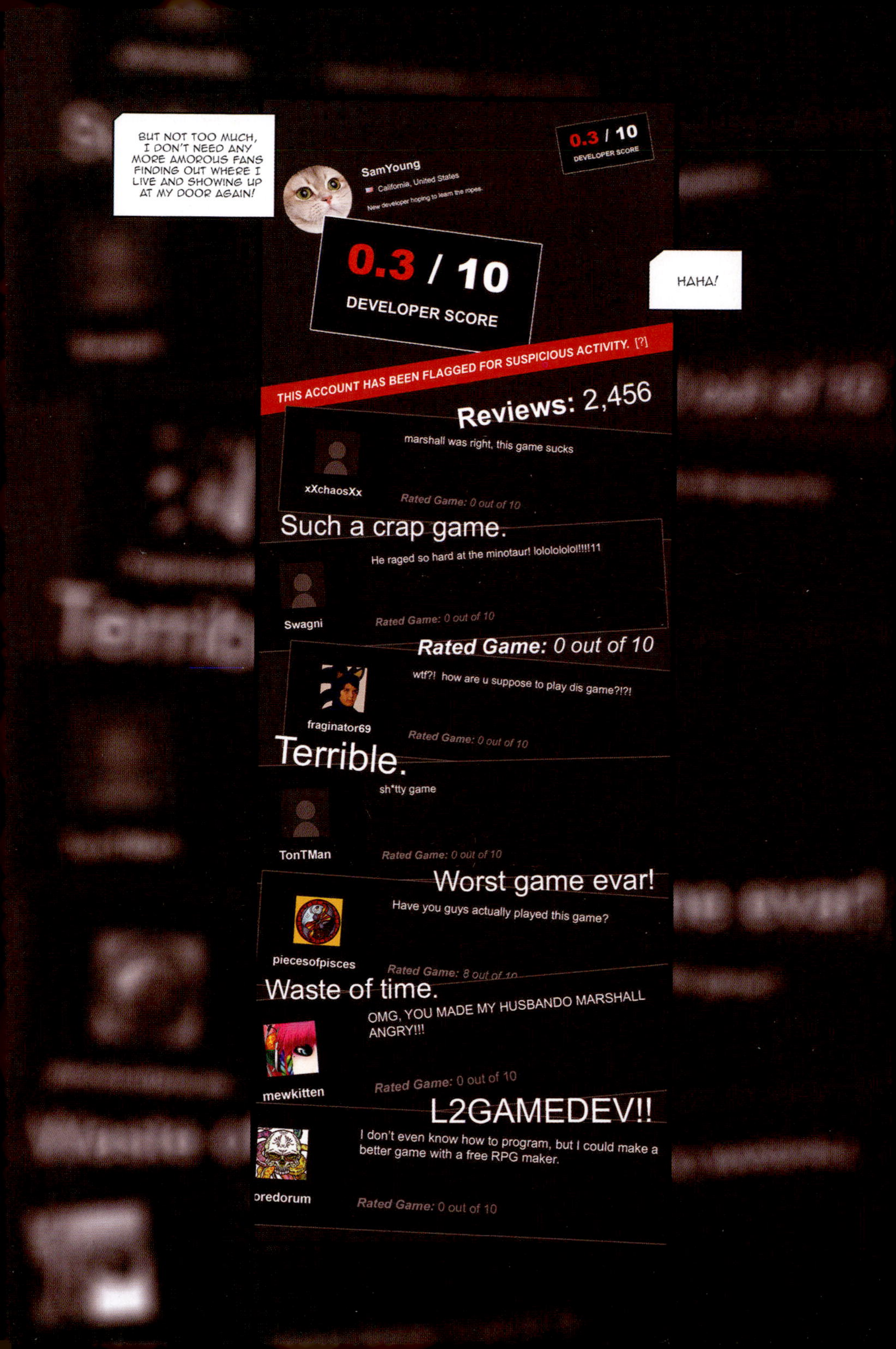
BUT NOT TOO MUCH, I DON'T NEED ANY MORE AMOROUS FANS FINDING OUT WHERE I LIVE AND SHOWING UP AT MY DOOR AGAIN!
SamYoung
California, United States
New developer hoping to learn the ropes.
0.3 / 10
DEVELOPER SCORE
0.3 / 10
DEVELOPER SCORE
HAHA!
THIS ACCOUNT HAS BEEN FLAGGED FOR SUSPICIOUS ACTIVITY. [?]
Reviews: 2,456
marshall was right, this game sucks
xXchaosXx
Rated Game: 0 out of 10
Such a crap game.
He raged so hard at the minotaur! lolololololol!!!!11
Swagni
Rated Game: 0 out of 10
Rated Game: 0 out of 10
wtf?! how are u suppose to play dis game?!?!
fraginator69
Rated Game: 0 out of 10
Terrible.
sh*tty game
TonTMan
Rated Game: 0 out of 10
Worst game evar!
Have you guys actually played this game?
piecesofpisces
Rated Game: 8 out of 10
Waste of time.
OMG, YOU MADE MY HUSBANDO MARSHALL ANGRY!!!
mewkitten
Rated Game: 0 out of 10
L2GAMEDEV!!
I don't even know how to program, but I could make a better game with a free RPG maker.
predorum
Rated Game: 0 out of 10

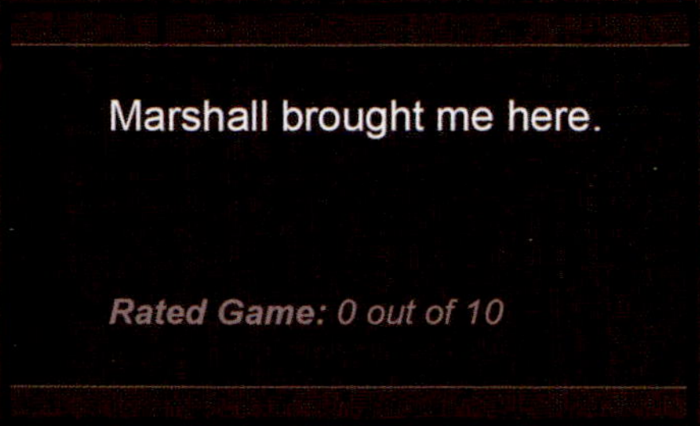
Marshall brought me here.
Rated Game: 0 out of 10

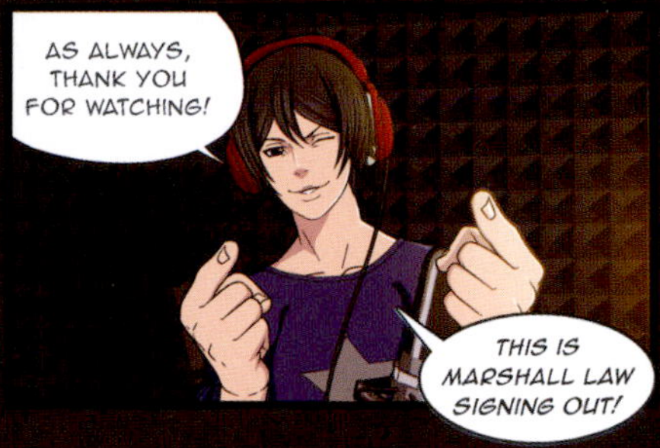
AS ALWAYS, THANK YOU FOR WATCHING!
THIS IS MARSHALL LAW SIGNING OUT!

IT SEEMED AS THOUGH
MY CAREER AS A DEVELOPER
WAS ALREADY OVER BEFORE
IT HAD TRULY STARTED.

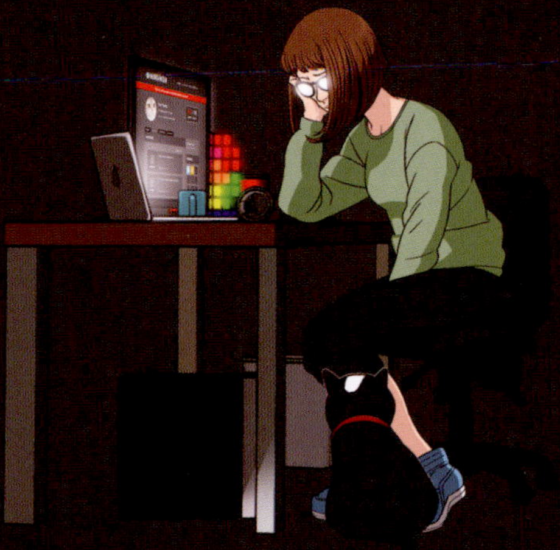

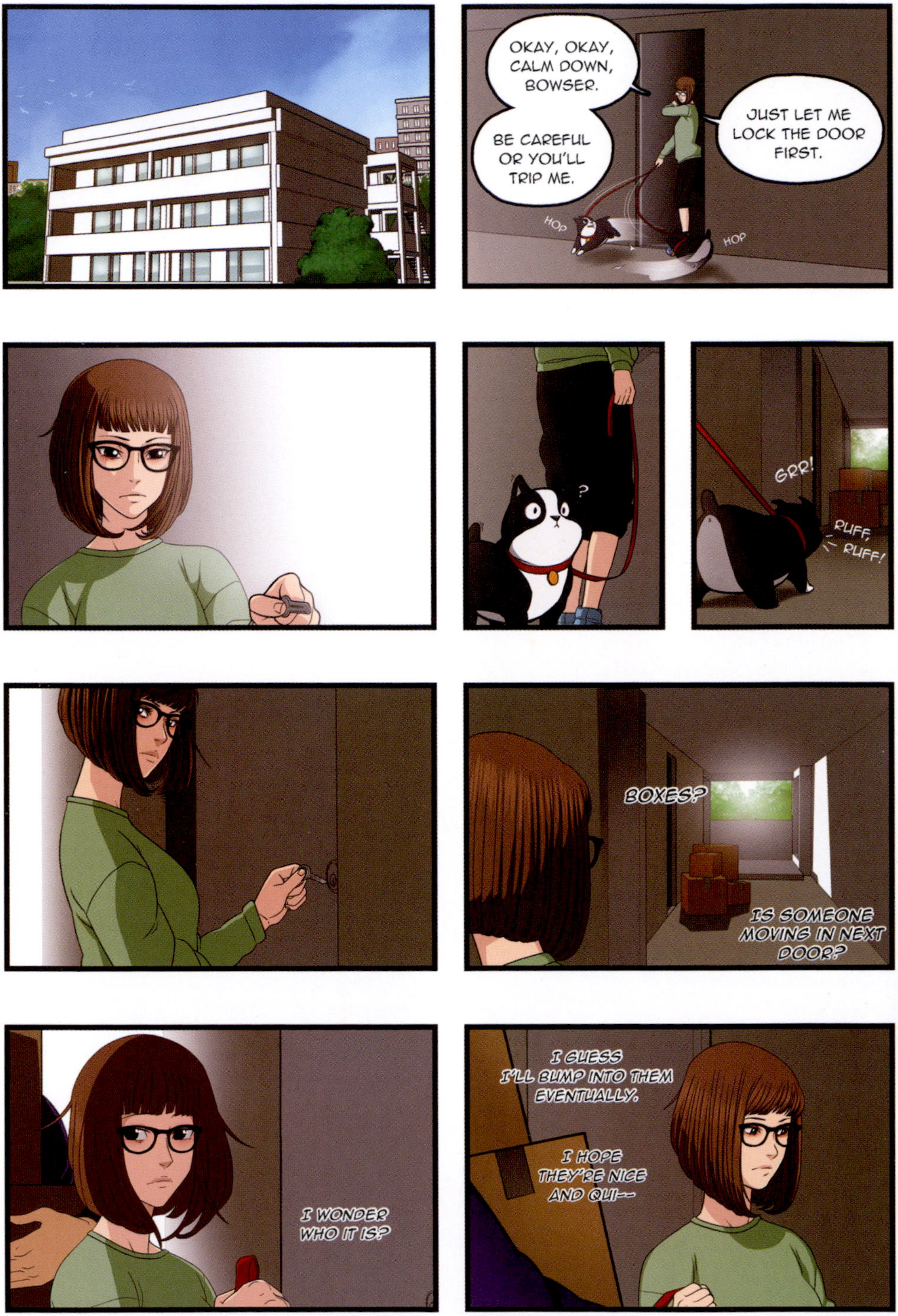
OKAY, OKAY, CALM DOWN, BOWSER.
BE CAREFUL OR YOU'LL TRIP ME.
JUST LET ME LOCK THE DOOR FIRST.
HOP
HOP
?
GRR!
RUFF, RUFF!
BOXES?
IS SOMEONE MOVING IN NEXT DOOR?
I WONDER WHO IT IS?
I GUESS I'LL BUMP INTO THEM EVENTUALLY.
I HOPE THEY'RE NICE AND QUI--

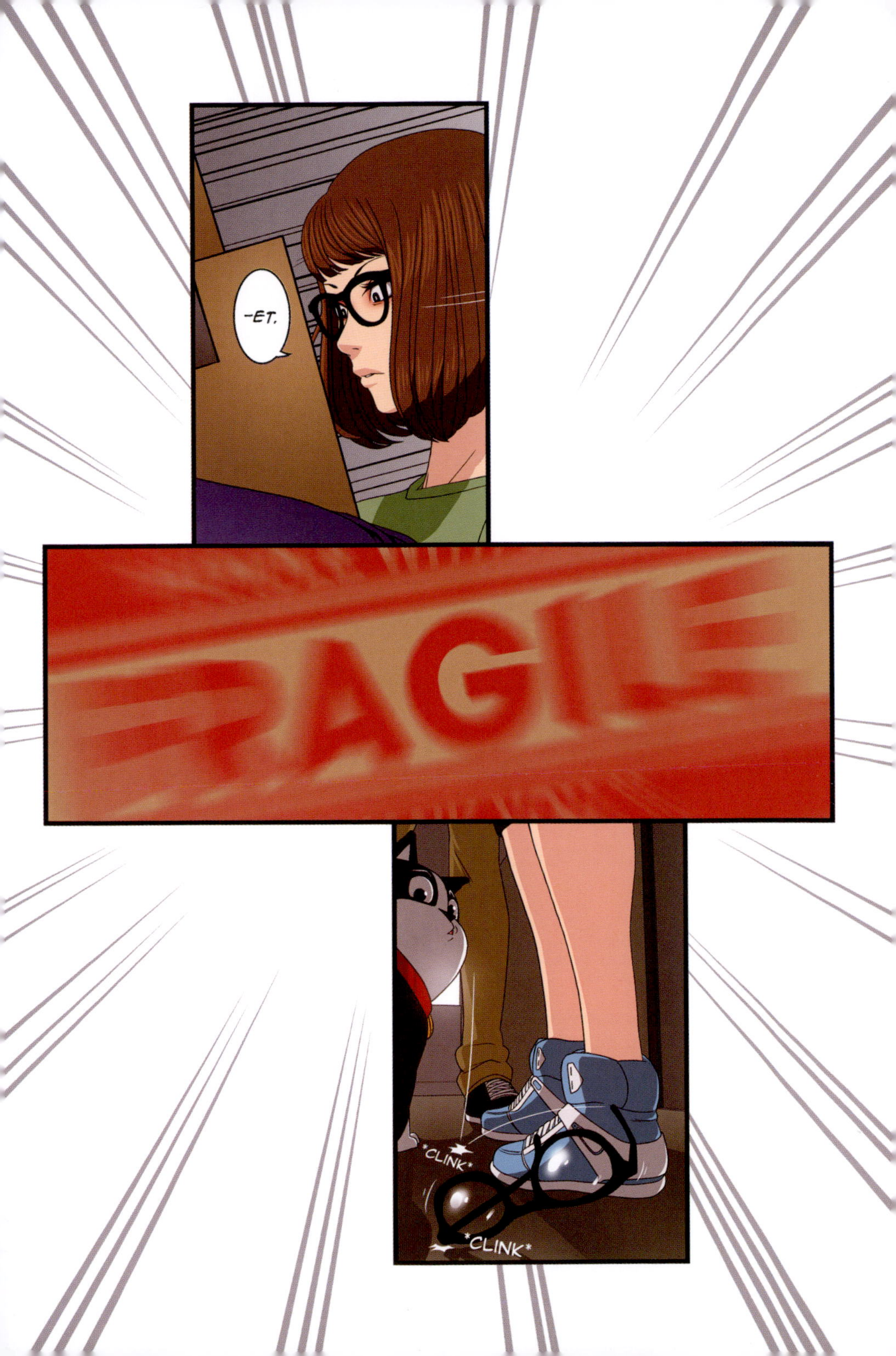
–ET.
CLINK
CLINK

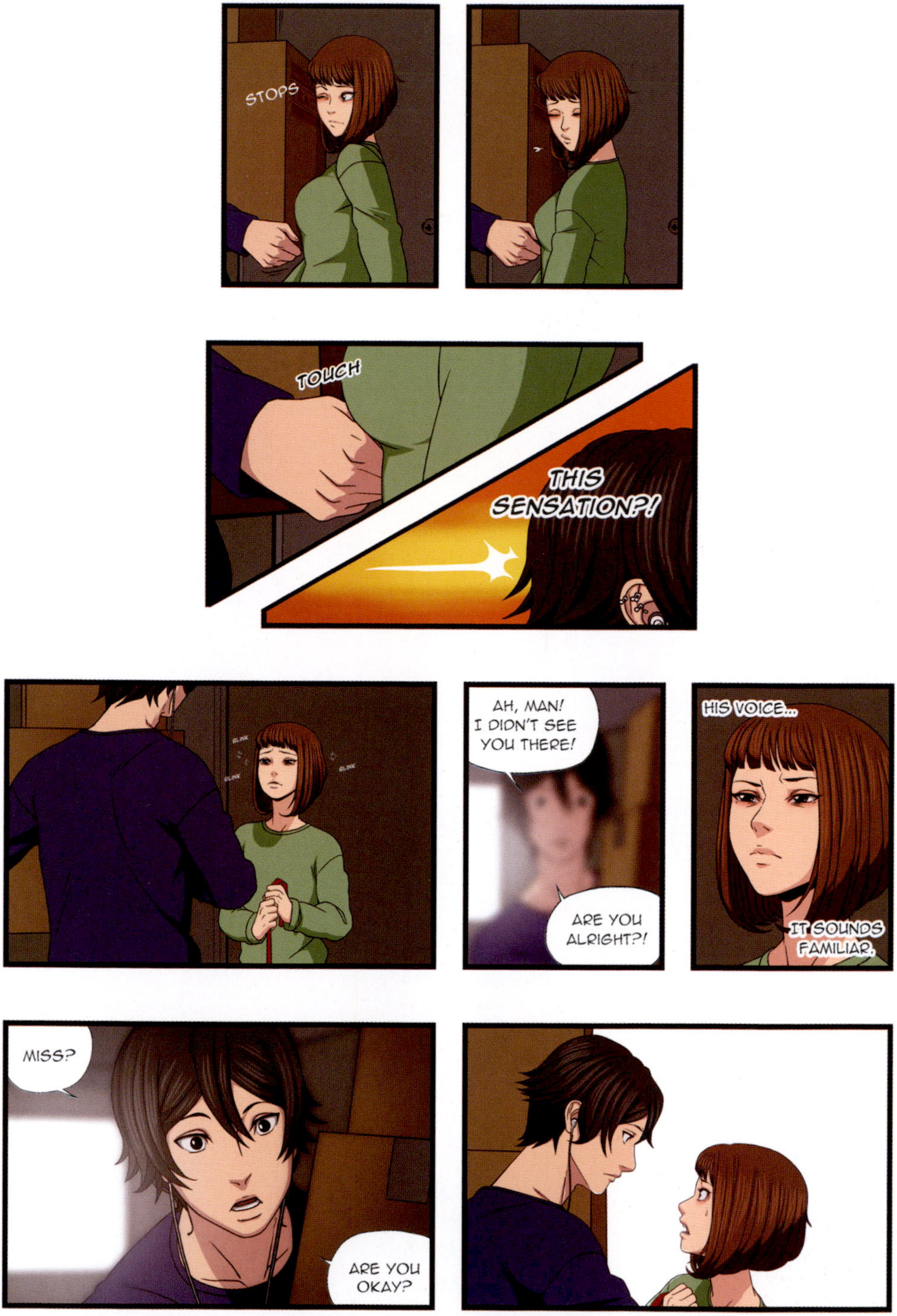
STOPS
TOUCH
THIS SENSATION?!
AH, MAN! I DIDN'T SEE YOU THERE!
ARE YOU ALRIGHT?!
HIS VOICE...
IT SOUNDS FAMILIAR.
MISS?
ARE YOU OKAY?

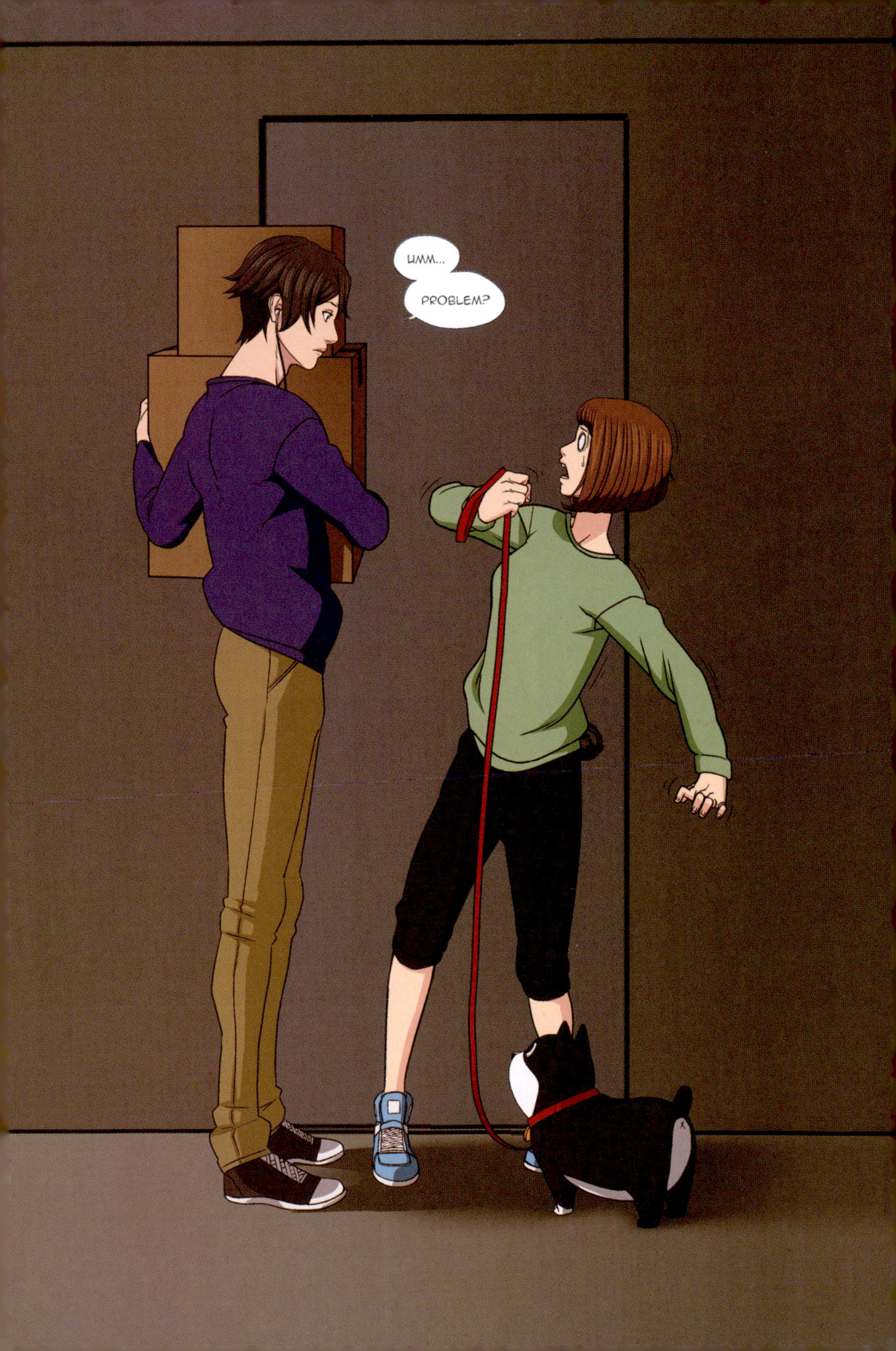
UMM...
PROBLEM?

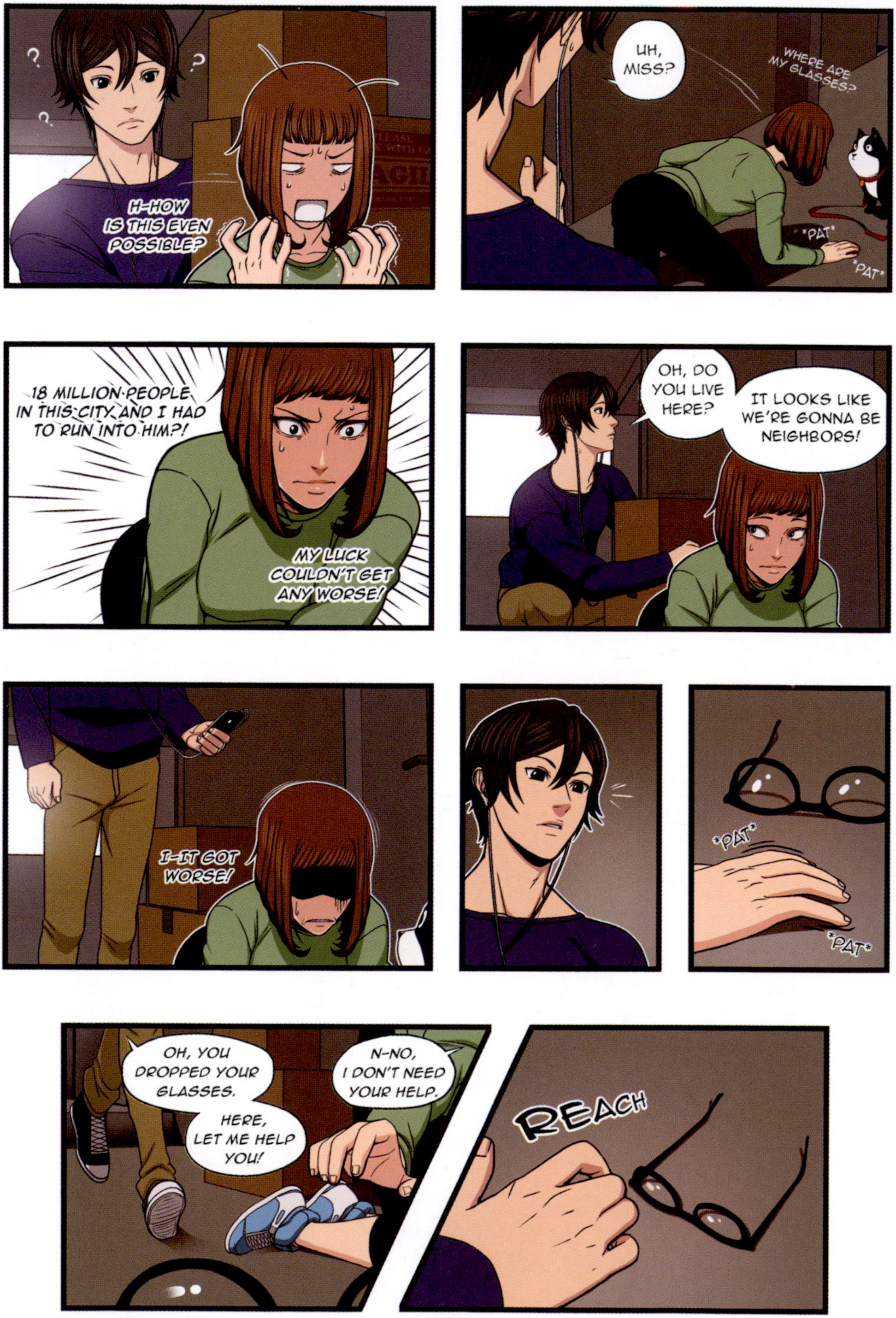

H-HOW IS THIS EVEN POSSIBLE?
UH, MISS?
WHERE ARE MY GLASSES?
PAT
PAT
18 MILLION PEOPLE IN THIS CITY AND I HAD TO RUN INTO HIM?!
MY LUCK COULDN'T GET ANY WORSE!
OH, DO YOU LIVE HERE?
IT LOOKS LIKE WE'RE GONNA BE NEIGHBORS!
I-IT GOT WORSE!
PAT
PAT
OH, YOU DROPPED YOUR GLASSES.
HERE, LET ME HELP YOU!
N-NO, I DON'T NEED YOUR HELP.
REACH

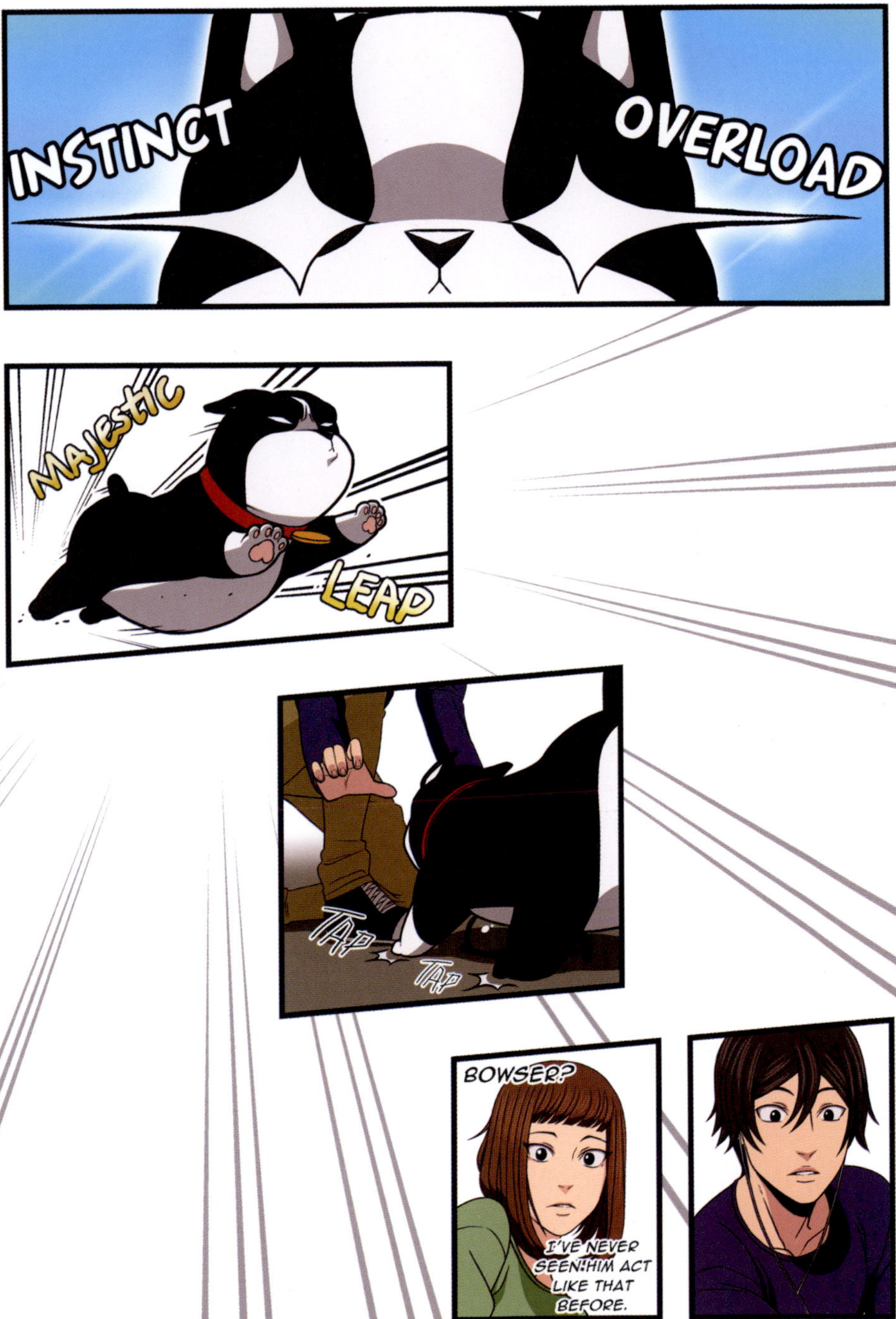
INSTINCT
OVERLOAD
Majestic
LEAP
TAP
TAP
BOWSER?
I'VE NEVER SEEN HIM ACT LIKE THAT BEFORE.

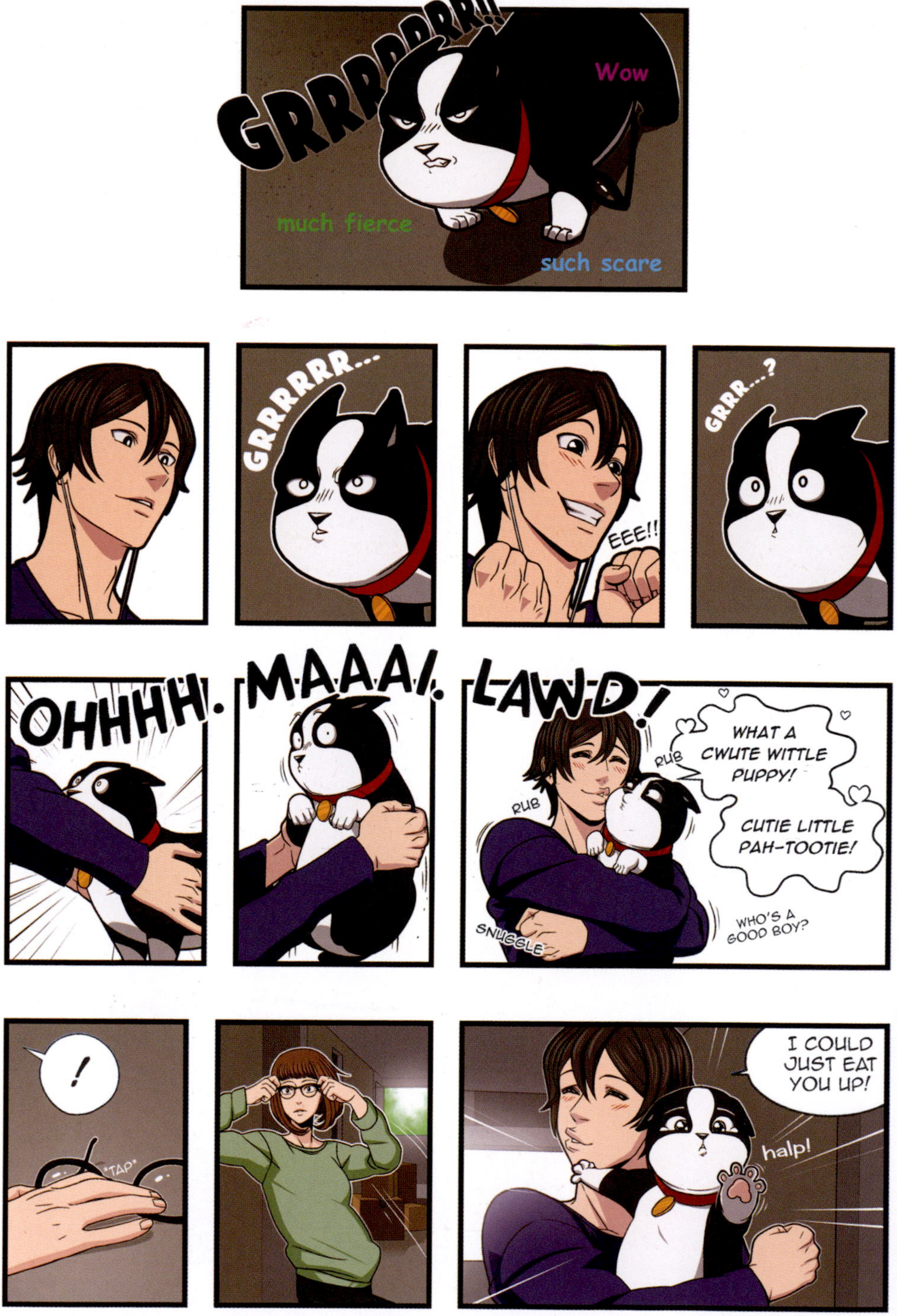
GRRRRRRR!!
Wow
much fierce
such scare
GRRRRRR...
EEE!!
GRRR...?
OHHHH. MAAAI. LAWD!
RUB
RUB
WHAT A CWUTE WITTLE PUPPY!
CUTIE LITTLE PAH-TOOTIE!
SNUGGLE
WHO'S A GOOD BOY?
!
TAP
I COULD JUST EAT YOU UP!
halp!

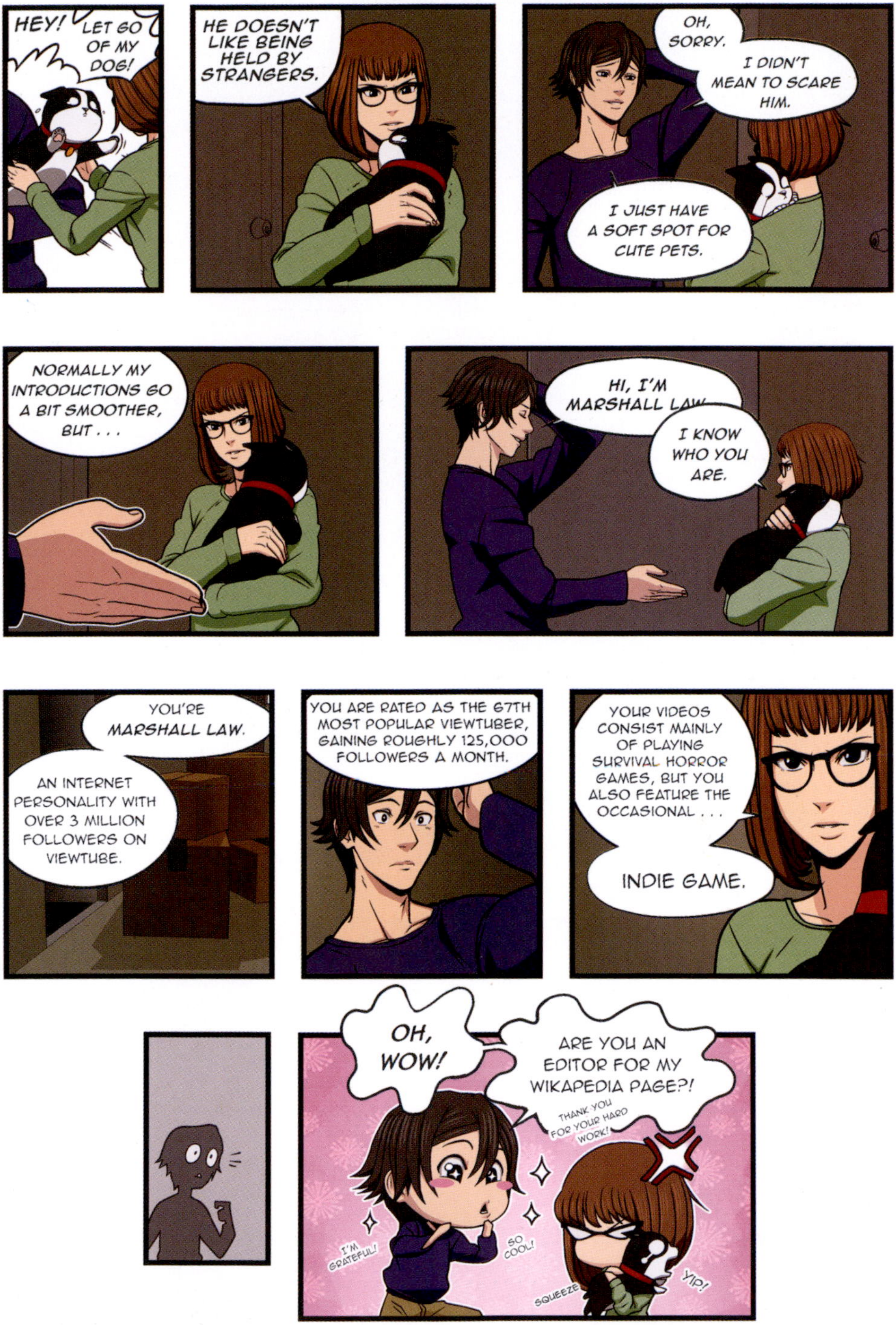
HEY!
LET GO OF MY DOG!
HE DOESN'T LIKE BEING HELD BY STRANGERS.
OH, SORRY.
I DIDN'T MEAN TO SCARE HIM.
I JUST HAVE A SOFT SPOT FOR CUTE PETS.
NORMALLY MY INTRODUCTIONS GO A BIT SMOOTHER, BUT . . .
HI, I'M MARSHALL LAW.
I KNOW WHO YOU ARE.
YOU'RE MARSHALL LAW.
AN INTERNET PERSONALITY WITH OVER 3 MILLION FOLLOWERS ON VIEWTUBE.
YOU ARE RATED AS THE 67TH MOST POPULAR VIEWTUBER, GAINING ROUGHLY 125,000 FOLLOWERS A MONTH.
YOUR VIDEOS CONSIST MAINLY OF PLAYING SURVIVAL HORROR GAMES, BUT YOU ALSO FEATURE THE OCCASIONAL . . .
INDIE GAME.
OH, WOW!
ARE YOU AN EDITOR FOR MY WIKAPEDIA PAGE?!
THANK YOU FOR YOUR HARD WORK!
I'M GRATEFUL!
SO COOL!
SQUEEZE
YIP!

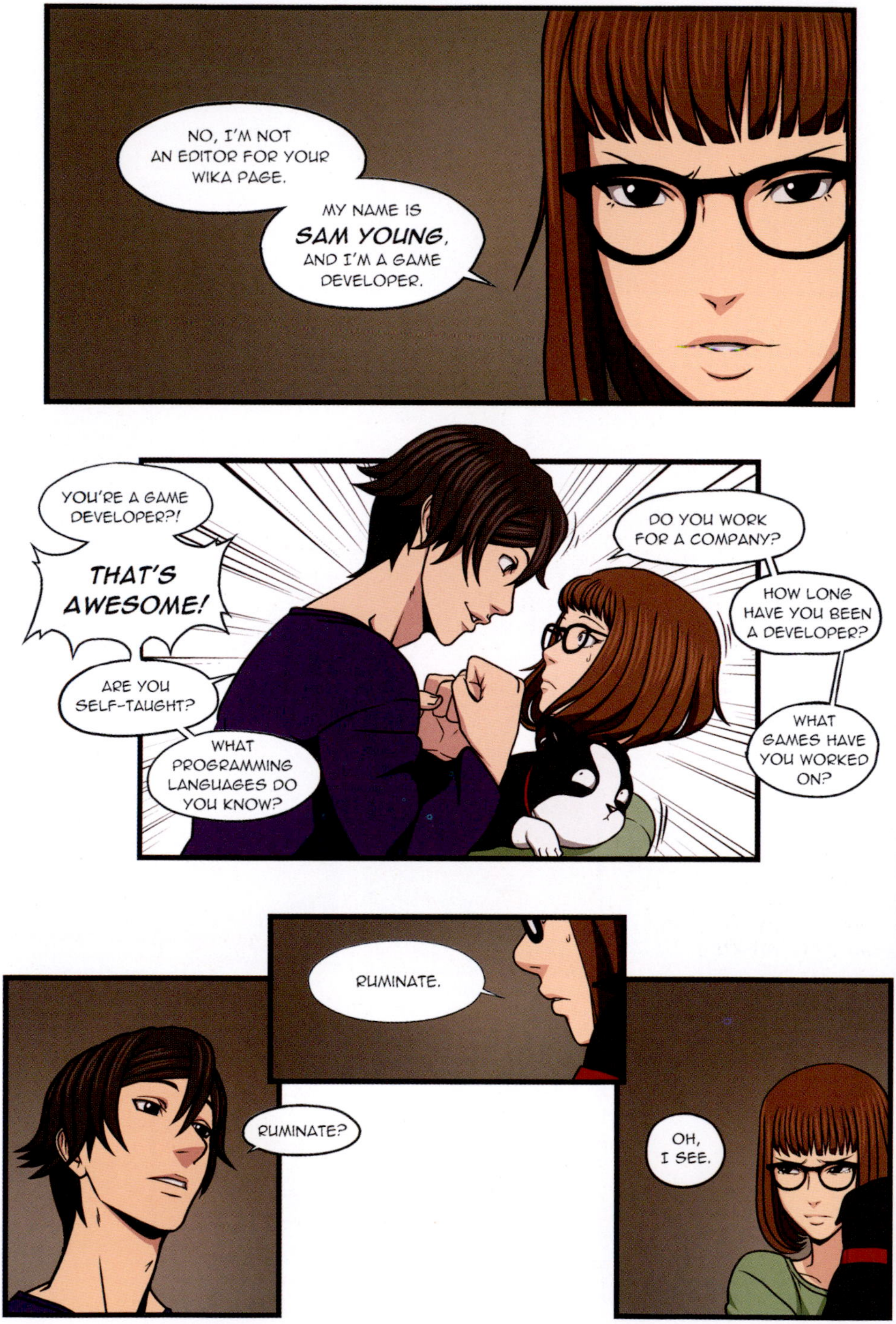
NO, I'M NOT AN EDITOR FOR YOUR WIKA PAGE.
MY NAME IS SAM YOUNG, AND I'M A GAME DEVELOPER.
YOU'RE A GAME DEVELOPER?!
THAT'S AWESOME!
ARE YOU SELF-TAUGHT?
WHAT PROGRAMMING LANGUAGES DO YOU KNOW?
DO YOU WORK FOR A COMPANY?
HOW LONG HAVE YOU BEEN A DEVELOPER?
WHAT GAMES HAVE YOU WORKED ON?
RUMINATE?
RUMINATE.
OH, I SEE.

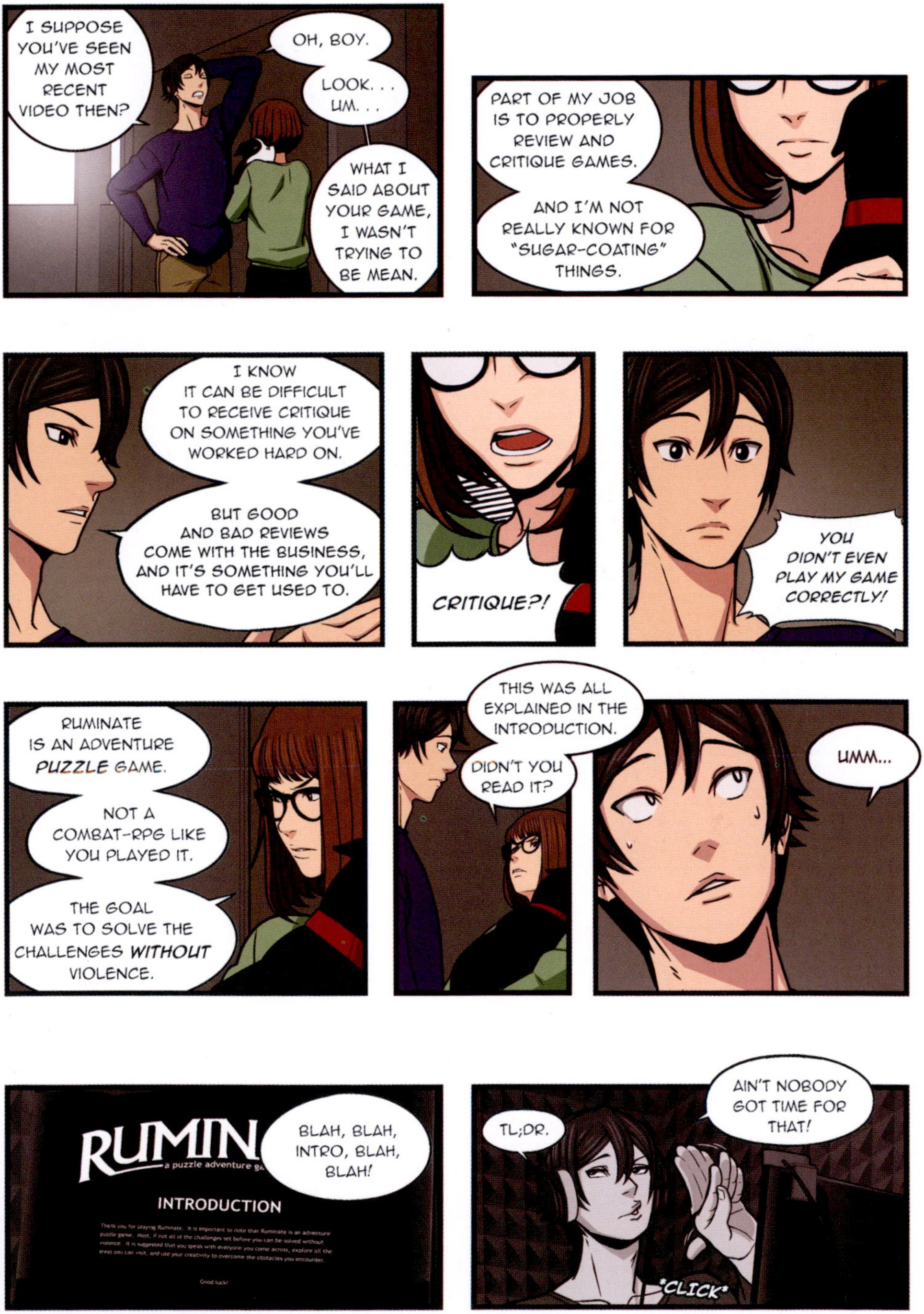
I SUPPOSE YOU'VE SEEN MY MOST RECENT VIDEO THEN?
OH, BOY.
LOOK. . . UM. . .
WHAT I SAID ABOUT YOUR GAME, I WASN'T TRYING TO BE MEAN.
PART OF MY JOB IS TO PROPERLY REVIEW AND CRITIQUE GAMES.
AND I'M NOT REALLY KNOWN FOR "SUGAR-COATING" THINGS.
I KNOW IT CAN BE DIFFICULT TO RECEIVE CRITIQUE ON SOMETHING YOU'VE WORKED HARD ON.
BUT GOOD AND BAD REVIEWS COME WITH THE BUSINESS, AND IT'S SOMETHING YOU'LL HAVE TO GET USED TO.
CRITIQUE?!
YOU DIDN'T EVEN PLAY MY GAME CORRECTLY!
RUMINATE IS AN ADVENTURE PUZZLE GAME.
NOT A COMBAT-RPG LIKE YOU PLAYED IT.
THE GOAL WAS TO SOLVE THE CHALLENGES WITHOUT VIOLENCE.
THIS WAS ALL EXPLAINED IN THE INTRODUCTION.
DIDN'T YOU READ IT?
UMM...
RUMIN
INTRODUCTION
BLAH, BLAH, INTRO, BLAH, BLAH!
TL;DR.
AIN'T NOBODY GOT TIME FOR THAT!
CLICK

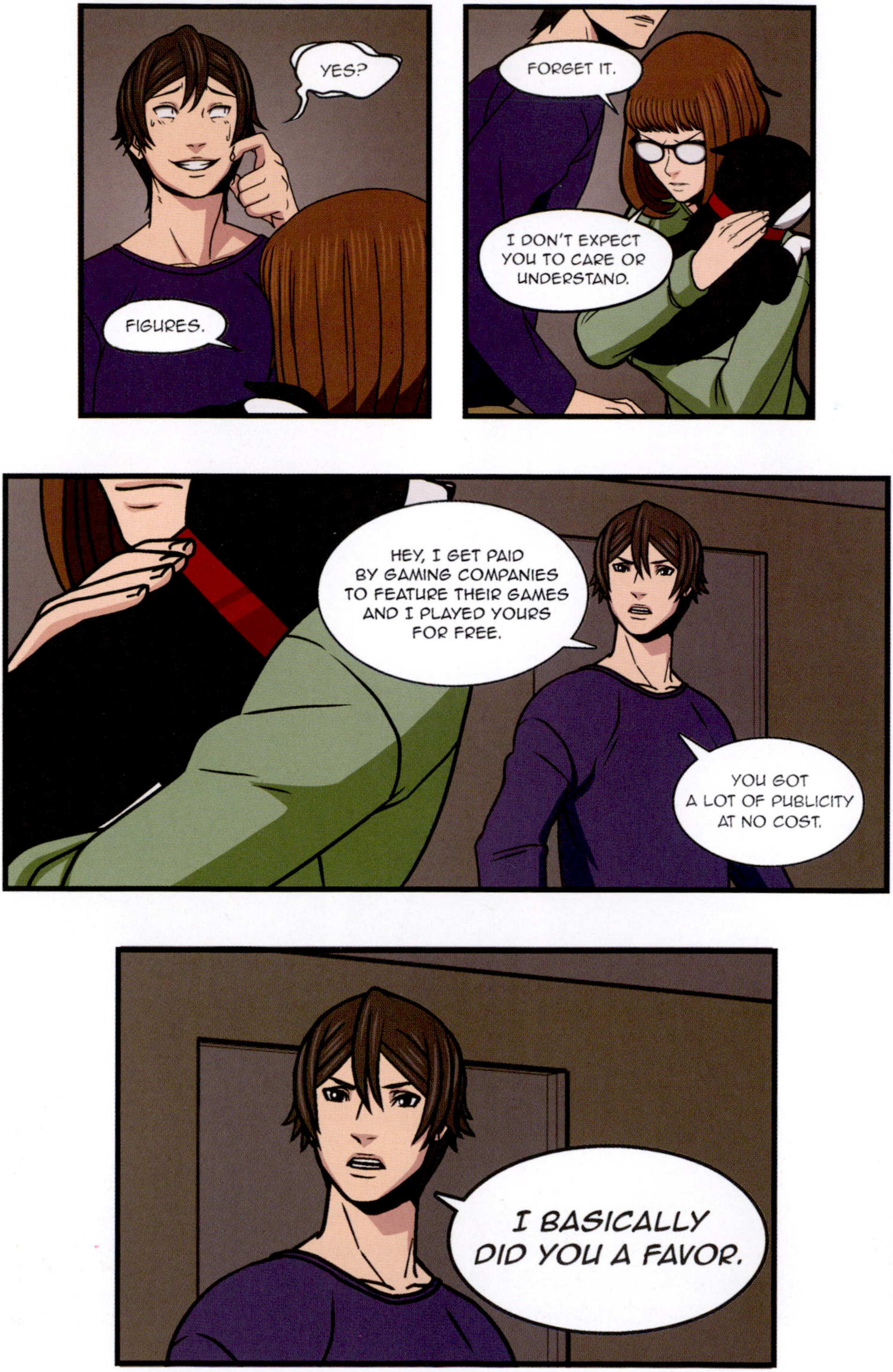
YES?
FIGURES.
FORGET IT.
I DON'T EXPECT YOU TO CARE OR UNDERSTAND.
HEY, I GET PAID BY GAMING COMPANIES TO FEATURE THEIR GAMES AND I PLAYED YOURS FOR FREE.
YOU GOT A LOT OF PUBLICITY AT NO COST.
I BASICALLY DID YOU A FAVOR.

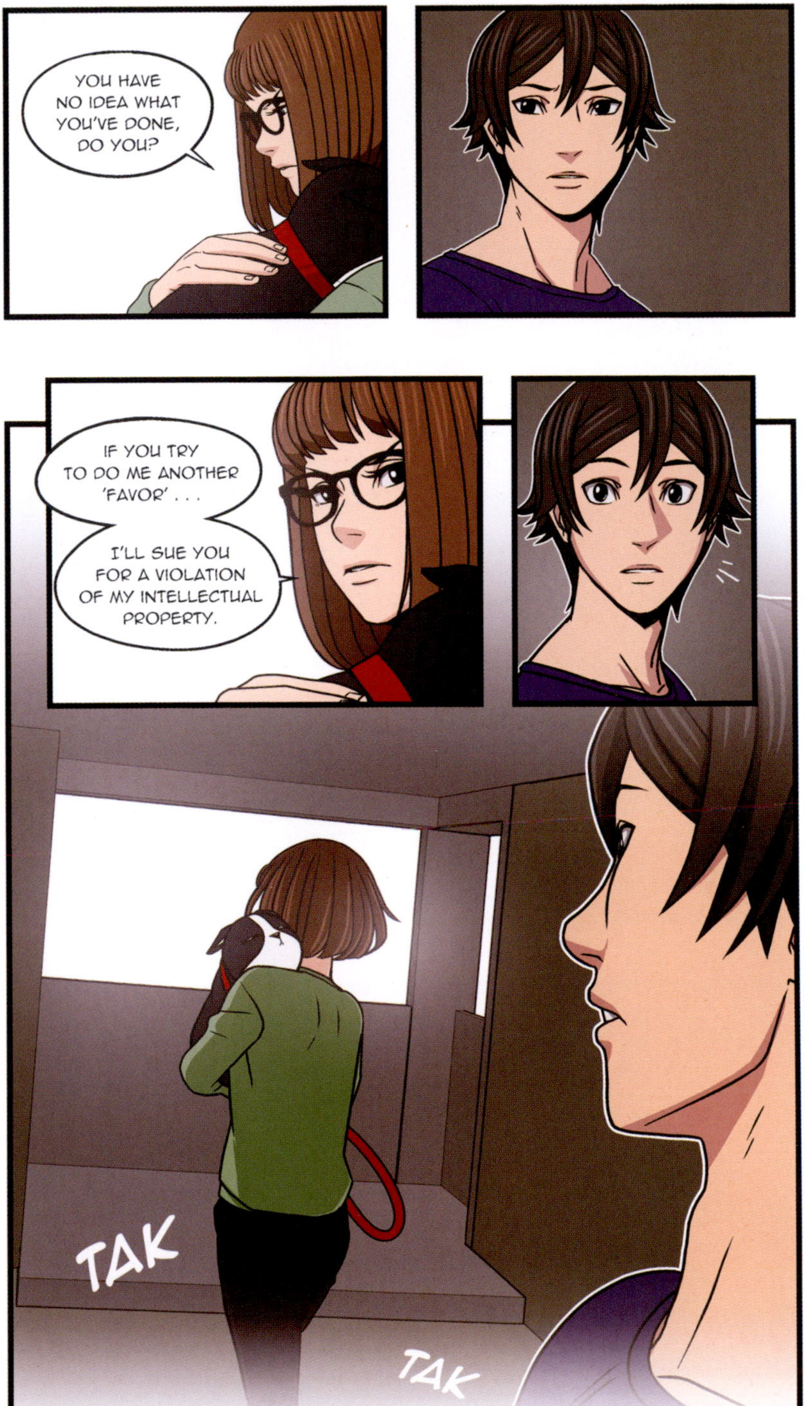
YOU HAVE NO IDEA WHAT YOU'VE DONE, DO YOU?
IF YOU TRY TO DO ME ANOTHER 'FAVOR' . . .
I'LL SUE YOU FOR A VIOLATION OF MY INTELLECTUAL PROPERTY.
TAK
TAK

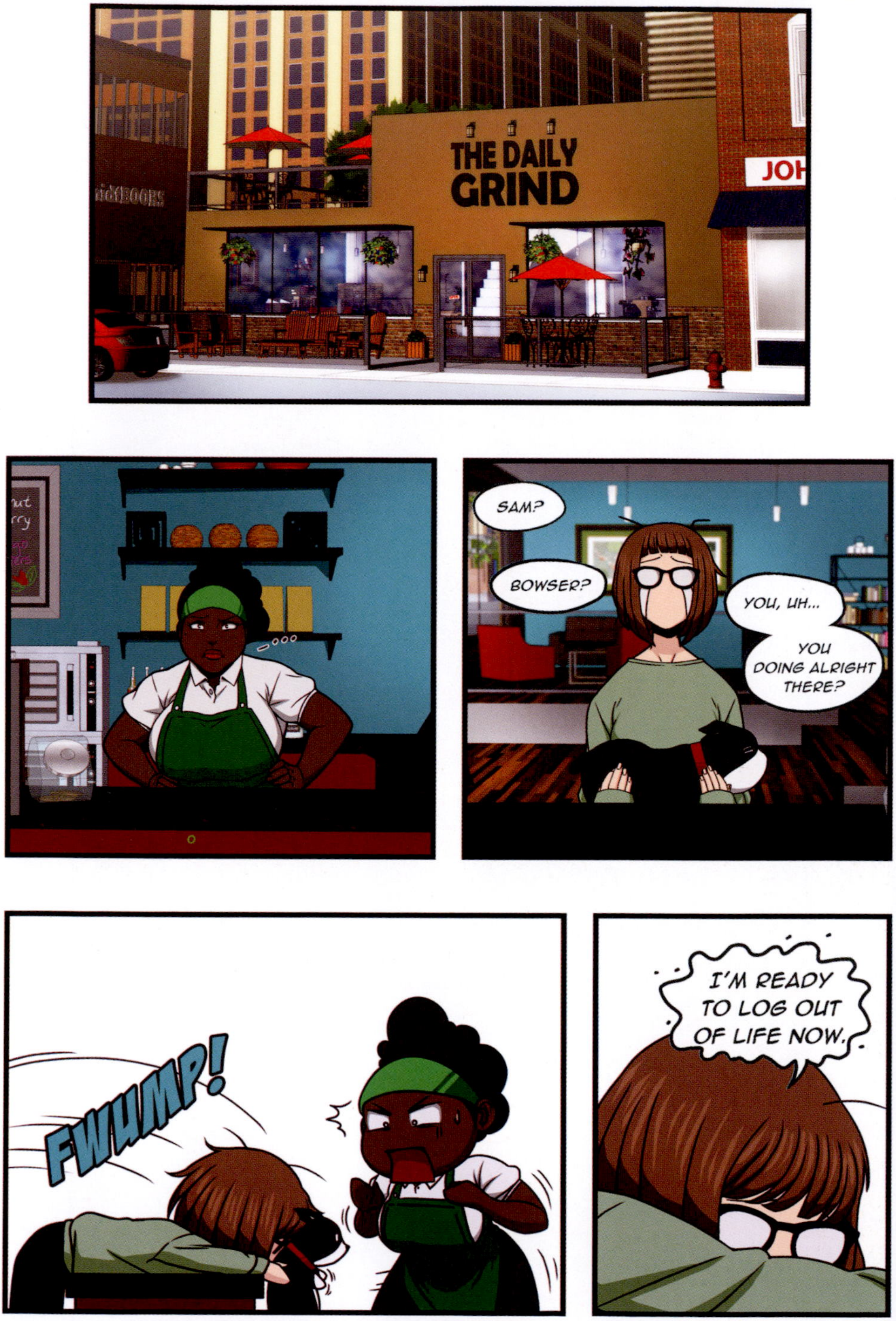
THE DAILY GRIND
SAM?
BOWSER?
YOU, UH...
YOU DOING ALRIGHT THERE?
FWUMP!
I'M READY TO LOG OUT OF LIFE NOW.

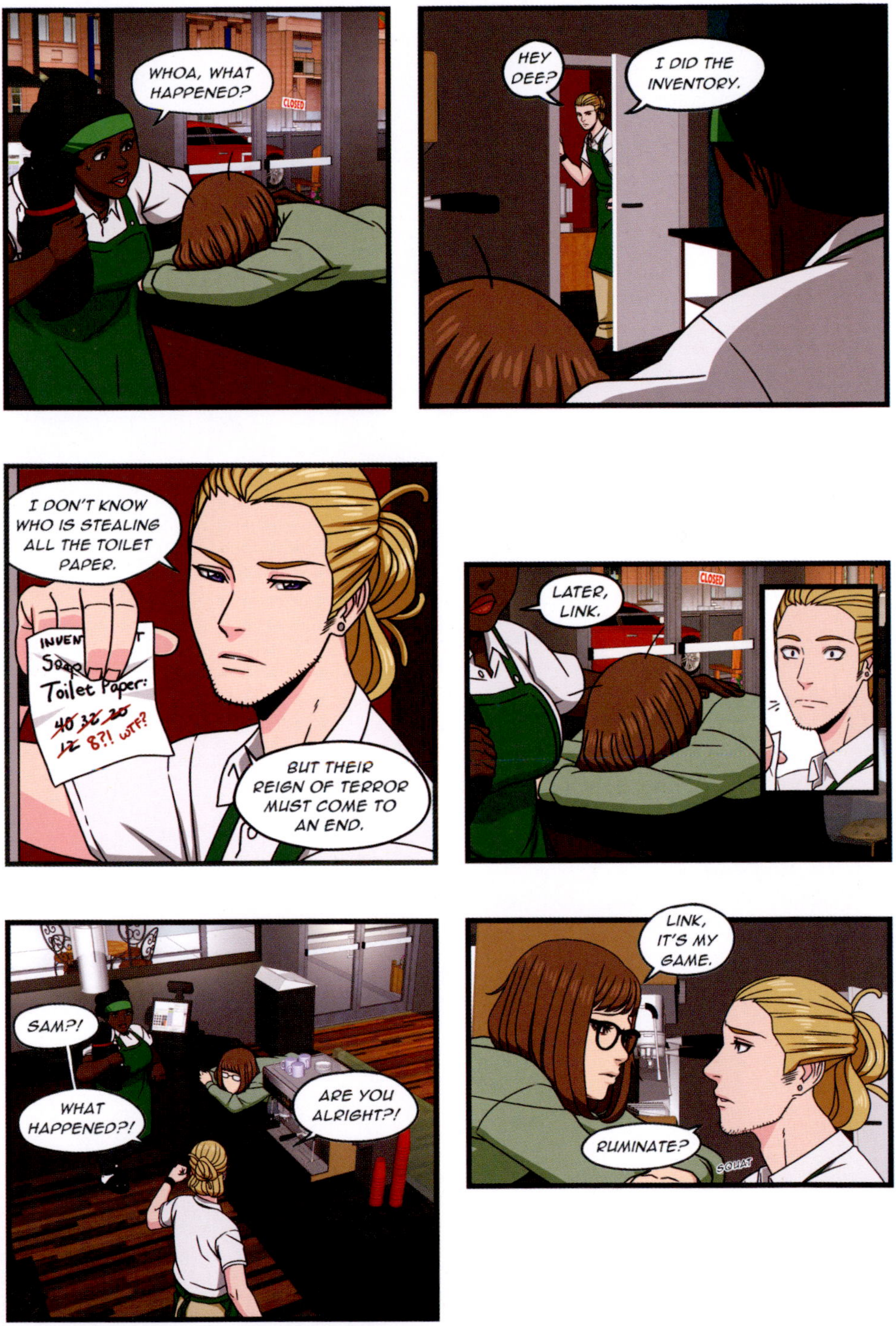
WHOA, WHAT HAPPENED?
CLOSED
HEY DEE?
I DID THE INVENTORY.
I DON'T KNOW WHO IS STEALING ALL THE TOILET PAPER.
Soap
Toilet Paper:
40 32 20 12 8?! WTF?
BUT THEIR REIGN OF TERROR MUST COME TO AN END.
LATER, LINK.
CLOSED
SAM?!
WHAT HAPPENED?!
ARE YOU ALRIGHT?!
LINK, IT'S MY GAME.
RUMINATE?
SQUAT

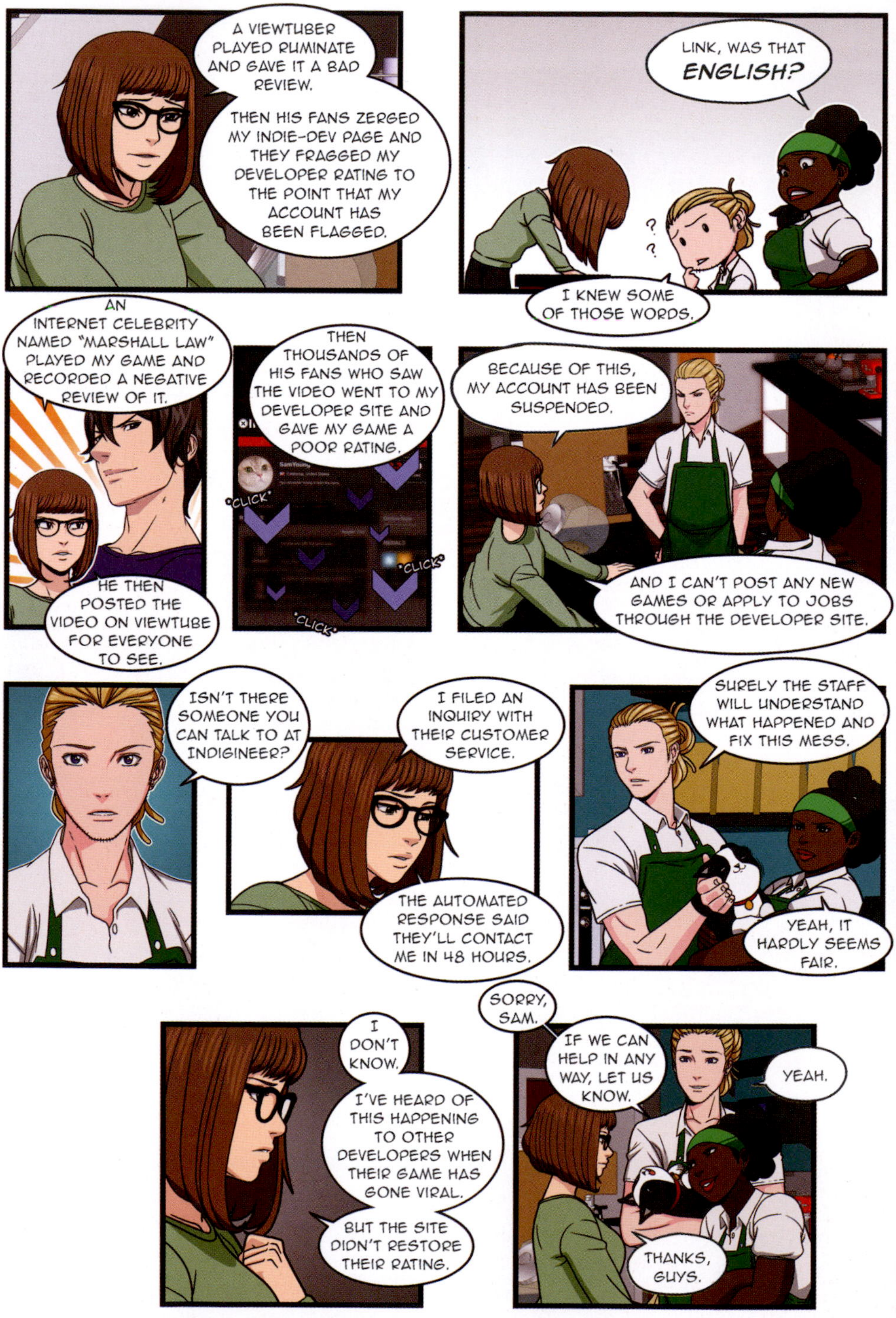
A VIEWTUBER PLAYED RUMINATE AND GAVE IT A BAD REVIEW.
THEN HIS FANS ZERGED MY INDIE-DEV PAGE AND THEY FRAGGED MY DEVELOPER RATING TO THE POINT THAT MY ACCOUNT HAS BEEN FLAGGED.
LINK, WAS THAT *ENGLISH?*
?
?
I KNEW SOME OF THOSE WORDS.
AN INTERNET CELEBRITY NAMED "MARSHALL LAW" PLAYED MY GAME AND RECORDED A NEGATIVE REVIEW OF IT.
HE THEN POSTED THE VIDEO ON VIEWTUBE FOR EVERYONE TO SEE.
THEN THOUSANDS OF HIS FANS WHO SAW THE VIDEO WENT TO MY DEVELOPER SITE AND GAVE MY GAME A POOR RATING.
CLICK
CLICK
CLICK
BECAUSE OF THIS, MY ACCOUNT HAS BEEN SUSPENDED.
AND I CAN'T POST ANY NEW GAMES OR APPLY TO JOBS THROUGH THE DEVELOPER SITE.
ISN'T THERE SOMEONE YOU CAN TALK TO AT INDIGINEER?
I FILED AN INQUIRY WITH THEIR CUSTOMER SERVICE.
THE AUTOMATED RESPONSE SAID THEY'LL CONTACT ME IN 48 HOURS.
SURELY THE STAFF WILL UNDERSTAND WHAT HAPPENED AND FIX THIS MESS.
YEAH, IT HARDLY SEEMS FAIR.
I DON'T KNOW.
I'VE HEARD OF THIS HAPPENING TO OTHER DEVELOPERS WHEN THEIR GAME HAS GONE VIRAL.
BUT THE SITE DIDN'T RESTORE THEIR RATING.
SORRY, SAM.
IF WE CAN HELP IN ANY WAY, LET US KNOW.
YEAH.
THANKS, GUYS.

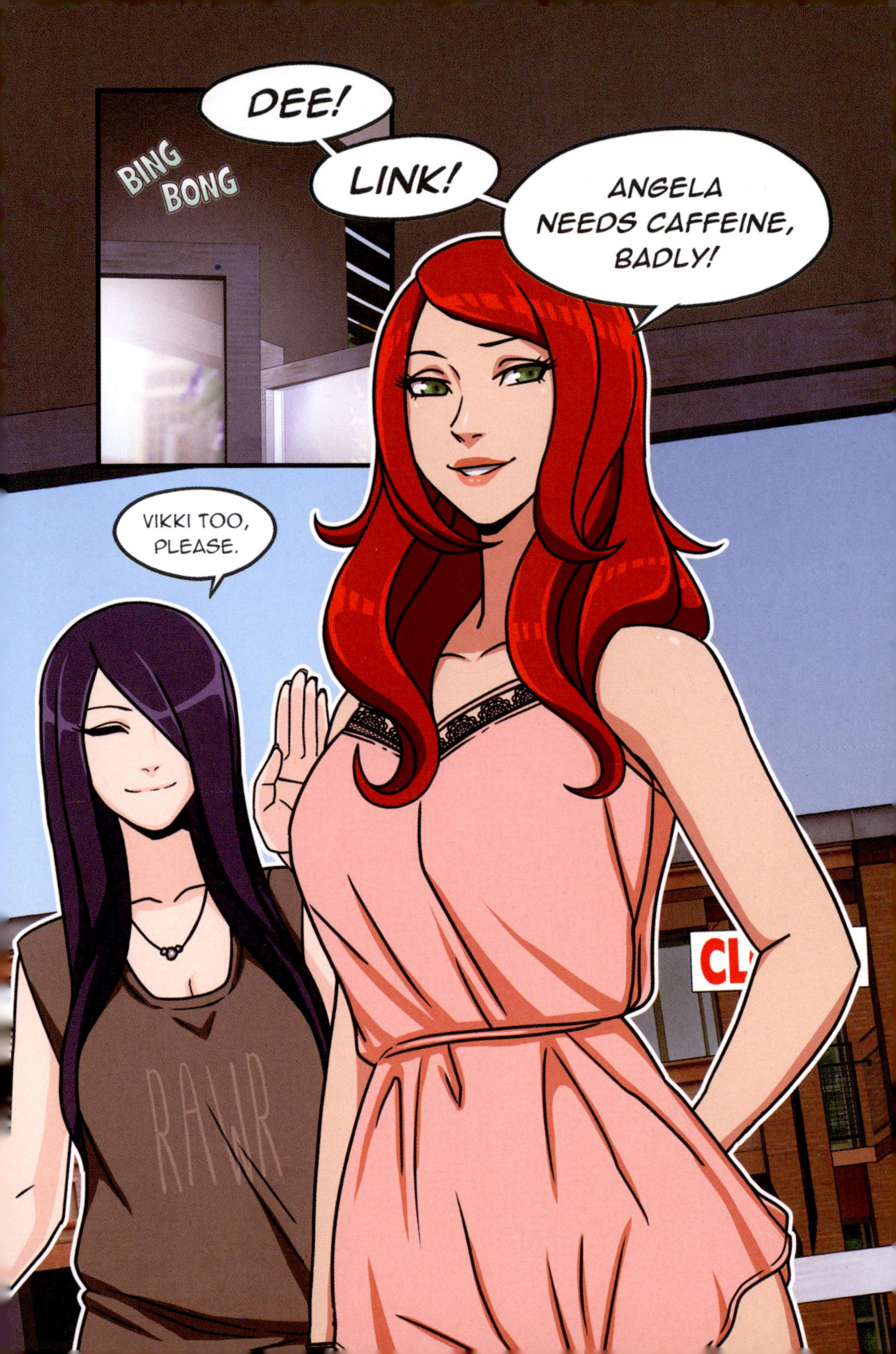
BING BONG
DEE!
LINK!
ANGELA NEEDS CAFFEINE, BADLY!
VIKKI TOO, PLEASE.
RAWR

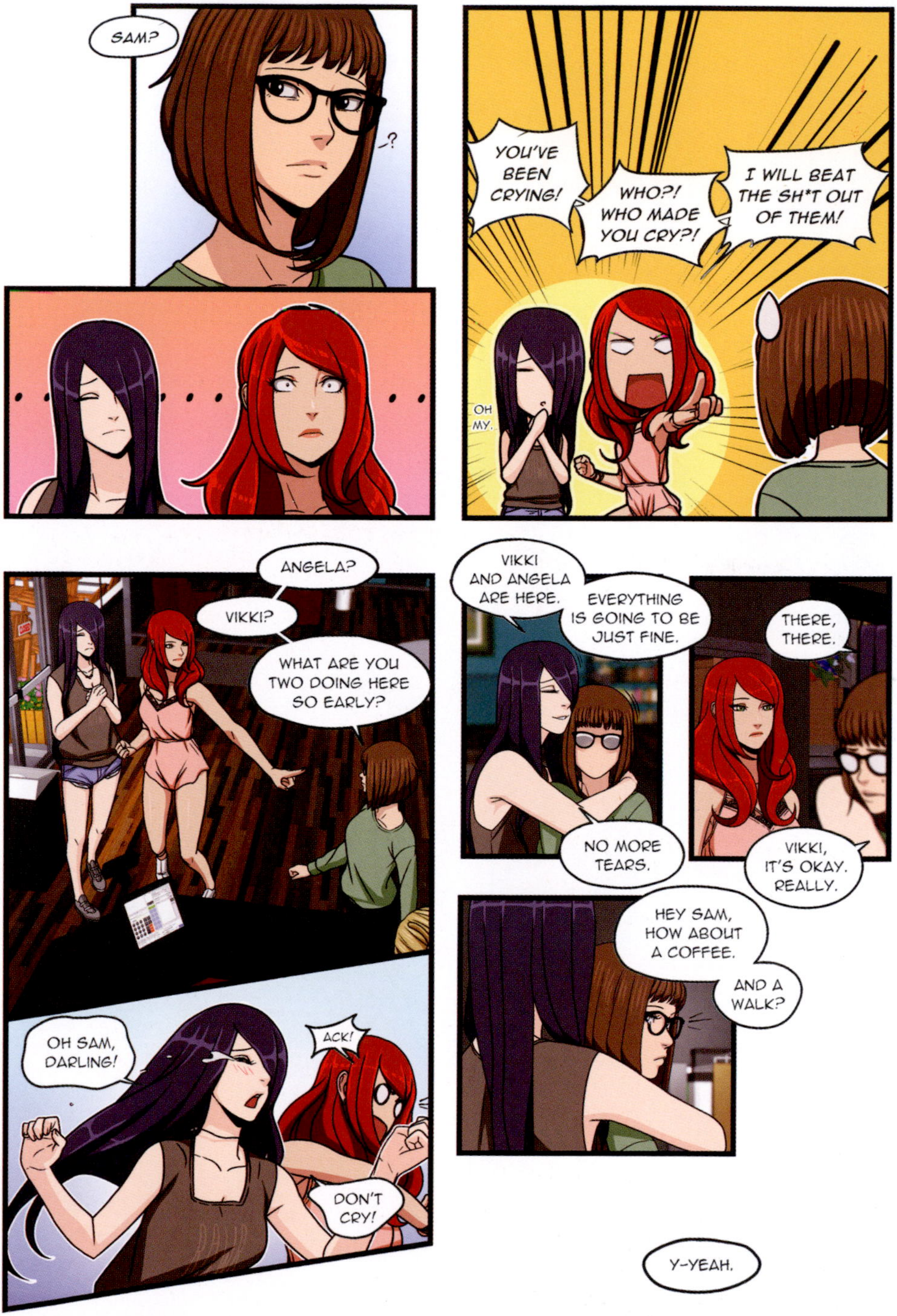
SAM?
?
. . . .
YOU'VE BEEN CRYING!
WHO?! WHO MADE YOU CRY?!
I WILL BEAT THE SH*T OUT OF THEM!
OH MY.
ANGELA?
VIKKI?
WHAT ARE YOU TWO DOING HERE SO EARLY?
OH SAM, DARLING!
ACK!
DON'T CRY!
VIKKI AND ANGELA ARE HERE.
EVERYTHING IS GOING TO BE JUST FINE.
NO MORE TEARS.
THERE, THERE.
VIKKI, IT'S OKAY. REALLY.
HEY SAM, HOW ABOUT A COFFEE.
AND A WALK?
Y-YEAH.

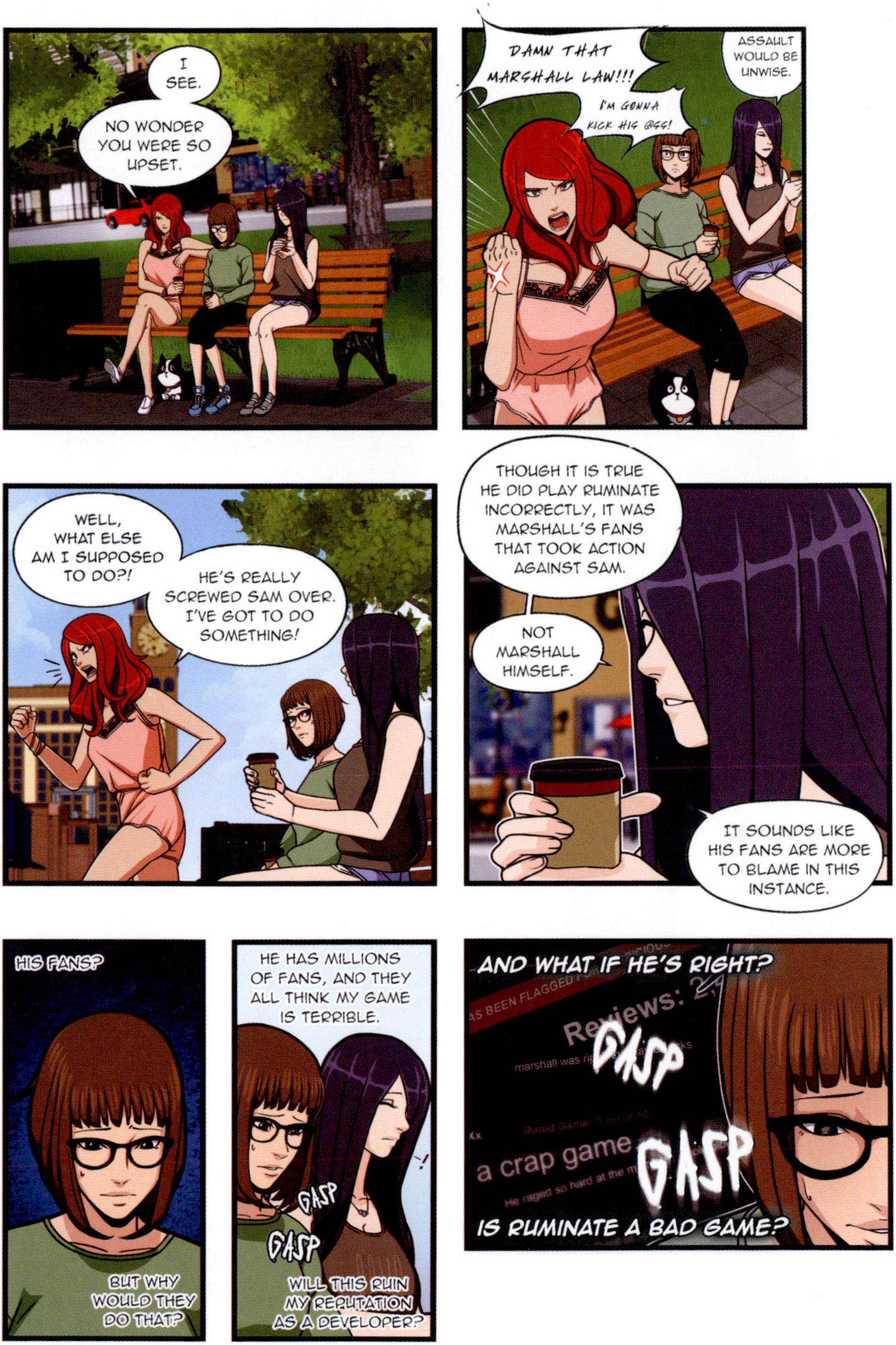
I SEE.
NO WONDER YOU WERE SO UPSET.
DAMN THAT MARSHALL LAW!!!
I'M GONNA KICK HIS @SS!
ASSAULT WOULD BE UNWISE.
WELL, WHAT ELSE AM I SUPPOSED TO DO?!
HE'S REALLY SCREWED SAM OVER. I'VE GOT TO DO SOMETHING!
THOUGH IT IS TRUE HE DID PLAY RUMINATE INCORRECTLY, IT WAS MARSHALL'S FANS THAT TOOK ACTION AGAINST SAM.
NOT MARSHALL HIMSELF.
IT SOUNDS LIKE HIS FANS ARE MORE TO BLAME IN THIS INSTANCE.
HIS FANS?
BUT WHY WOULD THEY DO THAT?
HE HAS MILLIONS OF FANS, AND THEY ALL THINK MY GAME IS TERRIBLE.
GASP
GASP
WILL THIS RUIN MY REPUTATION AS A DEVELOPER?
AND WHAT IF HE'S RIGHT?
GASP
a crap game
GASP
IS RUMINATE A BAD GAME?

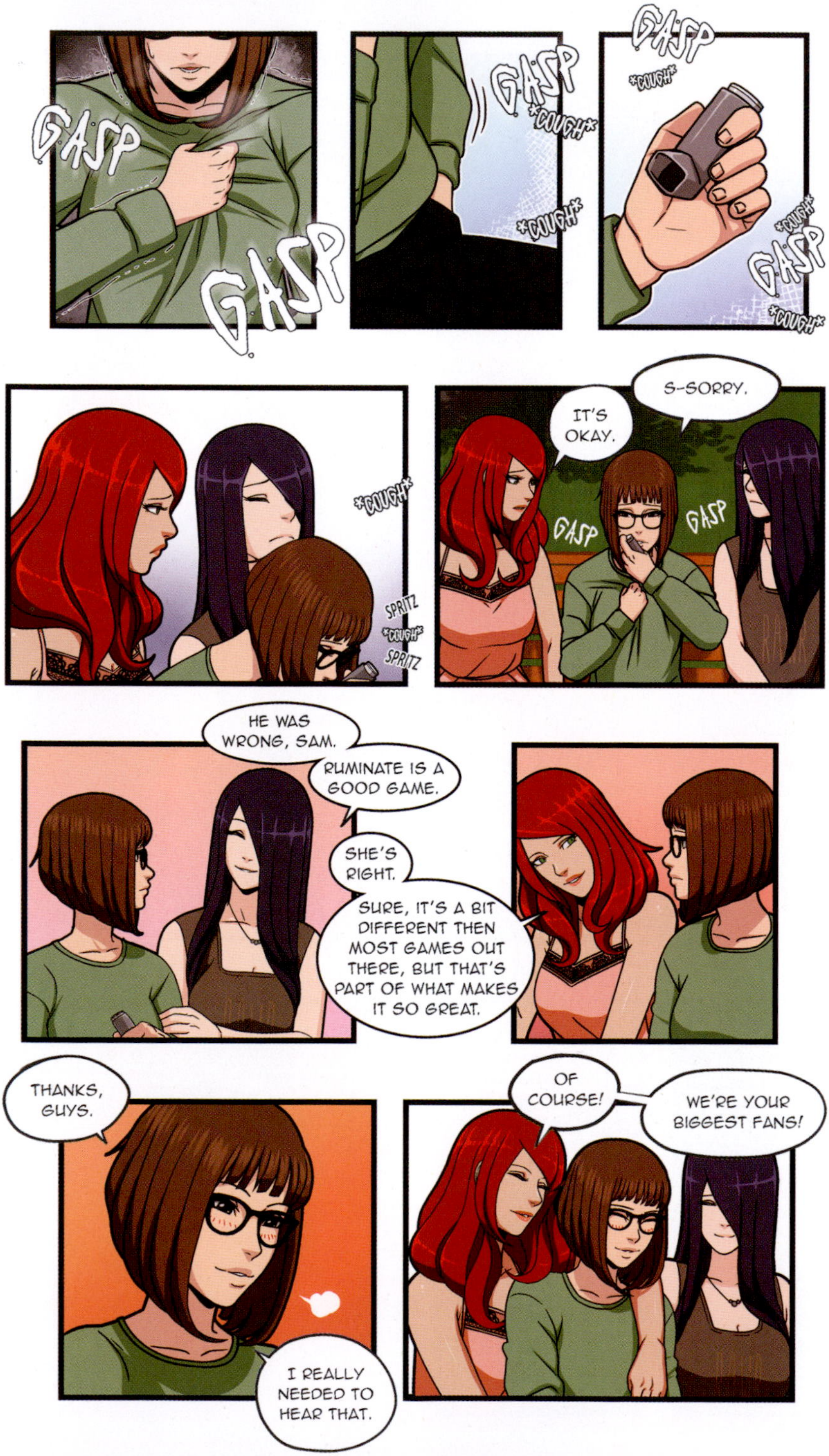

GASP
GASP
GASP
COUGH
COUGH
GASP
COUGH
COUGH
GASP
COUGH
COUGH
SPRITZ
COUGH
SPRITZ
IT'S OKAY.
S-SORRY.
GASP
GASP
HE WAS WRONG, SAM.
RUMINATE IS A GOOD GAME.
SHE'S RIGHT.
SURE, IT'S A BIT DIFFERENT THEN MOST GAMES OUT THERE, BUT THAT'S PART OF WHAT MAKES IT SO GREAT.
THANKS, GUYS.
I REALLY NEEDED TO HEAR THAT.
OF COURSE!
WE'RE YOUR BIGGEST FANS!

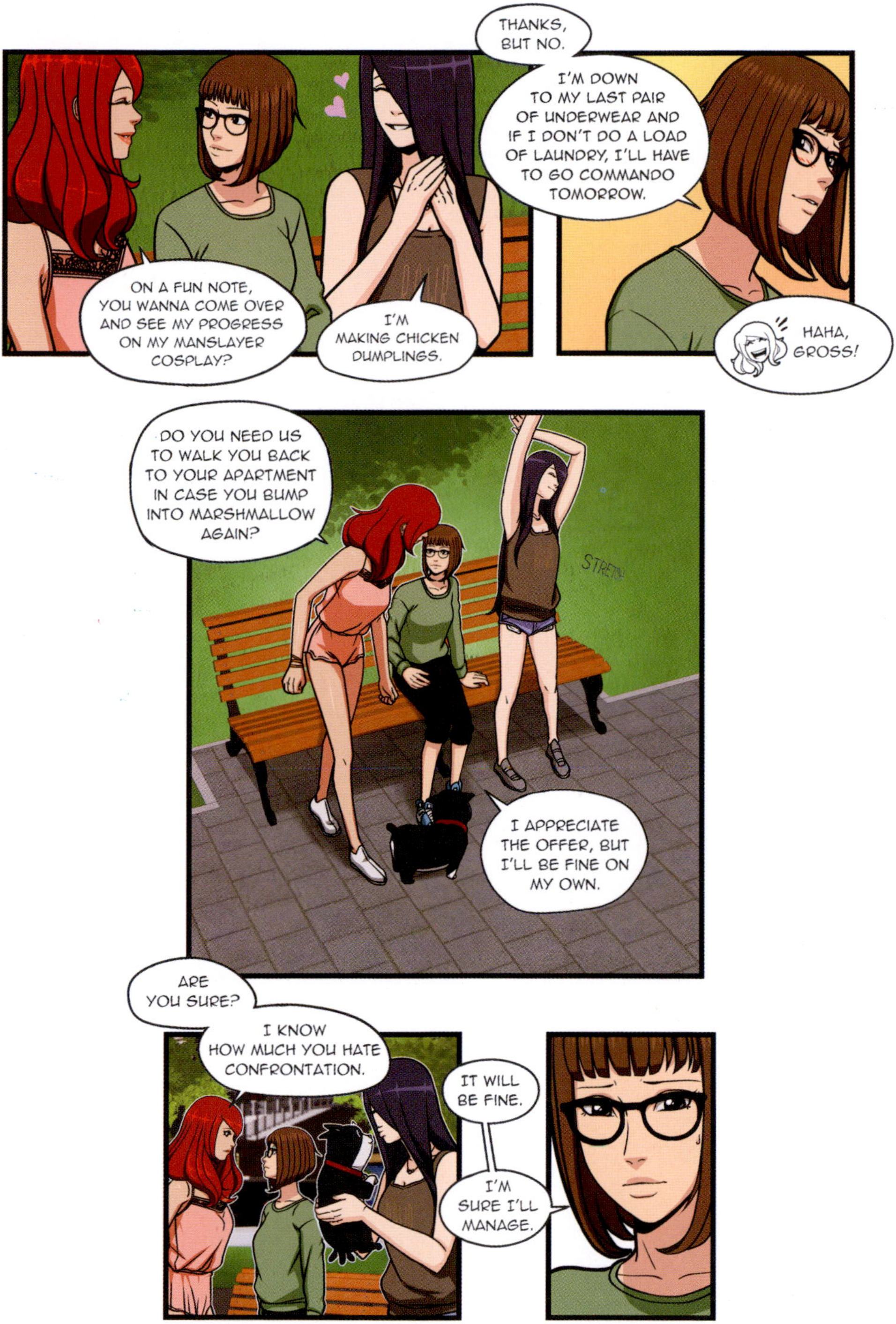
ON A FUN NOTE, YOU WANNA COME OVER AND SEE MY PROGRESS ON MY MANSLAYER COSPLAY?
I'M MAKING CHICKEN DUMPLINGS.
THANKS, BUT NO.
I'M DOWN TO MY LAST PAIR OF UNDERWEAR AND IF I DON'T DO A LOAD OF LAUNDRY, I'LL HAVE TO GO COMMANDO TOMORROW.
HAHA, GROSS!
DO YOU NEED US TO WALK YOU BACK TO YOUR APARTMENT IN CASE YOU BUMP INTO MARSHMALLOW AGAIN?
STRETCH
I APPRECIATE THE OFFER, BUT I'LL BE FINE ON MY OWN.
ARE YOU SURE?
I KNOW HOW MUCH YOU HATE CONFRONTATION.
IT WILL BE FINE.
I'M SURE I'LL MANAGE.

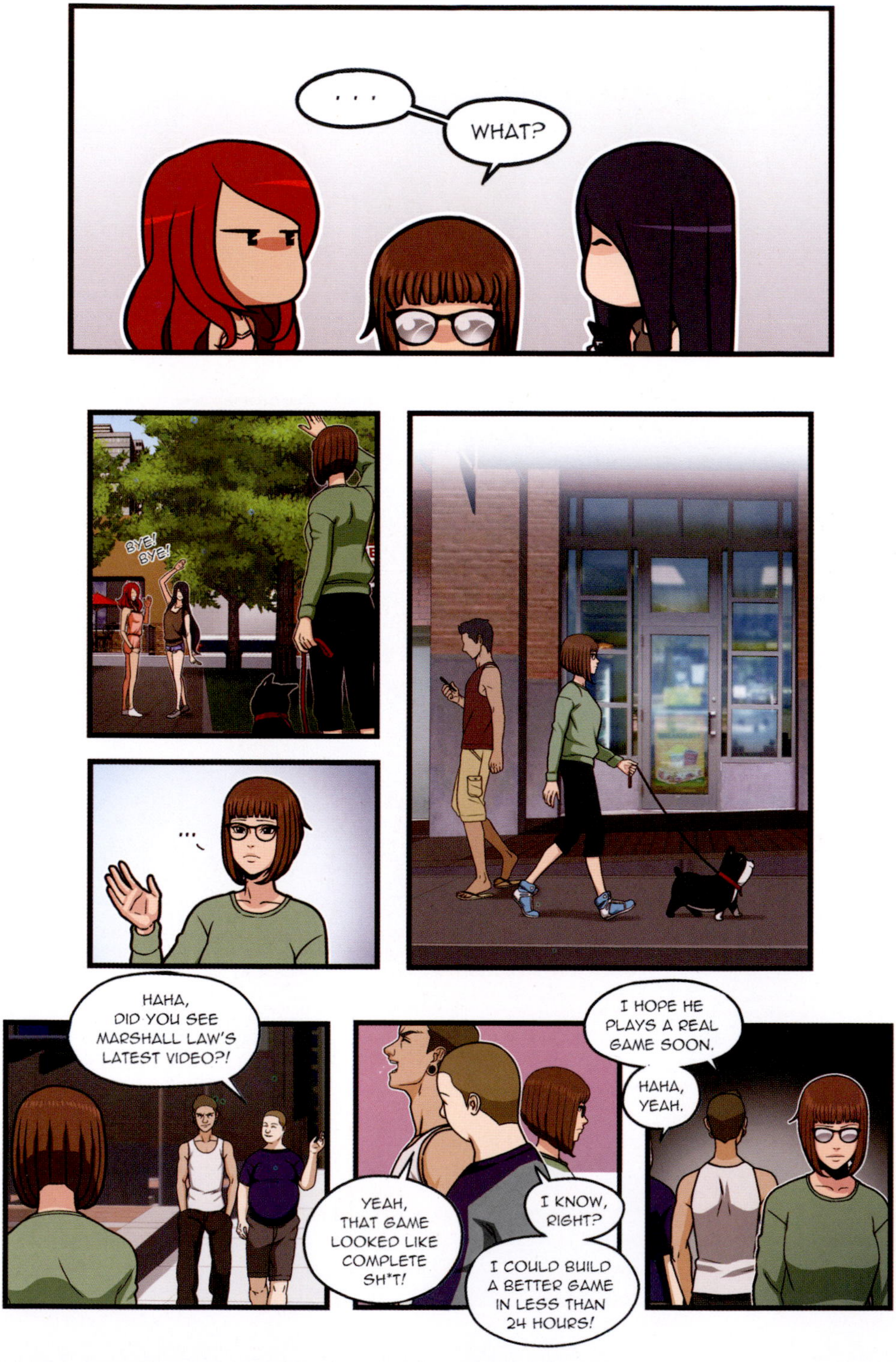
...
WHAT?
BYE!
BYE!
...
HAHA, DID YOU SEE MARSHALL LAW'S LATEST VIDEO?!
YEAH, THAT GAME LOOKED LIKE COMPLETE SH*T!
I KNOW, RIGHT?
I COULD BUILD A BETTER GAME IN LESS THAN 24 HOURS!
I HOPE HE PLAYS A REAL GAME SOON.
HAHA, YEAH.

I'M FINE, ANGELA.

YOU REALLY DON'T HAVE TO COME OVER HERE TO CHECK UP ON ME.

ARE YOU SURE, SAM?

I DON'T MIND.

YES, I'M SURE.

DID YOU RUN INTO MARSHMALLOW?

UMM.

NOT . . . EXACTLY.

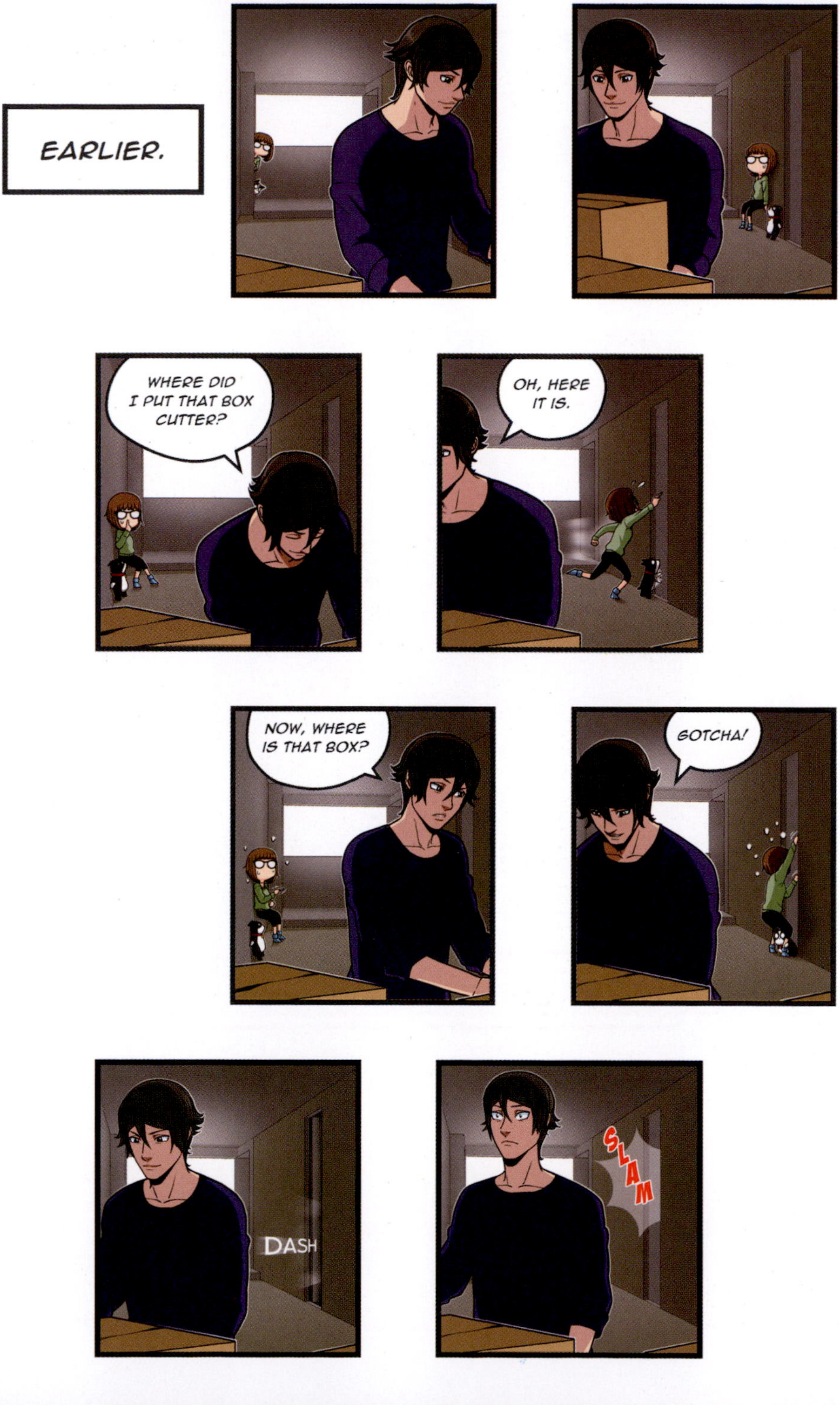
EARLIER.
WHERE DID I PUT THAT BOX CUTTER?
OH, HERE IT IS.
NOW, WHERE IS THAT BOX?
GOTCHA!
DASH
SLAM

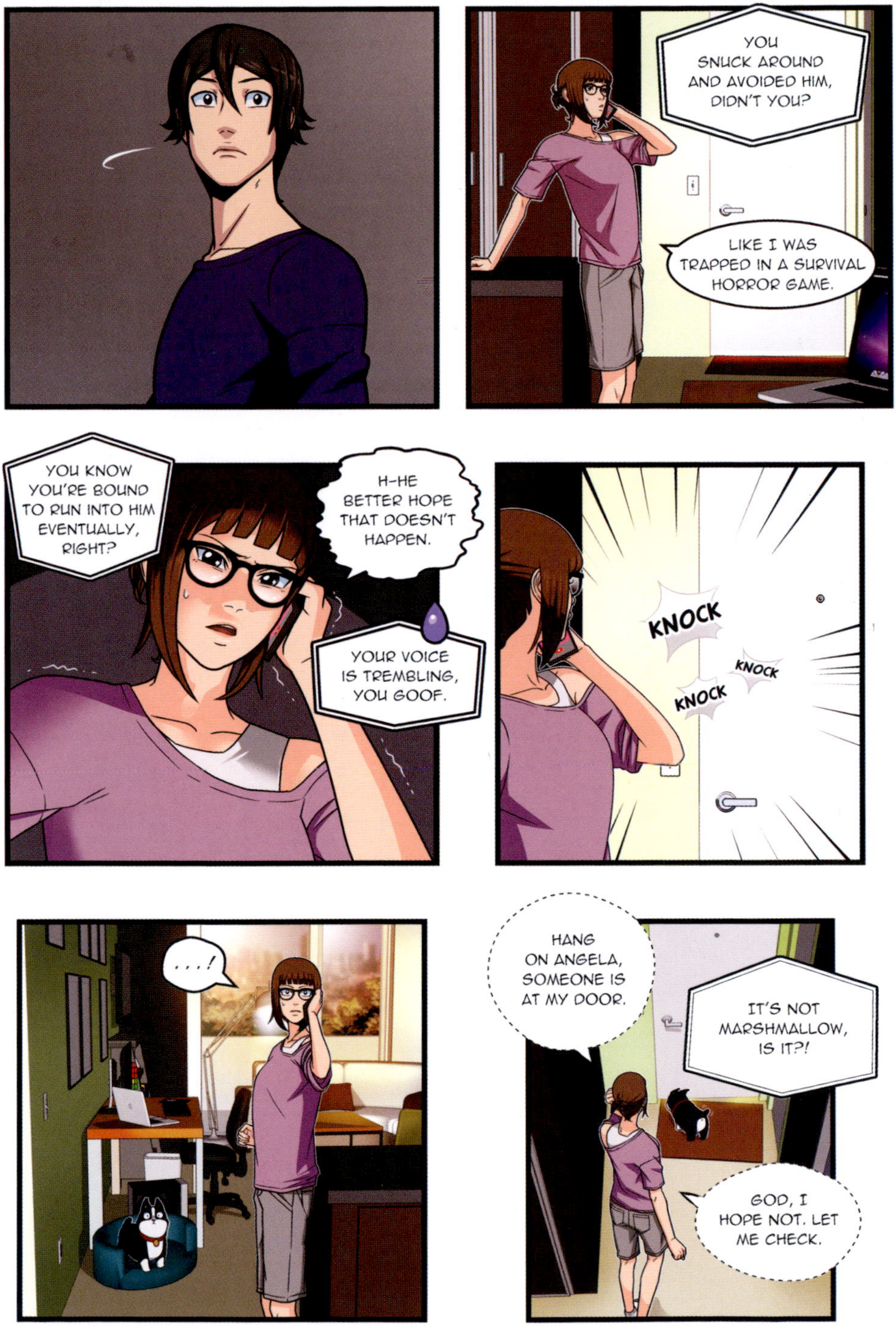
YOU SNUCK AROUND AND AVOIDED HIM, DIDN'T YOU?
LIKE I WAS TRAPPED IN A SURVIVAL HORROR GAME.
YOU KNOW YOU'RE BOUND TO RUN INTO HIM EVENTUALLY, RIGHT?
H-HE BETTER HOPE THAT DOESN'T HAPPEN.
YOUR VOICE IS TREMBLING, YOU GOOF.
KNOCK
KNOCK
KNOCK
...!
HANG ON ANGELA, SOMEONE IS AT MY DOOR.
IT'S NOT MARSHMALLOW, IS IT?!
GOD, I HOPE NOT. LET ME CHECK.

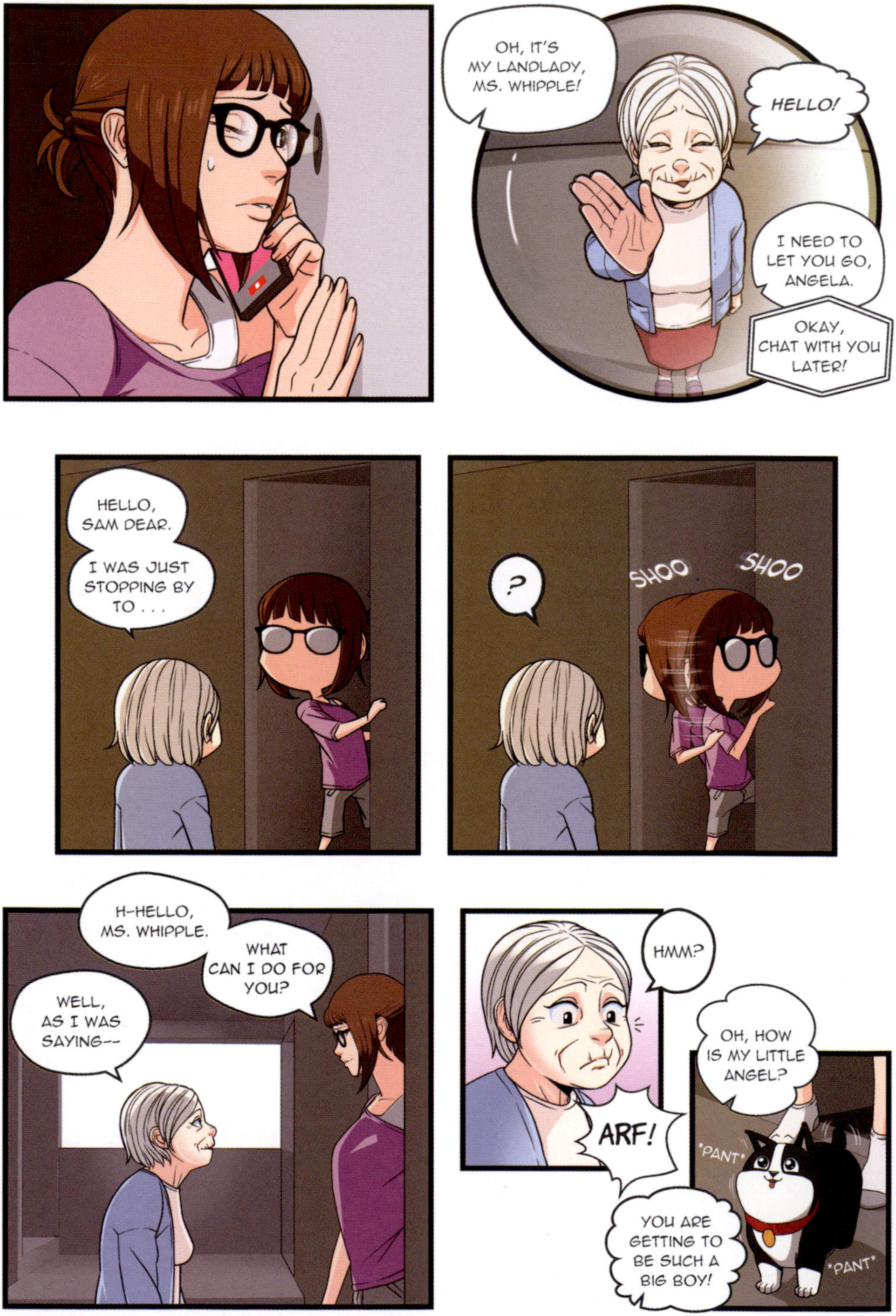

OH, IT'S MY LANDLADY, MS. WHIPPLE!
HELLO!
I NEED TO LET YOU GO, ANGELA.
OKAY, CHAT WITH YOU LATER!
HELLO, SAM DEAR.
I WAS JUST STOPPING BY TO . . .
?
SHOO
SHOO
H-HELLO, MS. WHIPPLE.
WHAT CAN I DO FOR YOU?
WELL, AS I WAS SAYING--
HMM?
ARF!
OH, HOW IS MY LITTLE ANGEL?
PANT
PANT
YOU ARE GETTING TO BE SUCH A BIG BOY!

OKAY, BOWSER. I'LL PICK YOU UP.

SAM, DEAR. I STOPPED BY TO LET YOU KNOW YOU HAVE A NEW NEIGHBOR.

AH, YEAH WE'VE, UM . . . WE'VE MET.

HIS BOXES ARE GONE.

MARSHALL MUST BE DONE MOVING IN BY NOW.

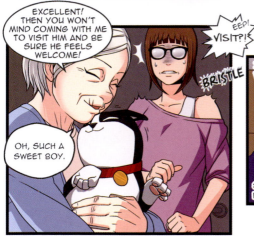

EXCELLENT! THEN YOU WON'T MIND COMING WITH ME TO VISIT HIM AND BE SURE HE FEELS WELCOME!

EEP! VISIT?!?

BRISTLE

OH, SUCH A SWEET BOY.

I CAN'T REALLY EXPLAIN TO HER WHAT HAPPENED.

SHE WOULDN'T UNDERSTAND AT ALL.

SORRY, MS. WHIPPLE.

I'M REALLY VERY BUSY AND WILL HAVE TO TAKE A RAIN CHECK.

I HAVE A BUNCH OF LAUNDRY TO DO, . . . AND MY TOILET TO CLEAN.

AND, AND . . .

THERE ISN'T SOME SORT OF CONFLICT BETWEEN TWO OF MY PRECIOUS TENANTS, IS THERE?

N-NO, MA'AM!

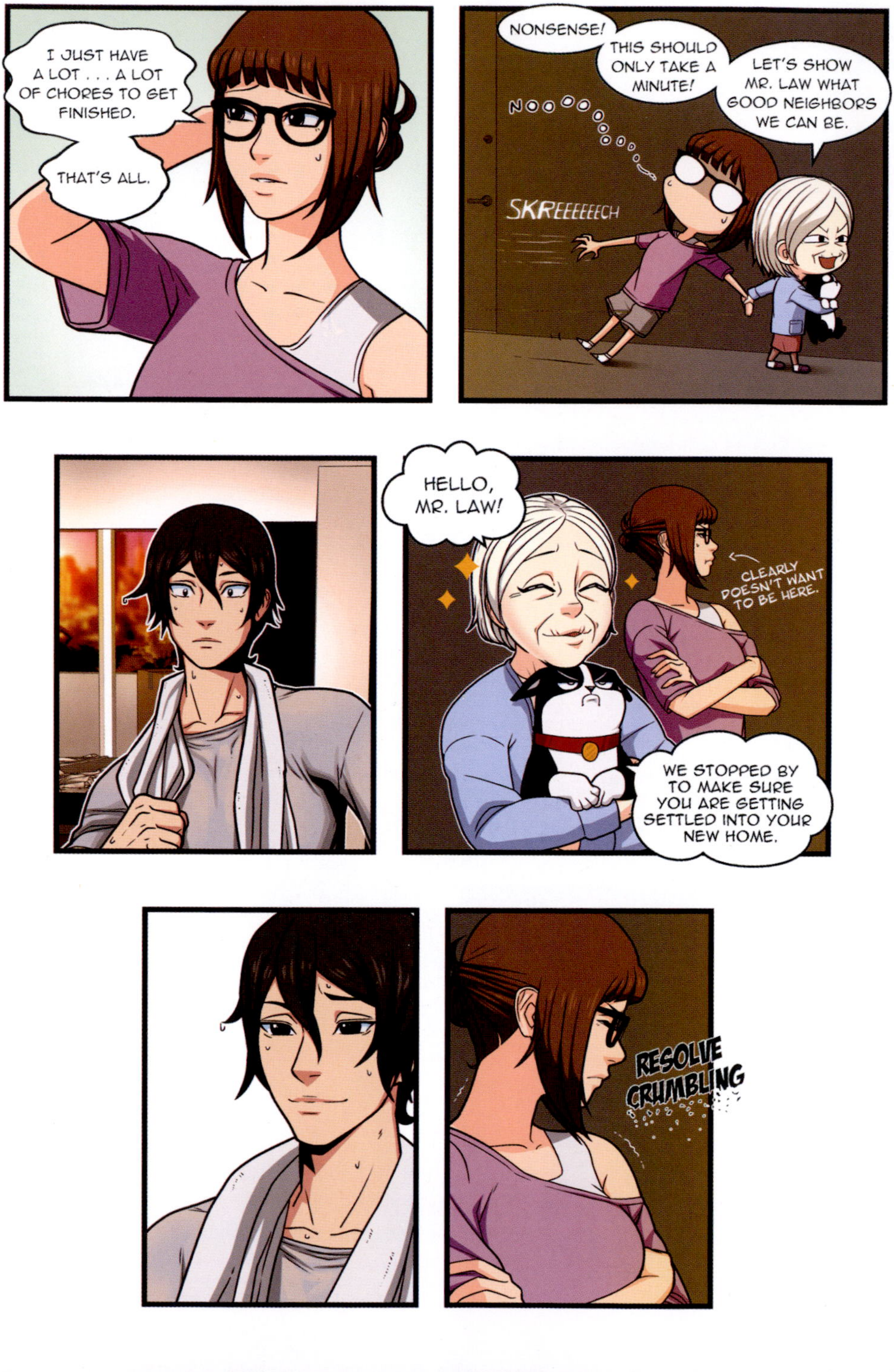

I JUST HAVE A LOT . . . A LOT OF CHORES TO GET FINISHED.
THAT'S ALL.
NONSENSE!
THIS SHOULD ONLY TAKE A MINUTE!
LET'S SHOW MR. LAW WHAT GOOD NEIGHBORS WE CAN BE.
NOOOOOOOOOO...
SKREEEEEECH
HELLO, MR. LAW!
CLEARLY DOESN'T WANT TO BE HERE.
WE STOPPED BY TO MAKE SURE YOU ARE GETTING SETTLED INTO YOUR NEW HOME.
RESOLVE CRUMBLING

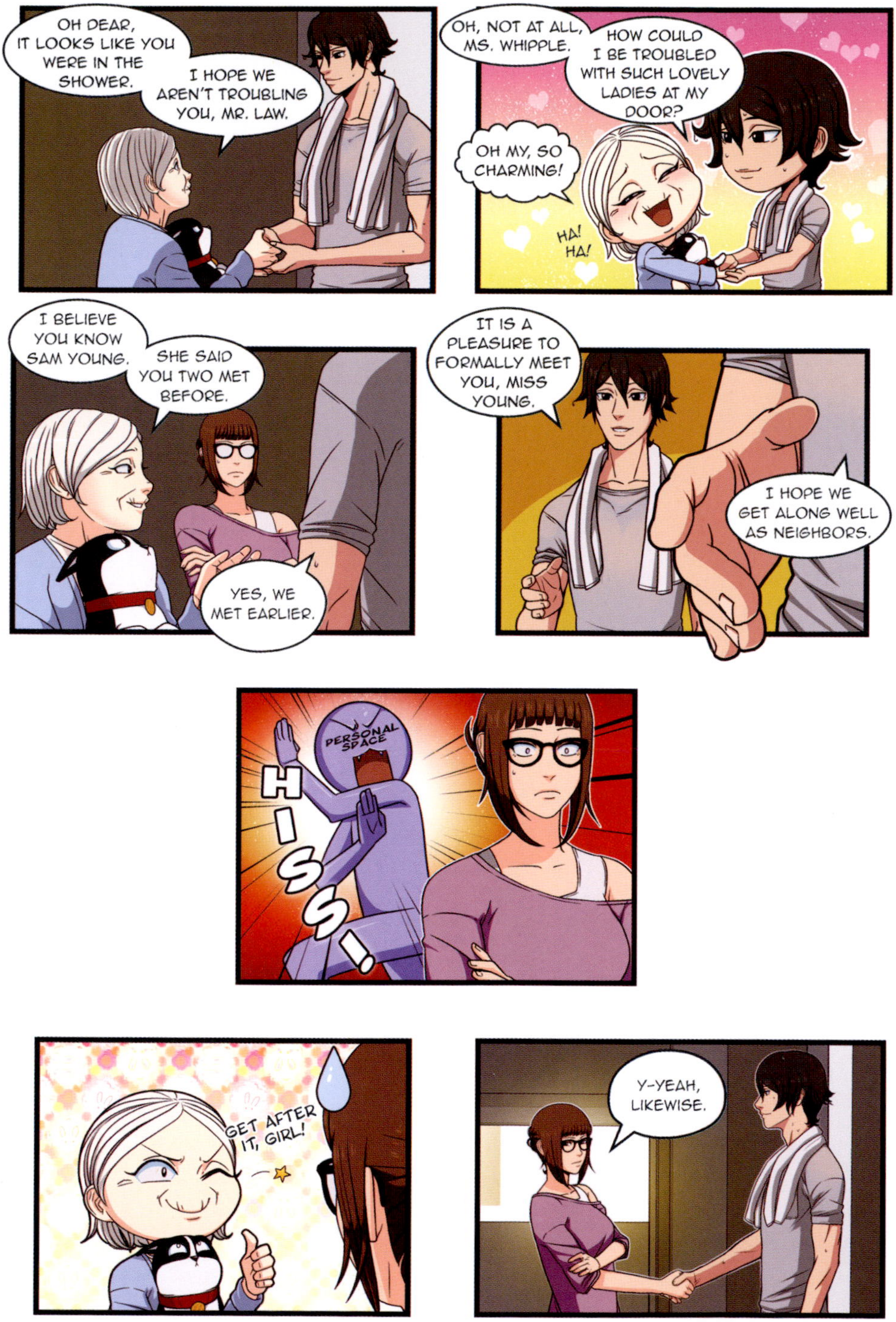
OH DEAR, IT LOOKS LIKE YOU WERE IN THE SHOWER.
I HOPE WE AREN'T TROUBLING YOU, MR. LAW.
OH, NOT AT ALL, MS. WHIPPLE.
HOW COULD I BE TROUBLED WITH SUCH LOVELY LADIES AT MY DOOR?
OH MY, SO CHARMING!
HA! HA!
I BELIEVE YOU KNOW SAM YOUNG.
SHE SAID YOU TWO MET BEFORE.
YES, WE MET EARLIER.
IT IS A PLEASURE TO FORMALLY MEET YOU, MISS YOUNG.
I HOPE WE GET ALONG WELL AS NEIGHBORS.
PERSONAL SPACE
HISS!
GET AFTER IT, GIRL!
Y-YEAH, LIKEWISE.

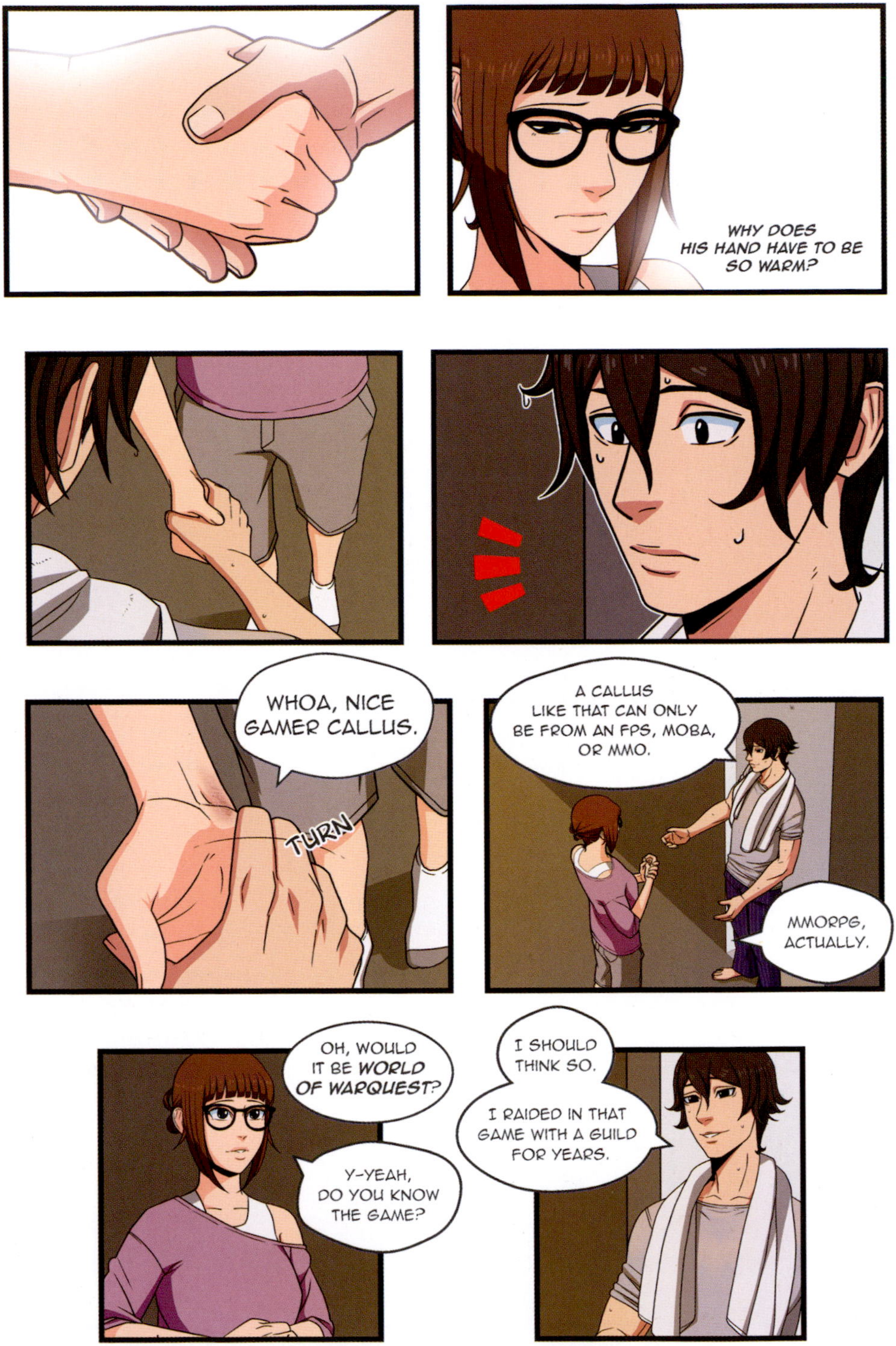
WHY DOES HIS HAND HAVE TO BE SO WARM?
WHOA, NICE GAMER CALLUS.
TURN
A CALLUS LIKE THAT CAN ONLY BE FROM AN FPS, MOBA, OR MMO.
MMORPG, ACTUALLY.
OH, WOULD IT BE *WORLD OF WARQUEST*?
Y-YEAH, DO YOU KNOW THE GAME?
I SHOULD THINK SO.
I RAIDED IN THAT GAME WITH A GUILD FOR YEARS.

WHAT—REALLY?! WHAT WAS THE LAST DUNGEON YOU RAIDED?

HALL OF THE TROLL KING.

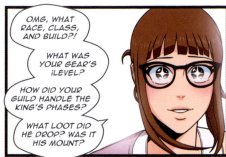

OMG, WHAT RACE, CLASS, AND BUILD?!

WHAT WAS YOUR GEAR'S iLEVEL?

HOW DID YOUR GUILD HANDLE THE KING'S PHASES?

WHAT LOOT DID HE DROP? WAS IT HIS MOUNT?

CHUCKLES

FROZEN

WHAT ON EARTH AM I DOING? I'M FURIOUS WITH HIM, I SHOULDN'T BE TALKING TO HIM LIKE THERE ISN'T ANYTHING WRONG!

DAMN HIM FOR ASKING ABOUT MY FAVORITE MMO, MY ONE TRUE WEAKNESS!!!

MOBA, AND FPS?

YOU KIDS AND YOUR HIP LINGO.

NOW, LET'S SEE HOW WELL YOU'RE GETTING SETTLED IN, MR. LAW.

STEP

STEP

AH, WAIT MS. WHIPPLE! THE PLACE IS A MESS!

WELL OF COURSE. YOU JUST MOVED IN TODAY. FUFU!

A BED IN YOUR LIVING ROOM, AND AN OFFICE IN YOUR BEDROOM?

THAT'S ODD.

PLEASE BE CAREFUL MS. WHIPPLE!

THERE IS A LOT OF SENSITIVE EQUIPMENT IN THERE!

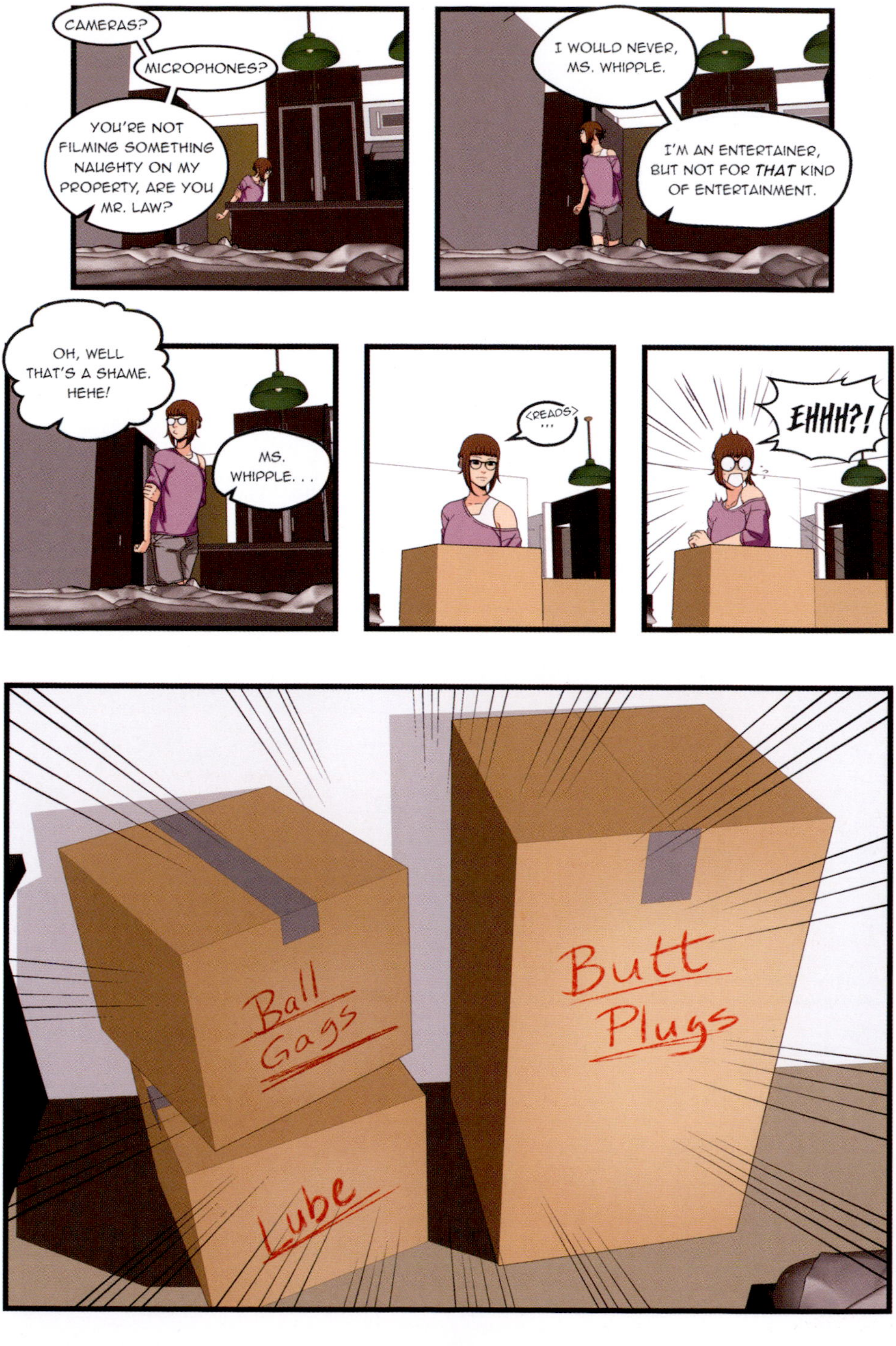
CAMERAS?
MICROPHONES?
YOU'RE NOT FILMING SOMETHING NAUGHTY ON MY PROPERTY, ARE YOU MR. LAW?
I WOULD NEVER, MS. WHIPPLE.
I'M AN ENTERTAINER, BUT NOT FOR *THAT* KIND OF ENTERTAINMENT.
OH, WELL THAT'S A SHAME. HEHE!
MS. WHIPPLE. . .
<READS> ...
EHHH?!
Ball Gags
Butt Plugs
Lube

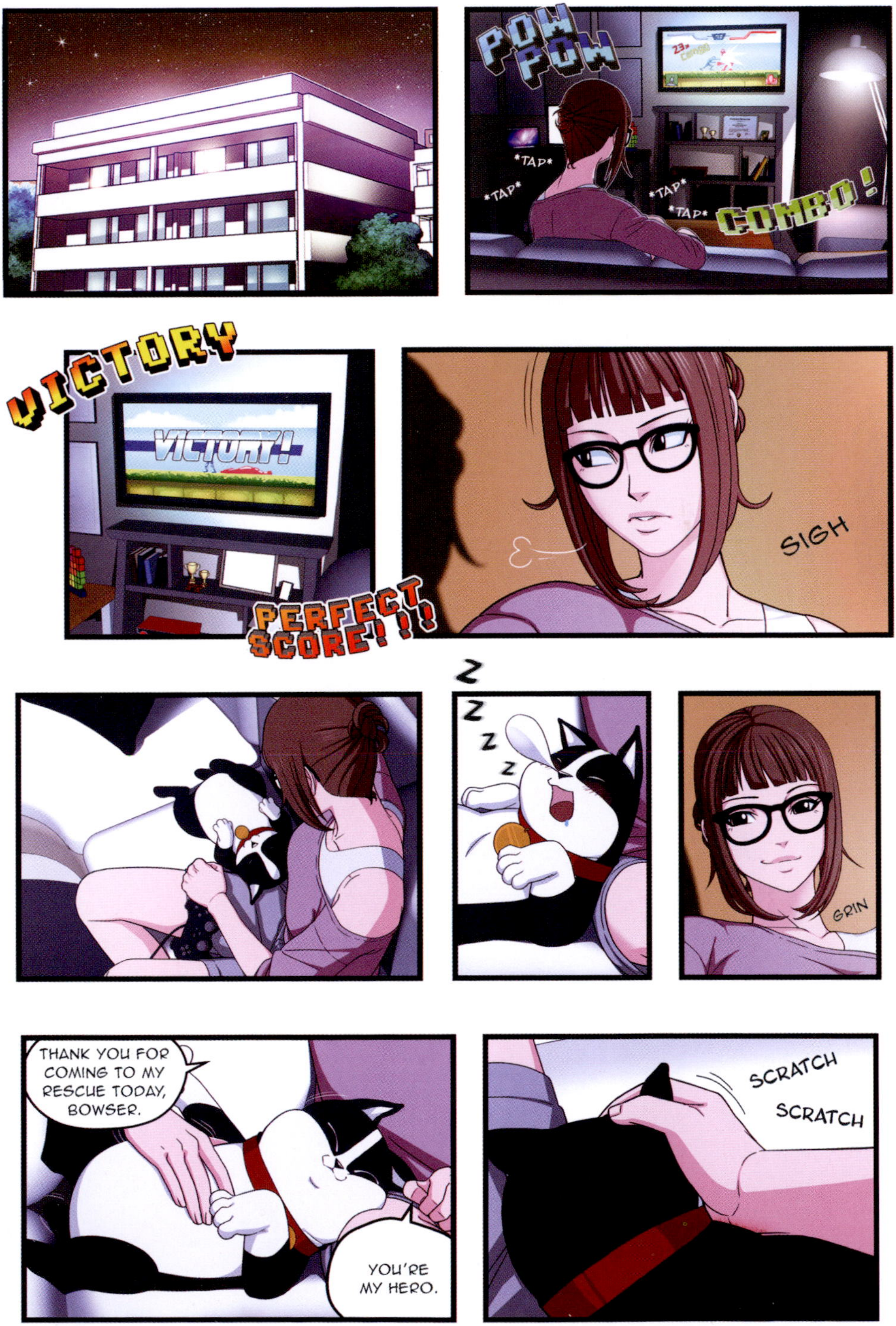
POW POW
TAP
TAP
TAP
TAP
COMBO!
VICTORY
VICTORY!
PERFECT SCORE!!!
SIGH
Z
Z
Z
Z
GRIN
THANK YOU FOR COMING TO MY RESCUE TODAY, BOWSER.
YOU'RE MY HERO.
SCRATCH
SCRATCH

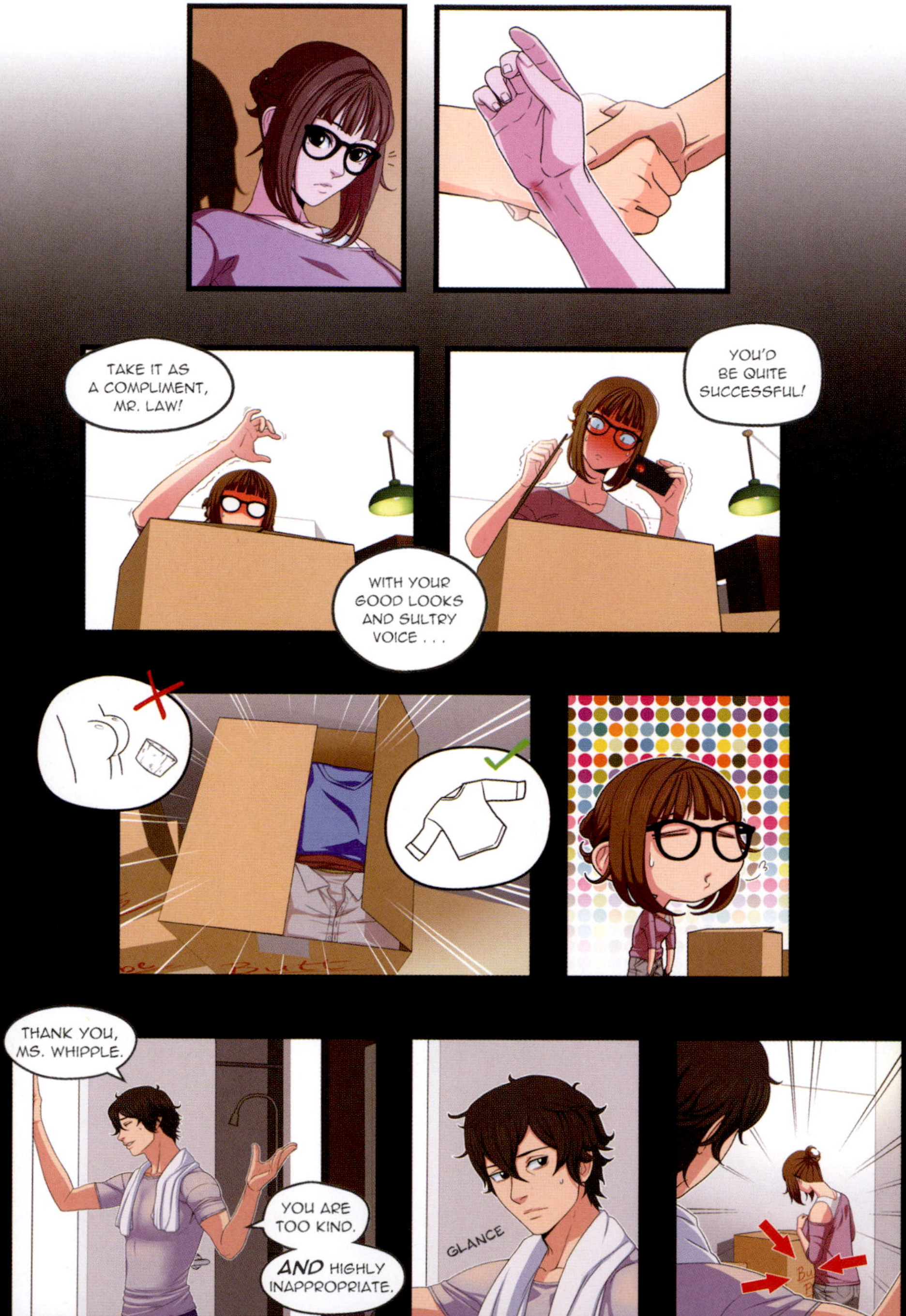
TAKE IT AS A COMPLIMENT, MR. LAW!
YOU'D BE QUITE SUCCESSFUL!
WITH YOUR GOOD LOOKS AND SULTRY VOICE . . .
THANK YOU, MS. WHIPPLE.
YOU ARE TOO KIND.
AND HIGHLY INAPPROPRIATE.
GLANCE

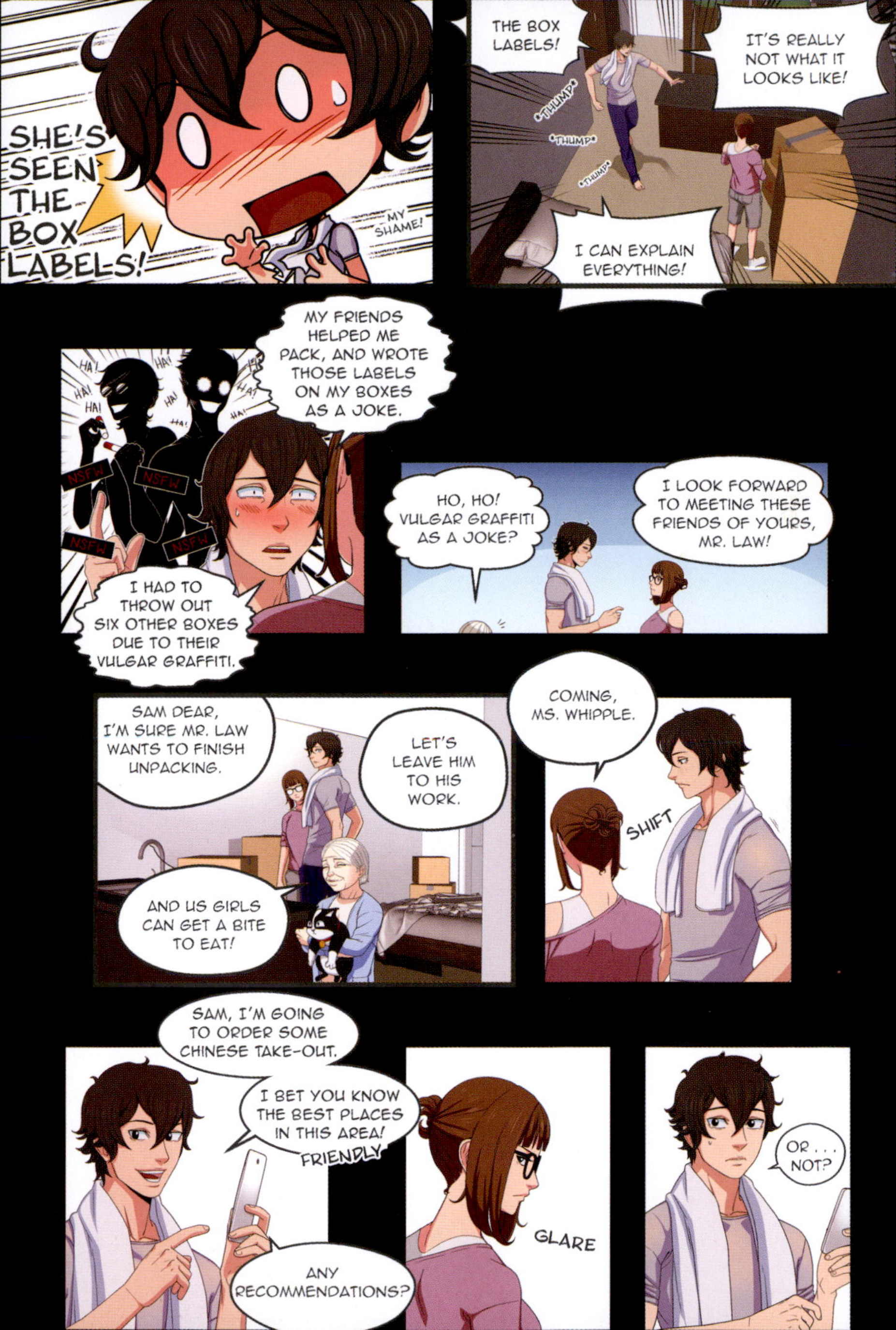
SHE'S SEEN THE BOX LABELS!
MY SHAME!
THE BOX LABELS!
IT'S REALLY NOT WHAT IT LOOKS LIKE!
THUMP
THUMP
THUMP
I CAN EXPLAIN EVERYTHING!
MY FRIENDS HELPED ME PACK, AND WROTE THOSE LABELS ON MY BOXES AS A JOKE.
HA! HA! HA! HA! HA! HA! HA! HA!
NSFW
NSFW
NSFW
NSFW
I HAD TO THROW OUT SIX OTHER BOXES DUE TO THEIR VULGAR GRAFFITI.
HO, HO! VULGAR GRAFFITI AS A JOKE?
I LOOK FORWARD TO MEETING THESE FRIENDS OF YOURS, MR. LAW!
SAM DEAR, I'M SURE MR. LAW WANTS TO FINISH UNPACKING.
LET'S LEAVE HIM TO HIS WORK.
AND US GIRLS CAN GET A BITE TO EAT!
COMING, MS. WHIPPLE.
SHIFT
SAM, I'M GOING TO ORDER SOME CHINESE TAKE-OUT.
I BET YOU KNOW THE BEST PLACES IN THIS AREA!
FRIENDLY
ANY RECOMMENDATIONS?
GLARE
OR . . . NOT?

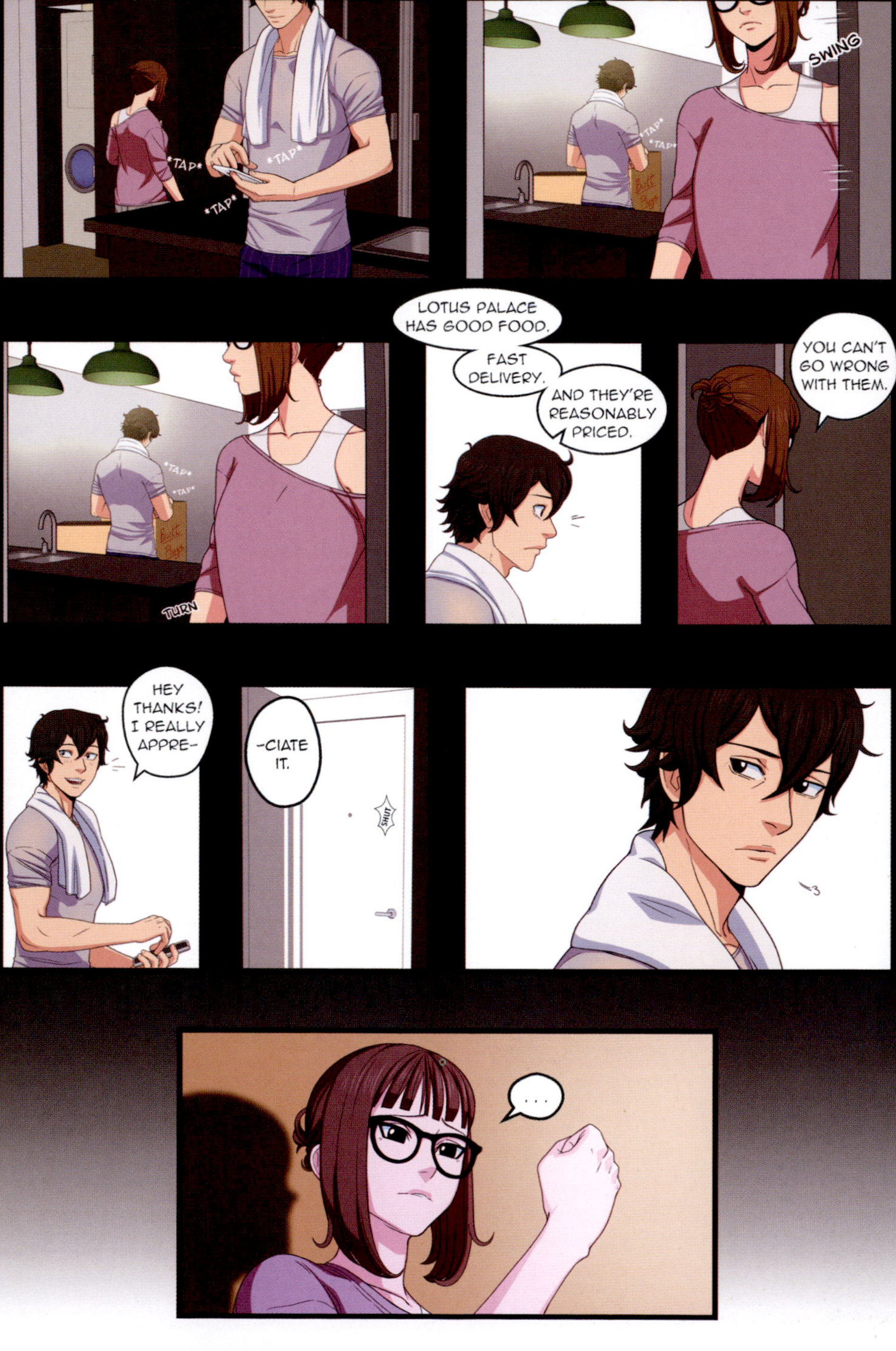
TAP
TAP
TAP
SWING
TAP
TAP
TURN
LOTUS PALACE HAS GOOD FOOD.
FAST DELIVERY.
AND THEY'RE REASONABLY PRICED.
YOU CAN'T GO WRONG WITH THEM.
HEY THANKS! I REALLY APPRE-
-CIATE IT.
SHUT
. . .

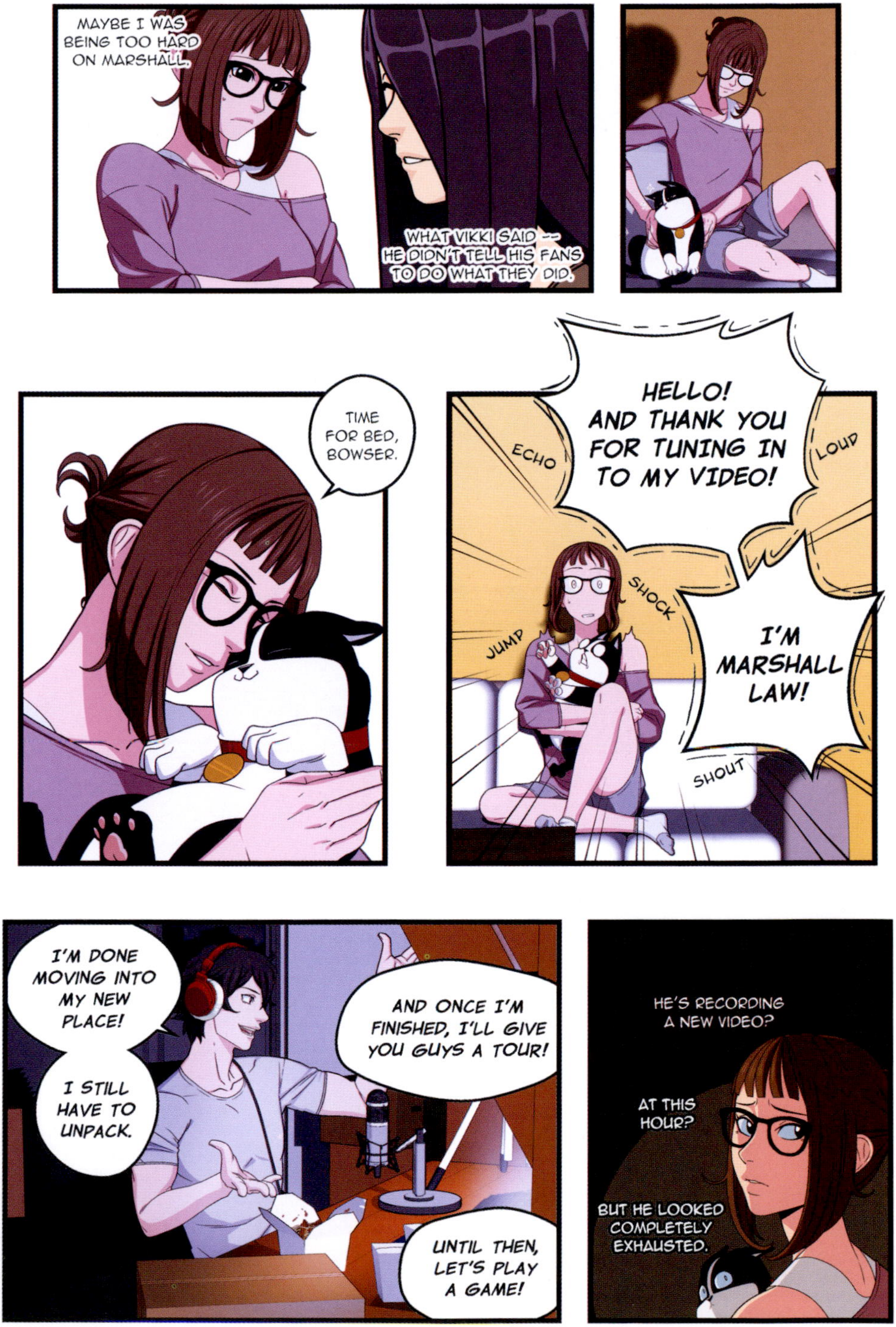
MAYBE I WAS BEING TOO HARD ON MARSHALL.
WHAT VIKKI SAID -- HE DIDN'T TELL HIS FANS TO DO WHAT THEY DID.
TIME FOR BED, BOWSER.
HELLO! AND THANK YOU FOR TUNING IN TO MY VIDEO!
ECHO
LOUD
SHOCK
JUMP
I'M MARSHALL LAW!
SHOUT
I'M DONE MOVING INTO MY NEW PLACE!
I STILL HAVE TO UNPACK.
AND ONCE I'M FINISHED, I'LL GIVE YOU GUYS A TOUR!
UNTIL THEN, LET'S PLAY A GAME!
HE'S RECORDING A NEW VIDEO?
AT THIS HOUR?
BUT HE LOOKED COMPLETELY EXHAUSTED.

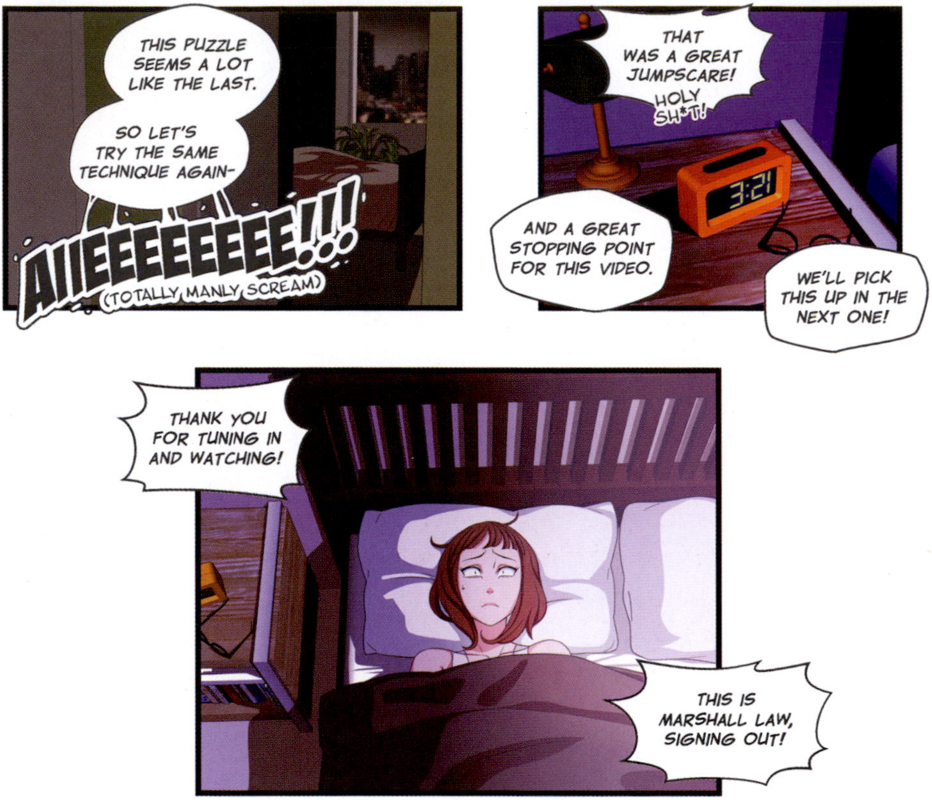
THIS PUZZLE SEEMS A LOT LIKE THE LAST.
SO LET'S TRY THE SAME TECHNIQUE AGAIN-
AIIEEEEEEEEE!!!
(TOTALLY MANLY SCREAM)
THAT WAS A GREAT JUMPSCARE!
HOLY SH*T!
AND A GREAT STOPPING POINT FOR THIS VIDEO.
WE'LL PICK THIS UP IN THE NEXT ONE!
THANK YOU FOR TUNING IN AND WATCHING!
THIS IS MARSHALL LAW, SIGNING OUT!

The next morning.

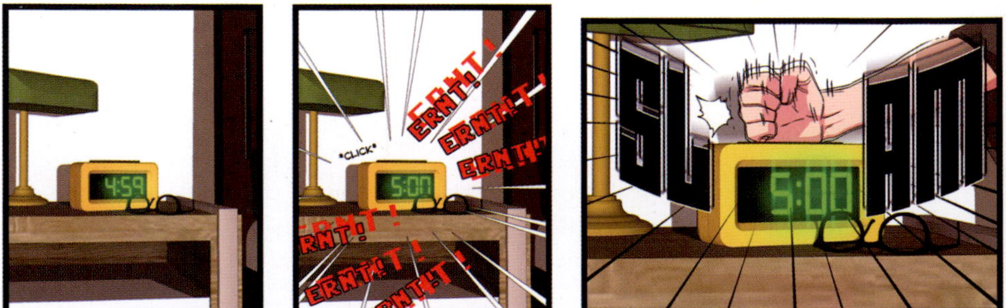
CLICK
ERNT!
ERNT!
ERNT!
ERNT!
ERNT!
ERNT!
SLAM

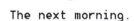

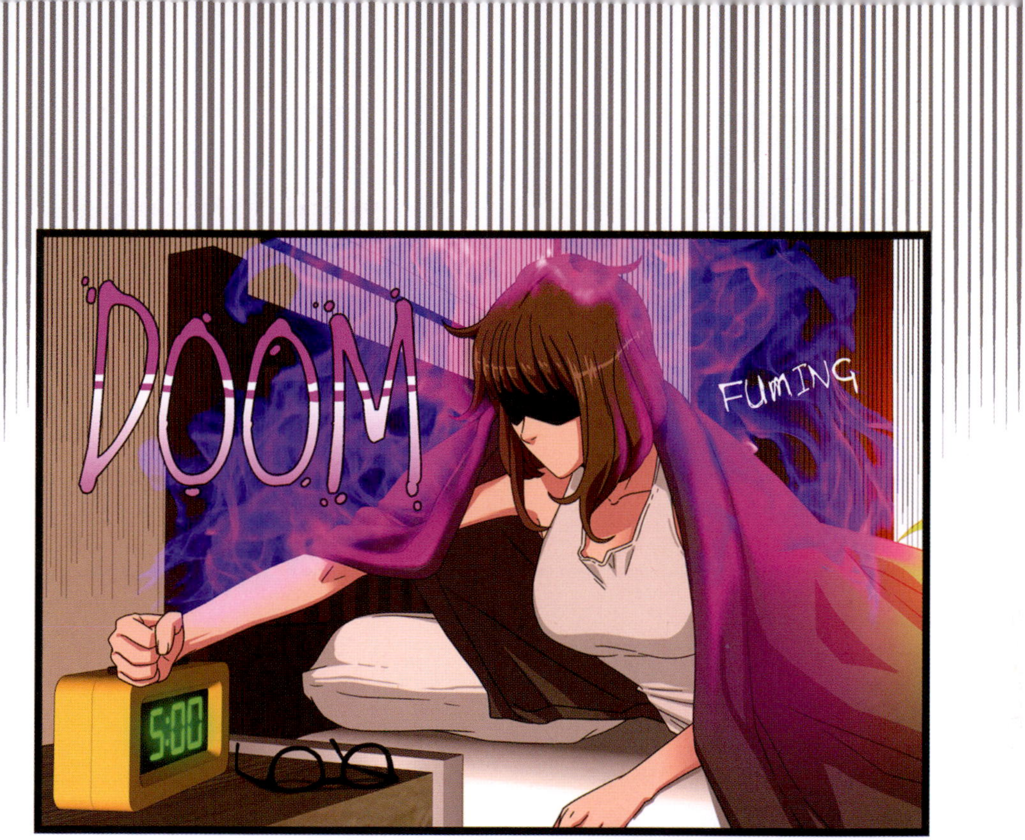
DOOM
FUMING

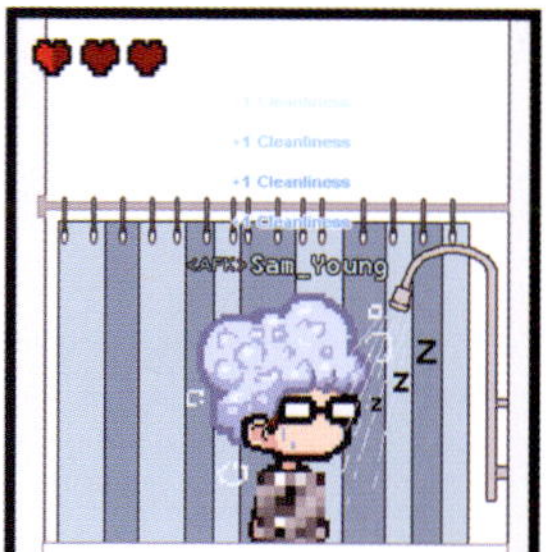
+1 Cleanliness
+1 Cleanliness
<AFK> Sam_Young
Z Z z

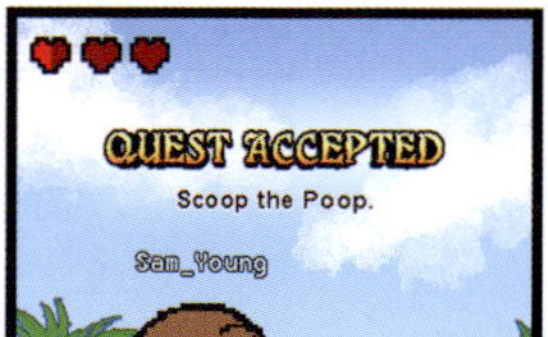
QUEST ACCEPTED
Scoop the Poop.
Sam_Young

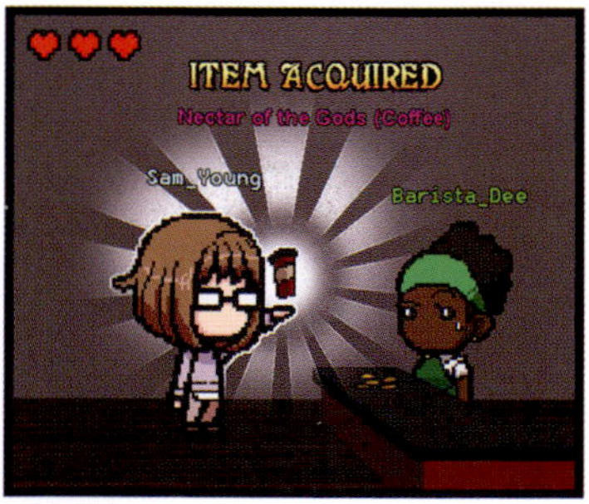
ITEM ACQUIRED
Nectar of the Gods (Coffee)
Sam_Young
Barista_Dee

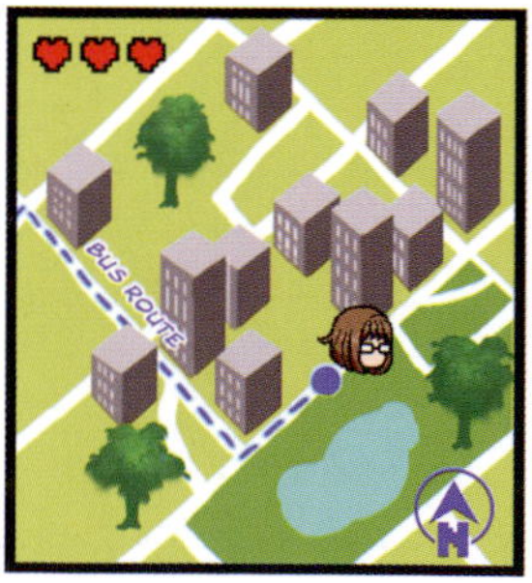
BUS ROUTE
N

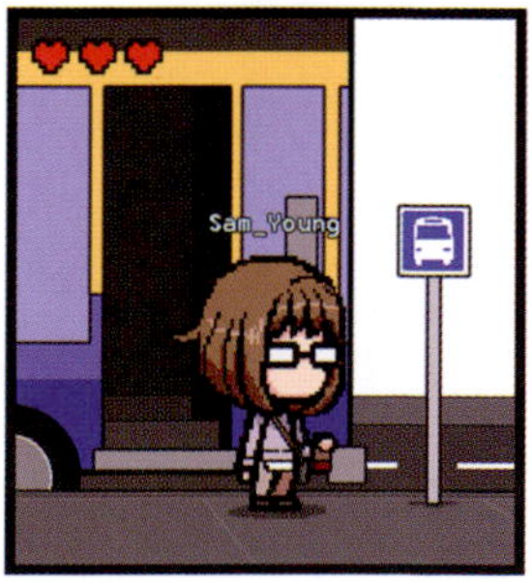
Sam_Young

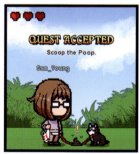

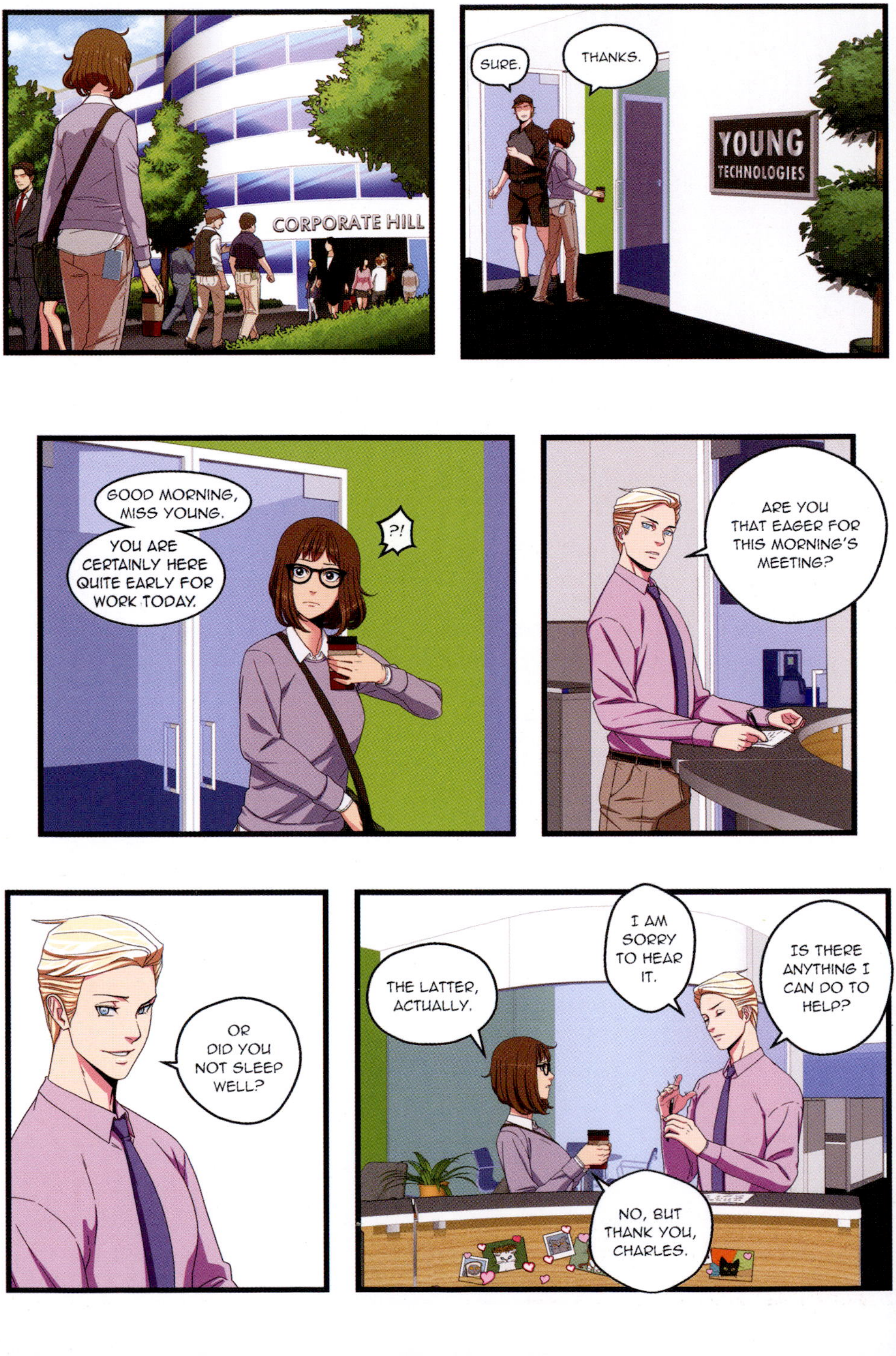
CORPORATE HILL
SURE.
THANKS.
YOUNG TECHNOLOGIES
GOOD MORNING, MISS YOUNG.
YOU ARE CERTAINLY HERE QUITE EARLY FOR WORK TODAY.
?!
ARE YOU THAT EAGER FOR THIS MORNING'S MEETING?
OR DID YOU NOT SLEEP WELL?
THE LATTER, ACTUALLY.
I AM SORRY TO HEAR IT.
IS THERE ANYTHING I CAN DO TO HELP?
NO, BUT THANK YOU, CHARLES.

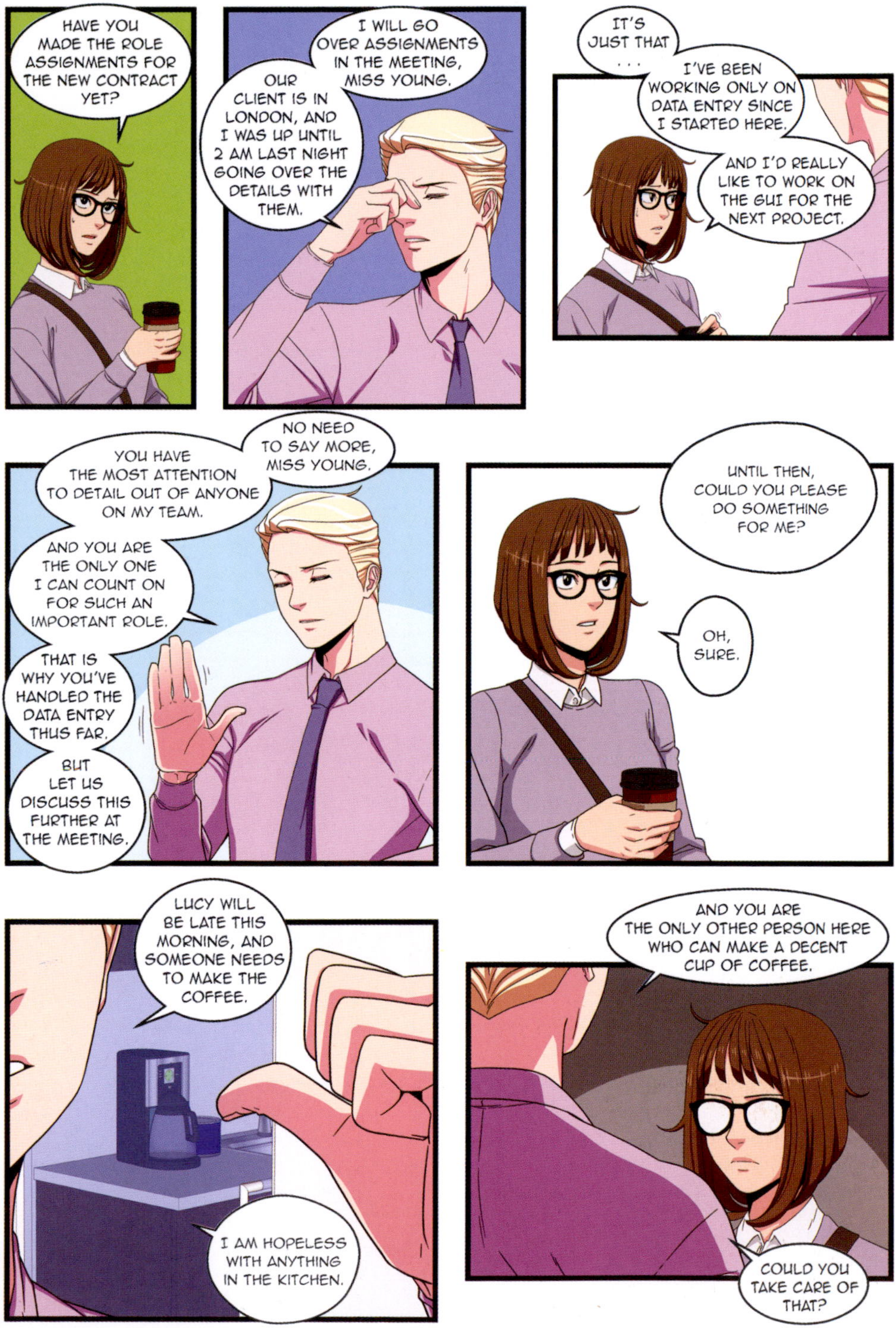
HAVE YOU MADE THE ROLE ASSIGNMENTS FOR THE NEW CONTRACT YET?
I WILL GO OVER ASSIGNMENTS IN THE MEETING, MISS YOUNG.
OUR CLIENT IS IN LONDON, AND I WAS UP UNTIL 2 AM LAST NIGHT GOING OVER THE DETAILS WITH THEM.
IT'S JUST THAT . . .
I'VE BEEN WORKING ONLY ON DATA ENTRY SINCE I STARTED HERE.
AND I'D REALLY LIKE TO WORK ON THE GUI FOR THE NEXT PROJECT.
YOU HAVE THE MOST ATTENTION TO DETAIL OUT OF ANYONE ON MY TEAM.
NO NEED TO SAY MORE, MISS YOUNG.
AND YOU ARE THE ONLY ONE I CAN COUNT ON FOR SUCH AN IMPORTANT ROLE.
THAT IS WHY YOU'VE HANDLED THE DATA ENTRY THUS FAR.
BUT LET US DISCUSS THIS FURTHER AT THE MEETING.
UNTIL THEN, COULD YOU PLEASE DO SOMETHING FOR ME?
OH, SURE.
LUCY WILL BE LATE THIS MORNING, AND SOMEONE NEEDS TO MAKE THE COFFEE.
I AM HOPELESS WITH ANYTHING IN THE KITCHEN.
AND YOU ARE THE ONLY OTHER PERSON HERE WHO CAN MAKE A DECENT CUP OF COFFEE.
COULD YOU TAKE CARE OF THAT?

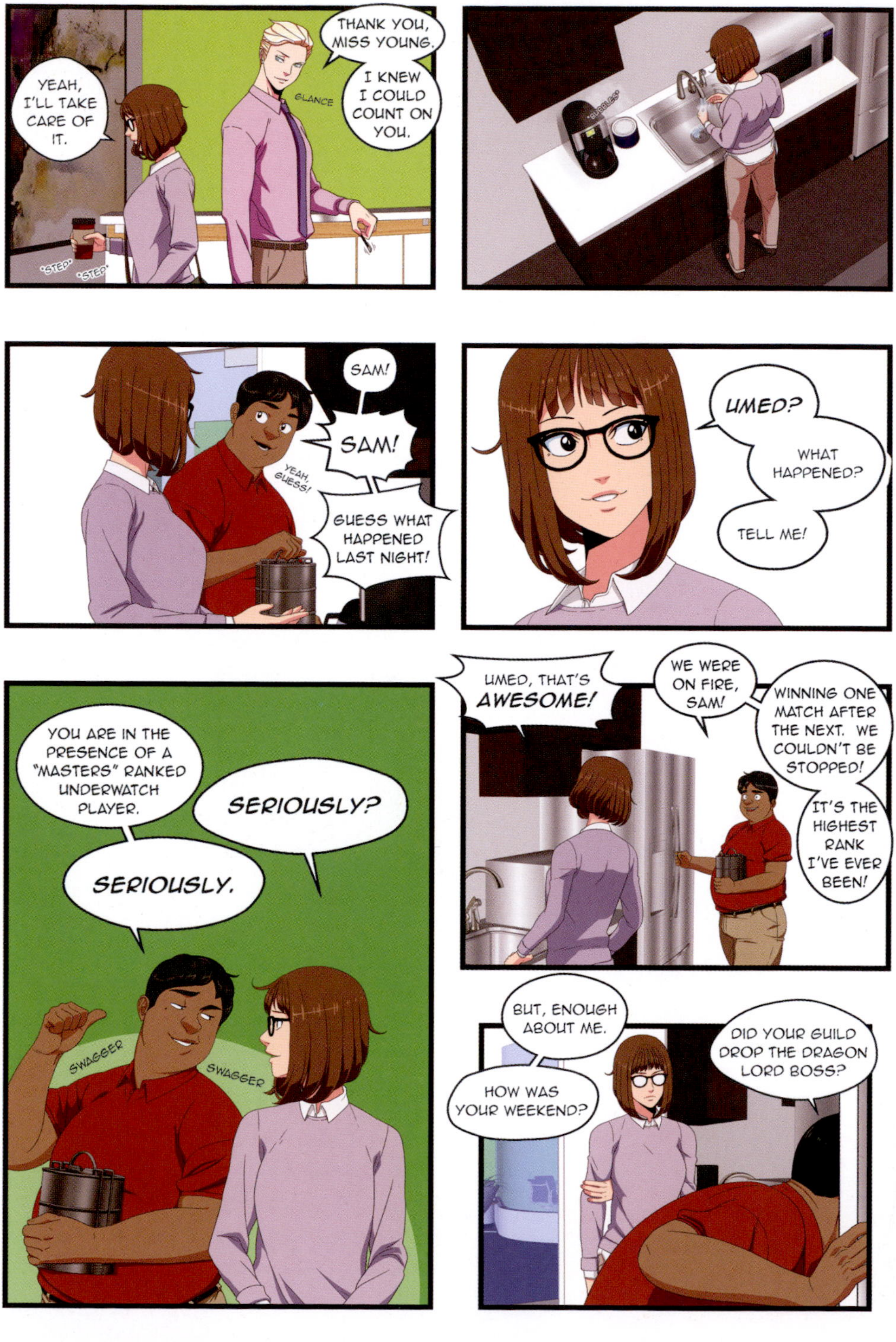
YEAH, I'LL TAKE CARE OF IT.
GLANCE
THANK YOU, MISS YOUNG.
I KNEW I COULD COUNT ON YOU.
STEP *STEP*
BUBBLES
SAM!
SAM!
YEAH, GUESS!
GUESS WHAT HAPPENED LAST NIGHT!
UMED?
WHAT HAPPENED?
TELL ME!
YOU ARE IN THE PRESENCE OF A "MASTERS" RANKED UNDERWATCH PLAYER.
SERIOUSLY?
SERIOUSLY.
SWAGGER
SWAGGER
UMED, THAT'S AWESOME!
WE WERE ON FIRE, SAM!
WINNING ONE MATCH AFTER THE NEXT. WE COULDN'T BE STOPPED!
IT'S THE HIGHEST RANK I'VE EVER BEEN!
BUT, ENOUGH ABOUT ME.
HOW WAS YOUR WEEKEND?
DID YOUR GUILD DROP THE DRAGON LORD BOSS?

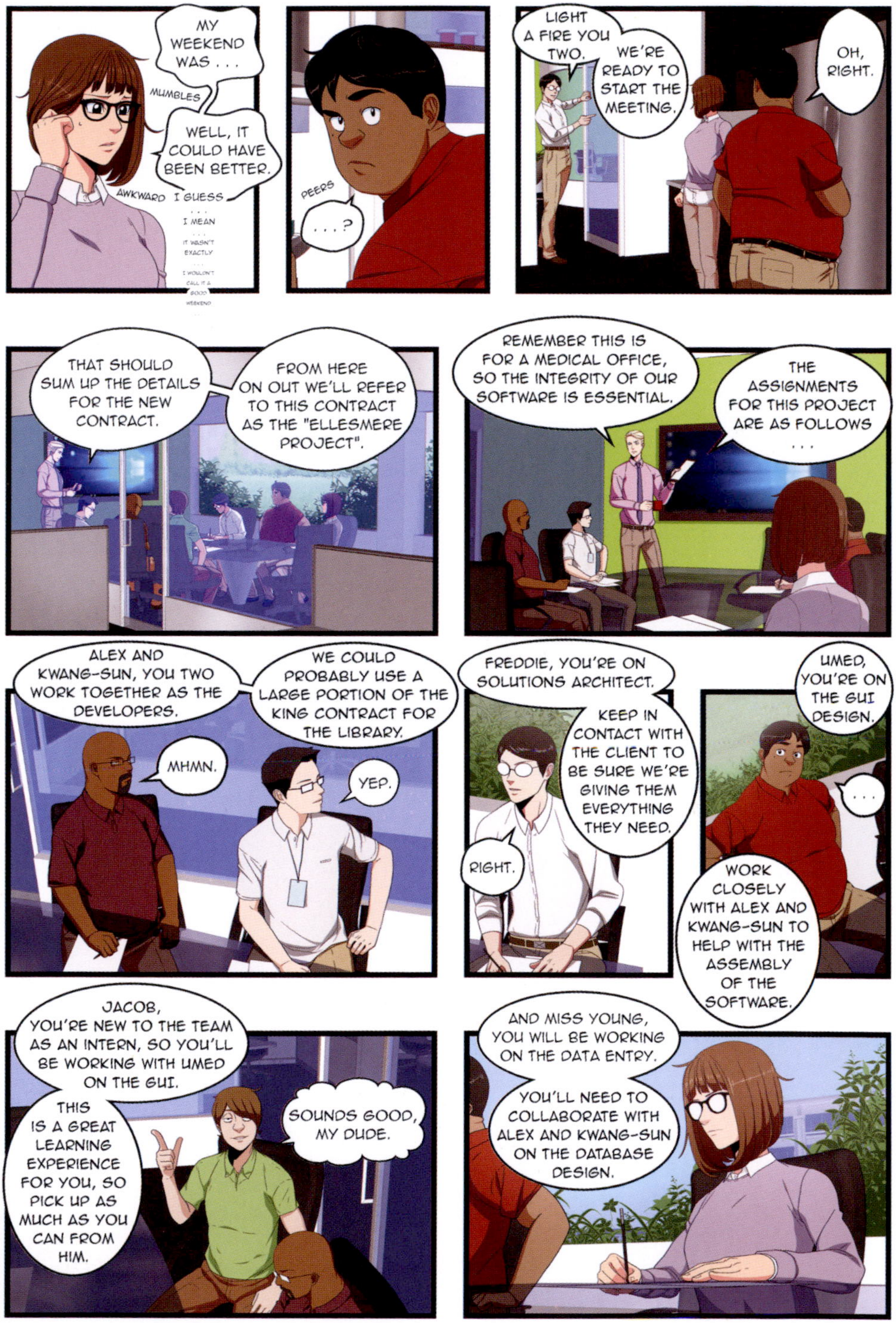
MY WEEKEND WAS . . .
MUMBLES
WELL, IT COULD HAVE BEEN BETTER.
AWKWARD
I GUESS . . . I MEAN . . . IT WASN'T EXACTLY . . . I WOULDN'T CALL IT A GOOD WEEKEND
PEERS
. . . ?
LIGHT A FIRE YOU TWO.
WE'RE READY TO START THE MEETING.
OH, RIGHT.
THAT SHOULD SUM UP THE DETAILS FOR THE NEW CONTRACT.
FROM HERE ON OUT WE'LL REFER TO THIS CONTRACT AS THE "ELLESMERE PROJECT".
REMEMBER THIS IS FOR A MEDICAL OFFICE, SO THE INTEGRITY OF OUR SOFTWARE IS ESSENTIAL.
THE ASSIGNMENTS FOR THIS PROJECT ARE AS FOLLOWS . . .
ALEX AND KWANG-SUN, YOU TWO WORK TOGETHER AS THE DEVELOPERS.
WE COULD PROBABLY USE A LARGE PORTION OF THE KING CONTRACT FOR THE LIBRARY.
MHMN.
YEP.
FREDDIE, YOU'RE ON SOLUTIONS ARCHITECT.
KEEP IN CONTACT WITH THE CLIENT TO BE SURE WE'RE GIVING THEM EVERYTHING THEY NEED.
RIGHT.
UMED, YOU'RE ON THE GUI DESIGN.
. . .
WORK CLOSELY WITH ALEX AND KWANG-SUN TO HELP WITH THE ASSEMBLY OF THE SOFTWARE.
JACOB, YOU'RE NEW TO THE TEAM AS AN INTERN, SO YOU'LL BE WORKING WITH UMED ON THE GUI.
THIS IS A GREAT LEARNING EXPERIENCE FOR YOU, SO PICK UP AS MUCH AS YOU CAN FROM HIM.
SOUNDS GOOD, MY DUDE.
AND MISS YOUNG, YOU WILL BE WORKING ON THE DATA ENTRY.
YOU'LL NEED TO COLLABORATE WITH ALEX AND KWANG-SUN ON THE DATABASE DESIGN.

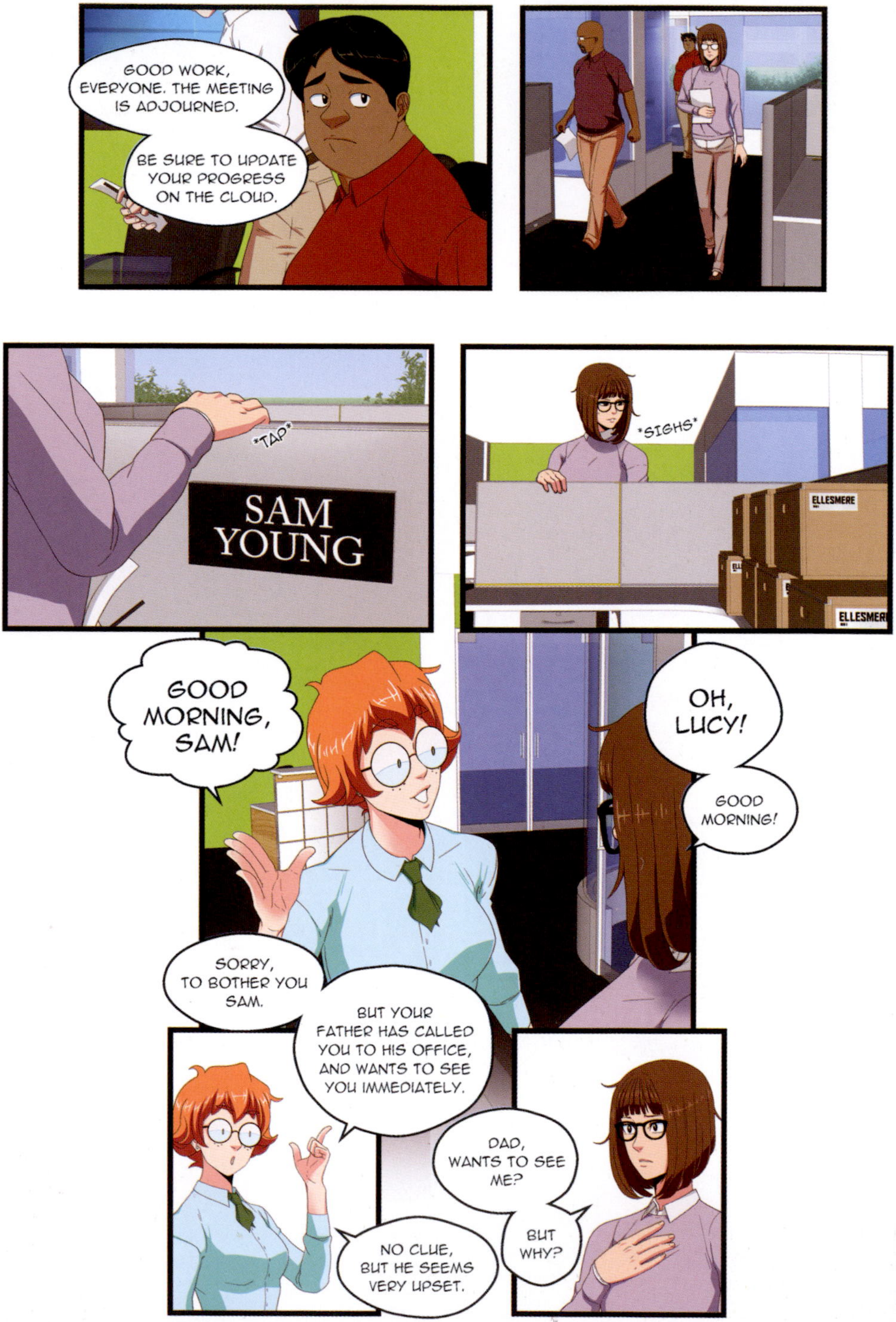
GOOD WORK, EVERYONE. THE MEETING IS ADJOURNED.
BE SURE TO UPDATE YOUR PROGRESS ON THE CLOUD.
TAP
SAM YOUNG
SIGHS
ELLESMERE
ELLESMERE
GOOD MORNING, SAM!
OH, LUCY!
GOOD MORNING!
SORRY, TO BOTHER YOU SAM.
BUT YOUR FATHER HAS CALLED YOU TO HIS OFFICE, AND WANTS TO SEE YOU IMMEDIATELY.
DAD, WANTS TO SEE ME?
BUT WHY?
NO CLUE, BUT HE SEEMS VERY UPSET.

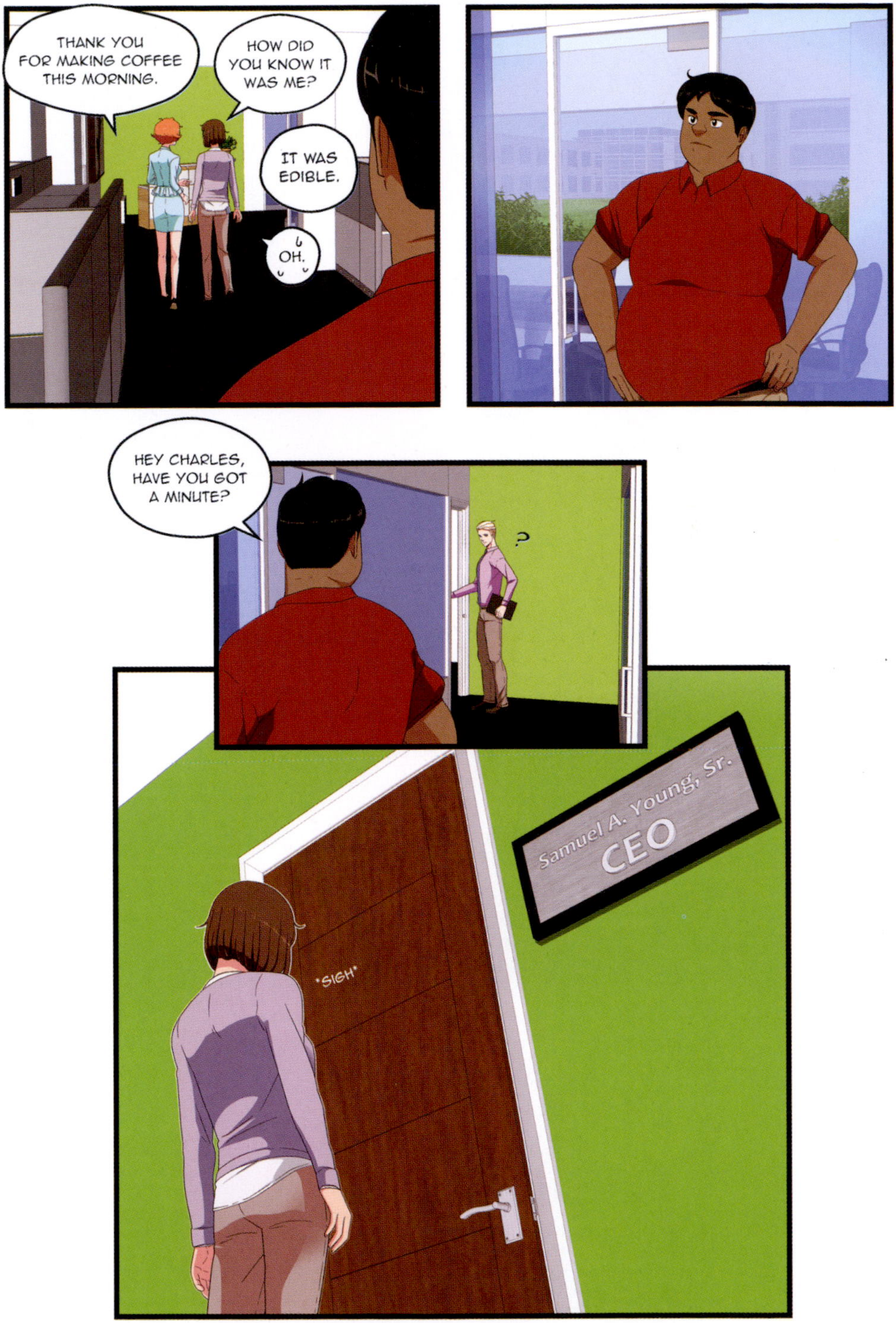
THANK YOU FOR MAKING COFFEE THIS MORNING.
HOW DID YOU KNOW IT WAS ME?
IT WAS EDIBLE.
OH.
HEY CHARLES, HAVE YOU GOT A MINUTE?
?
Samuel A. Young, Sr.
CEO
SIGH

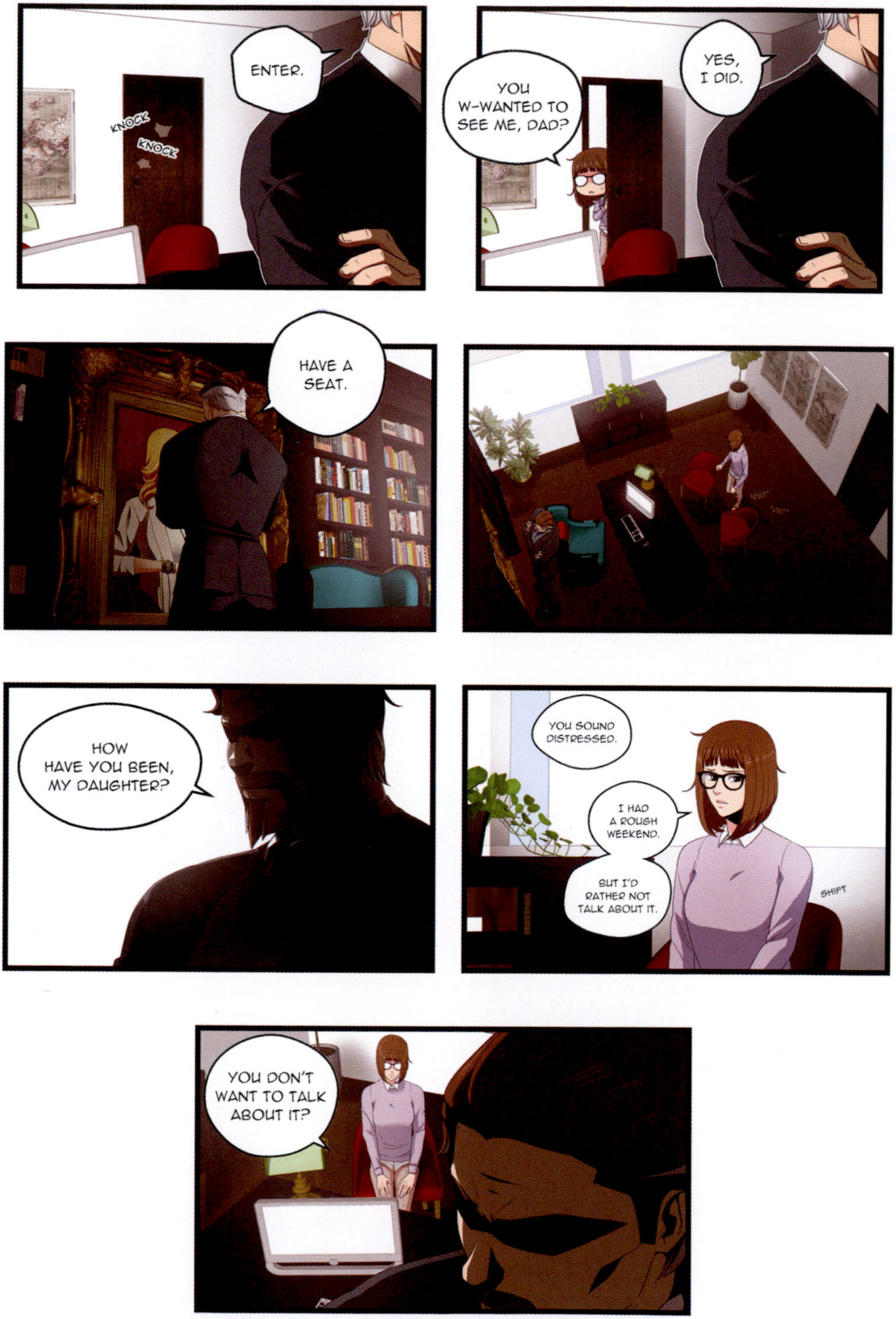
ENTER.
KNOCK
KNOCK
YOU W-WANTED TO SEE ME, DAD?
YES, I DID.
HAVE A SEAT.
HOW HAVE YOU BEEN, MY DAUGHTER?
YOU SOUND DISTRESSED.
I HAD A ROUGH WEEKEND.
BUT I'D RATHER NOT TALK ABOUT IT.
SHIFT
YOU DON'T WANT TO TALK ABOUT IT?

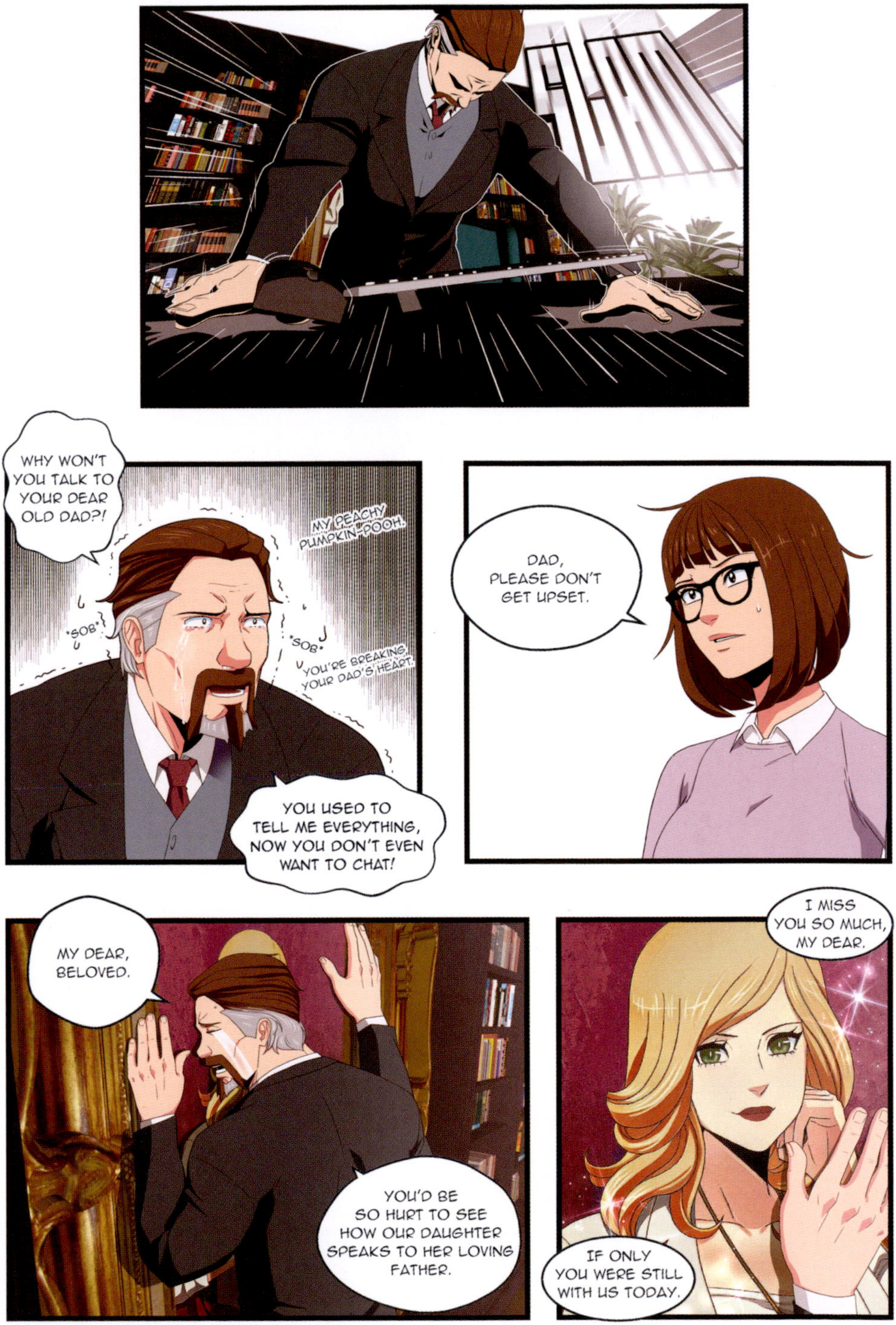
WHY WON'T YOU TALK TO YOUR DEAR OLD DAD?!
MY PEACHY PUMPKIN-POOH.
SOB
SOB
YOU'RE BREAKING YOUR DAD'S HEART.
YOU USED TO TELL ME EVERYTHING, NOW YOU DON'T EVEN WANT TO CHAT!
DAD, PLEASE DON'T GET UPSET.
MY DEAR, BELOVED.
YOU'D BE SO HURT TO SEE HOW OUR DAUGHTER SPEAKS TO HER LOVING FATHER.
I MISS YOU SO MUCH, MY DEAR.
IF ONLY YOU WERE STILL WITH US TODAY.

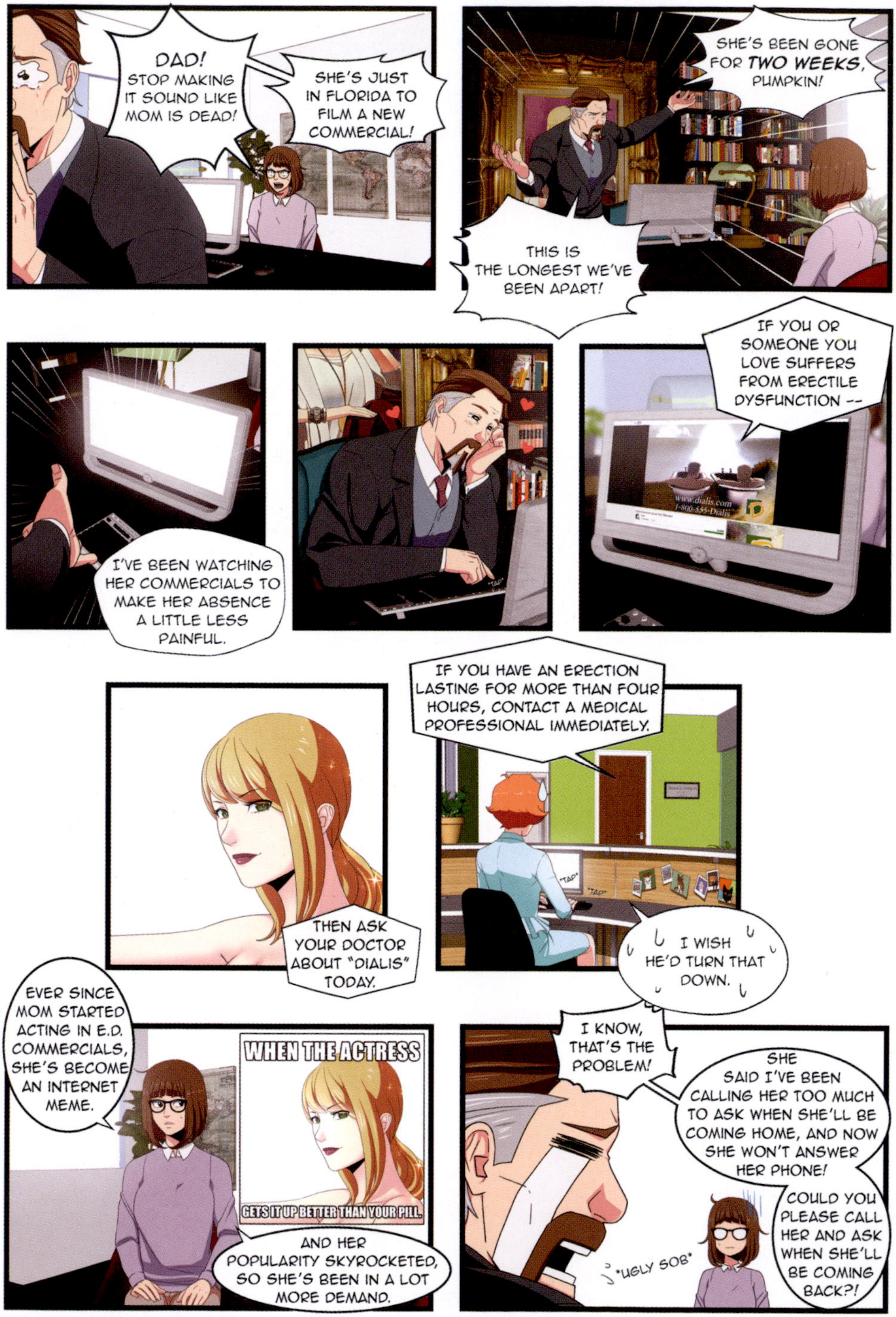
DAD! STOP MAKING IT SOUND LIKE MOM IS DEAD!
SHE'S JUST IN FLORIDA TO FILM A NEW COMMERCIAL!
SHE'S BEEN GONE FOR **TWO WEEKS**, PUMPKIN!
THIS IS THE LONGEST WE'VE BEEN APART!
I'VE BEEN WATCHING HER COMMERCIALS TO MAKE HER ABSENCE A LITTLE LESS PAINFUL.
TAP
IF YOU OR SOMEONE YOU LOVE SUFFERS FROM ERECTILE DYSFUNCTION --
www.dialis.com
1-800-555-Dialis
THEN ASK YOUR DOCTOR ABOUT "DIALIS" TODAY.
IF YOU HAVE AN ERECTION LASTING FOR MORE THAN FOUR HOURS, CONTACT A MEDICAL PROFESSIONAL IMMEDIATELY.
TAP
TAP
I WISH HE'D TURN THAT DOWN.
EVER SINCE MOM STARTED ACTING IN E.D. COMMERCIALS, SHE'S BECOME AN INTERNET MEME.
WHEN THE ACTRESS
GETS IT UP BETTER THAN YOUR PILL.
AND HER POPULARITY SKYROCKETED, SO SHE'S BEEN IN A LOT MORE DEMAND.
I KNOW, THAT'S THE PROBLEM!
SHE SAID I'VE BEEN CALLING HER TOO MUCH TO ASK WHEN SHE'LL BE COMING HOME, AND NOW SHE WON'T ANSWER HER PHONE!
COULD YOU PLEASE CALL HER AND ASK WHEN SHE'LL BE COMING BACK?!
UGLY SOB

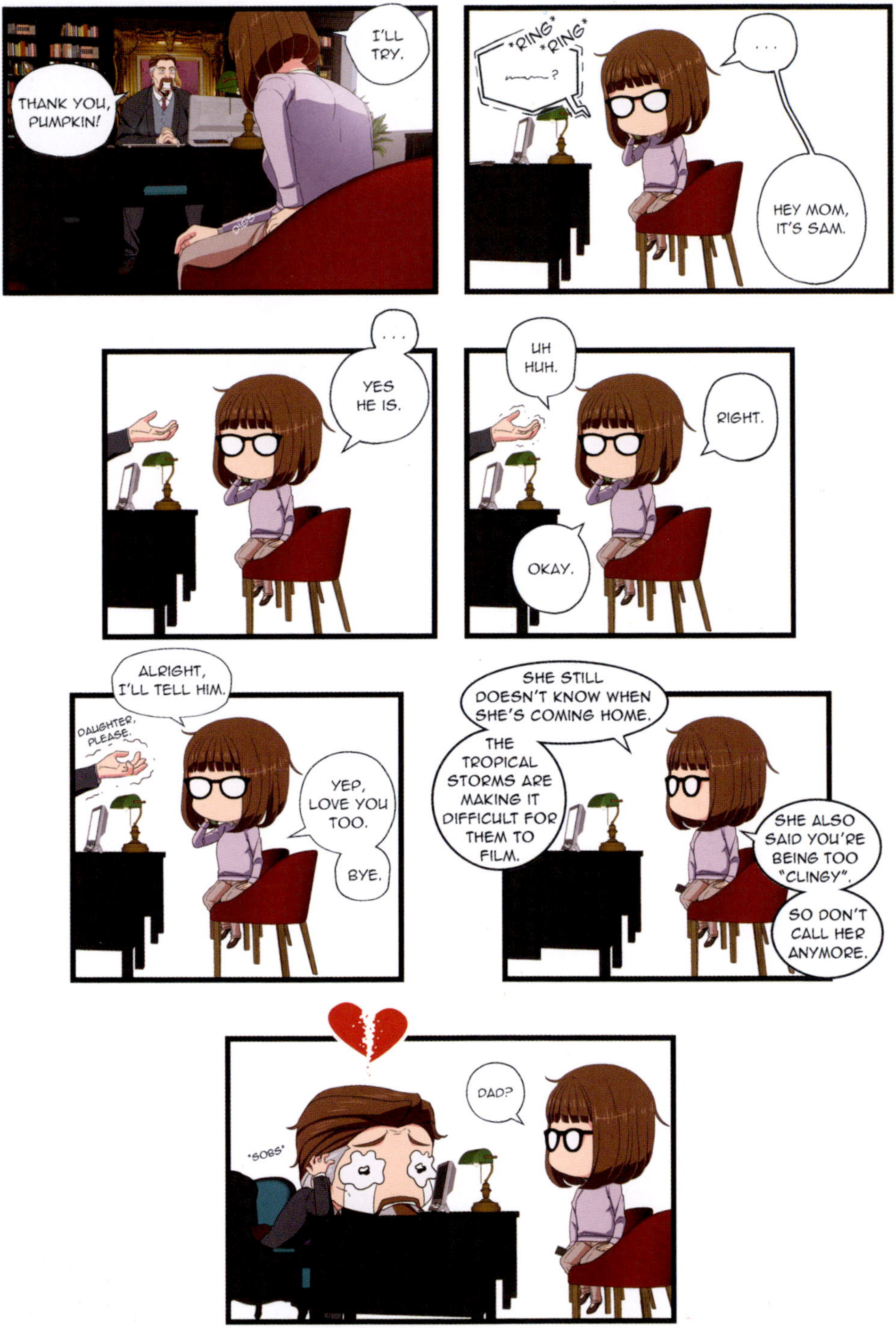
THANK YOU, PUMPKIN!
I'LL TRY.
RING *RING*
. . .
HEY MOM, IT'S SAM.
. . .
YES HE IS.
UH HUH.
RIGHT.
OKAY.
ALRIGHT, I'LL TELL HIM.
DAUGHTER, PLEASE.
YEP, LOVE YOU TOO.
BYE.
SHE STILL DOESN'T KNOW WHEN SHE'S COMING HOME.
THE TROPICAL STORMS ARE MAKING IT DIFFICULT FOR THEM TO FILM.
SHE ALSO SAID YOU'RE BEING TOO "CLINGY".
SO DON'T CALL HER ANYMORE.
SOBS
DAD?

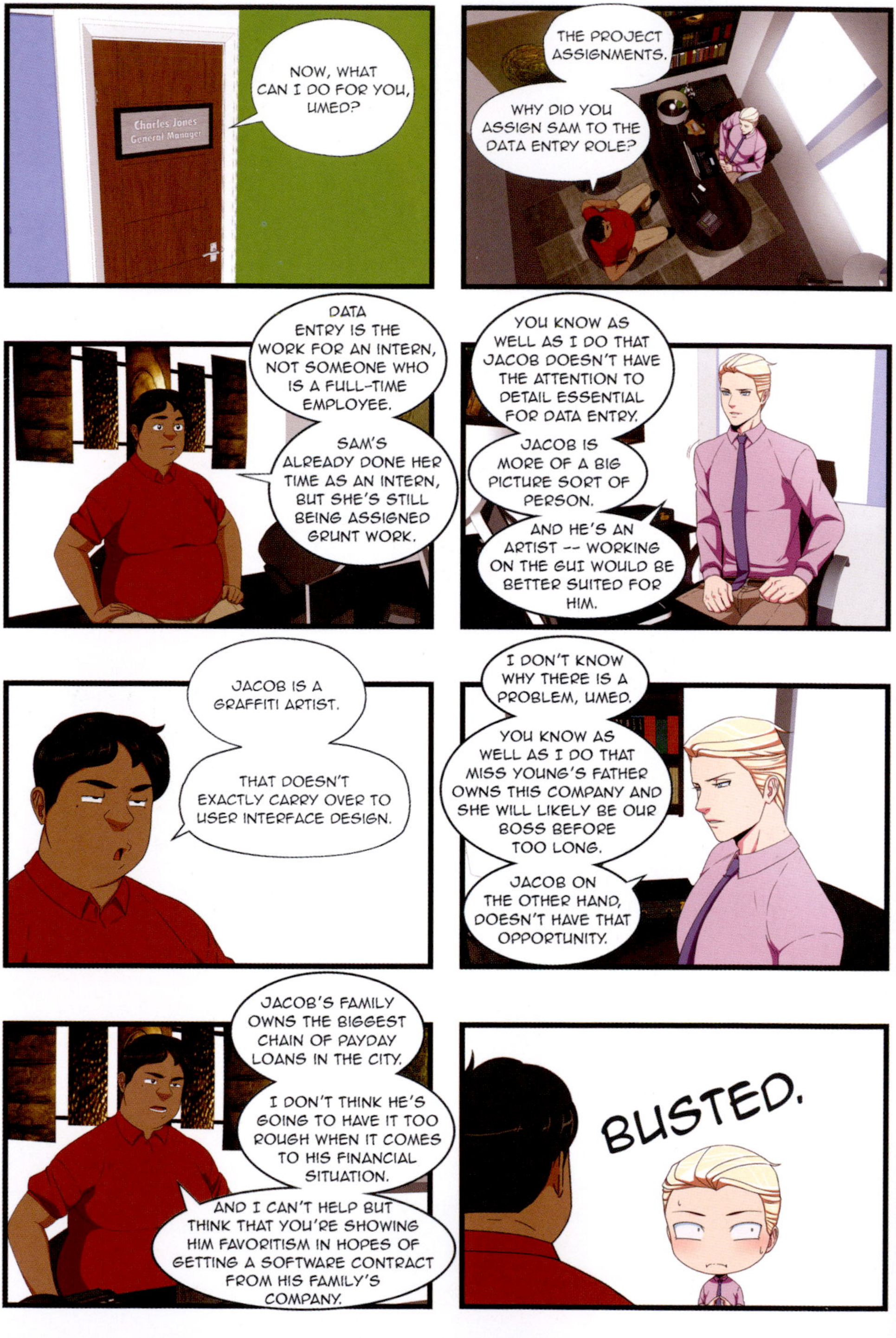
Charles Jones
General Manager
NOW, WHAT CAN I DO FOR YOU, UMED?
THE PROJECT ASSIGNMENTS.
WHY DID YOU ASSIGN SAM TO THE DATA ENTRY ROLE?
DATA ENTRY IS THE WORK FOR AN INTERN, NOT SOMEONE WHO IS A FULL-TIME EMPLOYEE.
SAM'S ALREADY DONE HER TIME AS AN INTERN, BUT SHE'S STILL BEING ASSIGNED GRUNT WORK.
YOU KNOW AS WELL AS I DO THAT JACOB DOESN'T HAVE THE ATTENTION TO DETAIL ESSENTIAL FOR DATA ENTRY.
JACOB IS MORE OF A BIG PICTURE SORT OF PERSON.
AND HE'S AN ARTIST -- WORKING ON THE GUI WOULD BE BETTER SUITED FOR HIM.
JACOB IS A GRAFFITI ARTIST.
THAT DOESN'T EXACTLY CARRY OVER TO USER INTERFACE DESIGN.
I DON'T KNOW WHY THERE IS A PROBLEM, UMED.
YOU KNOW AS WELL AS I DO THAT MISS YOUNG'S FATHER OWNS THIS COMPANY AND SHE WILL LIKELY BE OUR BOSS BEFORE TOO LONG.
JACOB ON THE OTHER HAND, DOESN'T HAVE THAT OPPORTUNITY.
JACOB'S FAMILY OWNS THE BIGGEST CHAIN OF PAYDAY LOANS IN THE CITY.
I DON'T THINK HE'S GOING TO HAVE IT TOO ROUGH WHEN IT COMES TO HIS FINANCIAL SITUATION.
AND I CAN'T HELP BUT THINK THAT YOU'RE SHOWING HIM FAVORITISM IN HOPES OF GETTING A SOFTWARE CONTRACT FROM HIS FAMILY'S COMPANY.
BUSTED.

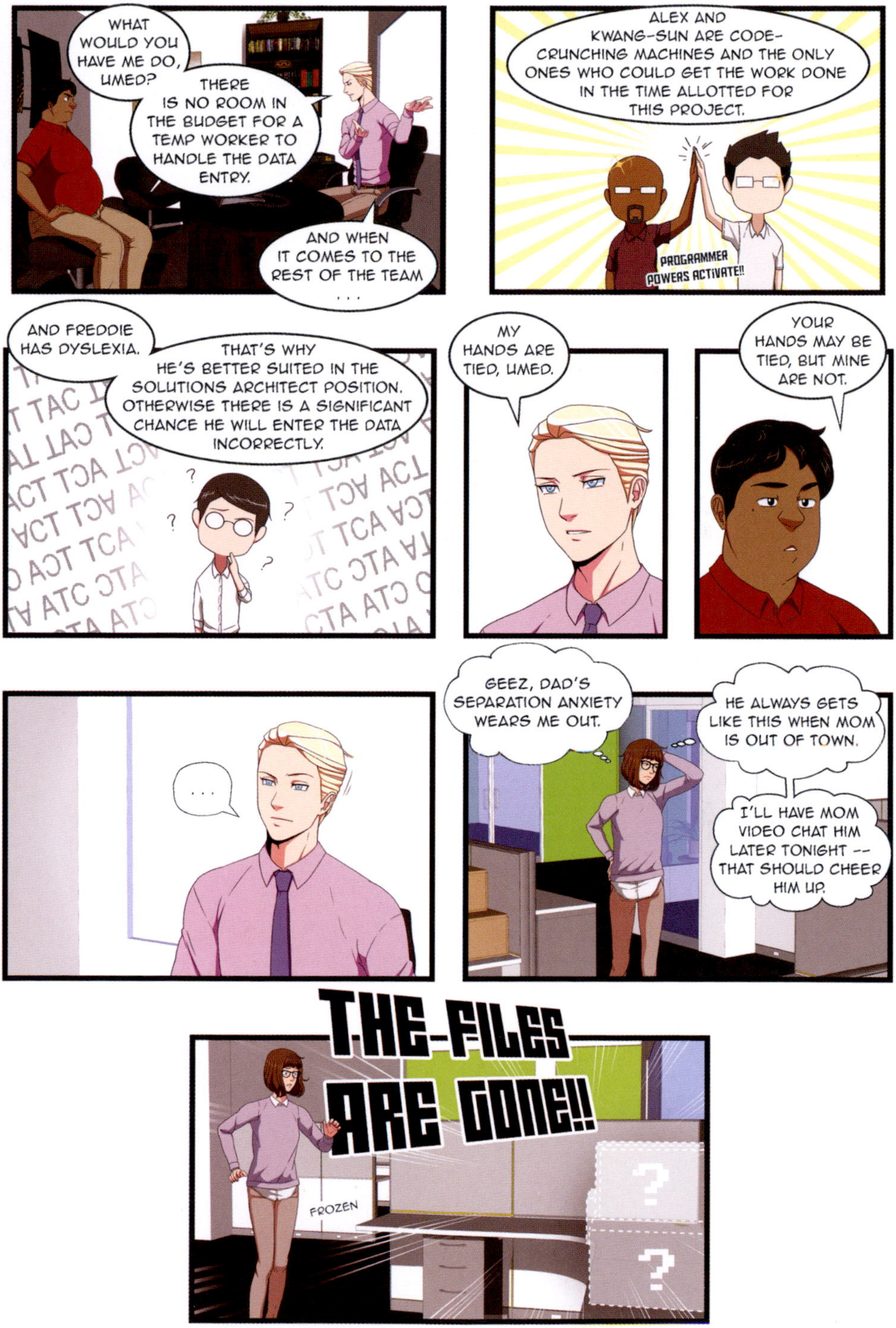
WHAT WOULD YOU HAVE ME DO, UMED?
THERE IS NO ROOM IN THE BUDGET FOR A TEMP WORKER TO HANDLE THE DATA ENTRY.
AND WHEN IT COMES TO THE REST OF THE TEAM . . .
ALEX AND KWANG-SUN ARE CODE-CRUNCHING MACHINES AND THE ONLY ONES WHO COULD GET THE WORK DONE IN THE TIME ALLOTTED FOR THIS PROJECT.
PROGRAMMER POWERS ACTIVATE!!
AND FREDDIE HAS DYSLEXIA.
THAT'S WHY HE'S BETTER SUITED IN THE SOLUTIONS ARCHITECT POSITION. OTHERWISE THERE IS A SIGNIFICANT CHANCE HE WILL ENTER THE DATA INCORRECTLY.
MY HANDS ARE TIED, UMED.
YOUR HANDS MAY BE TIED, BUT MINE ARE NOT.
. . .
GEEZ, DAD'S SEPARATION ANXIETY WEARS ME OUT.
HE ALWAYS GETS LIKE THIS WHEN MOM IS OUT OF TOWN.
I'LL HAVE MOM VIDEO CHAT HIM LATER TONIGHT -- THAT SHOULD CHEER HIM UP.
THE FILES ARE GONE!!
FROZEN

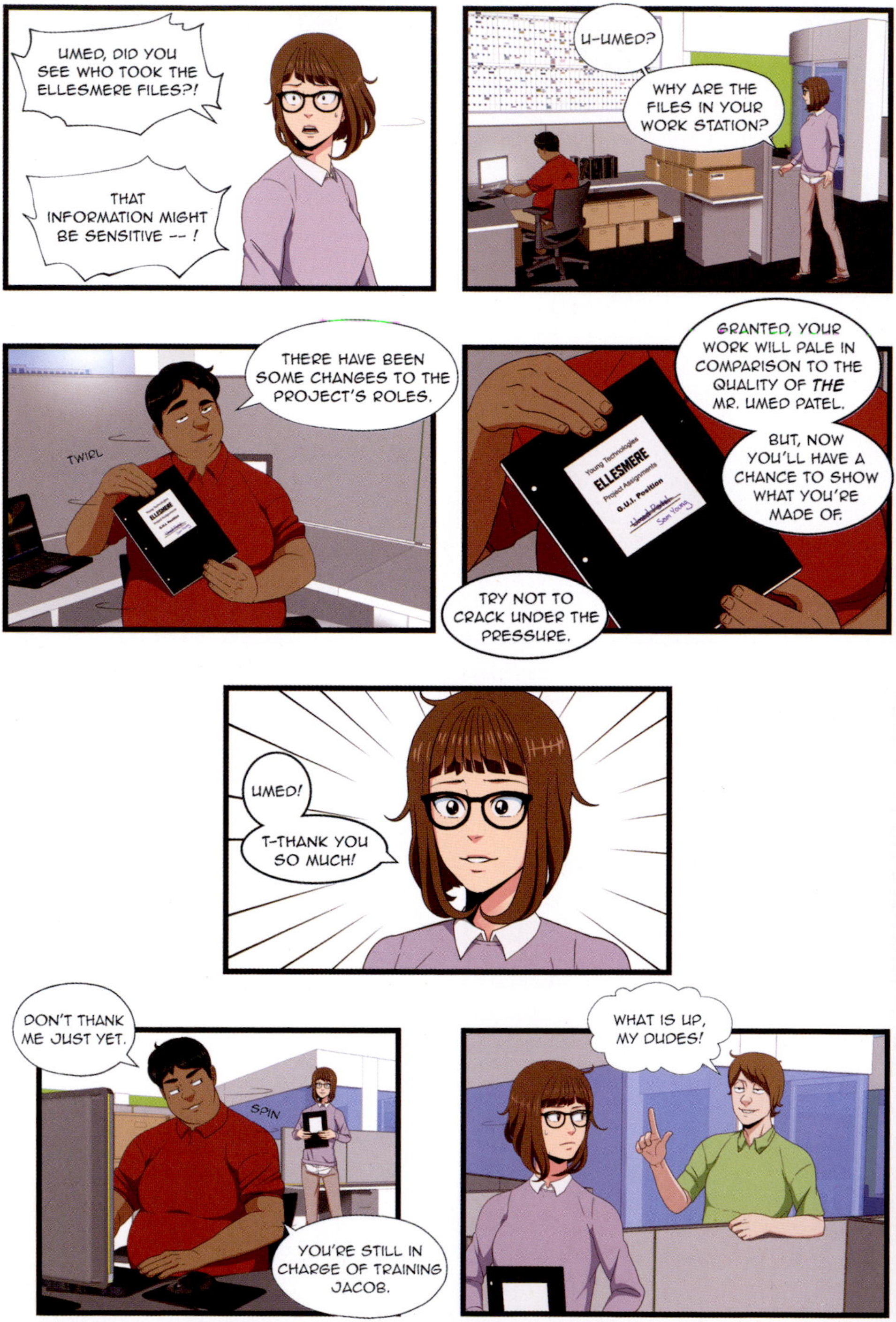
UMED, DID YOU SEE WHO TOOK THE ELLESMERE FILES?!
THAT INFORMATION MIGHT BE SENSITIVE -- !
U-UMED?
WHY ARE THE FILES IN YOUR WORK STATION?
TWIRL
THERE HAVE BEEN SOME CHANGES TO THE PROJECT'S ROLES.
GRANTED, YOUR WORK WILL PALE IN COMPARISON TO THE QUALITY OF *THE* MR. UMED PATEL.
BUT, NOW YOU'LL HAVE A CHANCE TO SHOW WHAT YOU'RE MADE OF.
Young Technologies
ELLESMERE
Project Assignments
G.U.I. Position
Sam Young
TRY NOT TO CRACK UNDER THE PRESSURE.
UMED!
T-THANK YOU SO MUCH!
DON'T THANK ME JUST YET.
SPIN
YOU'RE STILL IN CHARGE OF TRAINING JACOB.
WHAT IS UP, MY DUDES!

That night.

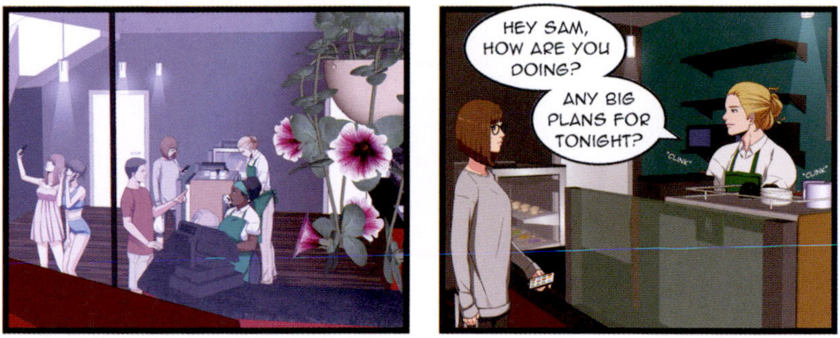
HEY SAM, HOW ARE YOU DOING?
ANY BIG PLANS FOR TONIGHT?
CLINK
CLINK

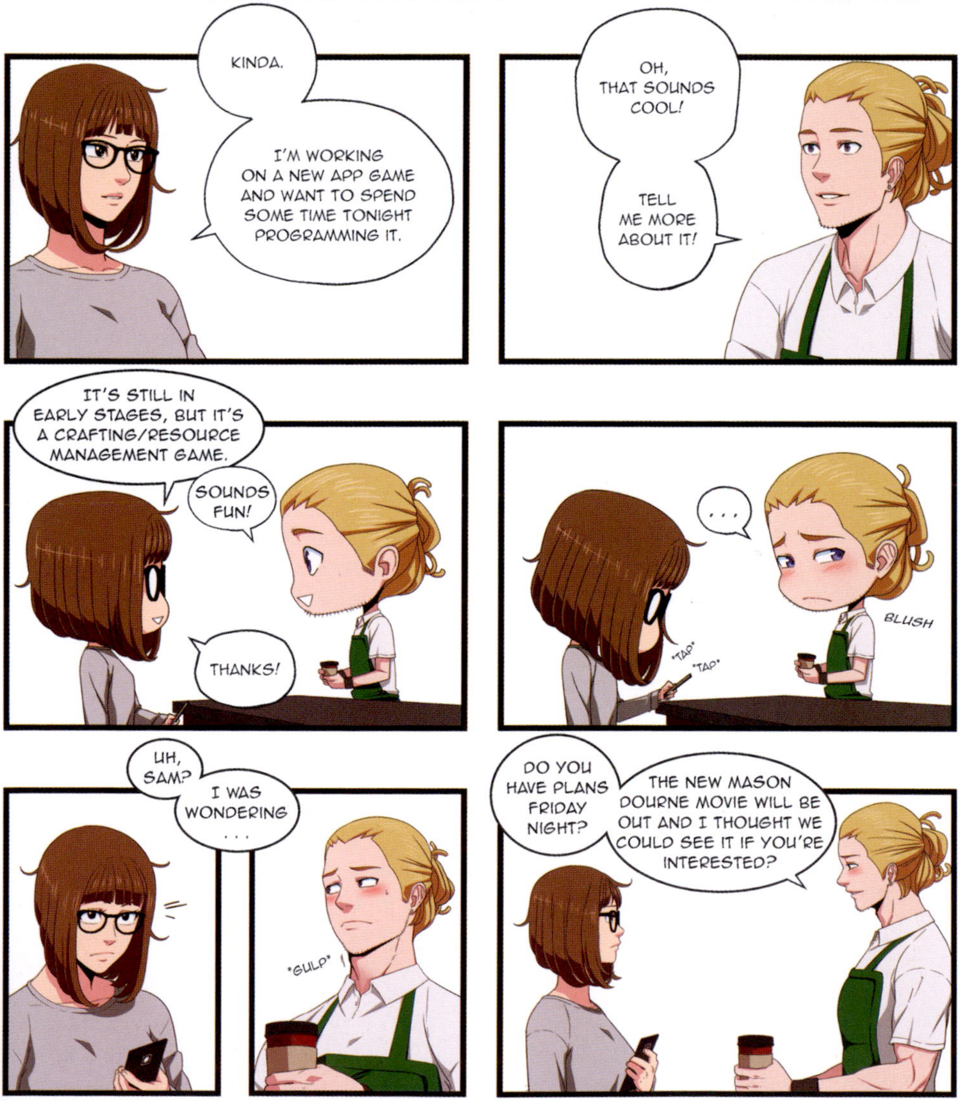
KINDA.
I'M WORKING ON A NEW APP GAME AND WANT TO SPEND SOME TIME TONIGHT PROGRAMMING IT.
OH, THAT SOUNDS COOL!
TELL ME MORE ABOUT IT!
IT'S STILL IN EARLY STAGES, BUT IT'S A CRAFTING/RESOURCE MANAGEMENT GAME.
SOUNDS FUN!
THANKS!
. . .
TAP
TAP
BLUSH
UH, SAM?
I WAS WONDERING . . .
GULP
DO YOU HAVE PLANS FRIDAY NIGHT?
THE NEW MASON DOURNE MOVIE WILL BE OUT AND I THOUGHT WE COULD SEE IT IF YOU'RE INTERESTED?

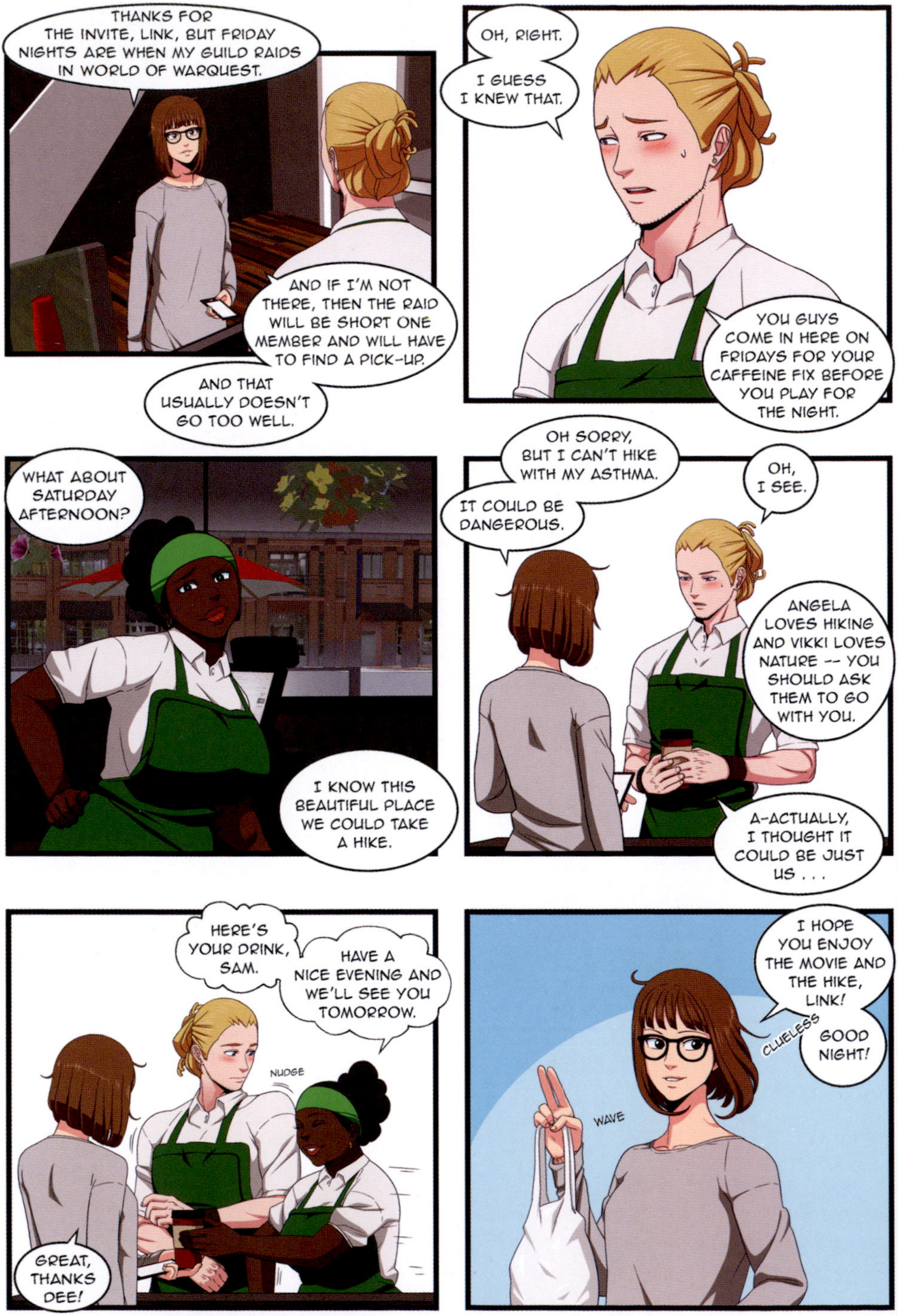
THANKS FOR THE INVITE, LINK, BUT FRIDAY NIGHTS ARE WHEN MY GUILD RAIDS IN WORLD OF WARQUEST.
AND IF I'M NOT THERE, THEN THE RAID WILL BE SHORT ONE MEMBER AND WILL HAVE TO FIND A PICK-UP.
AND THAT USUALLY DOESN'T GO TOO WELL.
OH, RIGHT.
I GUESS I KNEW THAT.
YOU GUYS COME IN HERE ON FRIDAYS FOR YOUR CAFFEINE FIX BEFORE YOU PLAY FOR THE NIGHT.
WHAT ABOUT SATURDAY AFTERNOON?
I KNOW THIS BEAUTIFUL PLACE WE COULD TAKE A HIKE.
OH SORRY, BUT I CAN'T HIKE WITH MY ASTHMA.
IT COULD BE DANGEROUS.
OH, I SEE.
ANGELA LOVES HIKING AND VIKKI LOVES NATURE -- YOU SHOULD ASK THEM TO GO WITH YOU.
A-ACTUALLY, I THOUGHT IT COULD BE JUST US . . .
HERE'S YOUR DRINK, SAM.
HAVE A NICE EVENING AND WE'LL SEE YOU TOMORROW.
NUDGE
GREAT, THANKS DEE!
I HOPE YOU ENJOY THE MOVIE AND THE HIKE, LINK!
CLUELESS
GOOD NIGHT!
WAVE

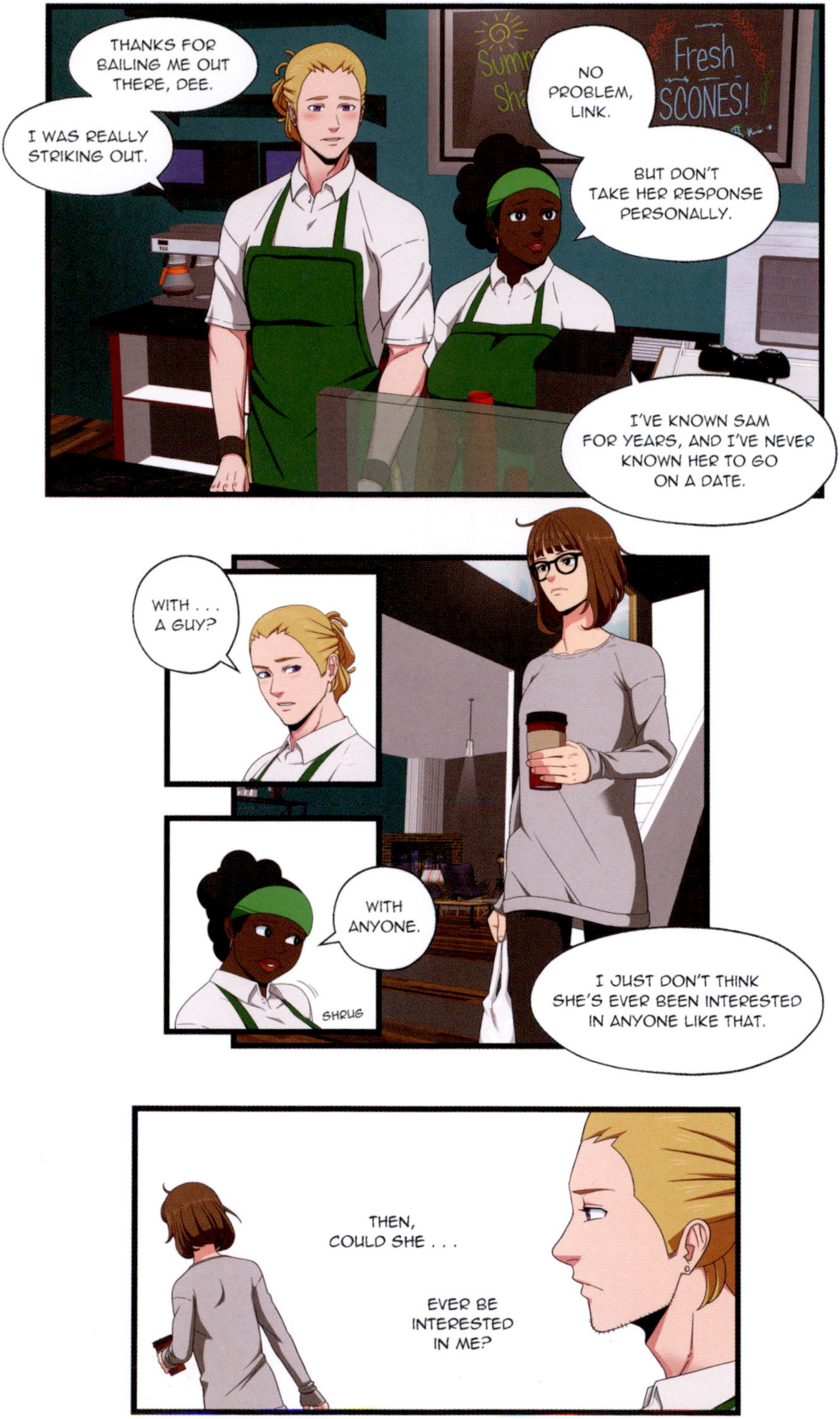
THANKS FOR BAILING ME OUT THERE, DEE.
I WAS REALLY STRIKING OUT.
Fresh SCONES!
NO PROBLEM, LINK.
BUT DON'T TAKE HER RESPONSE PERSONALLY.
I'VE KNOWN SAM FOR YEARS, AND I'VE NEVER KNOWN HER TO GO ON A DATE.
WITH . . . A GUY?
WITH ANYONE.
SHRUG
I JUST DON'T THINK SHE'S EVER BEEN INTERESTED IN ANYONE LIKE THAT.
THEN, COULD SHE . . .
EVER BE INTERESTED IN ME?

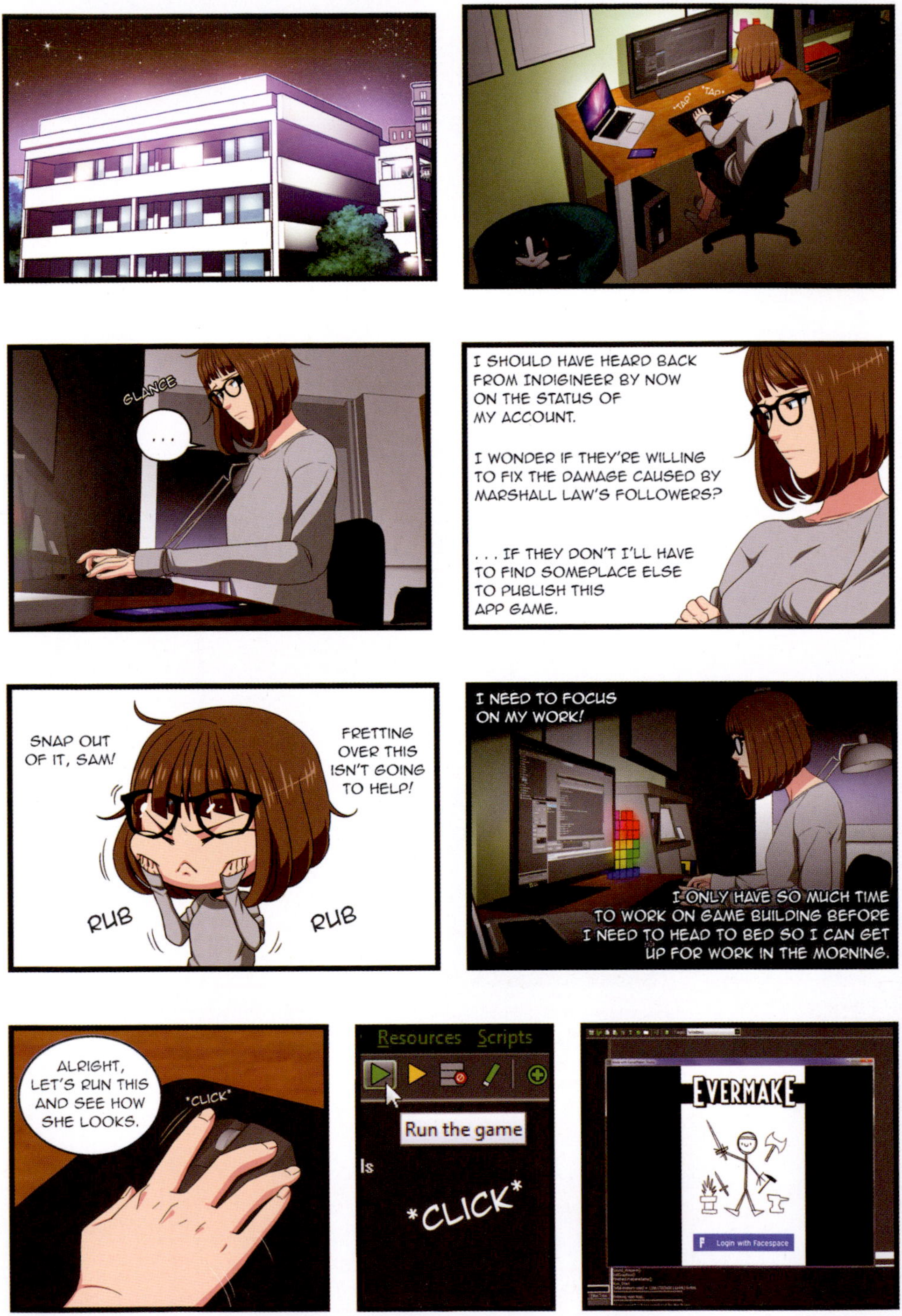
TAP *TAP*
GLANCE
. . .
I SHOULD HAVE HEARD BACK FROM INDIGINEER BY NOW ON THE STATUS OF MY ACCOUNT.
I WONDER IF THEY'RE WILLING TO FIX THE DAMAGE CAUSED BY MARSHALL LAW'S FOLLOWERS?
. . . IF THEY DON'T I'LL HAVE TO FIND SOMEPLACE ELSE TO PUBLISH THIS APP GAME.
SNAP OUT OF IT, SAM!
FRETTING OVER THIS ISN'T GOING TO HELP!
RUB
RUB
I NEED TO FOCUS ON MY WORK!
I ONLY HAVE SO MUCH TIME TO WORK ON GAME BUILDING BEFORE I NEED TO HEAD TO BED SO I CAN GET UP FOR WORK IN THE MORNING.
ALRIGHT, LET'S RUN THIS AND SEE HOW SHE LOOKS.
CLICK
Resources Scripts
Run the game
CLICK
EVERMAKE
Login with Facespace

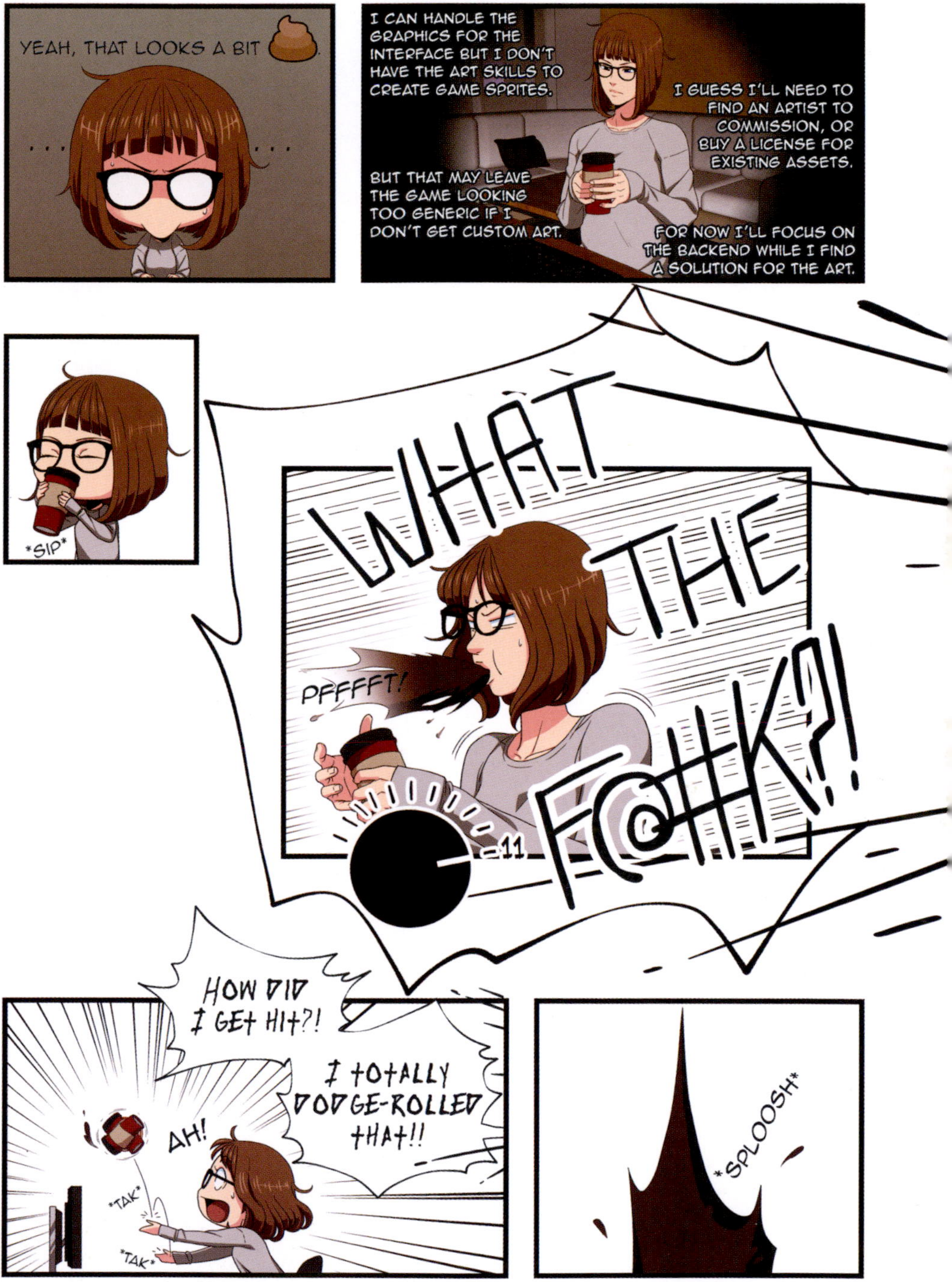
YEAH, THAT LOOKS A BIT
. . .
. . .
I CAN HANDLE THE GRAPHICS FOR THE INTERFACE BUT I DON'T HAVE THE ART SKILLS TO CREATE GAME SPRITES.
I GUESS I'LL NEED TO FIND AN ARTIST TO COMMISSION, OR BUY A LICENSE FOR EXISTING ASSETS.
BUT THAT MAY LEAVE THE GAME LOOKING TOO GENERIC IF I DON'T GET CUSTOM ART.
FOR NOW I'LL FOCUS ON THE BACKEND WHILE I FIND A SOLUTION FOR THE ART.
SIP
WHAT THE F@#K?!
PFFFFT!
-11
HOW DID I GET HIT?!
I TOTALLY DODGE-ROLLED THAT!!
AH!
TAK
TAK
SPLOOSH

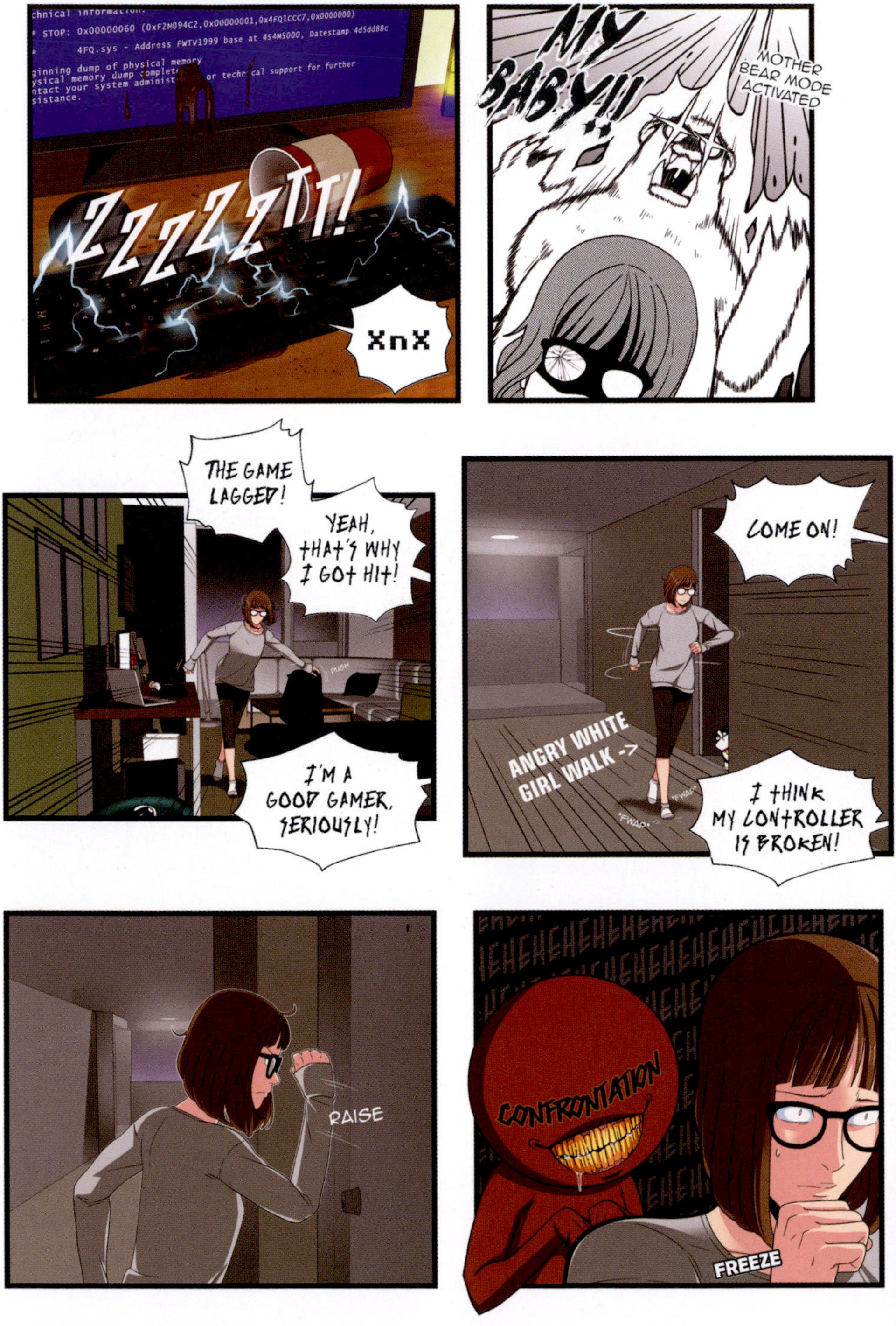
chnical information:
* STOP: 0x00000060 (0xF2M094C2,0x00000001,0x4FQ1CCC7,0x0000000)
4FQ.sys - Address FWTV1999 base at 4S4M5000, Datestamp 4d5dd88c
ginning dump of physical memory
ZZZZZTT!
XnX
MY BABY!!
MOTHER BEAR MODE ACTIVATED
THE GAME LAGGED!
YEAH, THAT'S WHY I GOT HIT!
PUSH
I'M A GOOD GAMER, SERIOUSLY!
COME ON!
ANGRY WHITE GIRL WALK ->
FWAP
FWAP
I THINK MY CONTROLLER IS BROKEN!
RAISE
CONFRONTATION
FREEZE

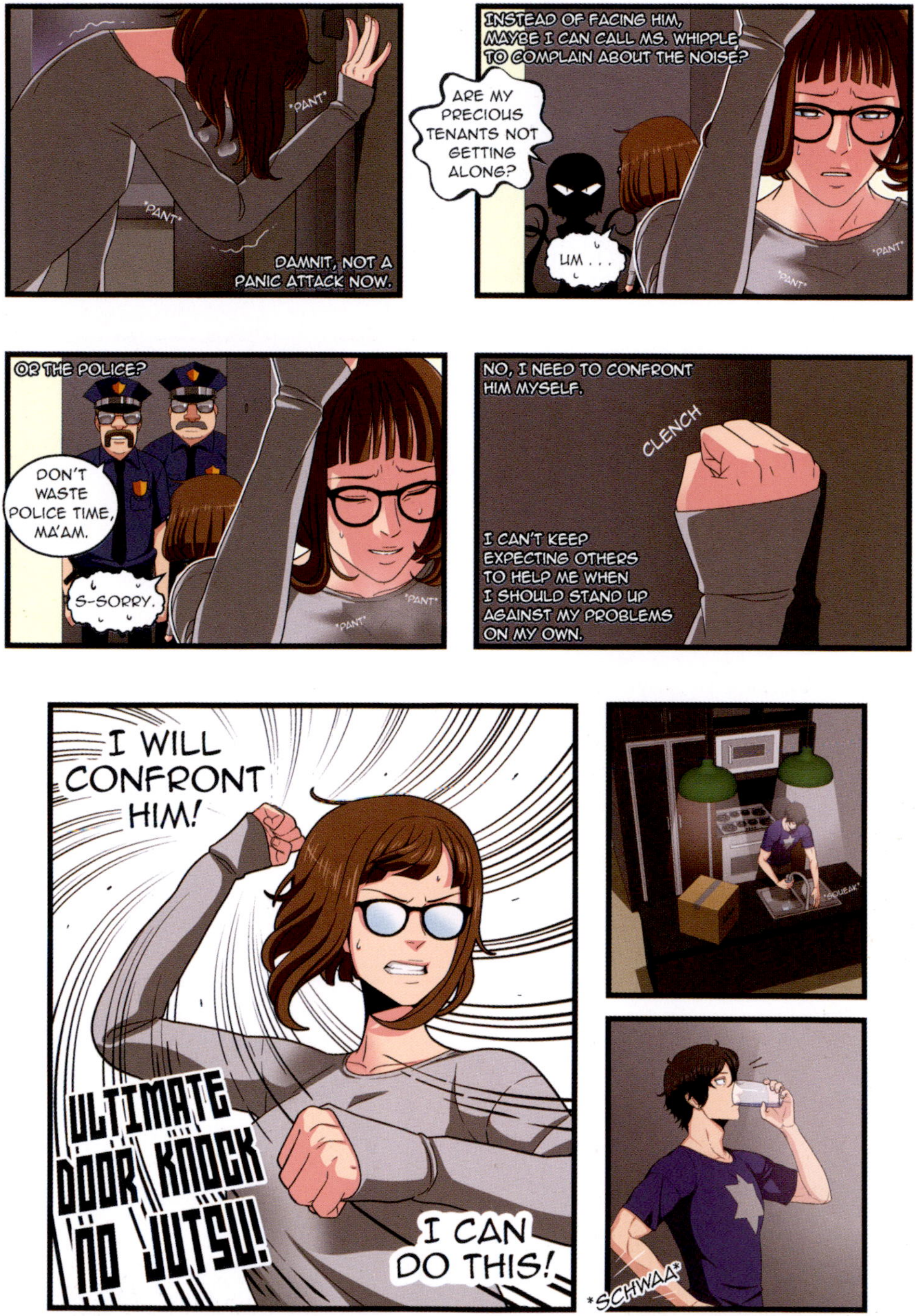
PANT
PANT
DAMNIT, NOT A PANIC ATTACK NOW.
INSTEAD OF FACING HIM, MAYBE I CAN CALL MS. WHIPPLE TO COMPLAIN ABOUT THE NOISE?
ARE MY PRECIOUS TENANTS NOT GETTING ALONG?
UM . . .
PANT
PANT
OR THE POLICE?
DON'T WASTE POLICE TIME, MA'AM.
S-SORRY.
PANT
PANT
NO, I NEED TO CONFRONT HIM MYSELF.
CLENCH
I CAN'T KEEP EXPECTING OTHERS TO HELP ME WHEN I SHOULD STAND UP AGAINST MY PROBLEMS ON MY OWN.
I WILL CONFRONT HIM!
ULTIMATE DOOR KNOCK NO JUTSU!
I CAN DO THIS!
SQUEAK
SCHWAA

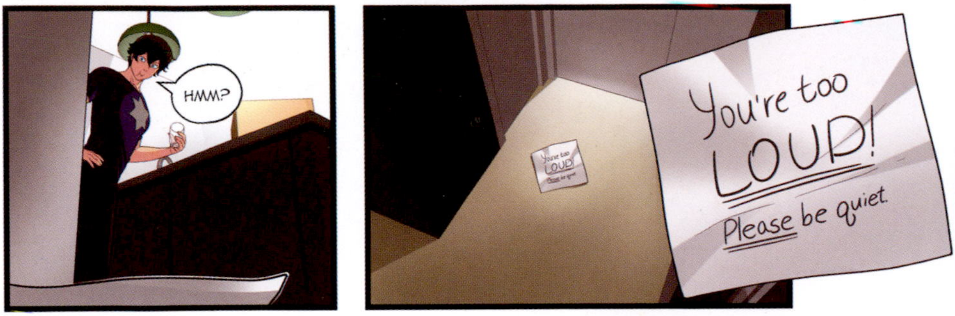
HMM?
You're too LOUD! Please be quiet.

The next morning.

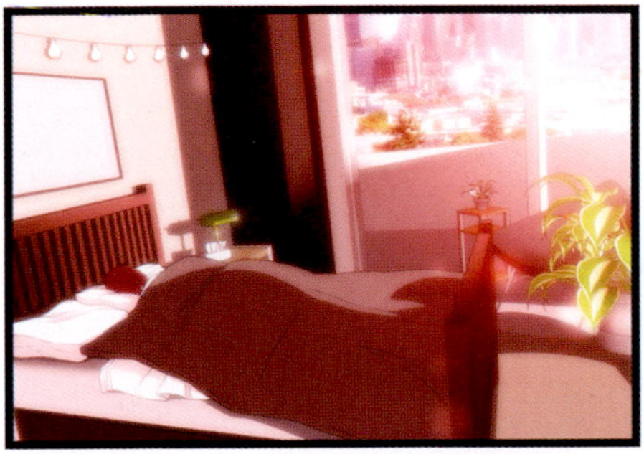

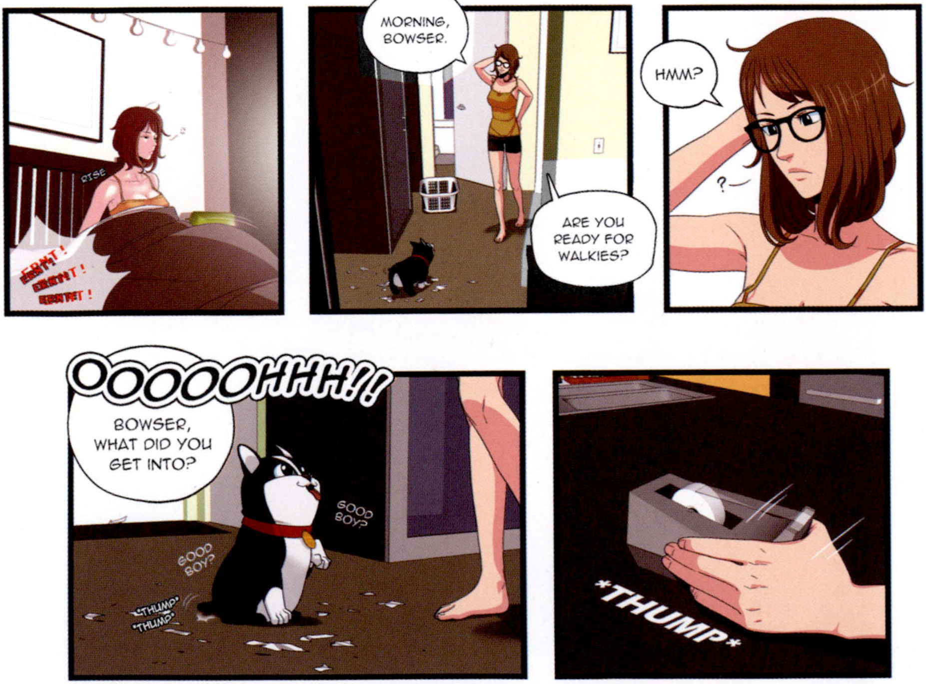
RISE
MORNING, BOWSER.
ARE YOU READY FOR WALKIES?
HMM?
?
OOOOOOHHHH!!
BOWSER, WHAT DID YOU GET INTO?
GOOD BOY?
GOOD BOY?
THUMP
THUMP
THUMP

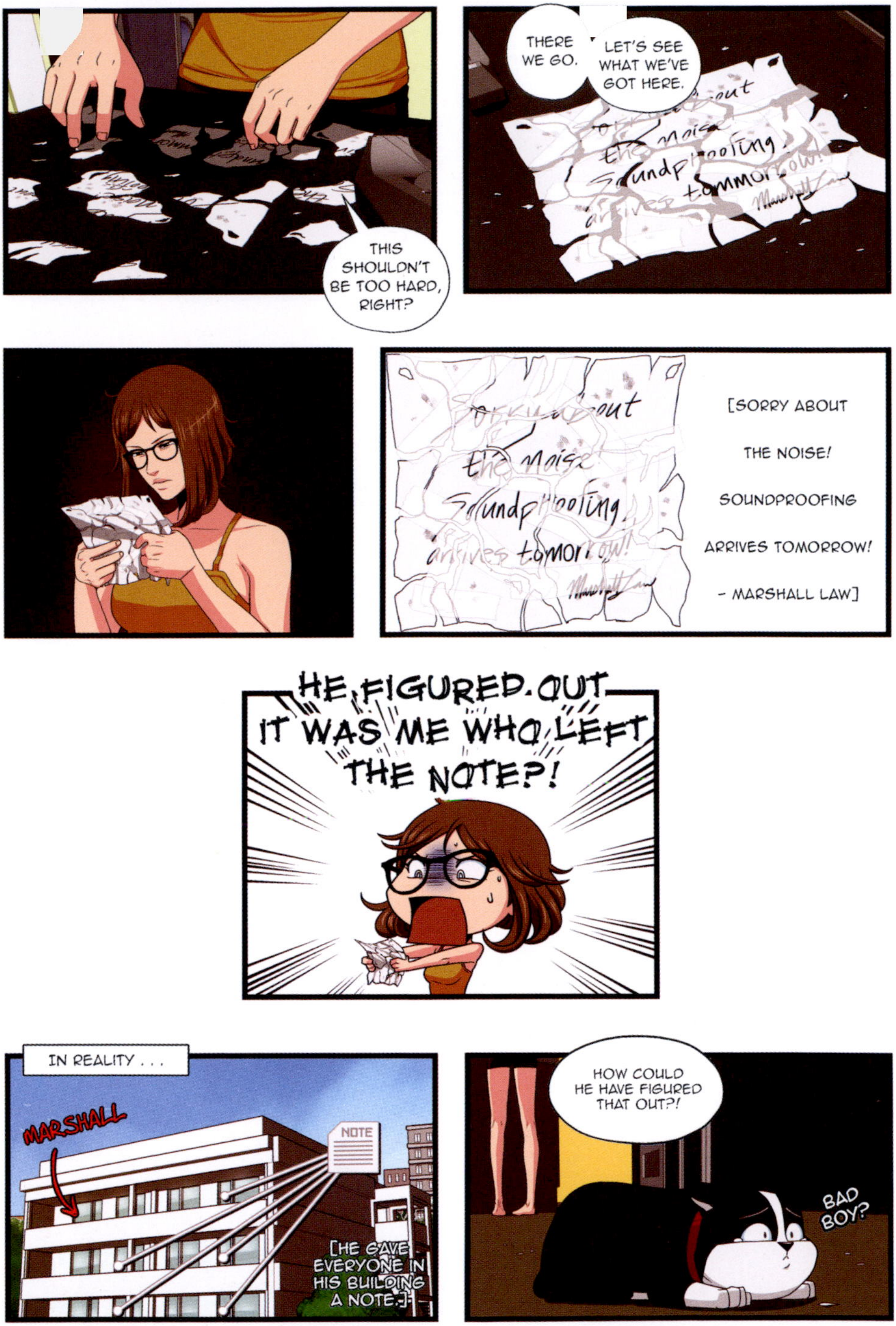
THIS SHOULDN'T BE TOO HARD, RIGHT?
THERE WE GO.
LET'S SEE WHAT WE'VE GOT HERE.
[SORRY ABOUT
THE NOISE!
SOUNDPROOFING
ARRIVES TOMORROW!
- MARSHALL LAW]
HE FIGURED OUT IT WAS ME WHO LEFT THE NOTE?!
IN REALITY . . .
MARSHALL
NOTE
[HE GAVE EVERYONE IN HIS BUILDING A NOTE.]
HOW COULD HE HAVE FIGURED THAT OUT?!
BAD BOY?

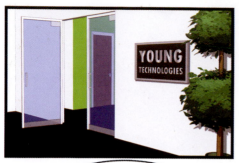

THAT SHOULD SUM UP SOME OF THE IMPORTANT BITS ON G.U.I. DESIGN, JACOB.

DID YOU HAVE ANY QUESTIONS FOR ME?

WHOA! SO WHAT YOU'RE SAYING IS THAT *G.U.I.* STANDS FOR *"GRAPHICAL USER INTERFACE"*?

I THOUGHT IT STOOD FOR *"GENIUS UNDER THE INFLUENCE"* AND WAS THINKING WE'D DO SOME SWEET SUBSTANCES.

N-NO, JACOB.

SQUEAKY

HAHA, I'M JUST JOSHIN YA, DUDE!

I KNOW WHAT IT MEANS.

HA, HA!

HAHA! GOOD ONE, JACOB!

THAT HURT MY HEART.

IF IT'S COOL FOR ME TO SAY, I DID HAVE A CONCERN WITH YOUR PROTOTYPE.

IN THIS EXAMPLE, YOU HAVE ALTERNATE SHADING STAGGERED BETWEEN EACH ROW OF THIS TABLE AND THE COLORS YOU CHOSE ARE A LIGHT ORANGE AND A LIGHT GREEN.
AND THOUGH THOSE COLORS MAY LOOK COMPLEMENTARY IN A LEDGER, IT MAY BE A PROBLEM FOR USERS WHO HAVE A RED-GREEN COLOR BLINDNESS CALLED DEUTERANOPIA.
NORMAL EYE
CORRECT UNDERSTANDING OF COLOR
DEUTERANOPIA
BLINDNESS TO GREEN
ALL THEY'LL SEE IS A LIGHT-YELLOW TABLE, OR THE COLOR VARIATION MAY BE SO SLIGHT THAT IT MAY EVEN CAUSE EYE STRAIN WHEN VIEWING THE TABLE FOR TOO LONG.
WITH DEUTERANOPIA
<- THIS
BECOMES THIS ->
AND SINCE DEUTERANOPIA IS THE MOST COMMON FORM OF COLOR BLINDNESS IN THE WORLD, IT'S SOMETHING TO KEEP IN MIND.
WHOA, JACOB . . .
HOW DO YOU KNOW THIS?
IMPRESSED
I'VE GOT A BUDDY WITH DEUTERANOPIA WHO SPRAYS SOLELY IN MONOCHROMATIC ART BECAUSE OF HIS COLORBLINDNESS.
RESIST
WE'VE TALKED ABOUT COLOR THEORY A FEW TIMES.
THANK YOU SO MUCH FOR THE INFORMATION, JACOB!
I'LL TAKE YOUR ADVICE INTO CONSIDERATION AND MAKE THE NECESSARY CHANGES TO THE SOFTWARE.
AND THANK YOU FOR LETTING ME VOICE MY CONCERNS IN A NON-HOSTILE ENVIRONMENT, MY DUDE.
I'LL RETURN TO MY STATION AND WORK ON THE CHECKLIST YOU GAVE ME.
LATERS!
SEE YOU, JACOB!
OH, I JUST GOT A TEXT.
DING

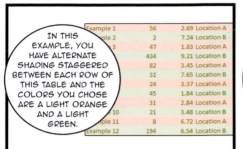

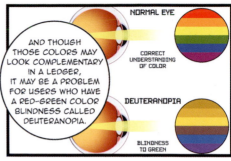

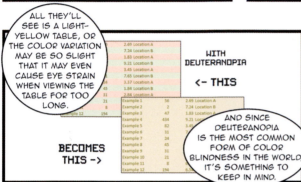

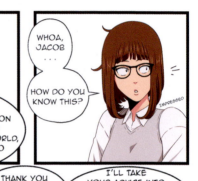

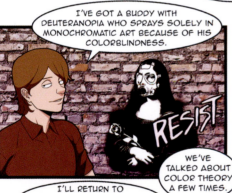

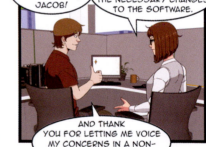

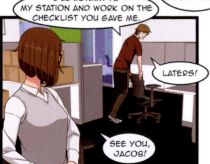

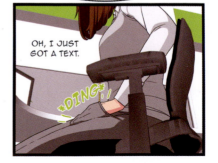

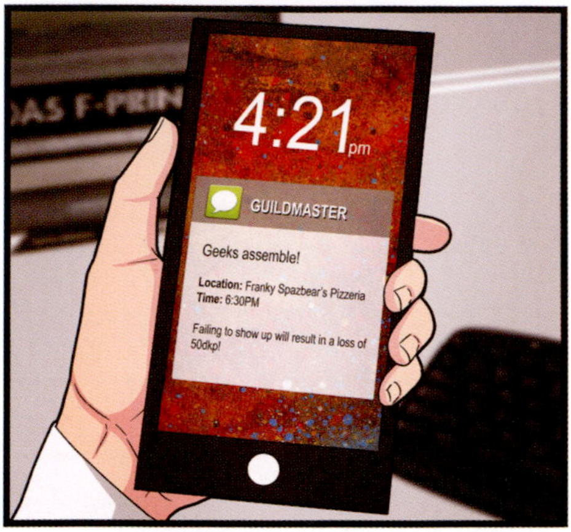
4:21pm
GUILDMASTER
Geeks assemble!
Location: Franky Spazbear's Pizzeria
Time: 6:30PM
Failing to show up will result in a loss of 50dkp!

DKP:

Stands for "Dragon Kill Points" or "Dungeon Kill Points." Used in mmorpgs as a form of currency within groups of players to bid on or "buy" items that are received in said dungeons. Awarded in different ways: time spent in the dungeon, how many bosses (main monsters) are killed, etc.

-UrbanDictionary.com

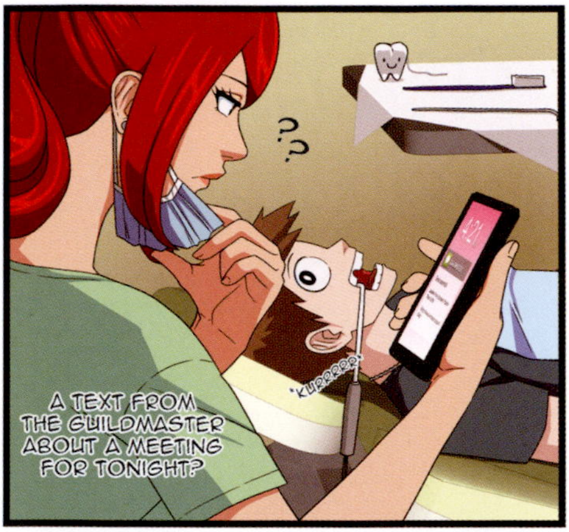
??
A TEXT FROM THE GUILDMASTER ABOUT A MEETING FOR TONIGHT?

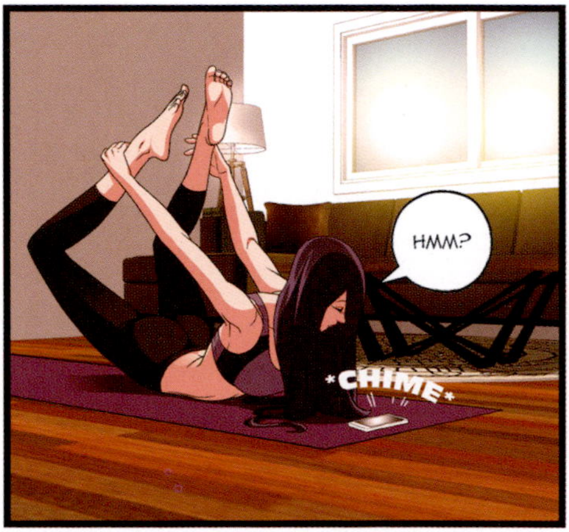
HMM?
CHIME

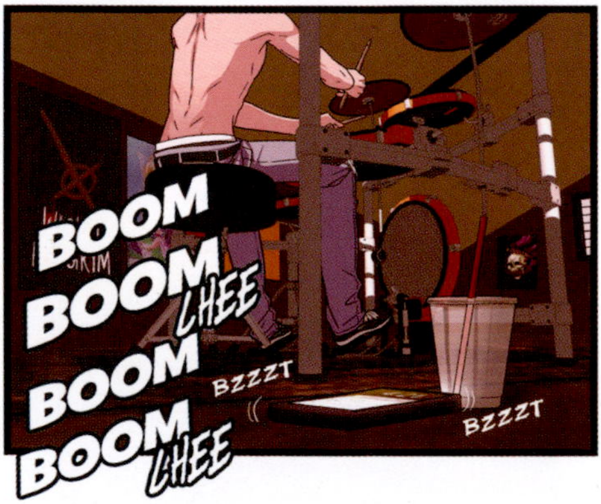
BOOM
BOOM
CHEE
BOOM
BOOM
CHEE
BZZZT
BZZZT

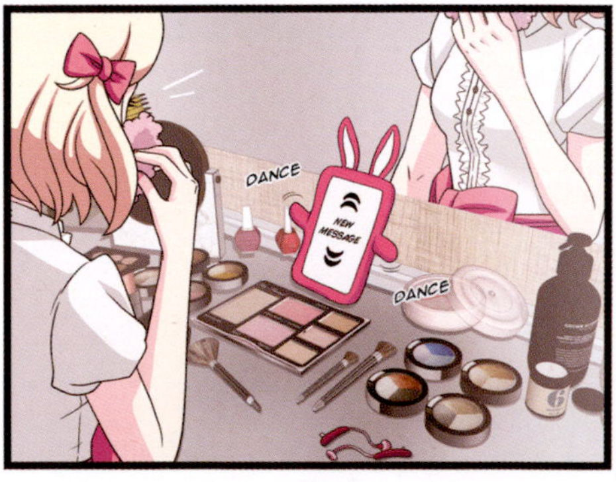
DANCE
NEW MESSAGE
DANCE

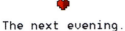

The next evening.

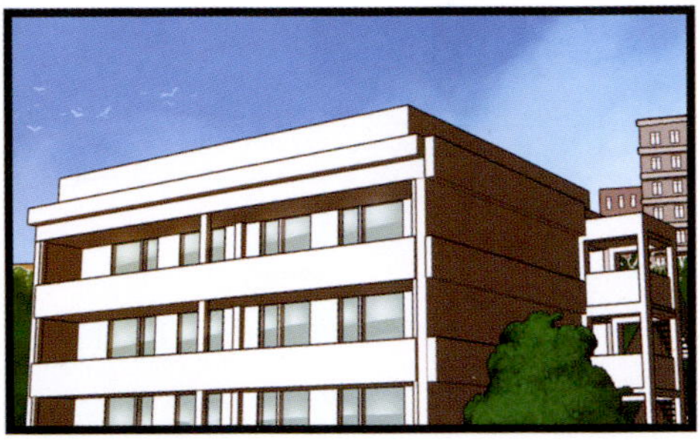

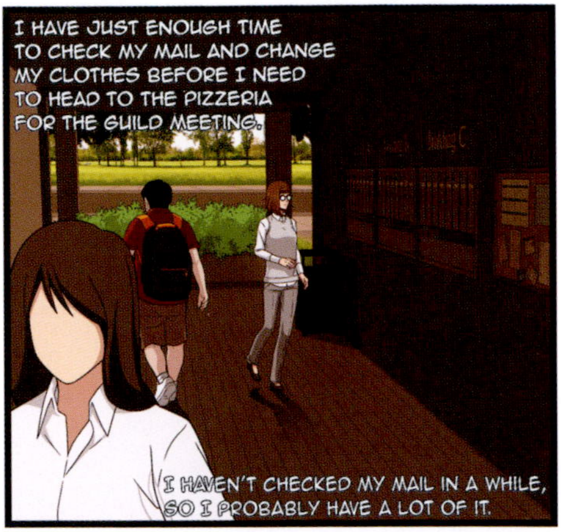
I HAVE JUST ENOUGH TIME TO CHECK MY MAIL AND CHANGE MY CLOTHES BEFORE I NEED TO HEAD TO THE PIZZERIA FOR THE GUILD MEETING.
I HAVEN'T CHECKED MY MAIL IN A WHILE, SO I PROBABLY HAVE A LOT OF IT.

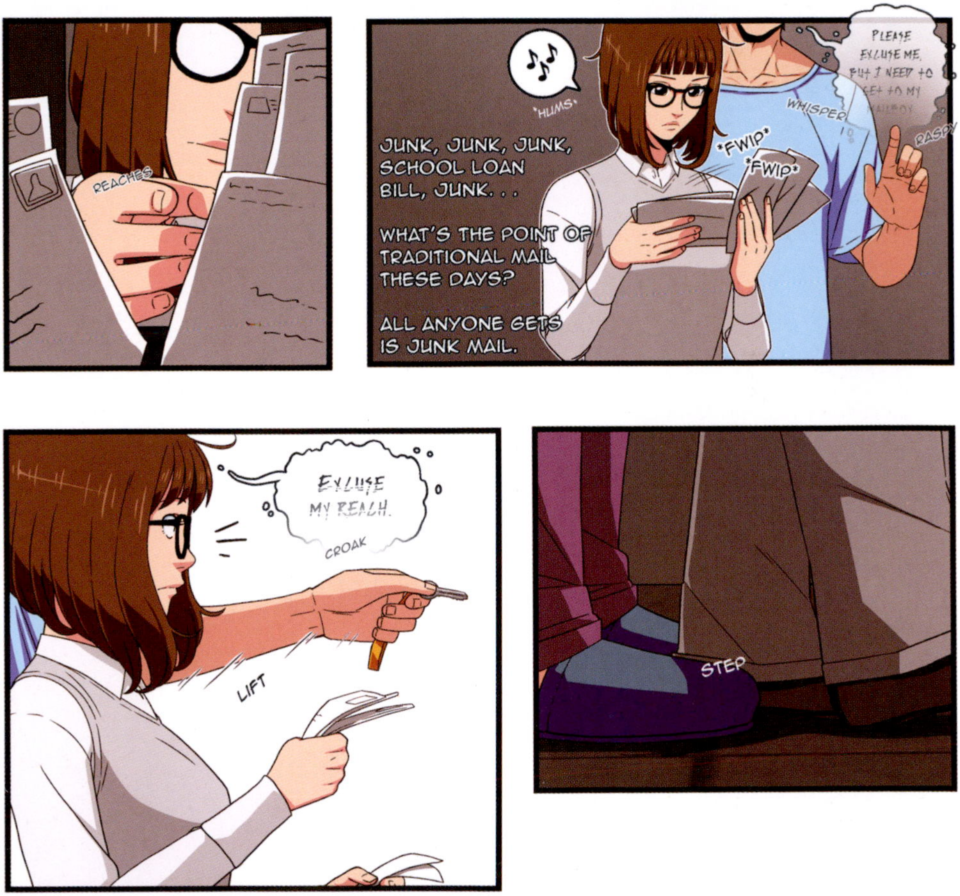
REACHES
HUMS
JUNK, JUNK, JUNK, SCHOOL LOAN BILL, JUNK. . .
WHAT'S THE POINT OF TRADITIONAL MAIL THESE DAYS?
ALL ANYONE GETS IS JUNK MAIL.
FWIP
FWIP
PLEASE EXCUSE ME, BUT I NEED TO GET TO MY MAILBOX
WHISPER
RASPY
EXCUSE MY REACH.
CROAK
LIFT
STEP

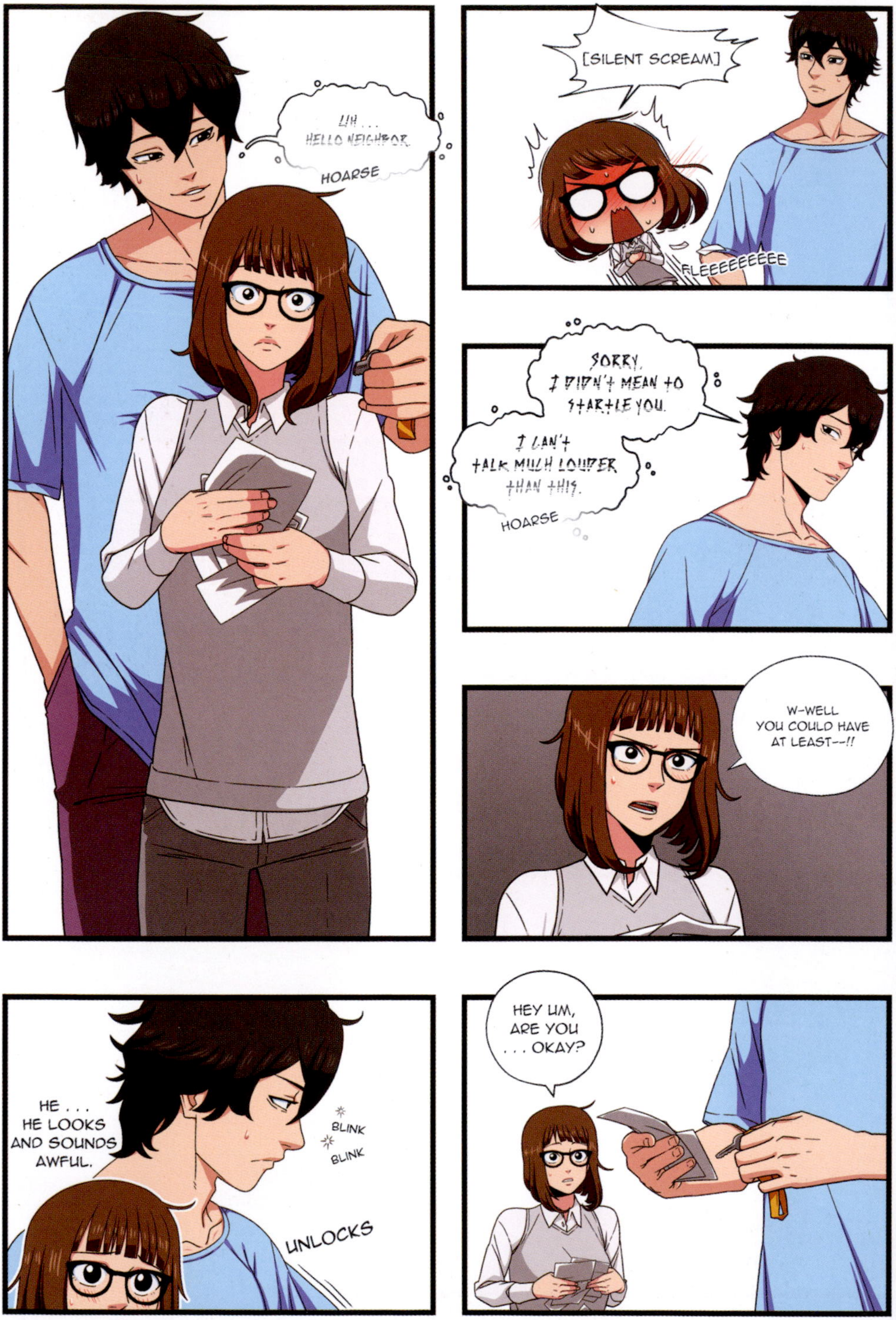
UH . . . HELLO NEIGHBOR.
HOARSE
[SILENT SCREAM]
FLEEEEEEEEE
SORRY, I DIDN'T MEAN TO STARTLE YOU.
I CAN'T TALK MUCH LOUDER THAN THIS.
HOARSE
W-WELL YOU COULD HAVE AT LEAST--!!
HE . . . HE LOOKS AND SOUNDS AWFUL.
BLINK
BLINK
UNLOCKS
HEY UM, ARE YOU . . . OKAY?

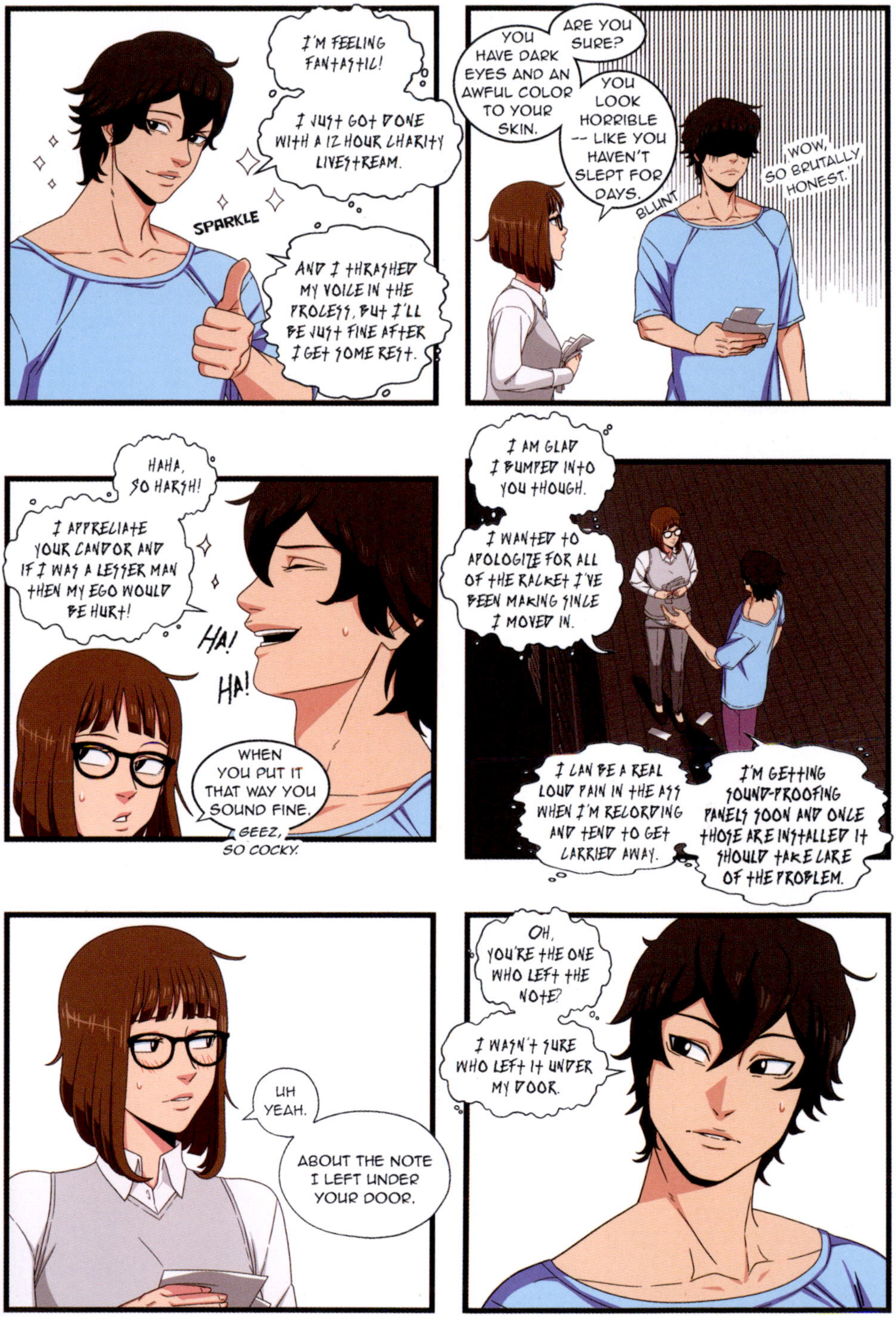
I'M FEELING FANTASTIC!
I JUST GOT DONE WITH A 12 HOUR CHARITY LIVESTREAM.
SPARKLE
AND I THRASHED MY VOICE IN THE PROCESS, BUT I'LL BE JUST FINE AFTER I GET SOME REST.
YOU HAVE DARK EYES AND AN AWFUL COLOR TO YOUR SKIN.
ARE YOU SURE?
YOU LOOK HORRIBLE -- LIKE YOU HAVEN'T SLEPT FOR DAYS.
BLUNT
WOW, SO BRUTALLY HONEST.
HAHA, SO HARSH!
I APPRECIATE YOUR CANDOR AND IF I WAS A LESSER MAN THEN MY EGO WOULD BE HURT!
HA! HA!
WHEN YOU PUT IT THAT WAY YOU SOUND FINE.
GEEZ, SO COCKY.
I AM GLAD I BUMPED INTO YOU THOUGH.
I WANTED TO APOLOGIZE FOR ALL OF THE RACKET I'VE BEEN MAKING SINCE I MOVED IN.
I CAN BE A REAL LOUD PAIN IN THE ASS WHEN I'M RECORDING AND TEND TO GET CARRIED AWAY.
I'M GETTING SOUND-PROOFING PANELS SOON AND ONCE THOSE ARE INSTALLED IT SHOULD TAKE CARE OF THE PROBLEM.
UH YEAH.
ABOUT THE NOTE I LEFT UNDER YOUR DOOR.
OH, YOU'RE THE ONE WHO LEFT THE NOTE?
I WASN'T SURE WHO LEFT IT UNDER MY DOOR.

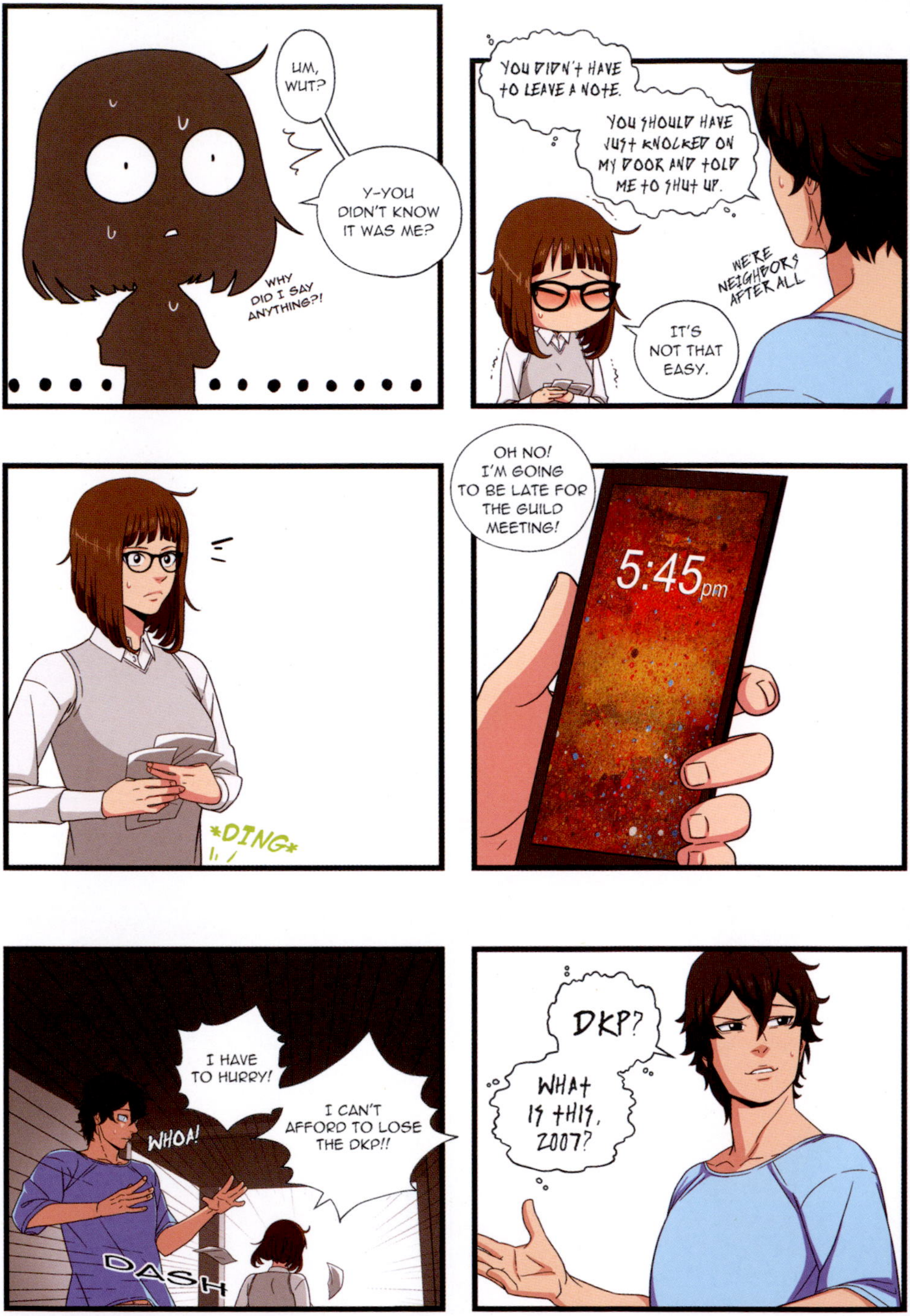
UM, WUT?
Y-YOU DIDN'T KNOW IT WAS ME?
WHY DID I SAY ANYTHING?!
YOU DIDN'T HAVE TO LEAVE A NOTE.
YOU SHOULD HAVE JUST KNOCKED ON MY DOOR AND TOLD ME TO SHUT UP.
WE'RE NEIGHBORS AFTER ALL
IT'S NOT THAT EASY.
DING
OH NO! I'M GOING TO BE LATE FOR THE GUILD MEETING!
5:45pm
I HAVE TO HURRY!
I CAN'T AFFORD TO LOSE THE DKP!!
WHOA!
DASH
DKP?
WHAT IS THIS, 2007?

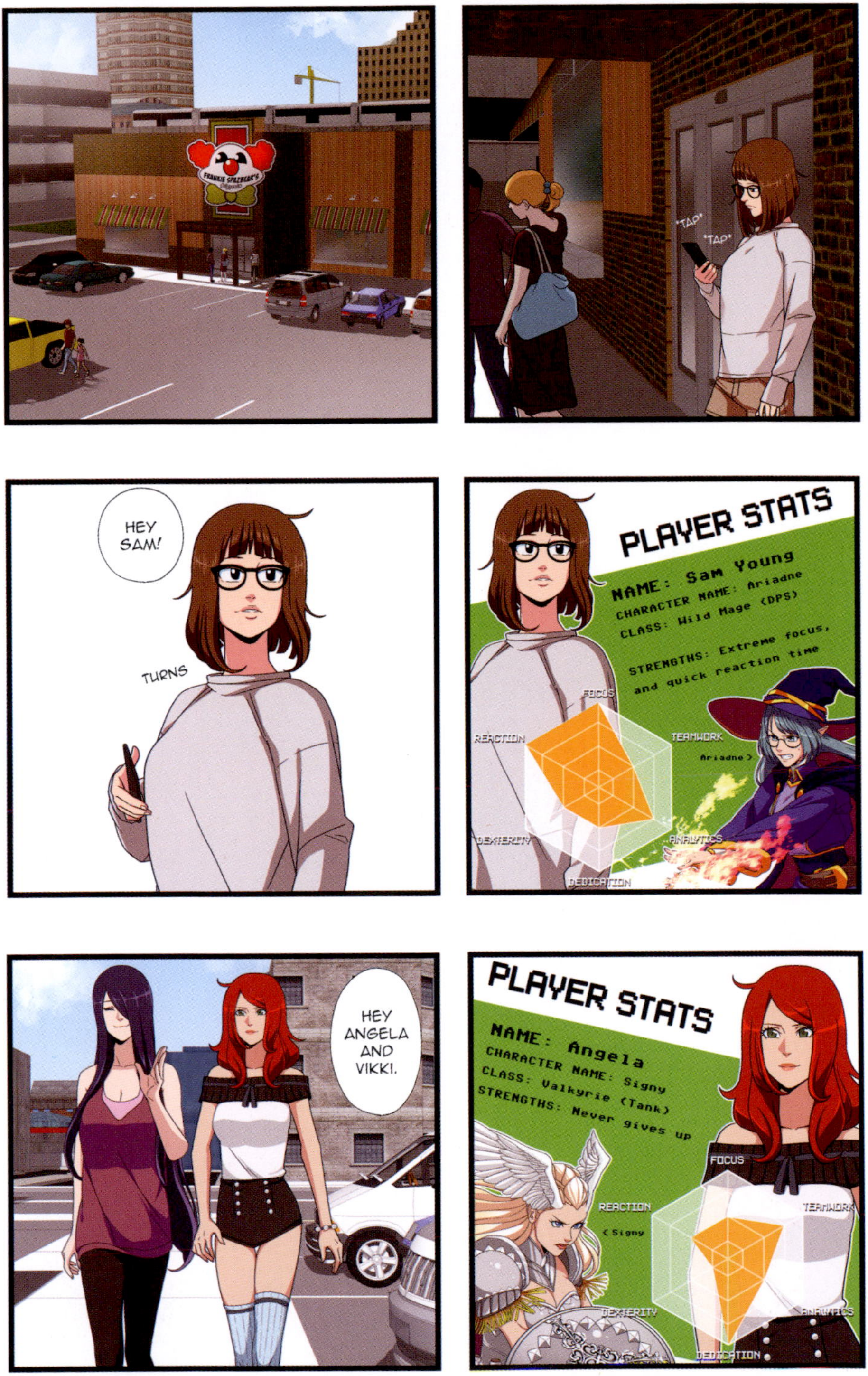
FRANKIE SPAZBEAR'S
TAP
TAP
HEY SAM!
TURNS
PLAYER STATS
NAME: Sam Young
CHARACTER NAME: Ariadne
CLASS: Wild Mage (DPS)
STRENGTHS: Extreme focus, and quick reaction time
FOCUS
REACTION
TEAMWORK
Ariadne >
DEXTERITY
ANALYTICS
DEDICATION
HEY ANGELA AND VIKKI.
PLAYER STATS
NAME: Angela
CHARACTER NAME: Signy
CLASS: Valkyrie (Tank)
STRENGTHS: Never gives up
FOCUS
REACTION
TEAMWORK
< Signy
DEXTERITY
ANALYTICS
DEDICATION

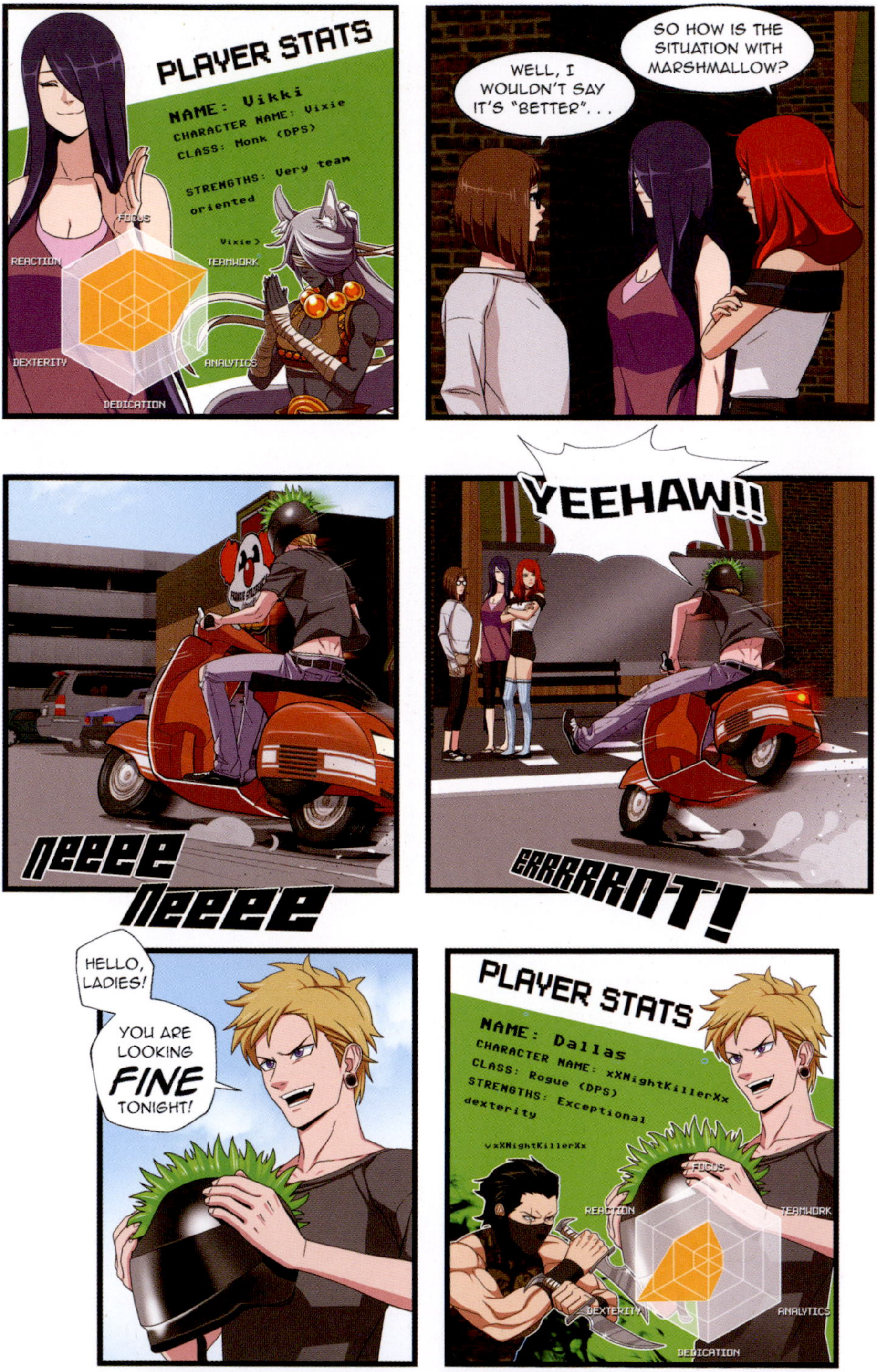
PLAYER STATS
NAME: Vikki
CHARACTER NAME: Vixie
CLASS: Monk (DPS)
STRENGTHS: Very team oriented
Vixie >
FOCUS
REACTION
TEAMWORK
DEXTERITY
ANALYTICS
DEDICATION
SO HOW IS THE SITUATION WITH MARSHMALLOW?
WELL, I WOULDN'T SAY IT'S "BETTER"...
NEEEE NEEEE
YEEHAW!!
ERRRRRNT!
HELLO, LADIES!
YOU ARE LOOKING FINE TONIGHT!
PLAYER STATS
NAME: Dallas
CHARACTER NAME: xXNightKillerXx
CLASS: Rogue (DPS)
STRENGTHS: Exceptional dexterity
xXNightKillerXx
FOCUS
REACTION
TEAMWORK
DEXTERITY
ANALYTICS
DEDICATION

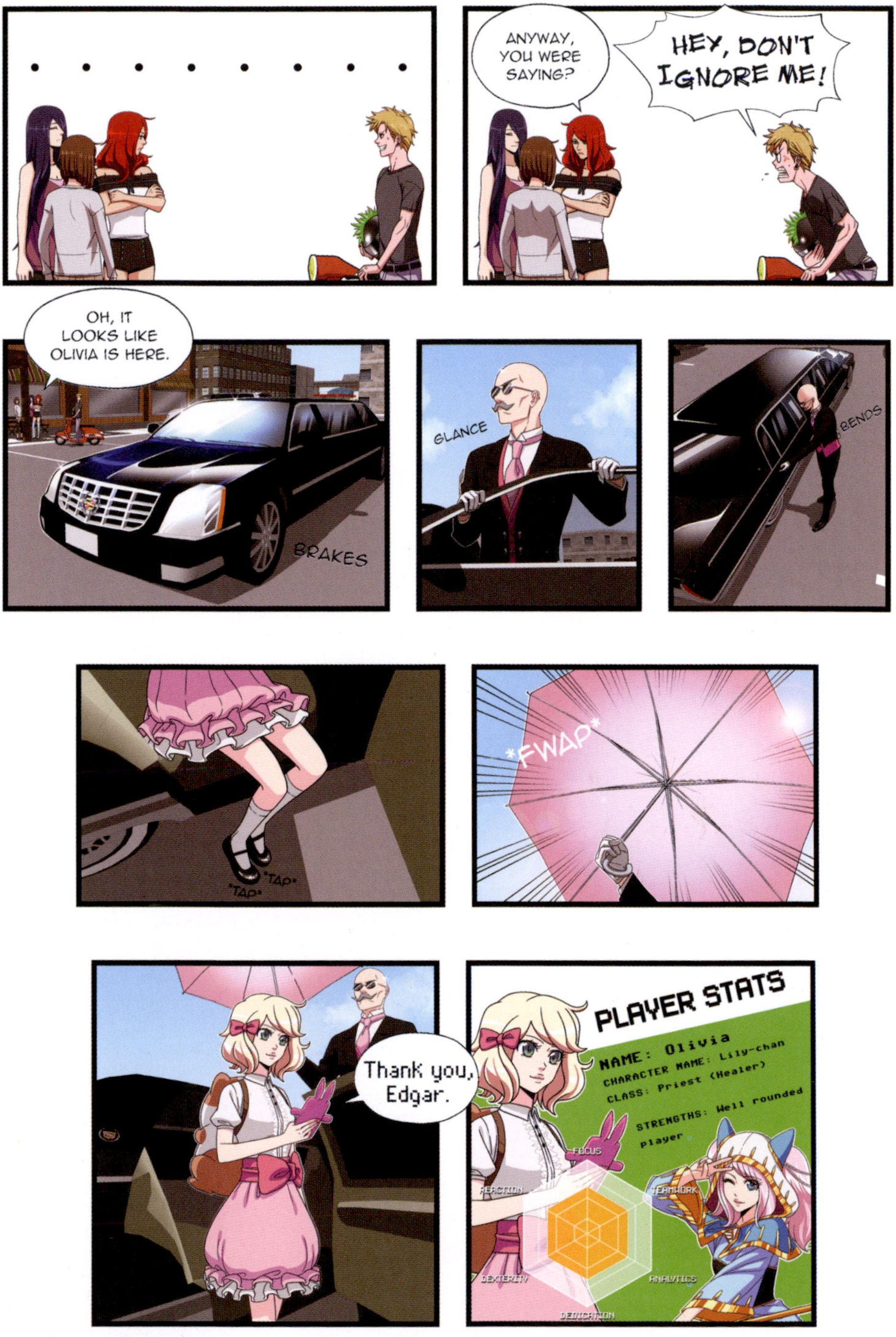
. . . .
ANYWAY, YOU WERE SAYING?
HEY, DON'T IGNORE ME!
OH, IT LOOKS LIKE OLIVIA IS HERE.
BRAKES
GLANCE
BENDS
TAP
TAP
FWAP
Thank you, Edgar.
PLAYER STATS
NAME: Olivia
CHARACTER NAME: Lily-chan
CLASS: Priest (Healer)
STRENGTHS: Well rounded player
FOCUS
REACTION
TEAMWORK
DEXTERITY
ANALYTICS
DEDICATION

DAMN OLIVIA, YOU'RE REALLY CHANNELING THAT "CREEPY DOLL" VIBE WITH THAT LOOK TODAY.

SHOVE

What did you say, you piece of trash?

D:<

SHUT UP YOU MORON!

YOU'RE COMMITTING A CARDINAL SIN OF MMO'S -- NEVER PISS OFF YOUR HEALER!

WHISPER

MMPH!

DON'T YOU REMEMBER WHAT HAPPENED LAST TIME YOU TICKED OLIVIA OFF?!

xXNIGHTKILLERXx

OLIVIA! HEAL ME ALREADY!!

SERIOUSLY, YOU HAVE THE EASIEST JOB IN THE WHOLE RAID!!!

SMILE

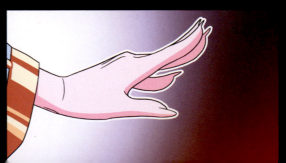

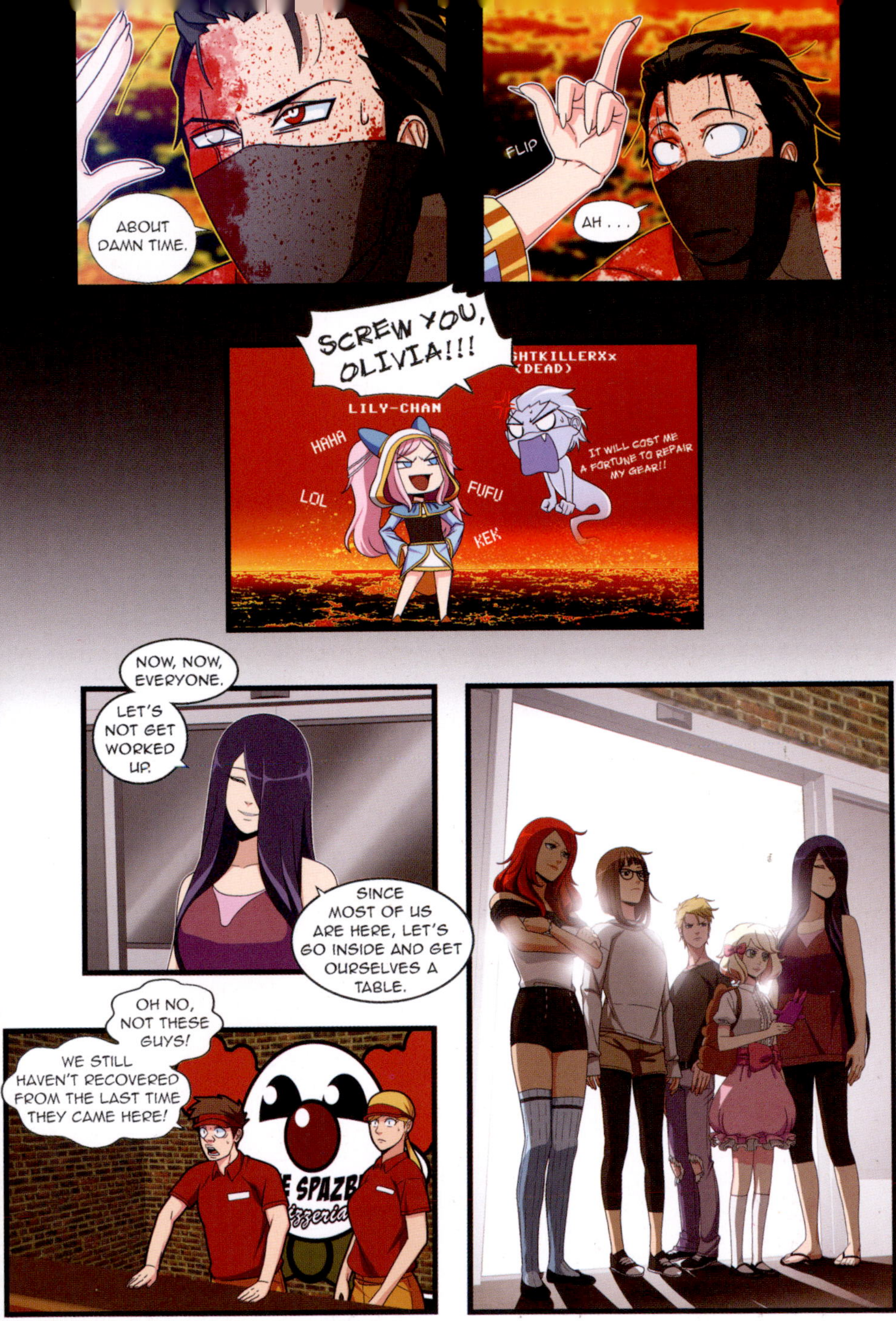

ABOUT DAMN TIME.
FLIP
AH . . .
SCREW YOU, OLIVIA!!!
LILY-CHAN
HAHA
LOL
FUFU
KEK
GHTKILLERXx (DEAD)
IT WILL COST ME A FORTUNE TO REPAIR MY GEAR!!
NOW, NOW, EVERYONE.
LET'S NOT GET WORKED UP.
SINCE MOST OF US ARE HERE, LET'S GO INSIDE AND GET OURSELVES A TABLE.
OH NO, NOT THESE GUYS!
WE STILL HAVEN'T RECOVERED FROM THE LAST TIME THEY CAME HERE!

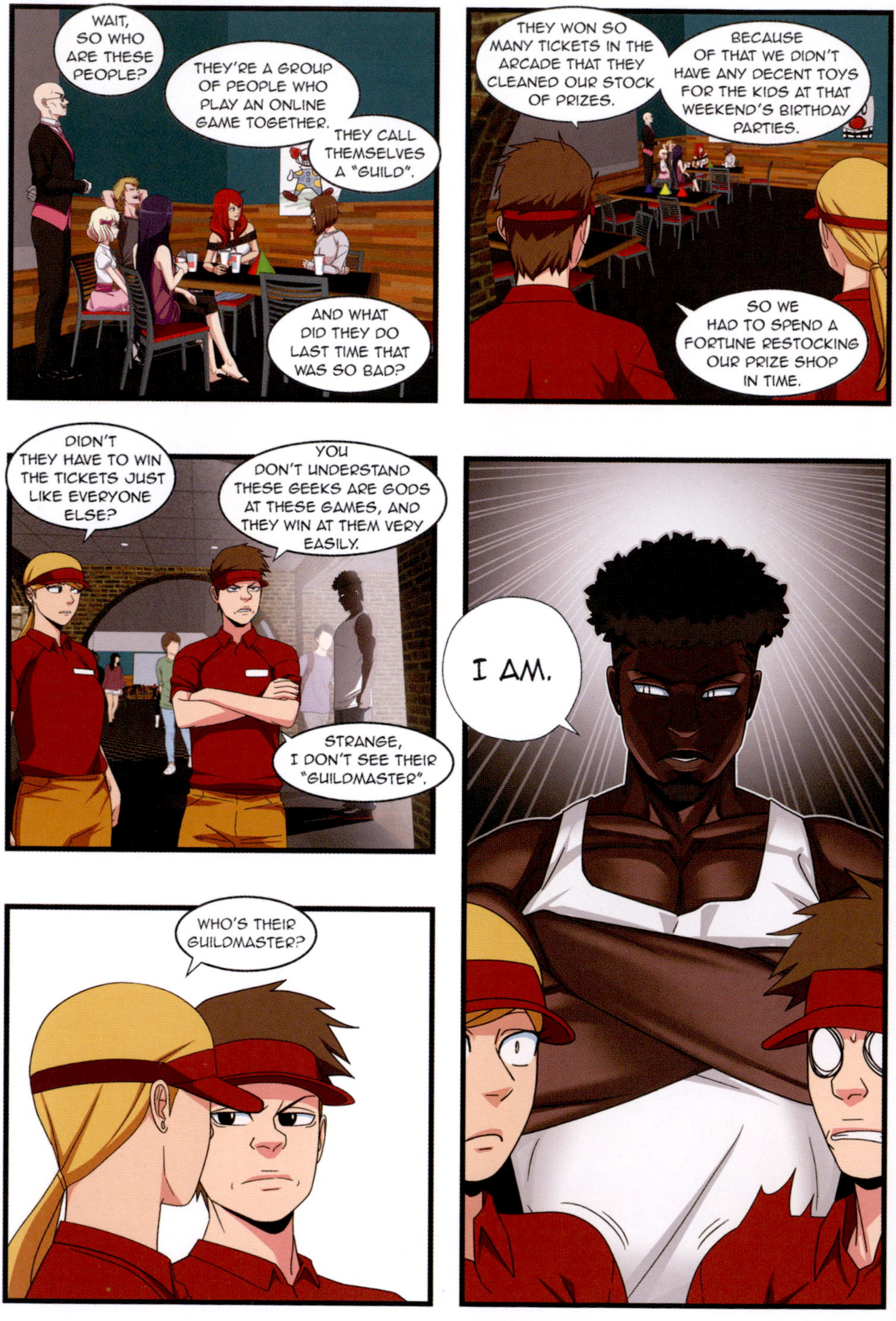
WAIT, SO WHO ARE THESE PEOPLE?
THEY'RE A GROUP OF PEOPLE WHO PLAY AN ONLINE GAME TOGETHER.
THEY CALL THEMSELVES A "GUILD".
AND WHAT DID THEY DO LAST TIME THAT WAS SO BAD?
THEY WON SO MANY TICKETS IN THE ARCADE THAT THEY CLEANED OUR STOCK OF PRIZES.
BECAUSE OF THAT WE DIDN'T HAVE ANY DECENT TOYS FOR THE KIDS AT THAT WEEKEND'S BIRTHDAY PARTIES.
SO WE HAD TO SPEND A FORTUNE RESTOCKING OUR PRIZE SHOP IN TIME.
DIDN'T THEY HAVE TO WIN THE TICKETS JUST LIKE EVERYONE ELSE?
YOU DON'T UNDERSTAND THESE GEEKS ARE GODS AT THESE GAMES, AND THEY WIN AT THEM VERY EASILY.
STRANGE, I DON'T SEE THEIR "GUILDMASTER".
WHO'S THEIR GUILDMASTER?
I AM.

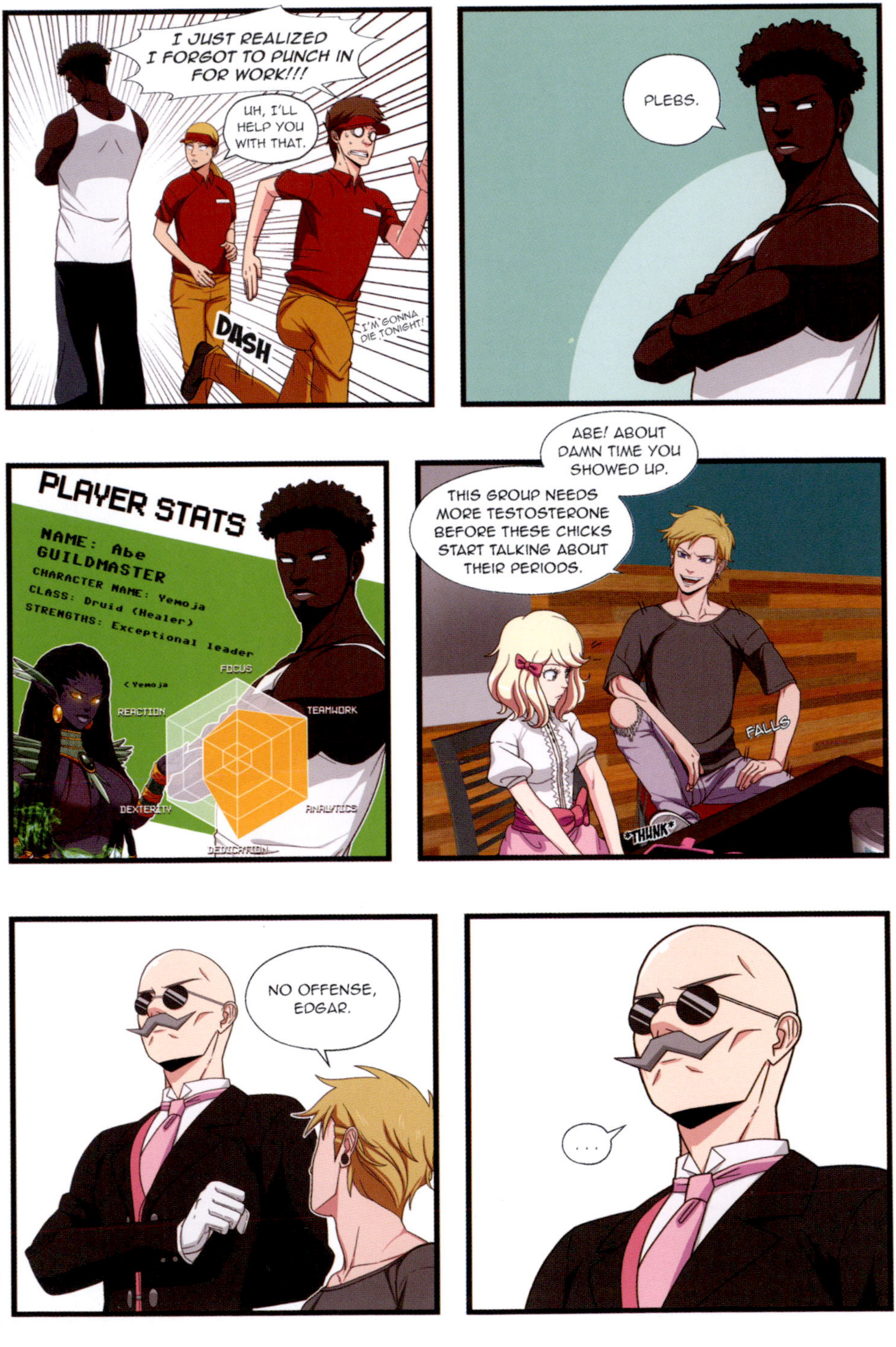
I JUST REALIZED I FORGOT TO PUNCH IN FOR WORK!!!
UH, I'LL HELP YOU WITH THAT.
DASH
I'M GONNA DIE TONIGHT!
PLEBS.
PLAYER STATS
NAME: Abe
GUILDMASTER
CHARACTER NAME: Yemoja
CLASS: Druid (Healer)
STRENGTHS: Exceptional leader
< Yemoja
FOCUS
TEAMWORK
ANALYTICS
DEDICATION
DEXTERITY
REACTION
ABE! ABOUT DAMN TIME YOU SHOWED UP.
THIS GROUP NEEDS MORE TESTOSTERONE BEFORE THESE CHICKS START TALKING ABOUT THEIR PERIODS.
FALLS
THUNK
NO OFFENSE, EDGAR.
...

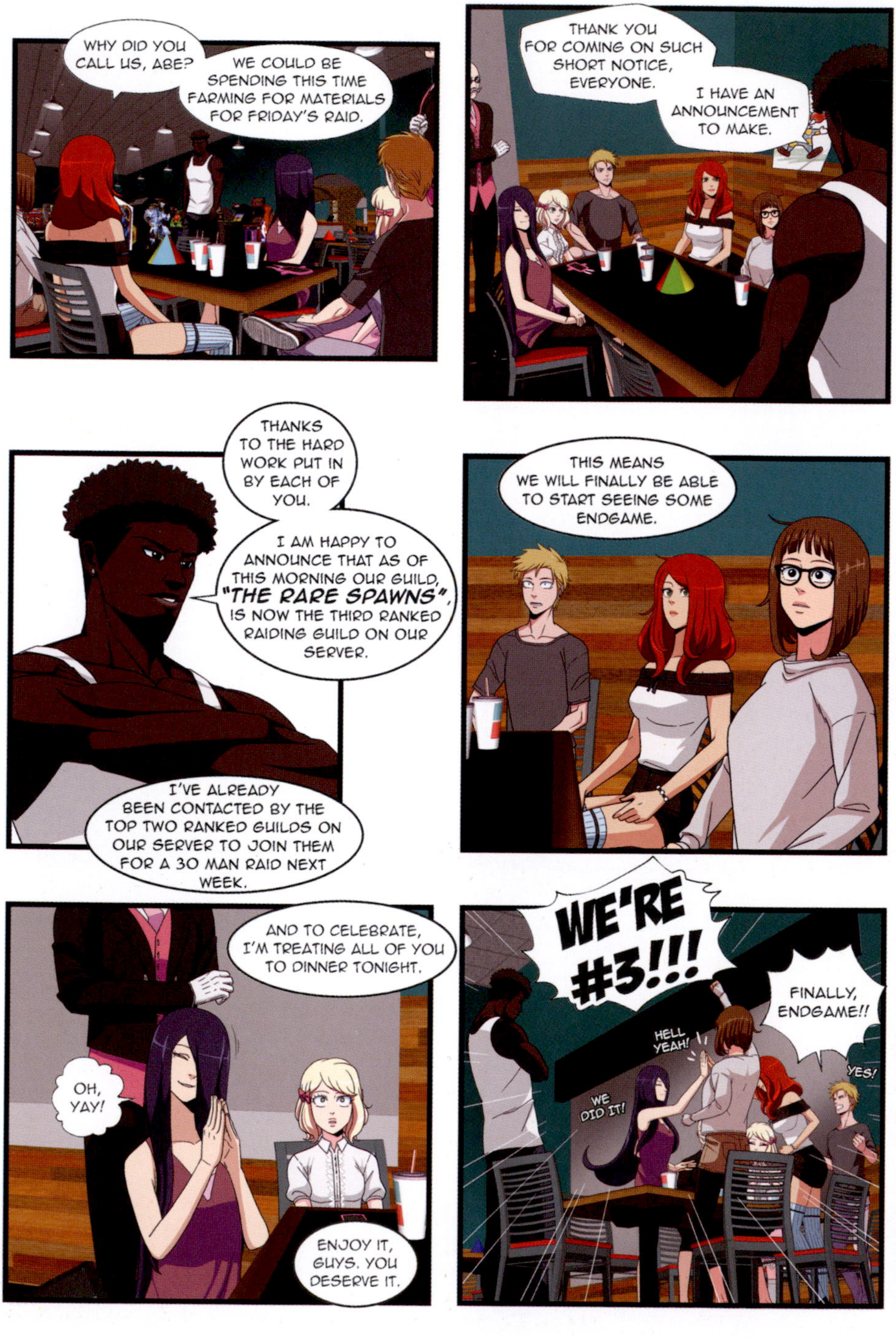
WHY DID YOU CALL US, ABE?
WE COULD BE SPENDING THIS TIME FARMING FOR MATERIALS FOR FRIDAY'S RAID.
THANK YOU FOR COMING ON SUCH SHORT NOTICE, EVERYONE.
I HAVE AN ANNOUNCEMENT TO MAKE.
THANKS TO THE HARD WORK PUT IN BY EACH OF YOU.
I AM HAPPY TO ANNOUNCE THAT AS OF THIS MORNING OUR GUILD, *"THE RARE SPAWNS"*, IS NOW THE THIRD RANKED RAIDING GUILD ON OUR SERVER.
I'VE ALREADY BEEN CONTACTED BY THE TOP TWO RANKED GUILDS ON OUR SERVER TO JOIN THEM FOR A 30 MAN RAID NEXT WEEK.
THIS MEANS WE WILL FINALLY BE ABLE TO START SEEING SOME ENDGAME.
AND TO CELEBRATE, I'M TREATING ALL OF YOU TO DINNER TONIGHT.
OH, YAY!
ENJOY IT, GUYS. YOU DESERVE IT.
WE'RE #3!!!
FINALLY, ENDGAME!!
HELL YEAH!
WE DID IT!
YES!

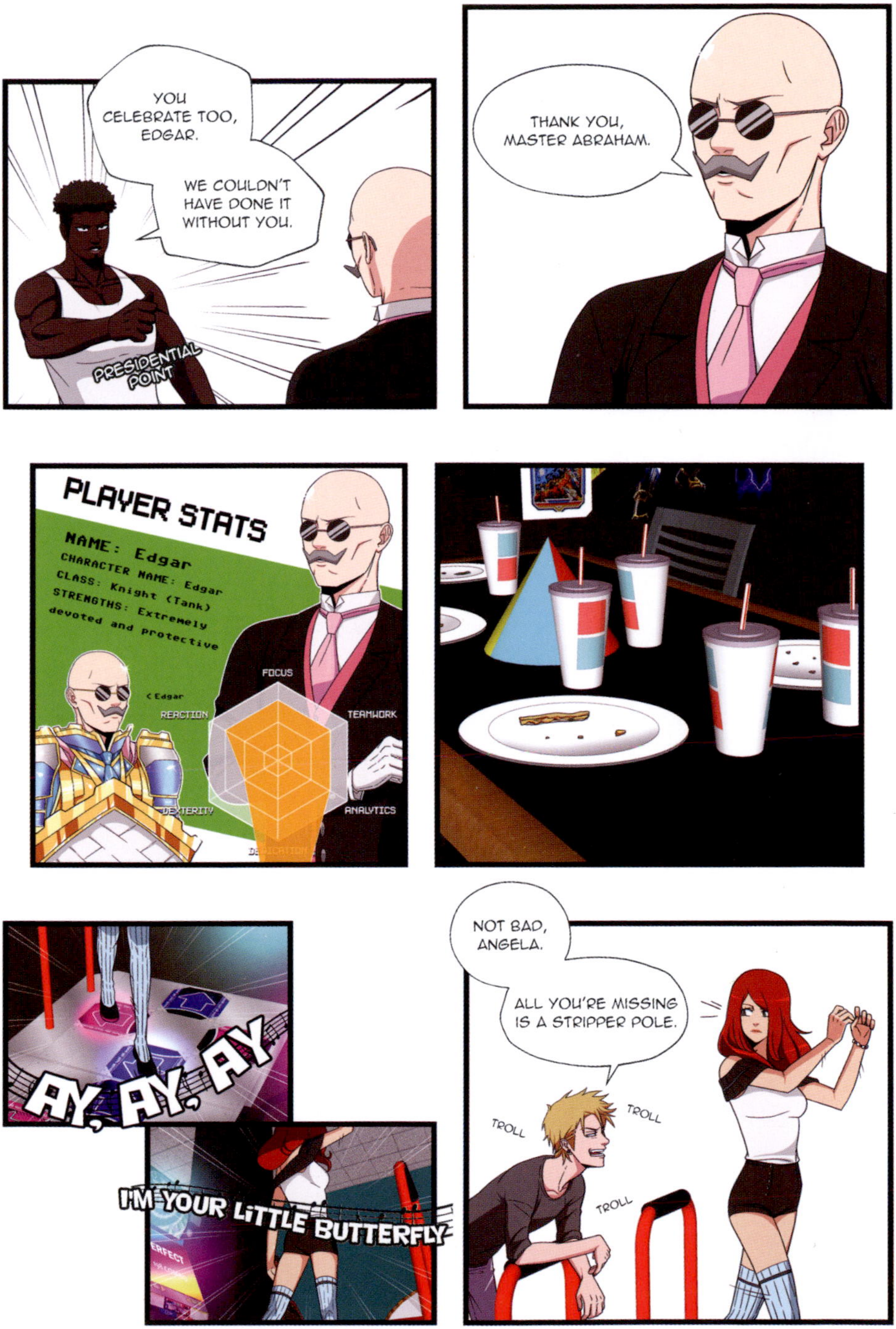

YOU CELEBRATE TOO, EDGAR.
WE COULDN'T HAVE DONE IT WITHOUT YOU.
PRESIDENTIAL POINT
THANK YOU, MASTER ABRAHAM.
PLAYER STATS
NAME: Edgar
CHARACTER NAME: Edgar
CLASS: Knight (Tank)
STRENGTHS: Extremely devoted and protective
< Edgar
FOCUS
REACTION
TEAMWORK
DEXTERITY
ANALYTICS
AY, AY, AY
I'M YOUR LITTLE BUTTERFLY
NOT BAD, ANGELA.
ALL YOU'RE MISSING IS A STRIPPER POLE.
TROLL
TROLL
TROLL

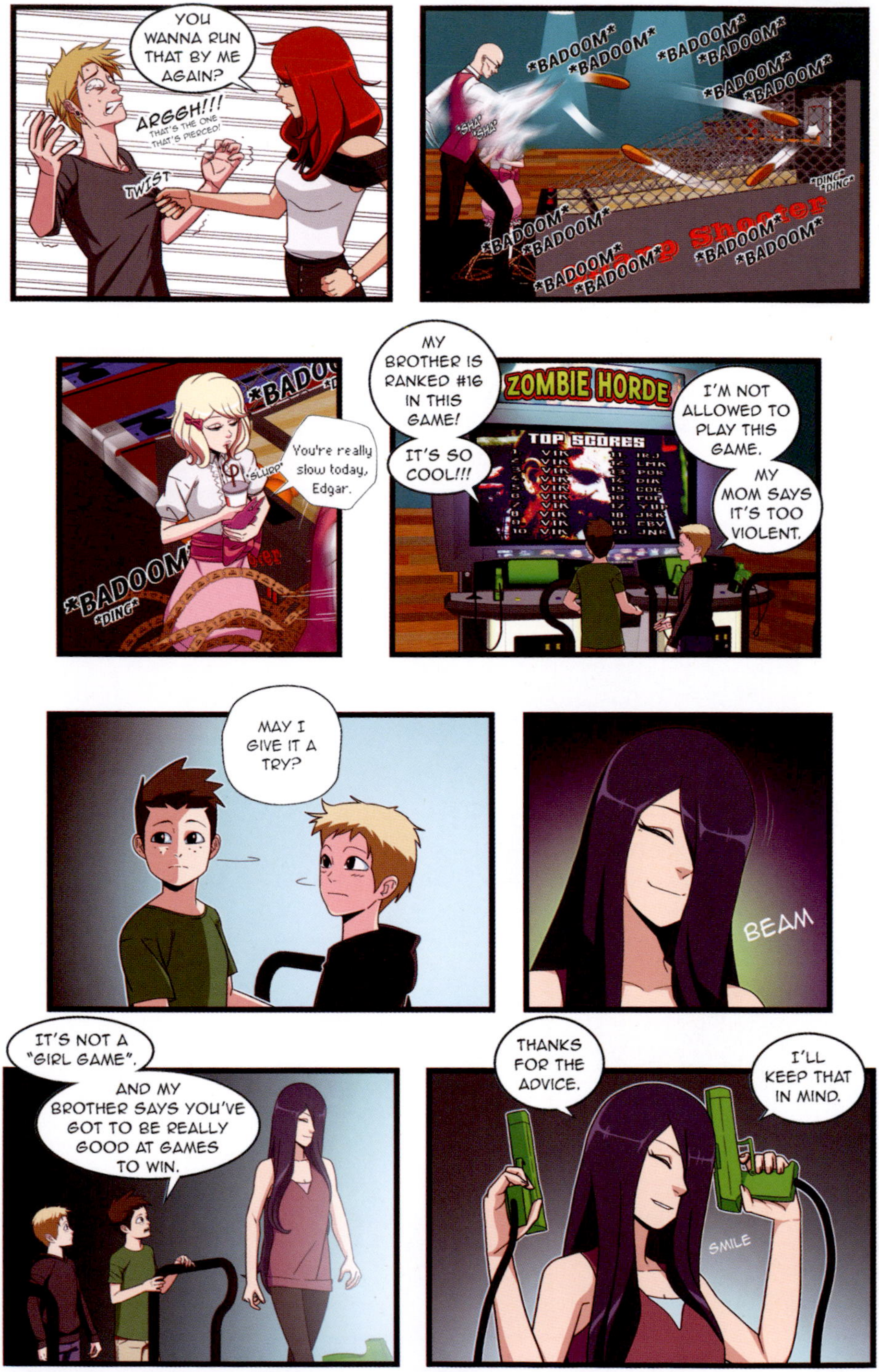

YOU WANNA RUN THAT BY ME AGAIN?
ARGGH!!!
THAT'S THE ONE THAT'S PIERCED!
TWIST
BADOOM *BADOOM*
BADOOM *BADOOM*
BADOOM *BADOOM*
SHA *SHA*
DING *DING*
BADOOM *BADOOM*
BADOOM *BADOOM*
BADOOM *BADOOM*
*BADOOM
SLURP
You're really slow today, Edgar.
*BADOOM
DING
MY BROTHER IS RANKED #16 IN THIS GAME!
IT'S SO COOL!!!
ZOMBIE HORDE
TOP SCORES
I'M NOT ALLOWED TO PLAY THIS GAME.
MY MOM SAYS IT'S TOO VIOLENT.
MAY I GIVE IT A TRY?
BEAM
IT'S NOT A "GIRL GAME".
AND MY BROTHER SAYS YOU'VE GOT TO BE REALLY GOOD AT GAMES TO WIN.
THANKS FOR THE ADVICE.
I'LL KEEP THAT IN MIND.
SMILE

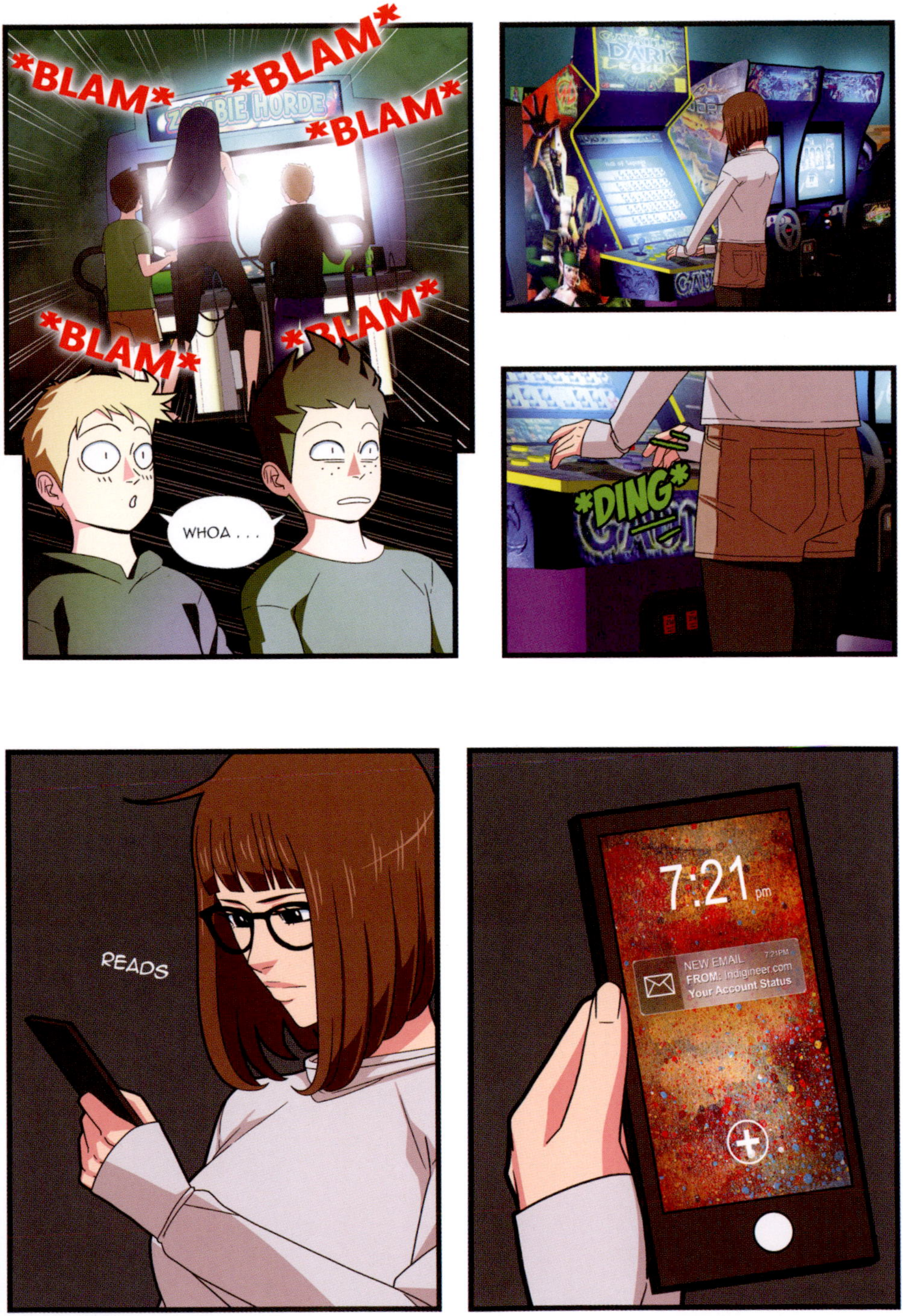
BLAM
BLAM
BLAM
BLAM
BLAM
WHOA . . .
DING
READS
7:21 pm
NEW EMAIL 7:21PM
FROM: Indigineer.com
Your Account Status

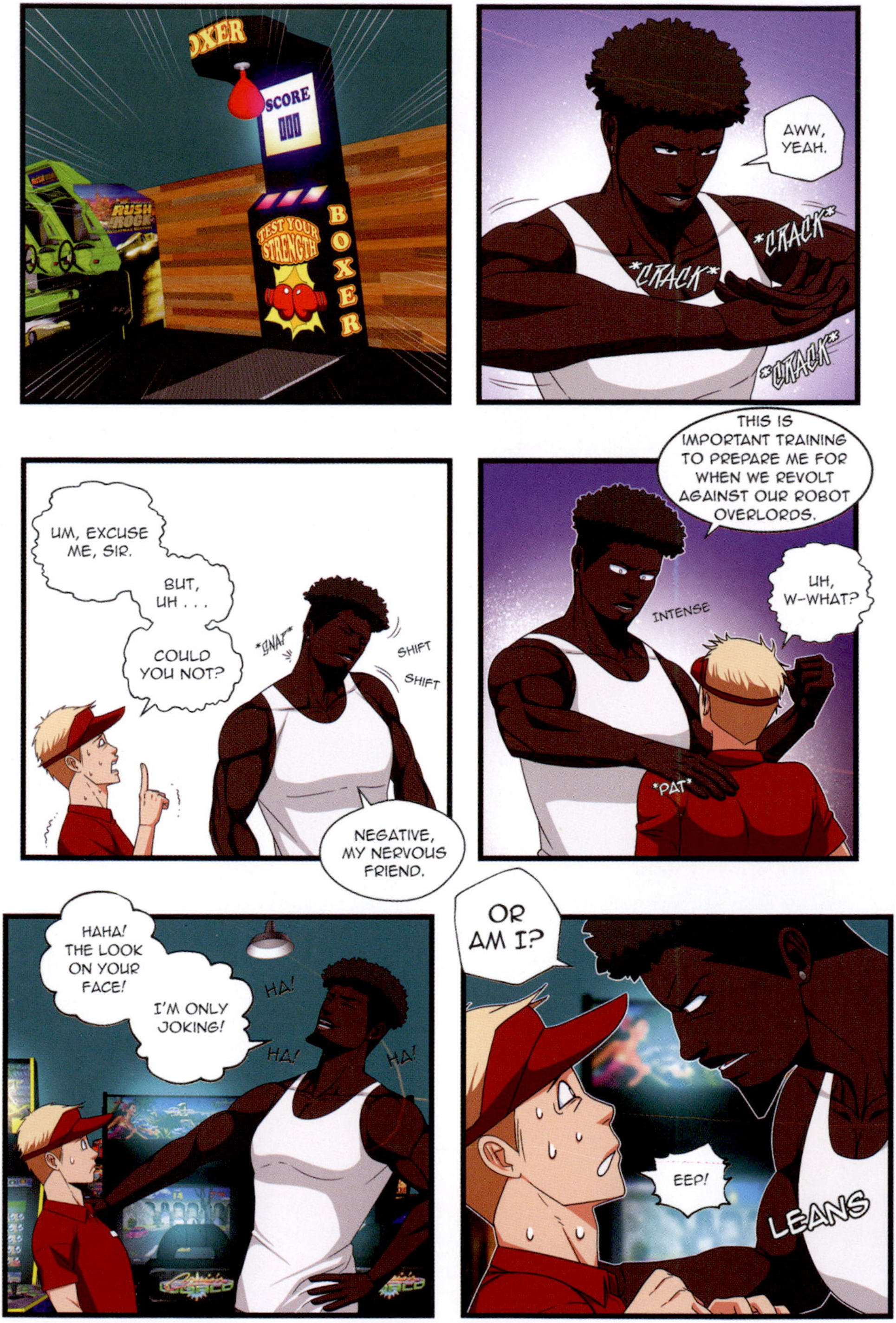
OXER
SCORE
RUSH ROCK
TEST YOUR STRENGTH
BOXER
AWW, YEAH.
CRACK
CRACK
CRACK
UM, EXCUSE ME, SIR.
BUT, UH . . .
COULD YOU NOT?
SHIFT
SHIFT
NEGATIVE, MY NERVOUS FRIEND.
THIS IS IMPORTANT TRAINING TO PREPARE ME FOR WHEN WE REVOLT AGAINST OUR ROBOT OVERLORDS.
INTENSE
UH, W-WHAT?
PAT
HAHA! THE LOOK ON YOUR FACE!
I'M ONLY JOKING!
HA!
HA!
HA!
OR AM I?
EEP!
LEANS

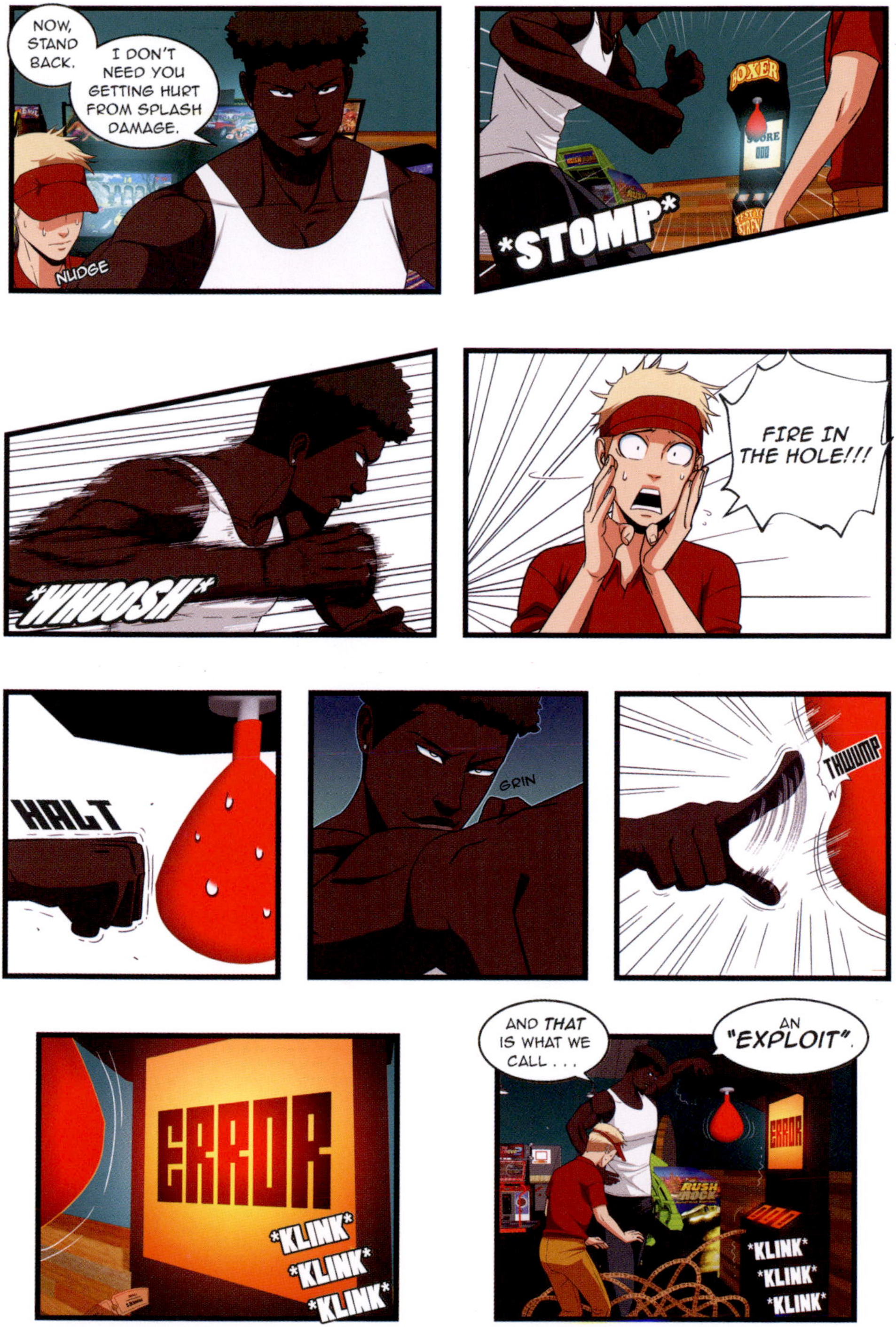
NOW, STAND BACK.
I DON'T NEED YOU GETTING HURT FROM SPLASH DAMAGE.
NUDGE
BOXER
SCORE
STOMP
WHOOSH
FIRE IN THE HOLE!!!
HALT
GRIN
THWUMP
ERROR
KLINK
KLINK
KLINK
AND THAT IS WHAT WE CALL . . .
AN "EXPLOIT".
ERROR
KLINK
KLINK
KLINK

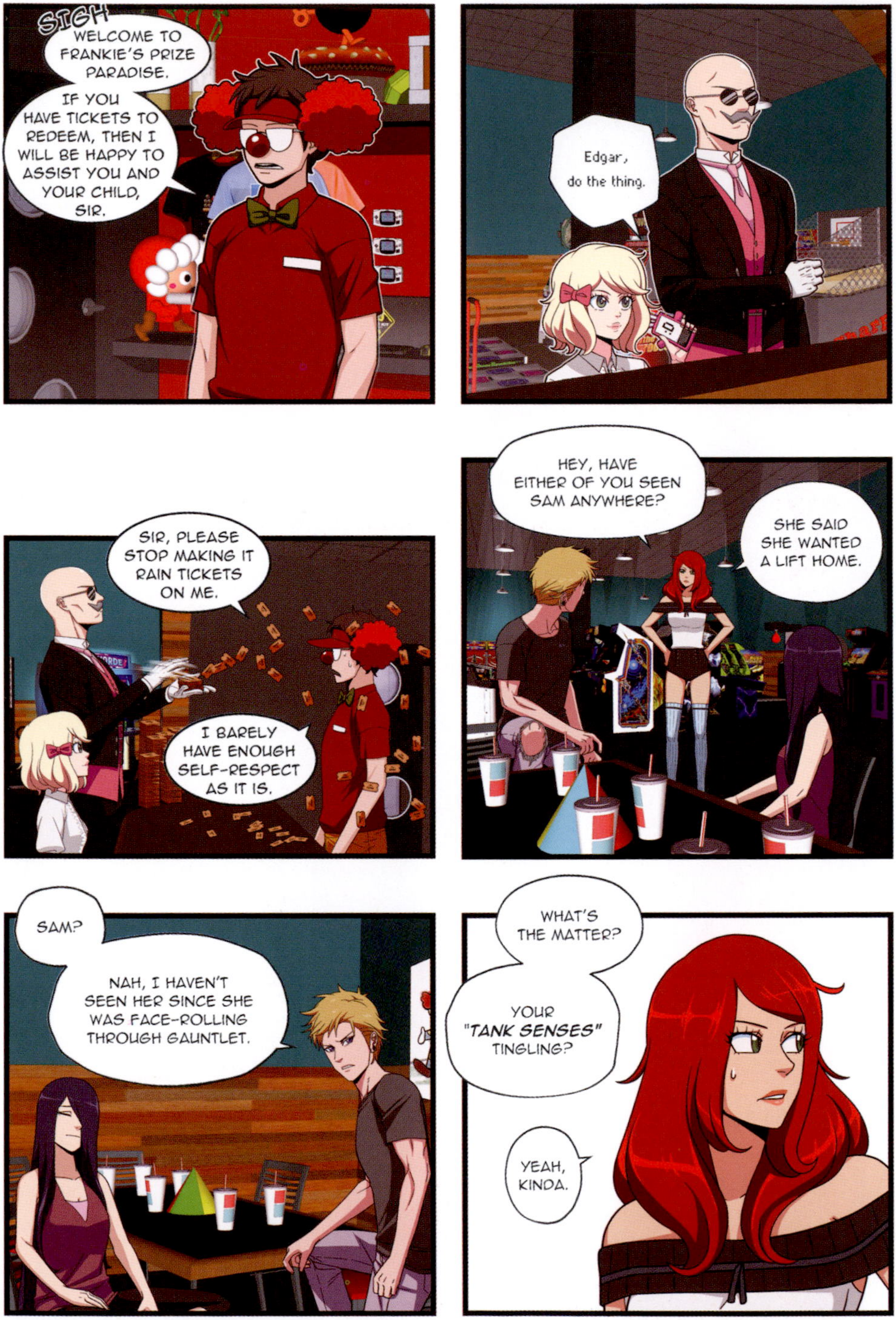
SIGH
WELCOME TO FRANKIE'S PRIZE PARADISE.
IF YOU HAVE TICKETS TO REDEEM, THEN I WILL BE HAPPY TO ASSIST YOU AND YOUR CHILD, SIR.
Edgar, do the thing.
SIR, PLEASE STOP MAKING IT RAIN TICKETS ON ME.
I BARELY HAVE ENOUGH SELF-RESPECT AS IT IS.
HEY, HAVE EITHER OF YOU SEEN SAM ANYWHERE?
SHE SAID SHE WANTED A LIFT HOME.
SAM?
NAH, I HAVEN'T SEEN HER SINCE SHE WAS FACE-ROLLING THROUGH GAUNTLET.
WHAT'S THE MATTER?
YOUR "TANK SENSES" TINGLING?
YEAH, KINDA.

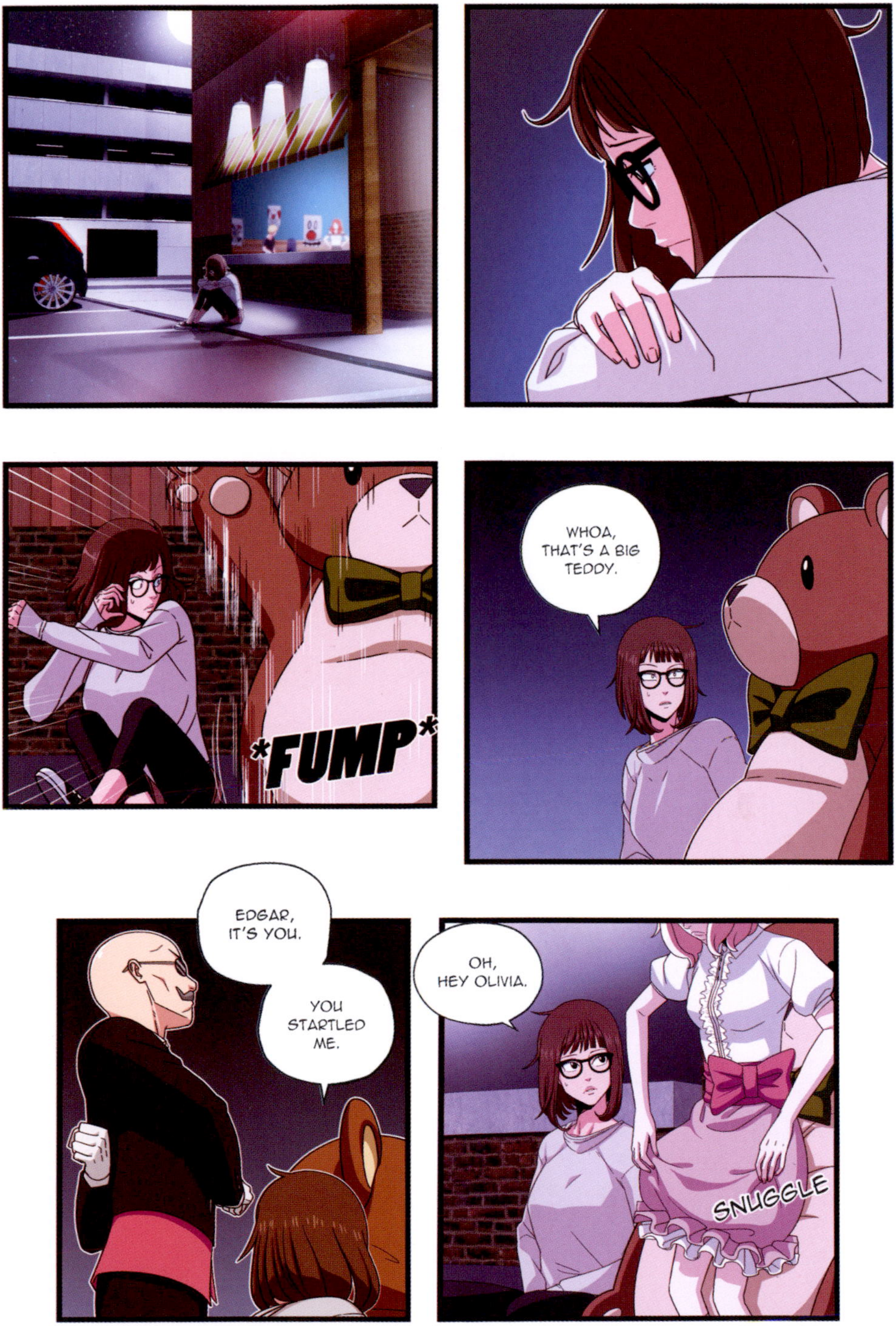
FUMP
WHOA, THAT'S A BIG TEDDY.
EDGAR, IT'S YOU.
YOU STARTLED ME.
OH, HEY OLIVIA.
SNUGGLE

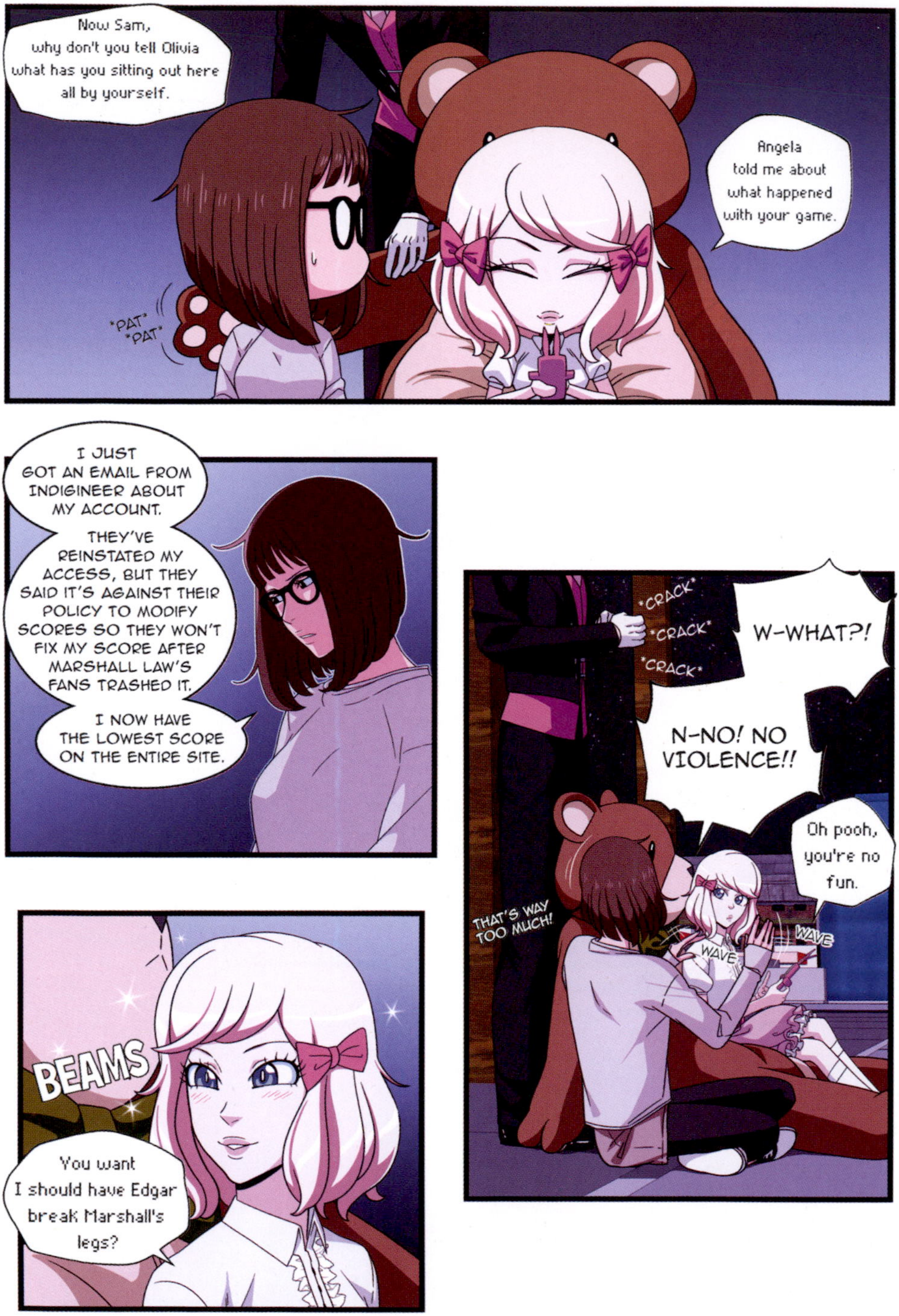
Now Sam, why don't you tell Olivia what has you sitting out here all by yourself.
Angela told me about what happened with your game.
PAT *PAT*
I JUST GOT AN EMAIL FROM INDIGINEER ABOUT MY ACCOUNT.
THEY'VE REINSTATED MY ACCESS, BUT THEY SAID IT'S AGAINST THEIR POLICY TO MODIFY SCORES SO THEY WON'T FIX MY SCORE AFTER MARSHALL LAW'S FANS TRASHED IT.
I NOW HAVE THE LOWEST SCORE ON THE ENTIRE SITE.
BEAMS
You want I should have Edgar break Marshall's legs?
CRACK
CRACK
CRACK
W-WHAT?!
N-NO! NO VIOLENCE!!
Oh pooh, you're no fun.
THAT'S WAY TOO MUCH!
WAVE
WAVE

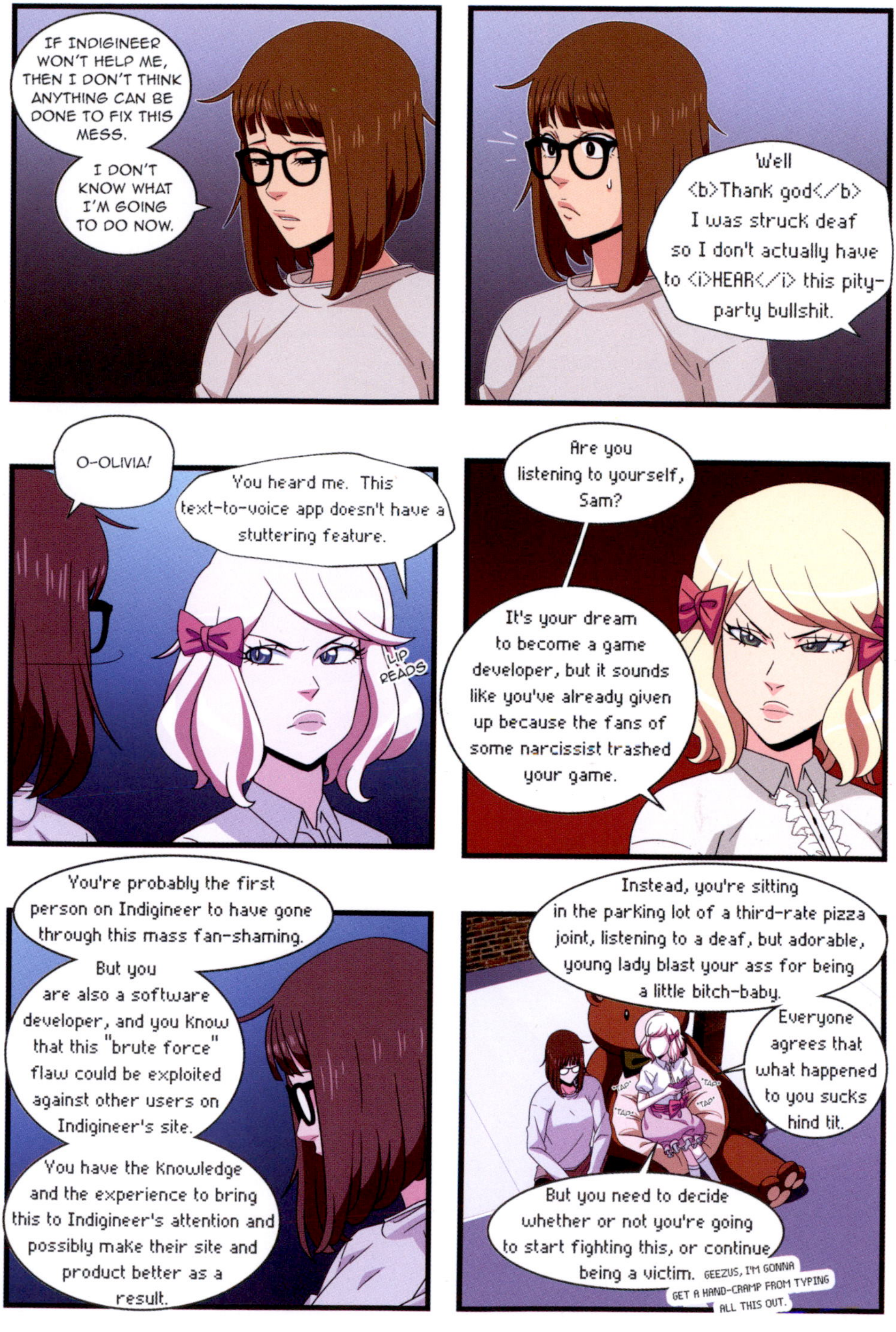
IF INDIGINEER WON'T HELP ME, THEN I DON'T THINK ANYTHING CAN BE DONE TO FIX THIS MESS.
I DON'T KNOW WHAT I'M GOING TO DO NOW.
Well <b>Thank god</b> I was struck deaf so I don't actually have to <i>HEAR</i> this pity-party bullshit.
O-OLIVIA!
You heard me. This text-to-voice app doesn't have a stuttering feature.
LIP READS
Are you listening to yourself, Sam?
It's your dream to become a game developer, but it sounds like you've already given up because the fans of some narcissist trashed your game.
You're probably the first person on Indigineer to have gone through this mass fan-shaming.
But you are also a software developer, and you know that this "brute force" flaw could be exploited against other users on Indigineer's site.
You have the knowledge and the experience to bring this to Indigineer's attention and possibly make their site and product better as a result.
Instead, you're sitting in the parking lot of a third-rate pizza joint, listening to a deaf, but adorable, young lady blast your ass for being a little bitch-baby.
Everyone agrees that what happened to you sucks hind tit.
TAP *TAP* *TAP* *TAP*
But you need to decide whether or not you're going to start fighting this, or continue being a victim.
GEEZUS, I'M GONNA GET A HAND-CRAMP FROM TYPING ALL THIS OUT.

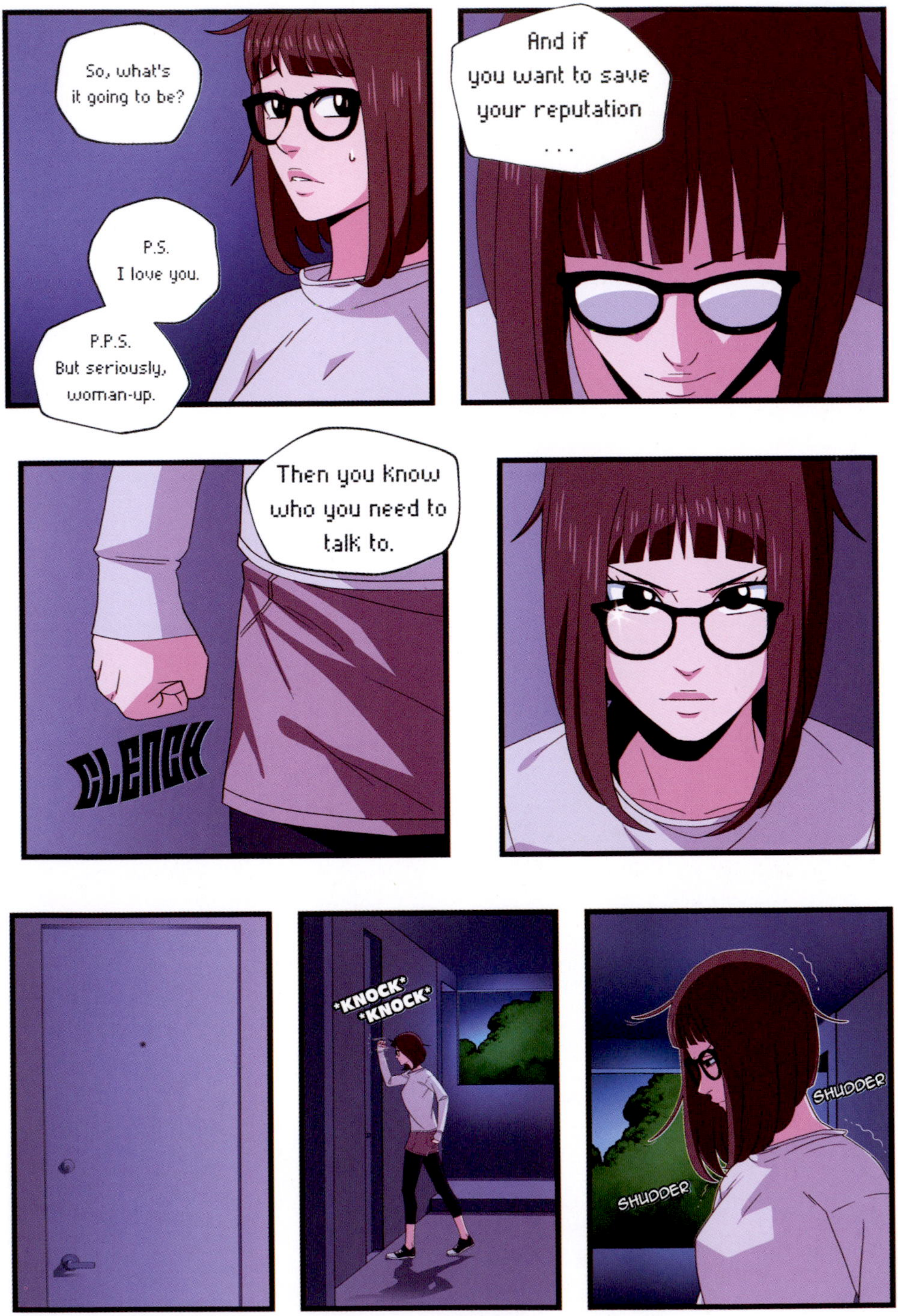
So, what's it going to be?
P.S. I love you.
P.P.S. But seriously, woman-up.
And if you want to save your reputation . . .
Then you know who you need to talk to.
CLENCH
KNOCK *KNOCK*
SHUDDER
SHUDDER

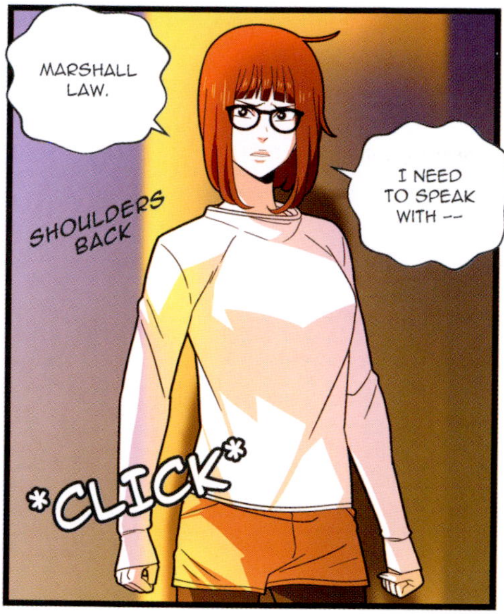
MARSHALL LAW.
SHOULDERS BACK
I NEED TO SPEAK WITH --
CLICK
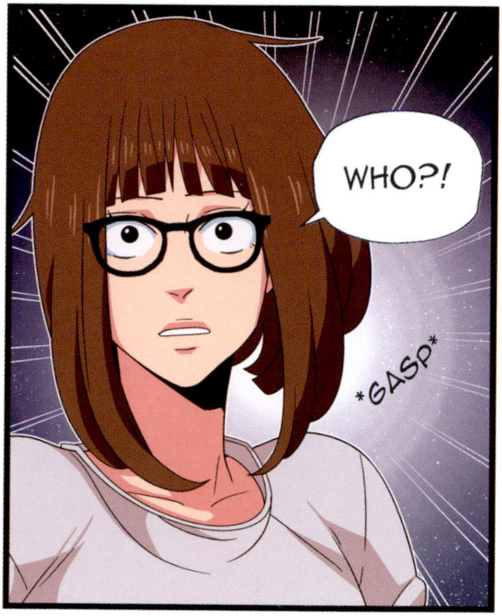
WHO?!
GASP
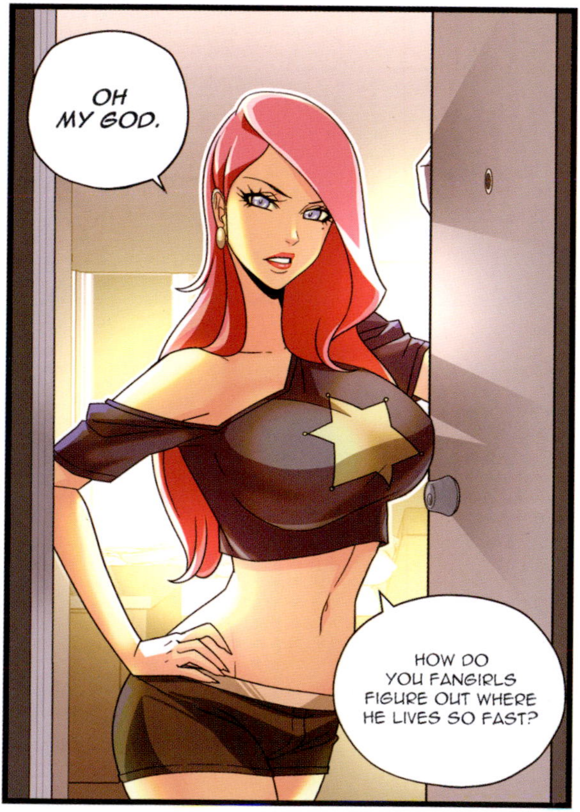
OH MY GOD.
HOW DO YOU FANGIRLS FIGURE OUT WHERE HE LIVES SO FAST?

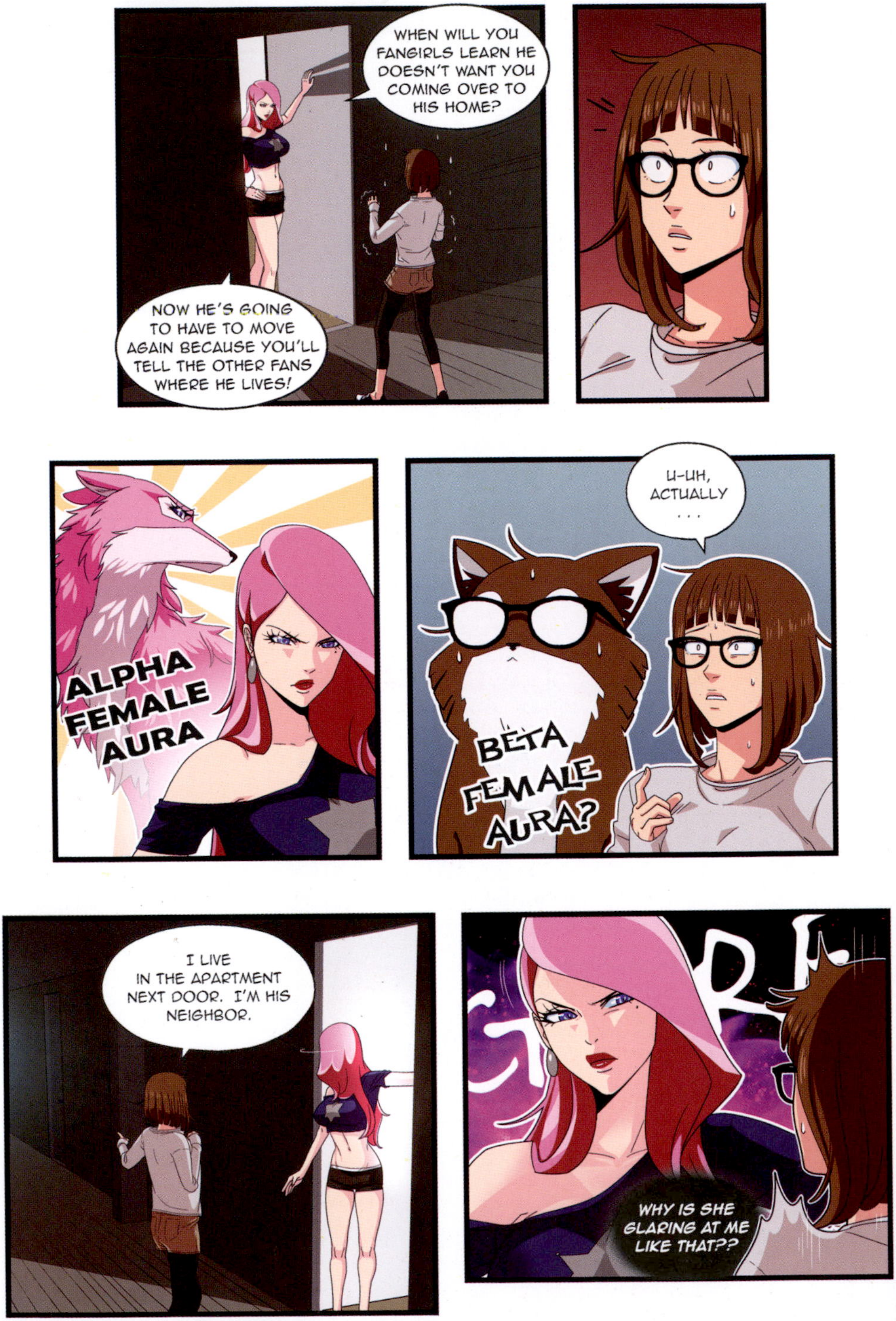
WHEN WILL YOU FANGIRLS LEARN HE DOESN'T WANT YOU COMING OVER TO HIS HOME?
NOW HE'S GOING TO HAVE TO MOVE AGAIN BECAUSE YOU'LL TELL THE OTHER FANS WHERE HE LIVES!
ALPHA FEMALE AURA
U-UH, ACTUALLY . . .
BETA FEMALE AURA?
I LIVE IN THE APARTMENT NEXT DOOR. I'M HIS NEIGHBOR.
WHY IS SHE GLARING AT ME LIKE THAT??

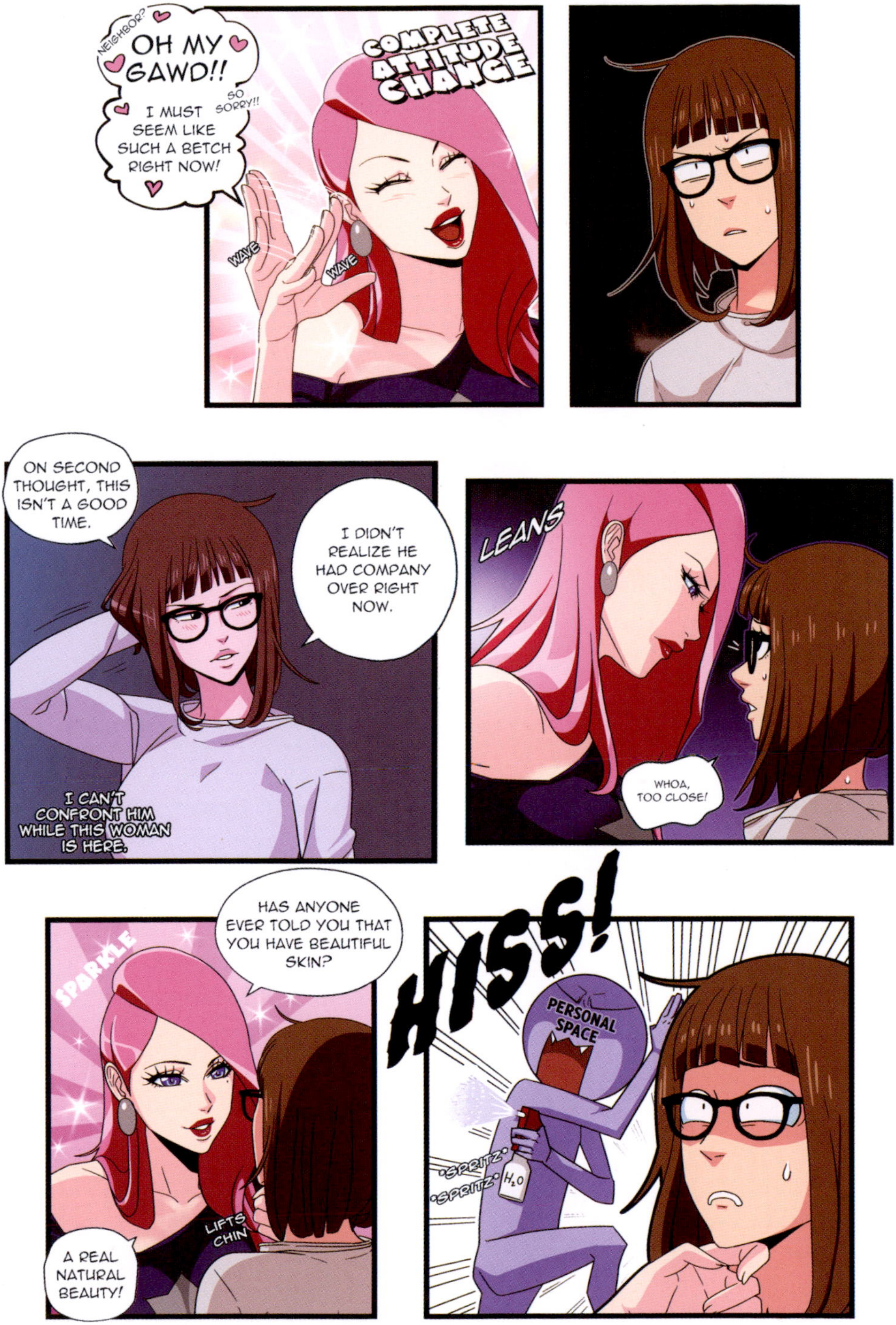
NEIGHBOR?
OH MY GAWD!!
SO SORRY!!
I MUST SEEM LIKE SUCH A BETCH RIGHT NOW!
COMPLETE ATTITUDE CHANGE
WAVE
WAVE
ON SECOND THOUGHT, THIS ISN'T A GOOD TIME.
I DIDN'T REALIZE HE HAD COMPANY OVER RIGHT NOW.
I CAN'T CONFRONT HIM WHILE THIS WOMAN IS HERE.
LEANS
WHOA, TOO CLOSE!
HAS ANYONE EVER TOLD YOU THAT YOU HAVE BEAUTIFUL SKIN?
SPARKLE
LIFTS CHIN
A REAL NATURAL BEAUTY!
HISS!
PERSONAL SPACE
SPRITZ
SPRITZ
H2O

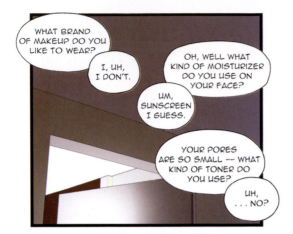

WHAT BRAND OF MAKEUP DO YOU LIKE TO WEAR?

I, UH, I DON'T.

OH, WELL WHAT KIND OF MOISTURIZER DO YOU USE ON YOUR FACE?

UM, SUNSCREEN I GUESS.

YOUR PORES ARE SO SMALL -- WHAT KIND OF TONER DO YOU USE?

UH, ...NO?

AH, I SEE.

PERHAPS I COULD BE OF SOME ASSISTANCE?

DIGS

MY CARD.

A BEAUTY VLOGGER?

Glitz Kitten
- Monica McKenzie -
WWW.VIEWTUBE.COM/USER/GLITZKITTEN
BEAUTY VLOGGER

OH, IT'S WARM.

THAT'S RIGHT, I'M MONICA MCKENZIE THE BEAUTY VLOGGER KNOWN AS "GLITZKITTEN"!

I HAVE OVER 2.5 MILLION SUBSCRIBERS ON VIEWTUBE.

AND 2 MILLION FOLLOWERS ON INSTAFRAME.

Glitz Kitten
I HAVE MY OWN FASHION AND MAKEUP LINE UNDER THE "GLITZKITTEN" BRAND.

AND TWICE A WEEK I UPLOAD MAKEUP AND FASHION VIDEO TUTORIALS HELPING VIEWERS FIND A MORE BEAUTIFUL YOU.

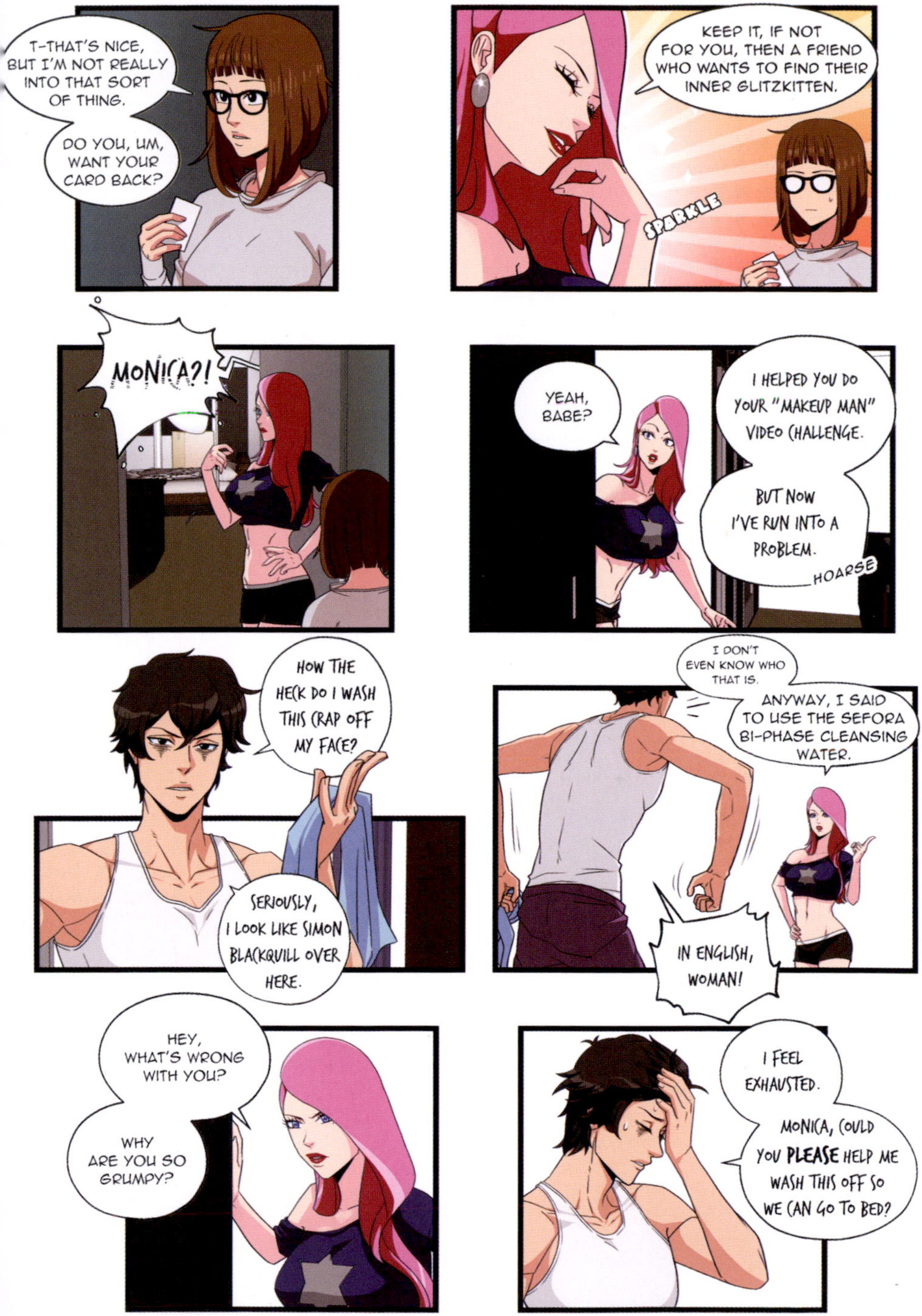
T-THAT'S NICE, BUT I'M NOT REALLY INTO THAT SORT OF THING.
DO YOU, UM, WANT YOUR CARD BACK?
KEEP IT, IF NOT FOR YOU, THEN A FRIEND WHO WANTS TO FIND THEIR INNER GLITZKITTEN.
SPARKLE
MONICA?!
YEAH, BABE?
I HELPED YOU DO YOUR "MAKEUP MAN" VIDEO CHALLENGE.
BUT NOW I'VE RUN INTO A PROBLEM.
HOARSE
HOW THE HECK DO I WASH THIS CRAP OFF MY FACE?
SERIOUSLY, I LOOK LIKE SIMON BLACKQUILL OVER HERE.
I DON'T EVEN KNOW WHO THAT IS.
ANYWAY, I SAID TO USE THE SEFORA BI-PHASE CLEANSING WATER.
IN ENGLISH, WOMAN!
HEY, WHAT'S WRONG WITH YOU?
WHY ARE YOU SO GRUMPY?
I FEEL EXHAUSTED.
MONICA, COULD YOU **PLEASE** HELP ME WASH THIS OFF SO WE CAN GO TO BED?

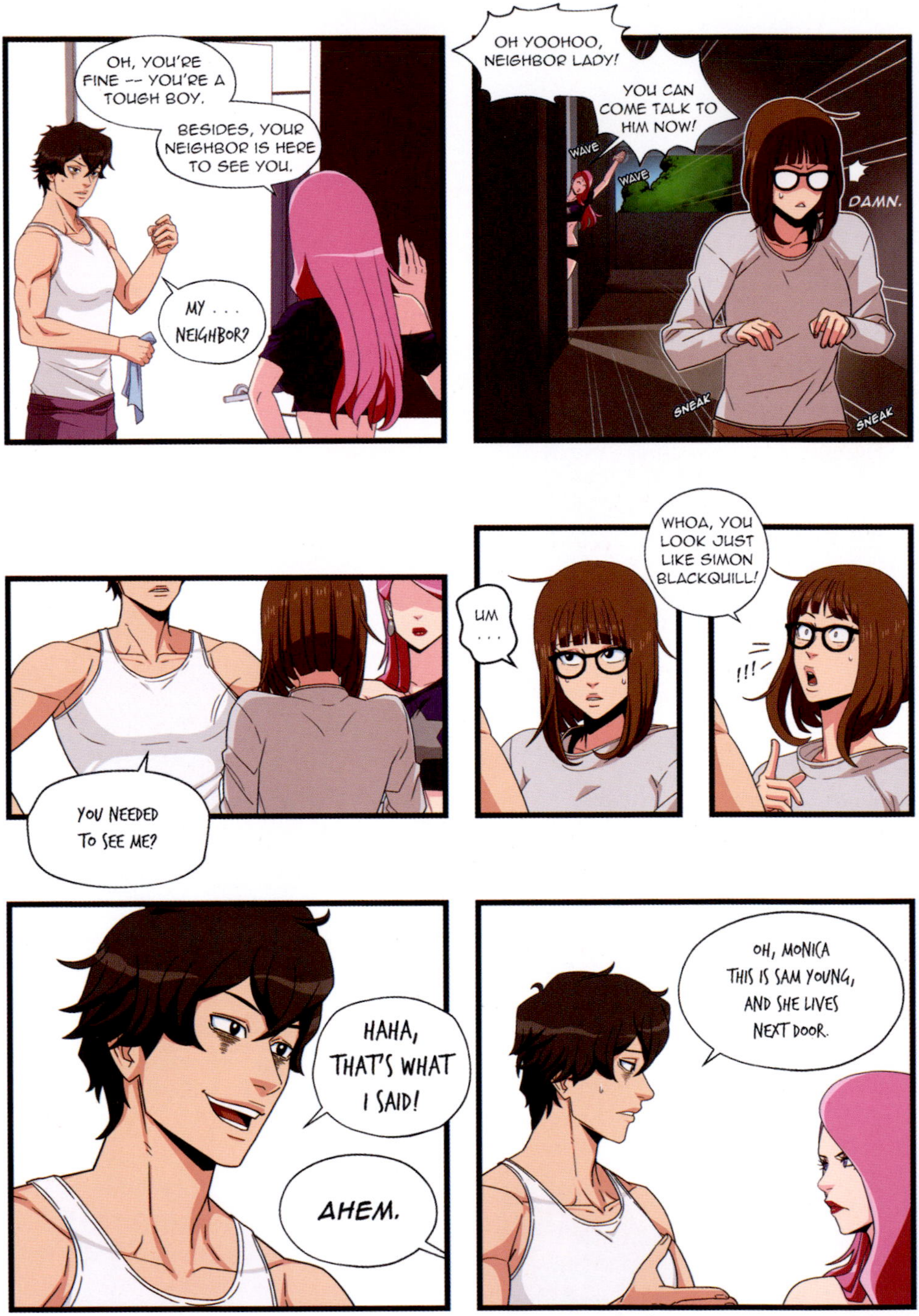
OH, YOU'RE FINE -- YOU'RE A TOUGH BOY.
BESIDES, YOUR NEIGHBOR IS HERE TO SEE YOU.
MY . . . NEIGHBOR?
OH YOOHOO, NEIGHBOR LADY!
YOU CAN COME TALK TO HIM NOW!
WAVE
WAVE
DAMN.
SNEAK
SNEAK
YOU NEEDED TO SEE ME?
UM . . .
WHOA, YOU LOOK JUST LIKE SIMON BLACKQUILL!
!!!
HAHA, THAT'S WHAT I SAID!
AHEM.
OH, MONICA THIS IS SAM YOUNG, AND SHE LIVES NEXT DOOR.

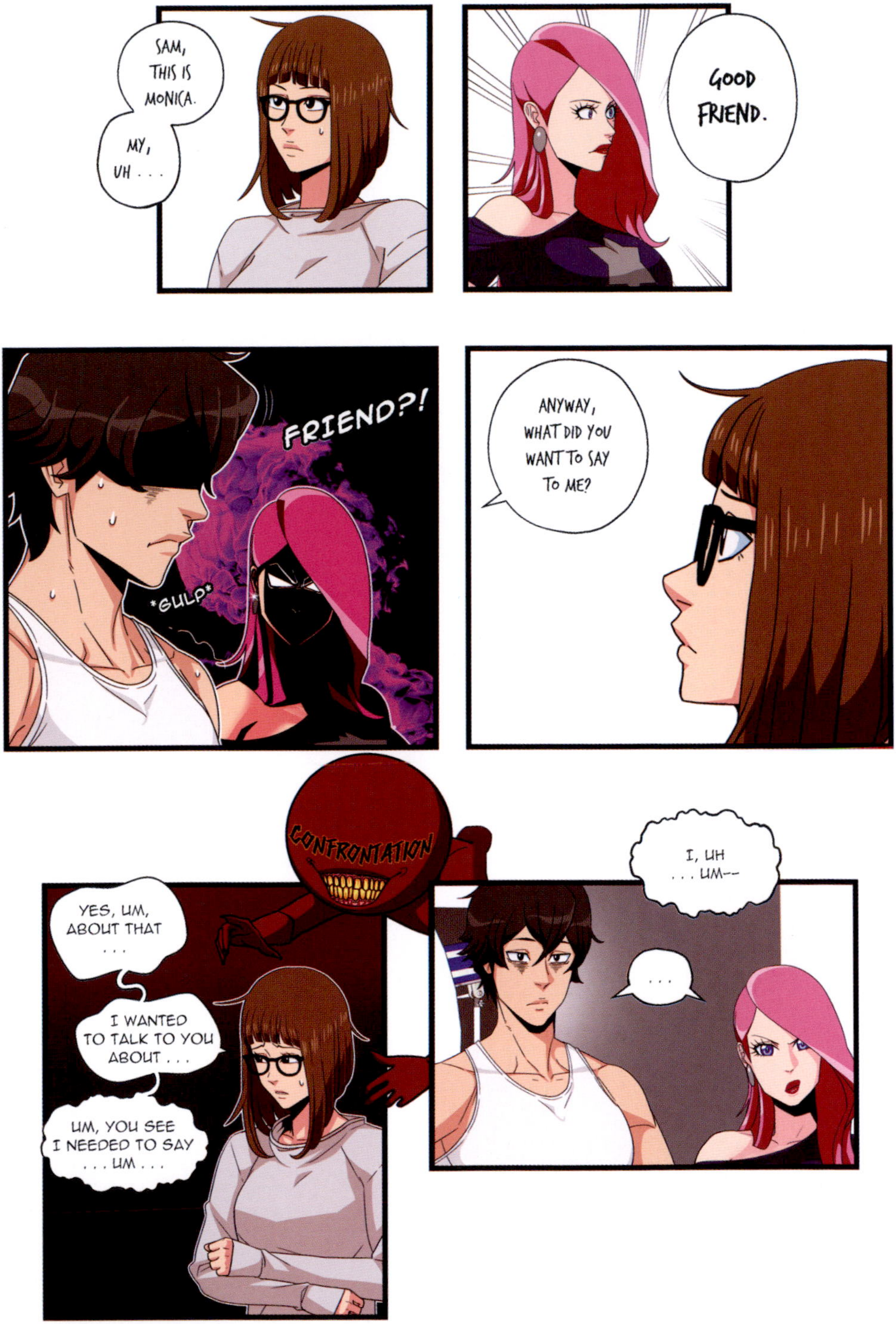
SAM, THIS IS MONICA.
MY, UH . . .
GOOD FRIEND.
FRIEND?!
GULP
ANYWAY, WHAT DID YOU WANT TO SAY TO ME?
CONFRONTATION
YES, UM, ABOUT THAT . . .
I WANTED TO TALK TO YOU ABOUT . . .
UM, YOU SEE I NEEDED TO SAY . . . UM . . .
I, UH . . . UM--
. . .

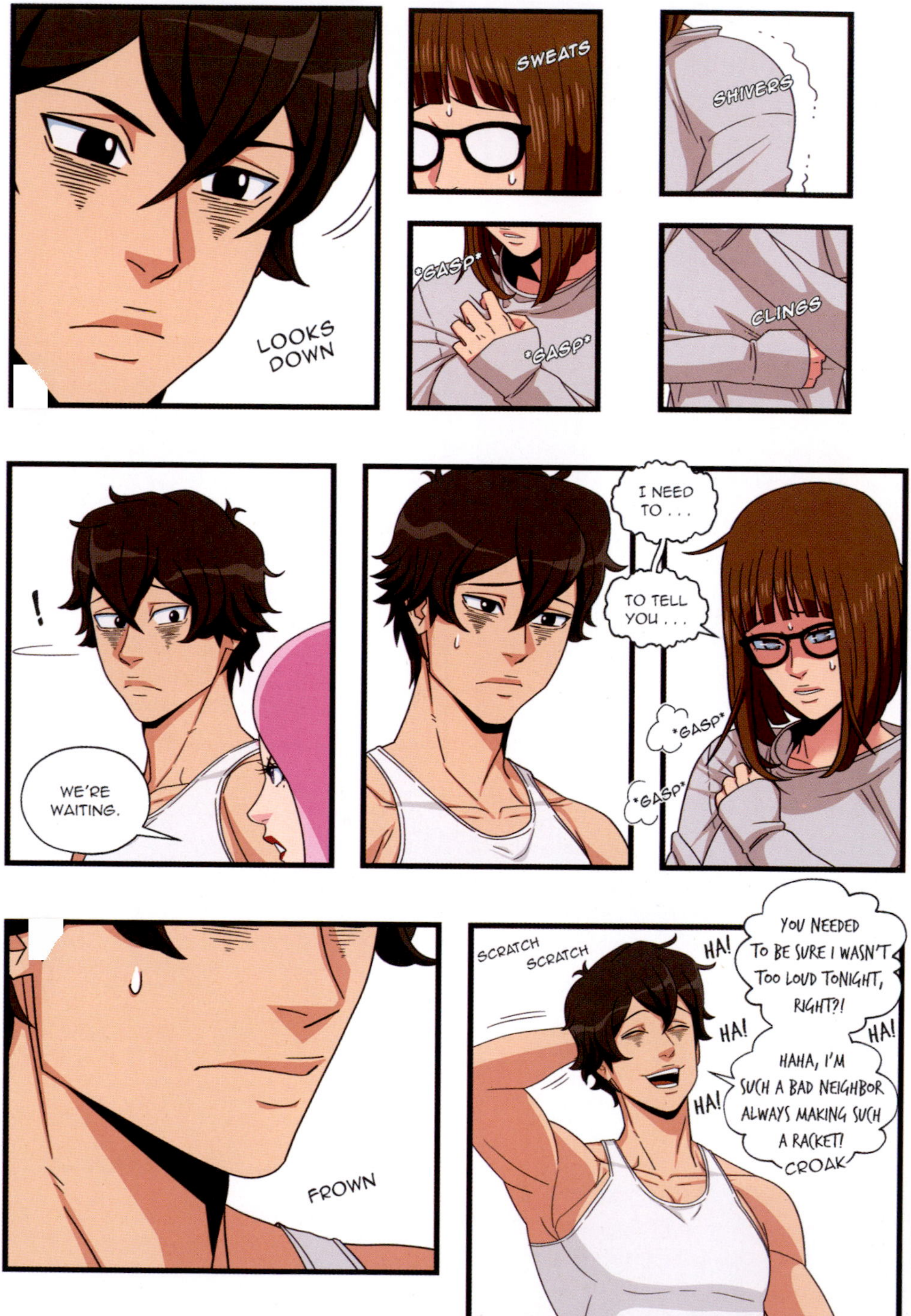
LOOKS DOWN
SWEATS
SHIVERS
GASP
GASP
CLINGS
!
WE'RE WAITING.
I NEED TO . . .
TO TELL YOU . . .
GASP
GASP
FROWN
SCRATCH SCRATCH
HA!
YOU NEEDED TO BE SURE I WASN'T TOO LOUD TONIGHT, RIGHT?!
HA!
HA!
HA!
HAHA, I'M SUCH A BAD NEIGHBOR ALWAYS MAKING SUCH A RACKET! CROAK

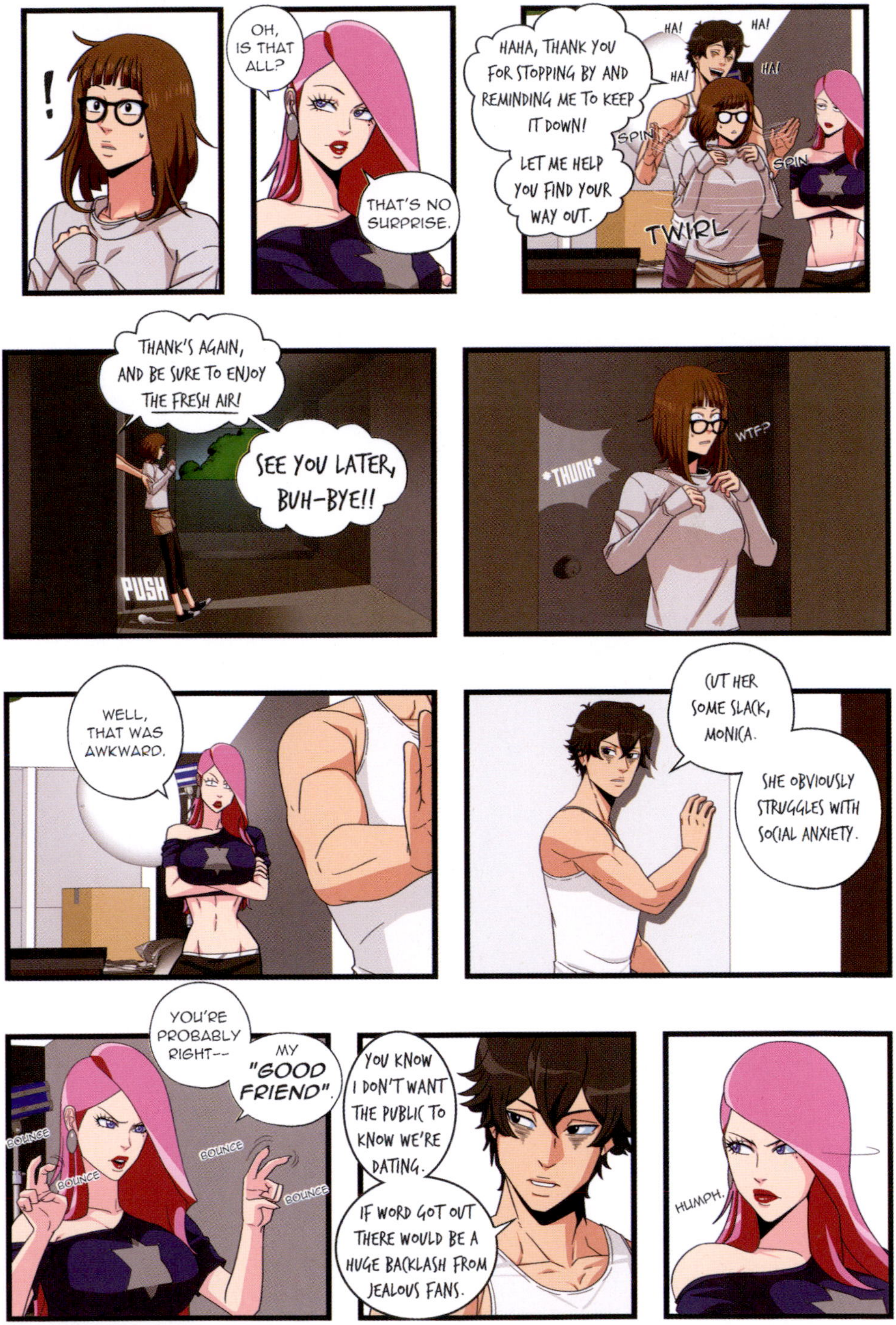
!
OH, IS THAT ALL?
THAT'S NO SURPRISE.
HAHA, THANK YOU FOR STOPPING BY AND REMINDING ME TO KEEP IT DOWN!
LET ME HELP YOU FIND YOUR WAY OUT.
HA! HA! HA! HA!
SPIN
SPIN
TWIRL
THANK'S AGAIN, AND BE SURE TO ENJOY THE FRESH AIR!
SEE YOU LATER, BUH-BYE!!
PUSH
THUNK
WTF?
WELL, THAT WAS AWKWARD.
CUT HER SOME SLACK, MONICA.
SHE OBVIOUSLY STRUGGLES WITH SOCIAL ANXIETY.
YOU'RE PROBABLY RIGHT--
MY "GOOD FRIEND".
BOUNCE
BOUNCE
BOUNCE
BOUNCE
YOU KNOW I DON'T WANT THE PUBLIC TO KNOW WE'RE DATING.
IF WORD GOT OUT THERE WOULD BE A HUGE BACKLASH FROM JEALOUS FANS.
HUMPH.

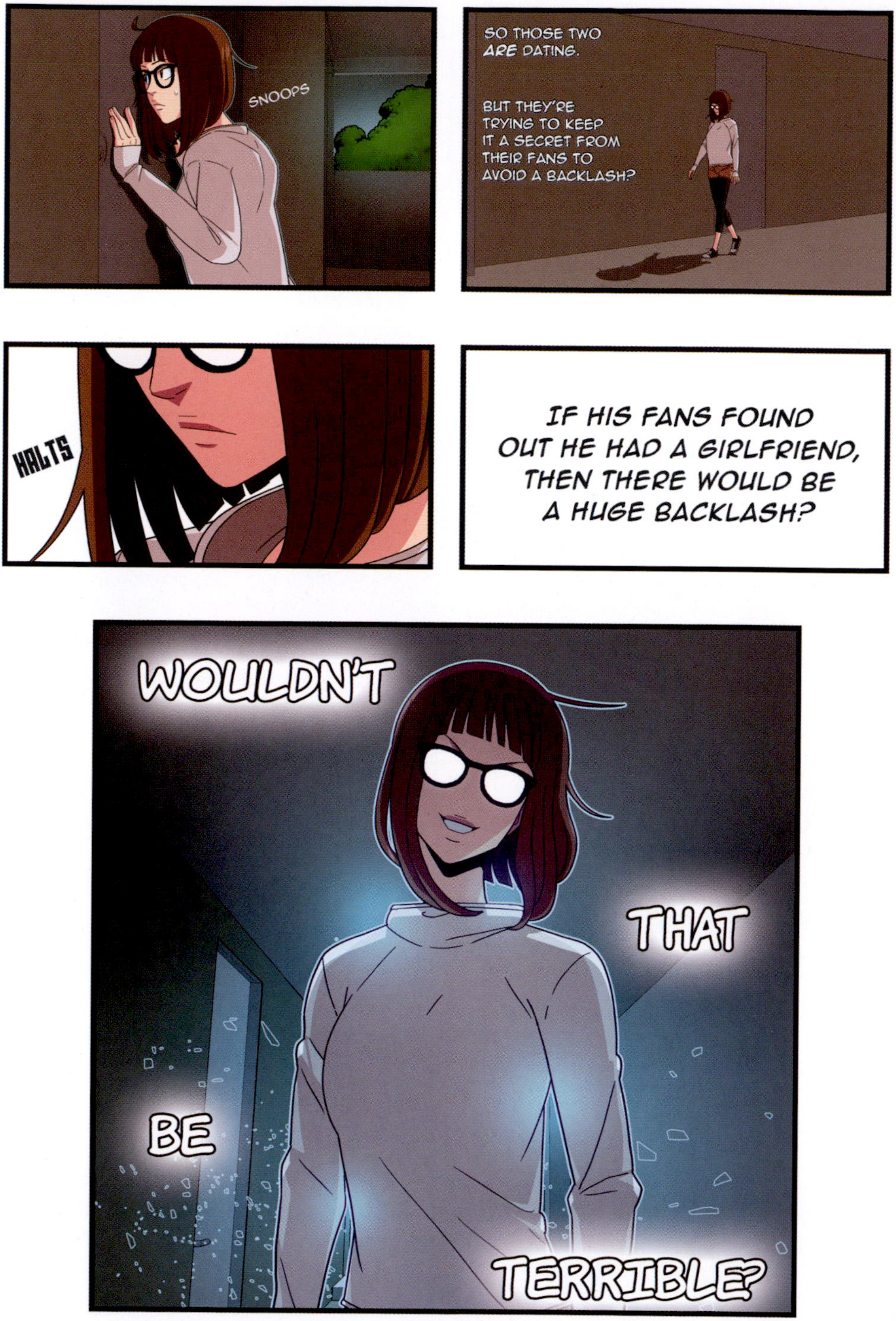
SNOOPS
SO THOSE TWO *ARE* DATING.
BUT THEY'RE TRYING TO KEEP IT A SECRET FROM THEIR FANS TO AVOID A BACKLASH?
HALTS
IF HIS FANS FOUND OUT HE HAD A GIRLFRIEND, THEN THERE WOULD BE A HUGE BACKLASH?
WOULDN'T
THAT
BE
TERRIBLE?

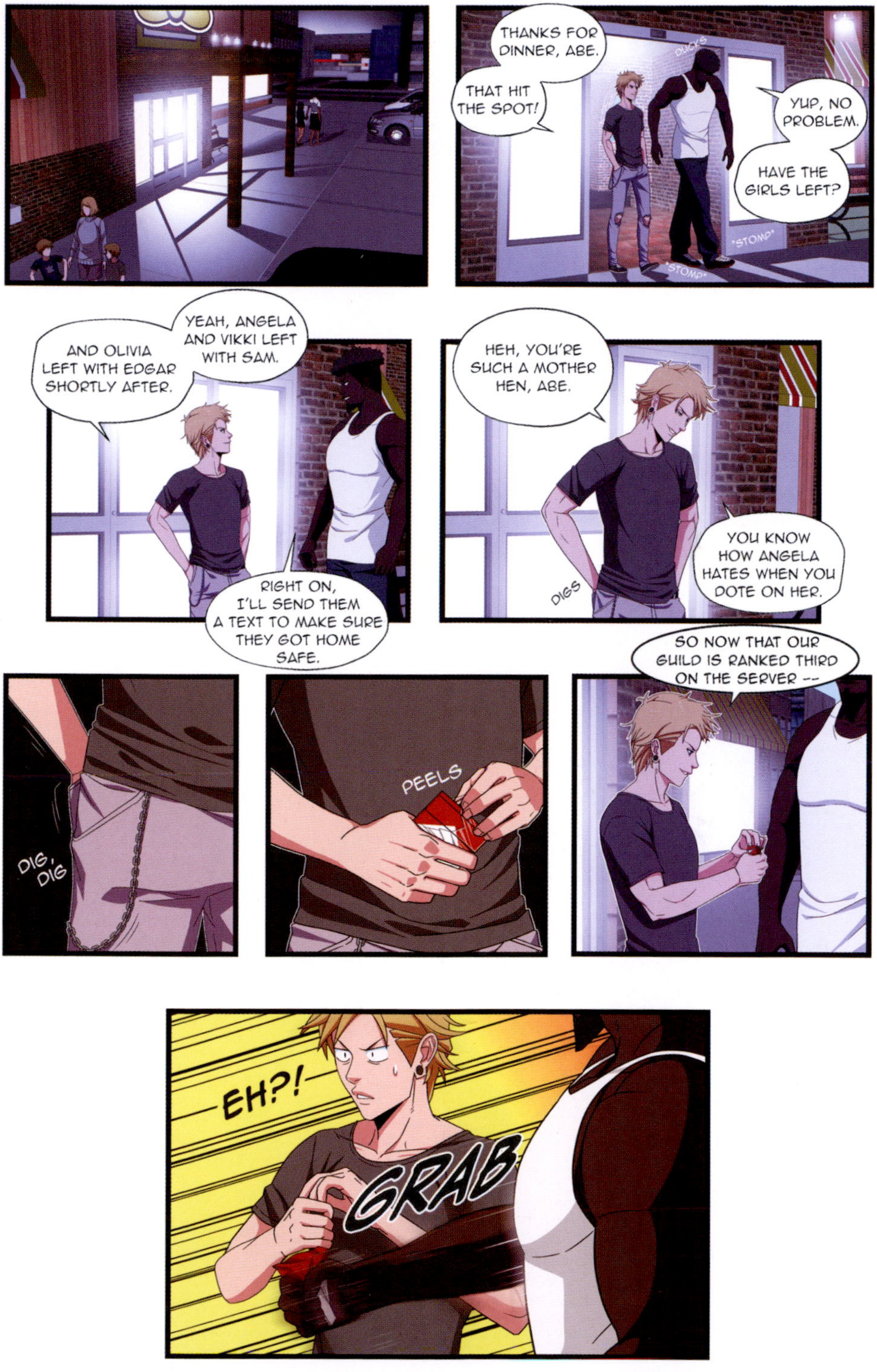
THANKS FOR DINNER, ABE.
THAT HIT THE SPOT!
DUCKS
YUP, NO PROBLEM.
HAVE THE GIRLS LEFT?
STOMP
STOMP
YEAH, ANGELA AND VIKKI LEFT WITH SAM.
AND OLIVIA LEFT WITH EDGAR SHORTLY AFTER.
RIGHT ON, I'LL SEND THEM A TEXT TO MAKE SURE THEY GOT HOME SAFE.
HEH, YOU'RE SUCH A MOTHER HEN, ABE.
DIGS
YOU KNOW HOW ANGELA HATES WHEN YOU DOTE ON HER.
DIG, DIG
PEELS
SO NOW THAT OUR GUILD IS RANKED THIRD ON THE SERVER --
EH?!
GRAB

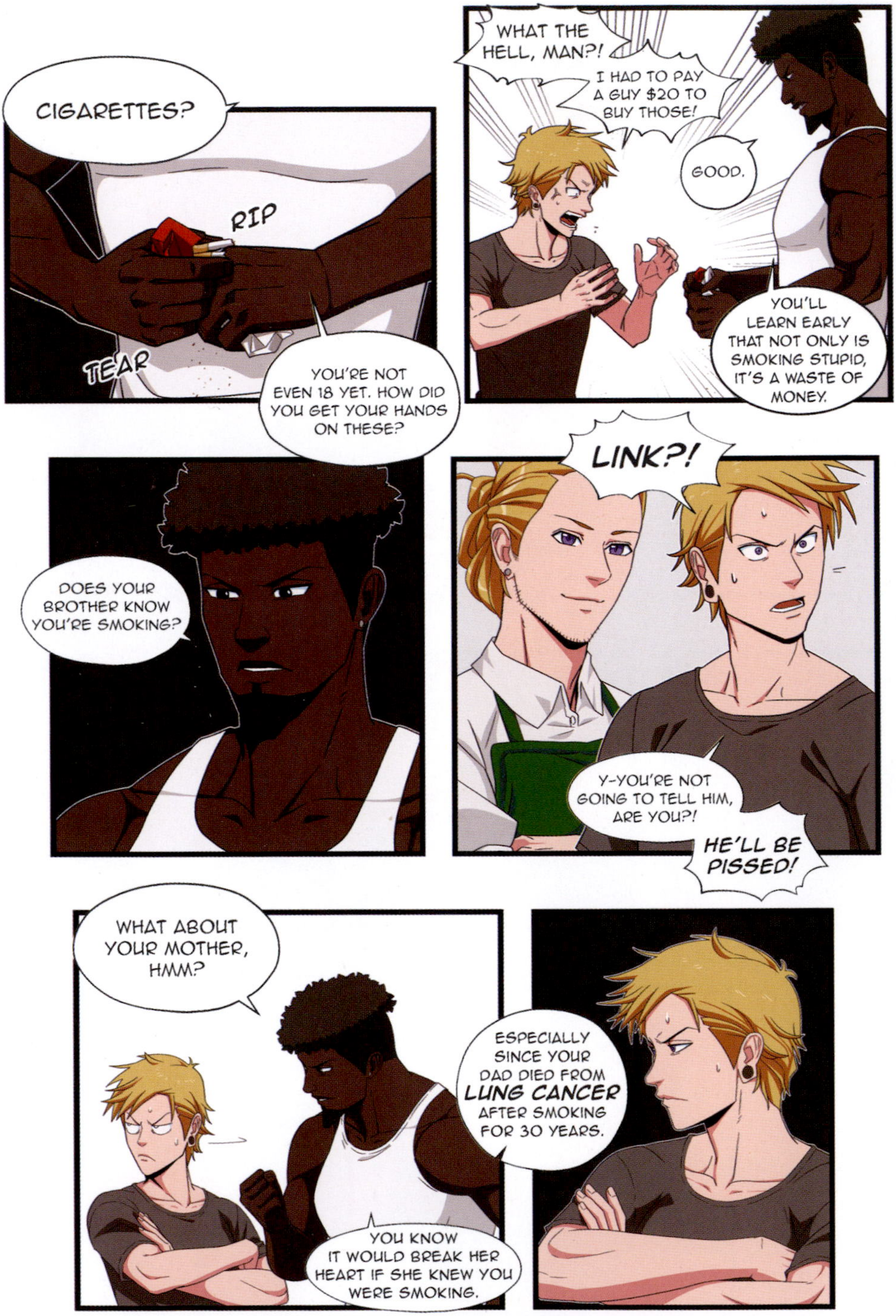
CIGARETTES?
RIP
TEAR
YOU'RE NOT EVEN 18 YET. HOW DID YOU GET YOUR HANDS ON THESE?
WHAT THE HELL, MAN?!
I HAD TO PAY A GUY $20 TO BUY THOSE!
GOOD.
YOU'LL LEARN EARLY THAT NOT ONLY IS SMOKING STUPID, IT'S A WASTE OF MONEY.
DOES YOUR BROTHER KNOW YOU'RE SMOKING?
LINK?!
Y-YOU'RE NOT GOING TO TELL HIM, ARE YOU?!
HE'LL BE PISSED!
WHAT ABOUT YOUR MOTHER, HMM?
YOU KNOW IT WOULD BREAK HER HEART IF SHE KNEW YOU WERE SMOKING.
ESPECIALLY SINCE YOUR DAD DIED FROM LUNG CANCER AFTER SMOKING FOR 30 YEARS.

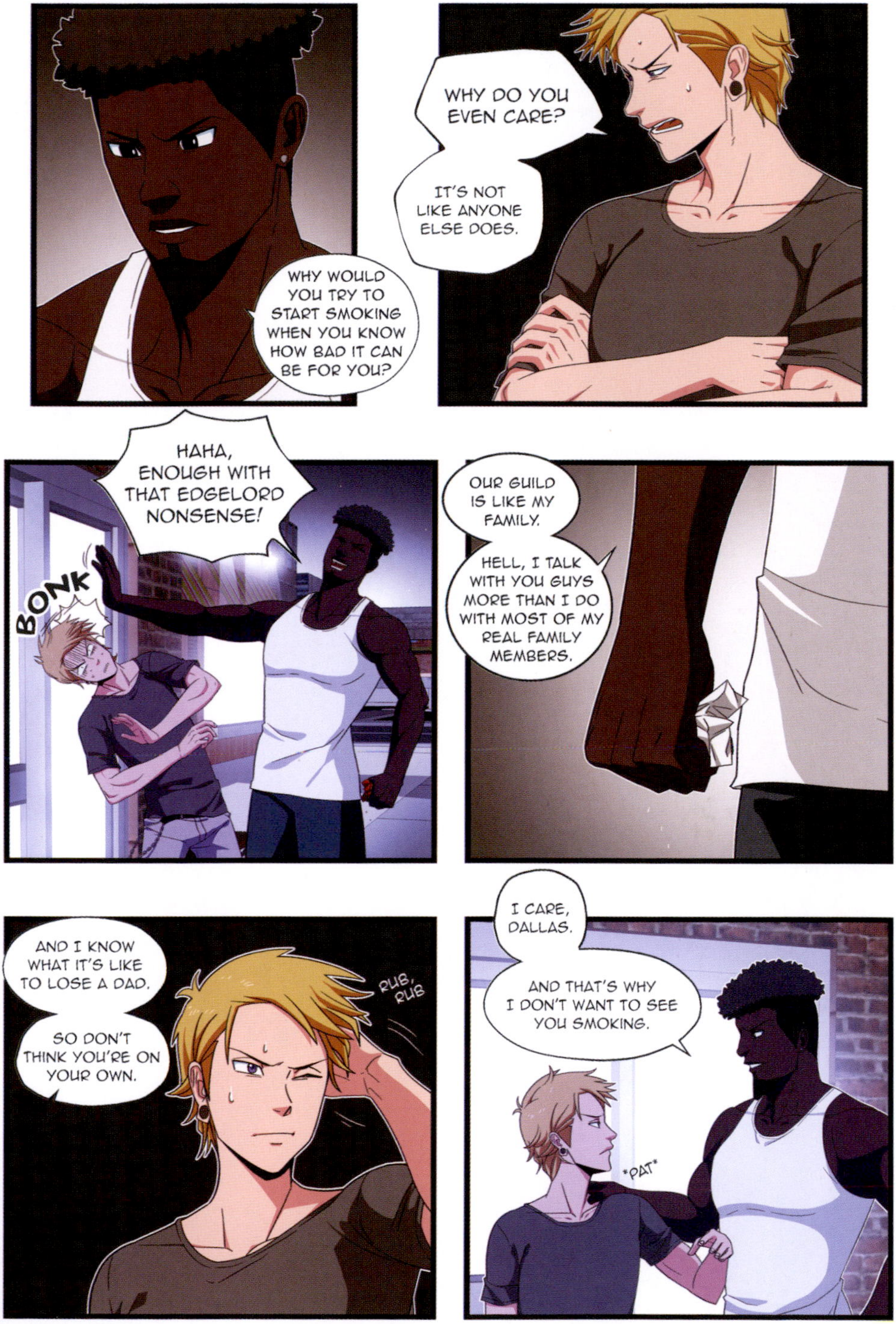
WHY WOULD YOU TRY TO START SMOKING WHEN YOU KNOW HOW BAD IT CAN BE FOR YOU?
WHY DO YOU EVEN CARE?
IT'S NOT LIKE ANYONE ELSE DOES.
HAHA, ENOUGH WITH THAT EDGELORD NONSENSE!
BONK
OUR GUILD IS LIKE MY FAMILY.
HELL, I TALK WITH YOU GUYS MORE THAN I DO WITH MOST OF MY REAL FAMILY MEMBERS.
AND I KNOW WHAT IT'S LIKE TO LOSE A DAD.
SO DON'T THINK YOU'RE ON YOUR OWN.
RUB, RUB
I CARE, DALLAS.
AND THAT'S WHY I DON'T WANT TO SEE YOU SMOKING.
PAT

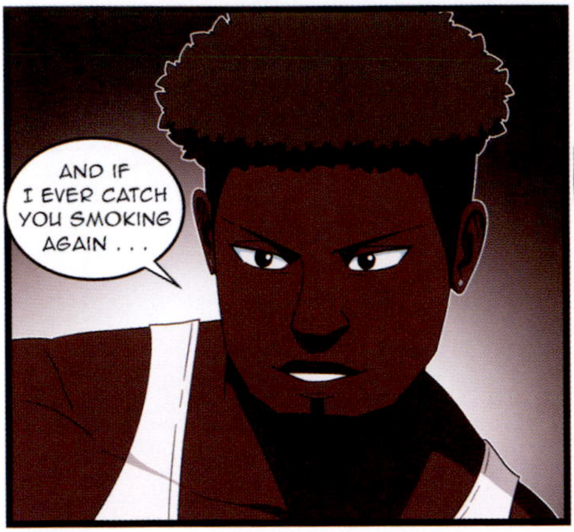
AND IF I EVER CATCH YOU SMOKING AGAIN . . .

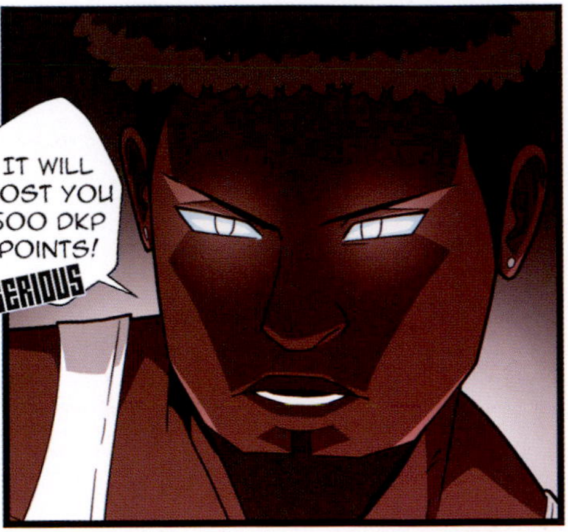
IT WILL COST YOU 500 DKP POINTS!
SERIOUS

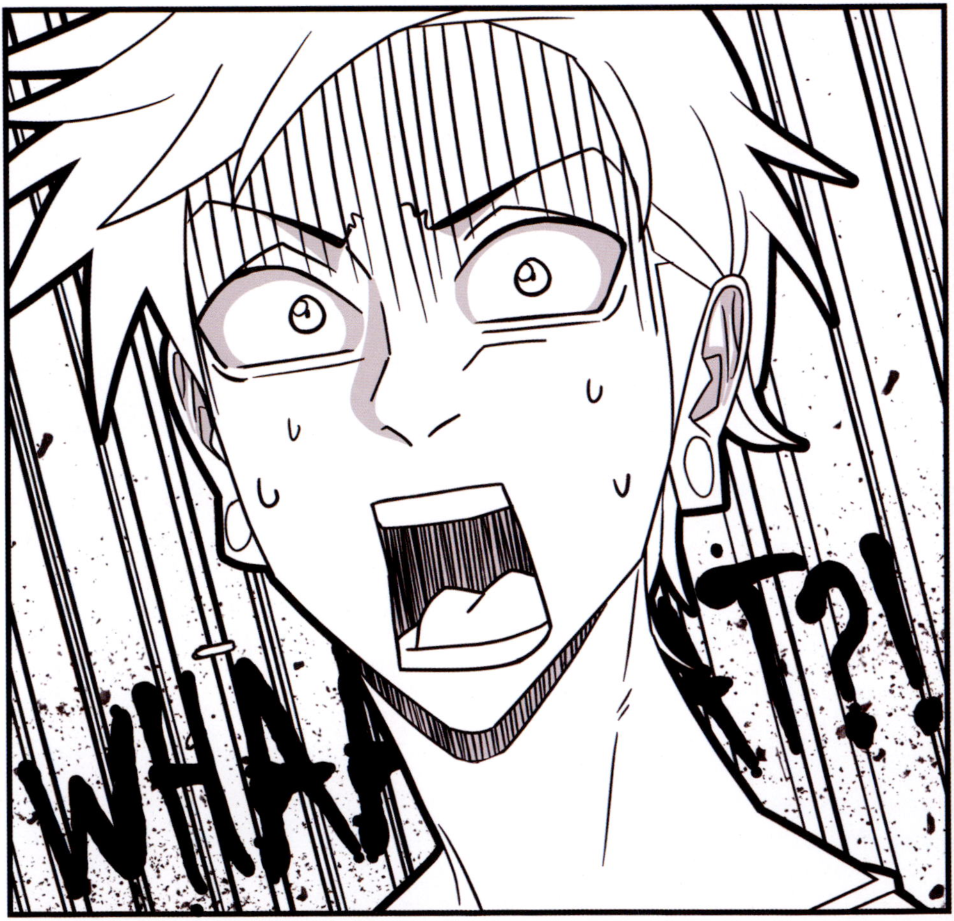
WHAT?!

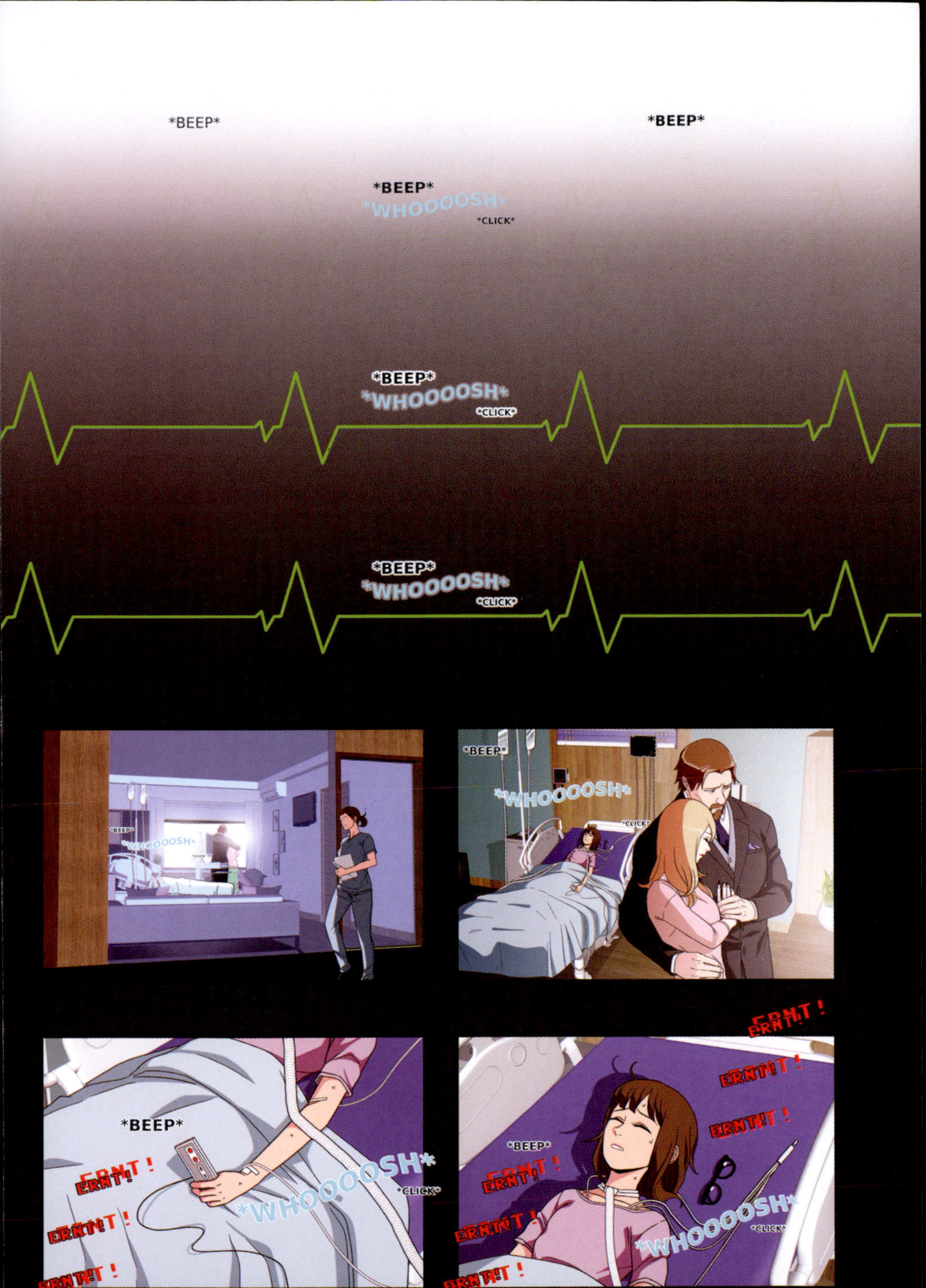

BEEP
BEEP
BEEP
WHOOOOSH
CLICK
BEEP
WHOOOOSH
CLICK
BEEP
WHOOOOSH
CLICK
BEEP
WHOOOOSH
CLICK
BEEP
WHOOOOSH
CLICK
BEEP
WHOOOOSH
CLICK
ERNT!
BEEP
WHOOOOSH
CLICK
ERNT!

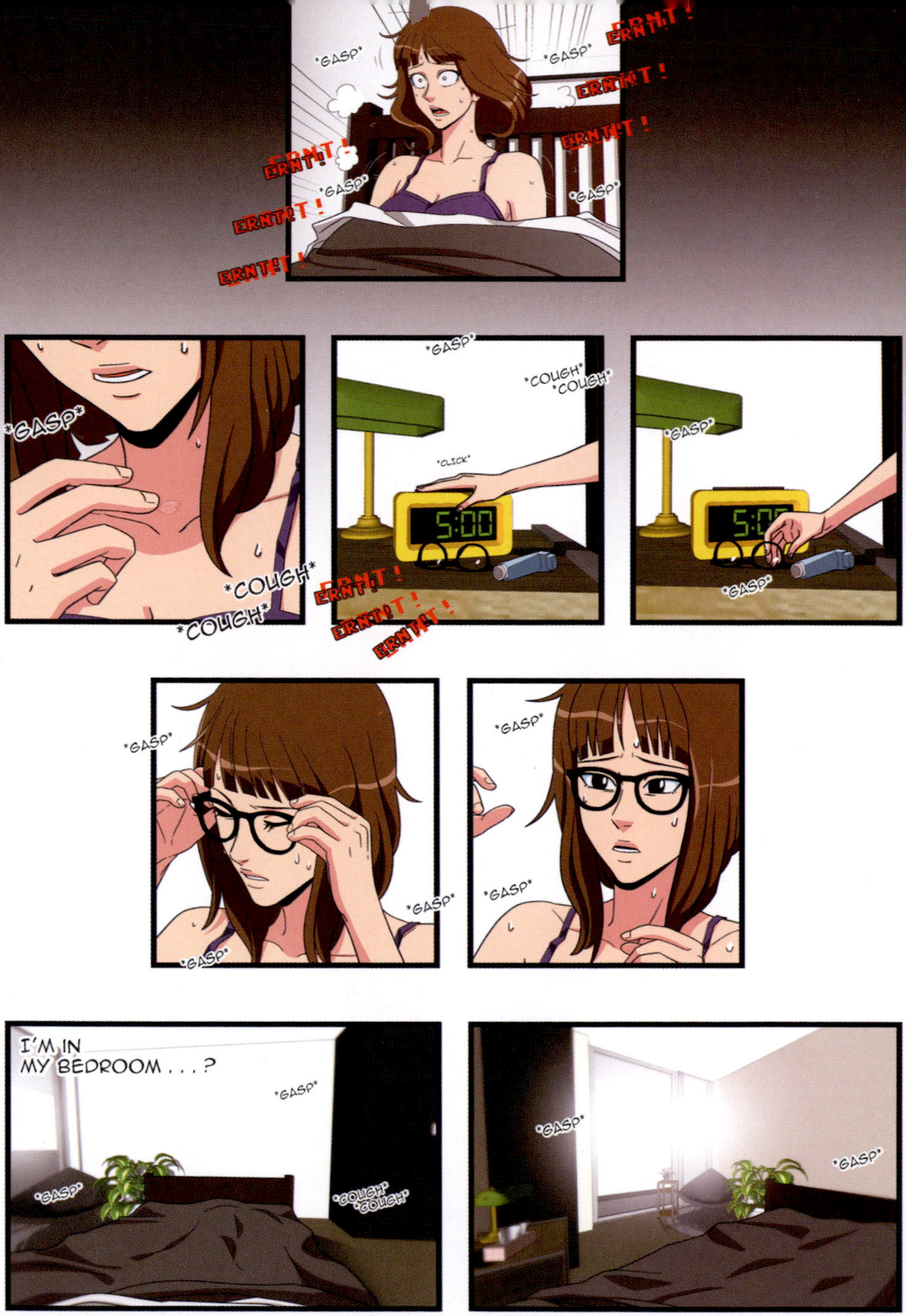
GASP
GASP
ERNT!T!
ERNT!T!
ERNT!T!
ERNT!T!
GASP
ERNT!T!
ERNT!T!
GASP
GASP
COUGH
COUGH
GASP
COUGH
COUGH
CLICK
ERNT!T!
ERNT!T!
ERNT!T!
GASP
GASP
GASP
GASP
GASP
GASP
GASP
I'M IN
MY BEDROOM . . . ?
GASP
GASP
COUGH
COUGH
GASP
GASP

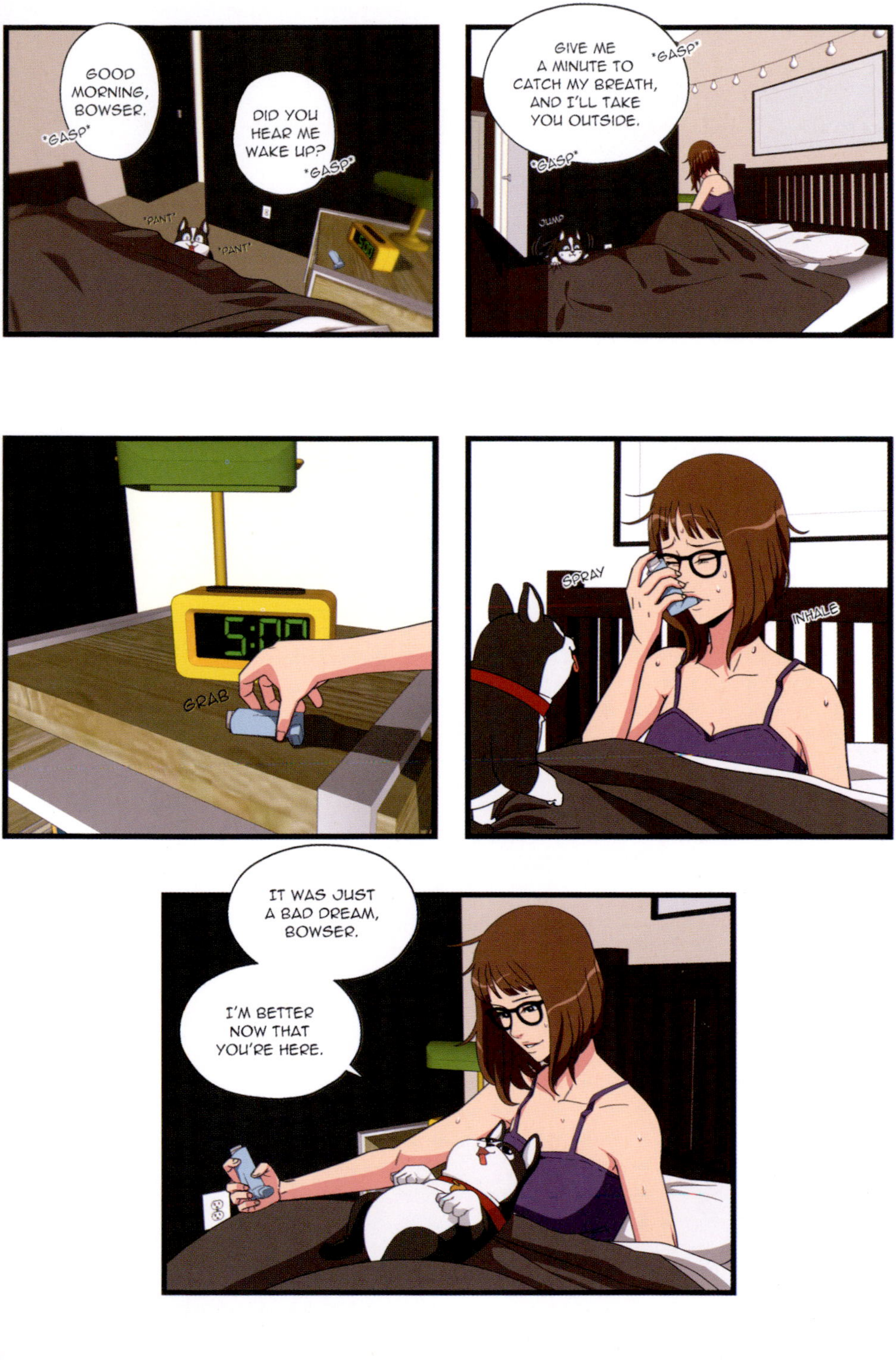
GOOD MORNING, BOWSER.
GASP
PANT
PANT
DID YOU HEAR ME WAKE UP?
GASP
GIVE ME A MINUTE TO CATCH MY BREATH, AND I'LL TAKE YOU OUTSIDE.
GASP
GASP
JUMP
GRAB
SPRAY
INHALE
IT WAS JUST A BAD DREAM, BOWSER.
I'M BETTER NOW THAT YOU'RE HERE.

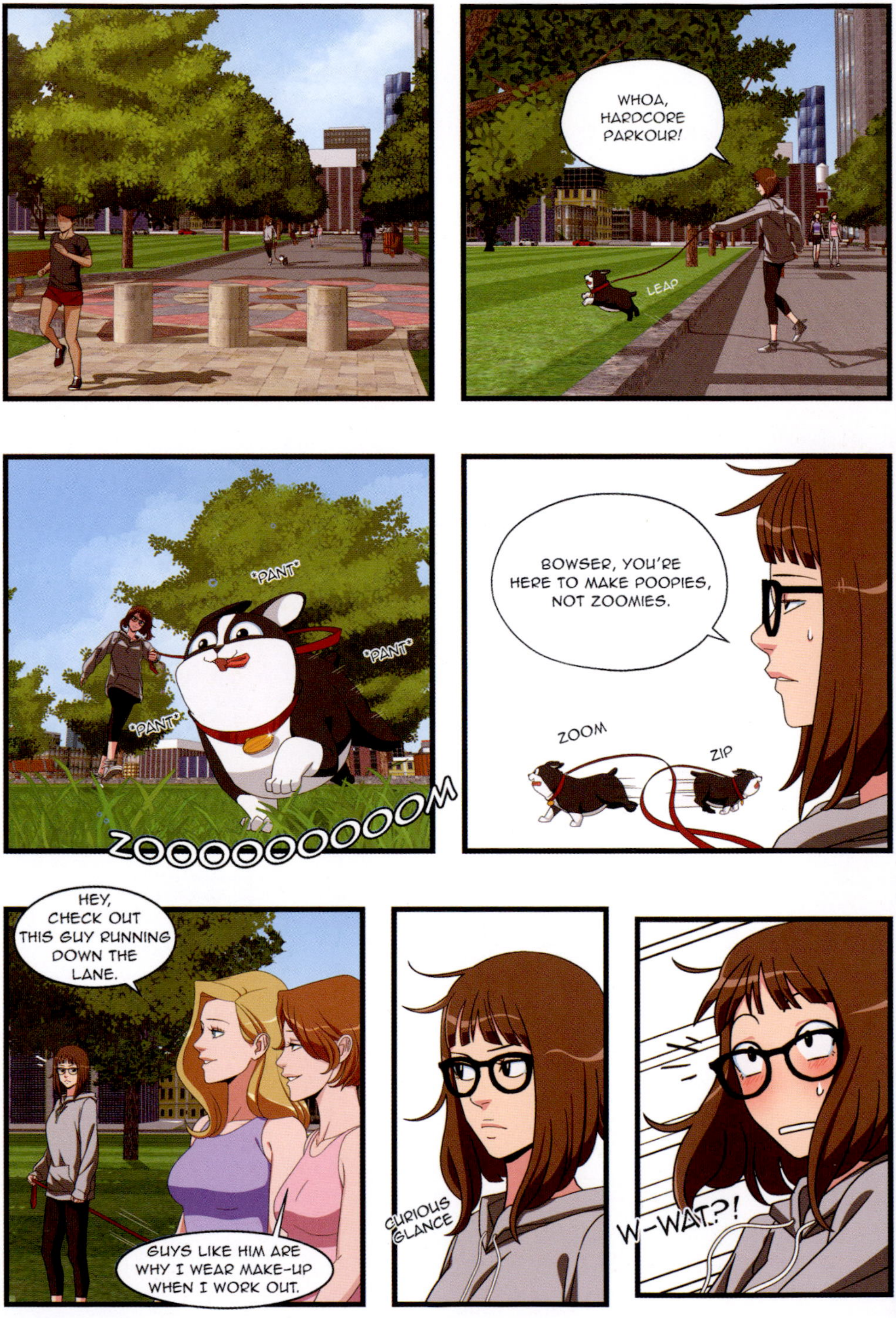
WHOA, HARDCORE PARKOUR!
LEAP
PANT
PANT
PANT
ZOOOOOOOOOM
BOWSER, YOU'RE HERE TO MAKE POOPIES, NOT ZOOMIES.
ZOOM
ZIP
HEY, CHECK OUT THIS GUY RUNNING DOWN THE LANE.
GUYS LIKE HIM ARE WHY I WEAR MAKE-UP WHEN I WORK OUT.
CURIOUS GLANCE
W-WAT?!

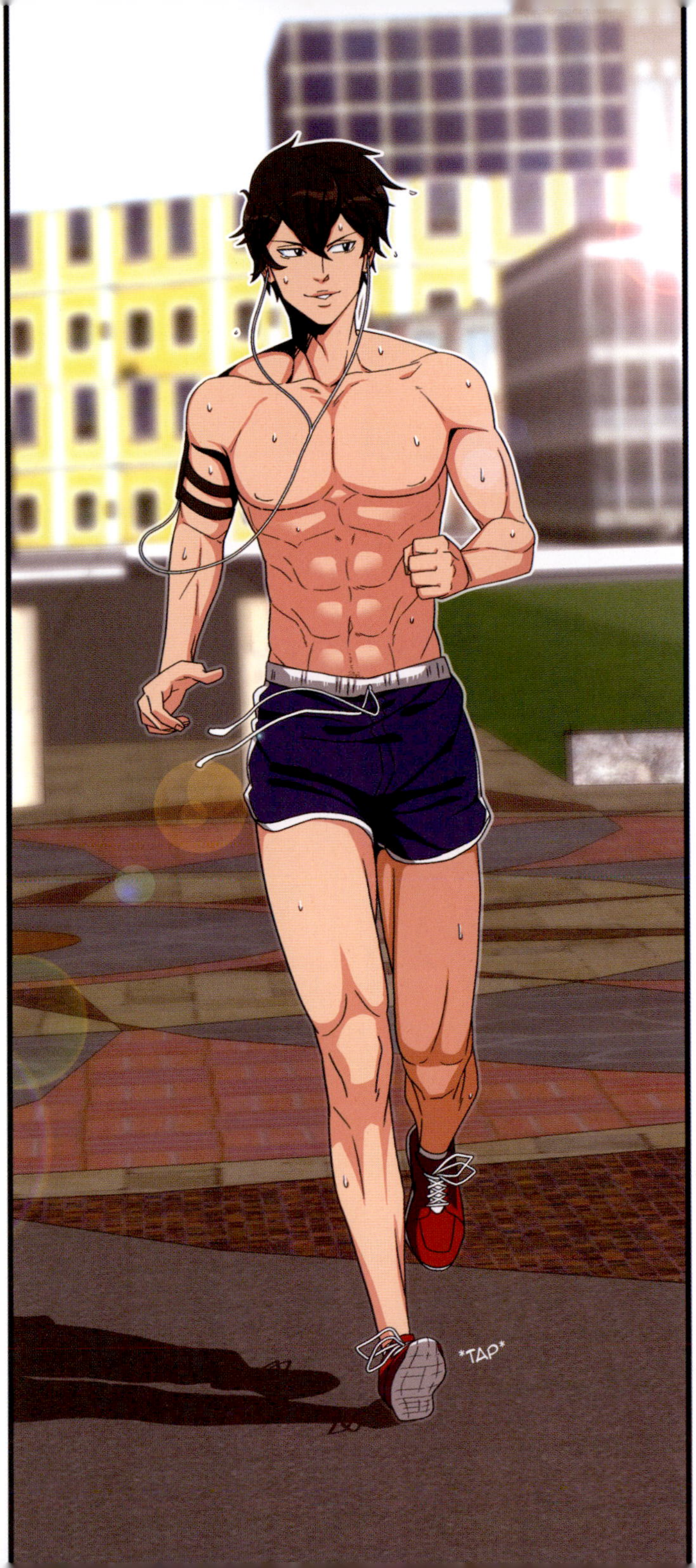
TAP

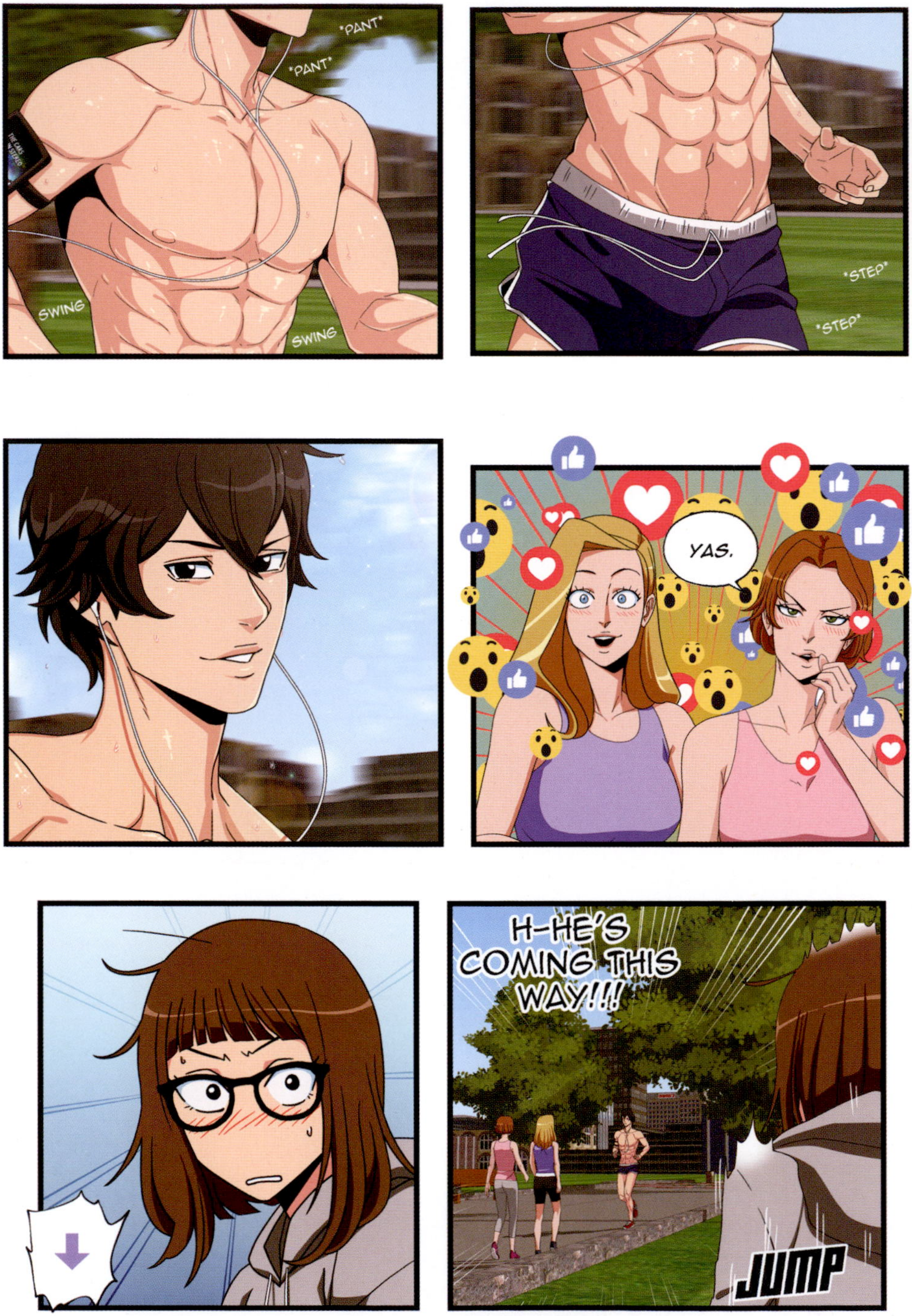
PANT
PANT
SWING
SWING
STEP
STEP
YAS.
H-HE'S COMING THIS WAY!!!
JUMP

CRAP, I . . . I GOTTA HIDE!
!
!
GOOD MORNING, LADIES.
MORNING.
KEEP UP THE HARD WORK.
TAP
HALTS
HEY, DID YOU SEE THE SIZE OF HIS FEET?
HOW COULD I MISS THEM?
THEY'RE HUGE!
Average Male Height & Shoe Size in the U.S.: 5'9.5" (177cm) Size: 10
Marshall Law: 6'3" (191cm) Size: 15
Sasquatch: ~8' (244cm) Size: ~16+
YOU KNOW WHAT THEY SAY ABOUT A GUY WITH BIG FEET, RIGHT?
THAT I'D LOVE TO SEE THEM AT THE FOOT OF MY BED?
HAHA, YOU'RE TERRIBLE!
THORCH
BIGFOOT
OF ALL THE THINGS THEY HAD TO POINT OUT.
WHY DID IT HAVE TO BE MY FEET? ;_;
Marshall Law's Greatest Insecurity:
THE SIZE OF HIS FREAKISHLY LARGE FEET

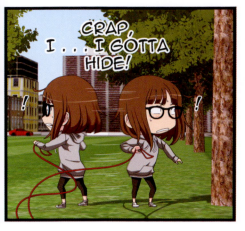

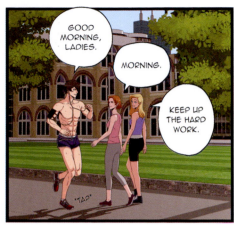

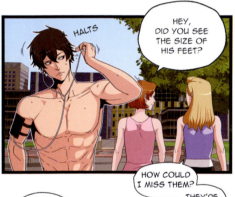

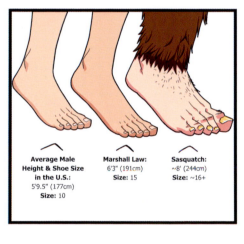

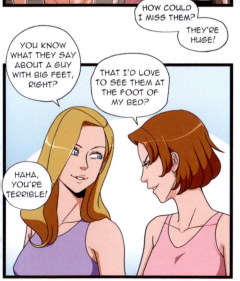

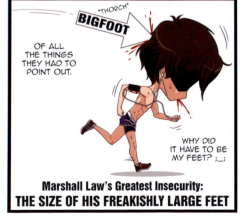

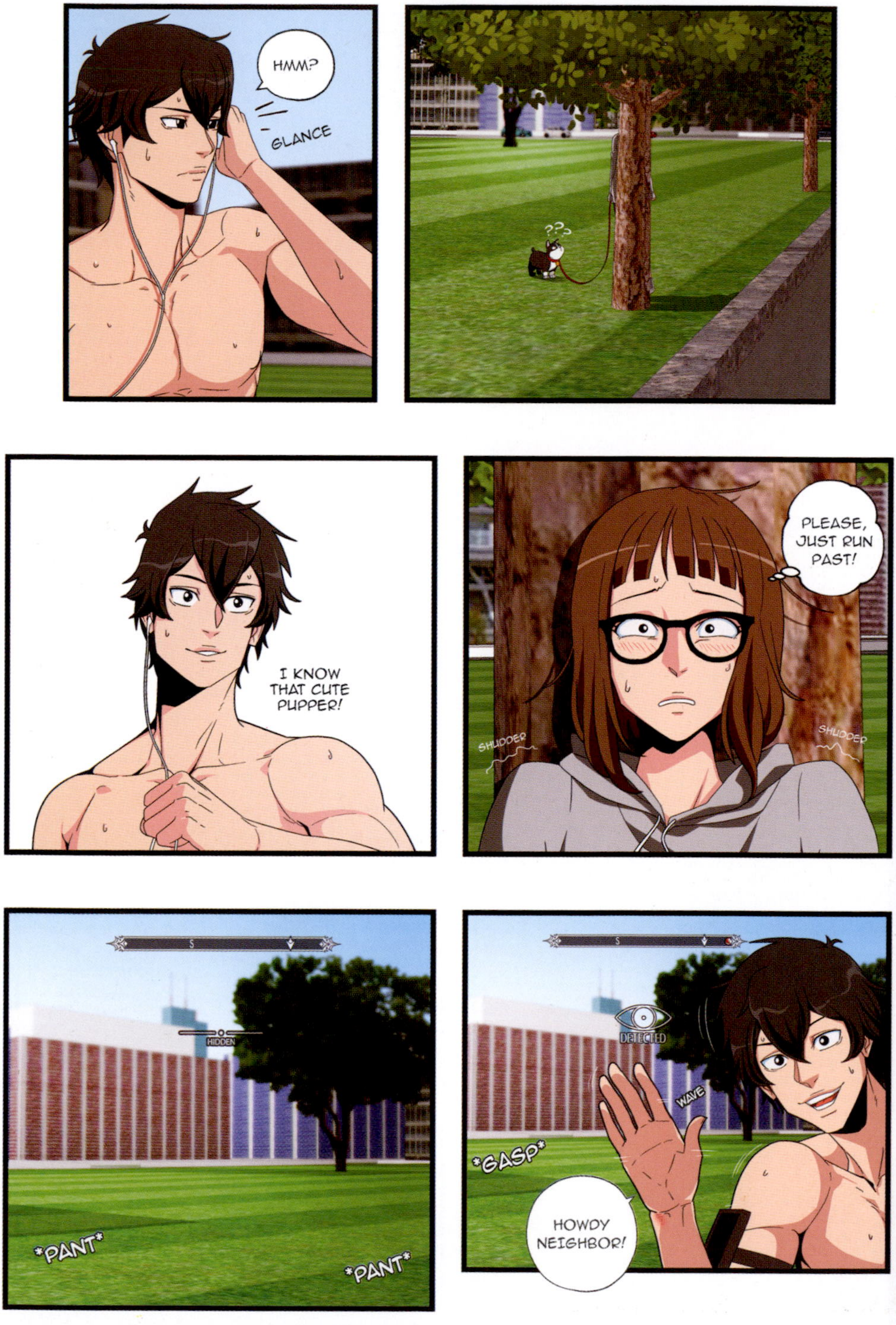
HMM?
GLANCE
???
I KNOW THAT CUTE PUPPER!
PLEASE, JUST RUN PAST!
SHUDDER
SHUDDER
HIDDEN
PANT
PANT
DETECTED
WAVE
GASP
HOWDY NEIGHBOR!

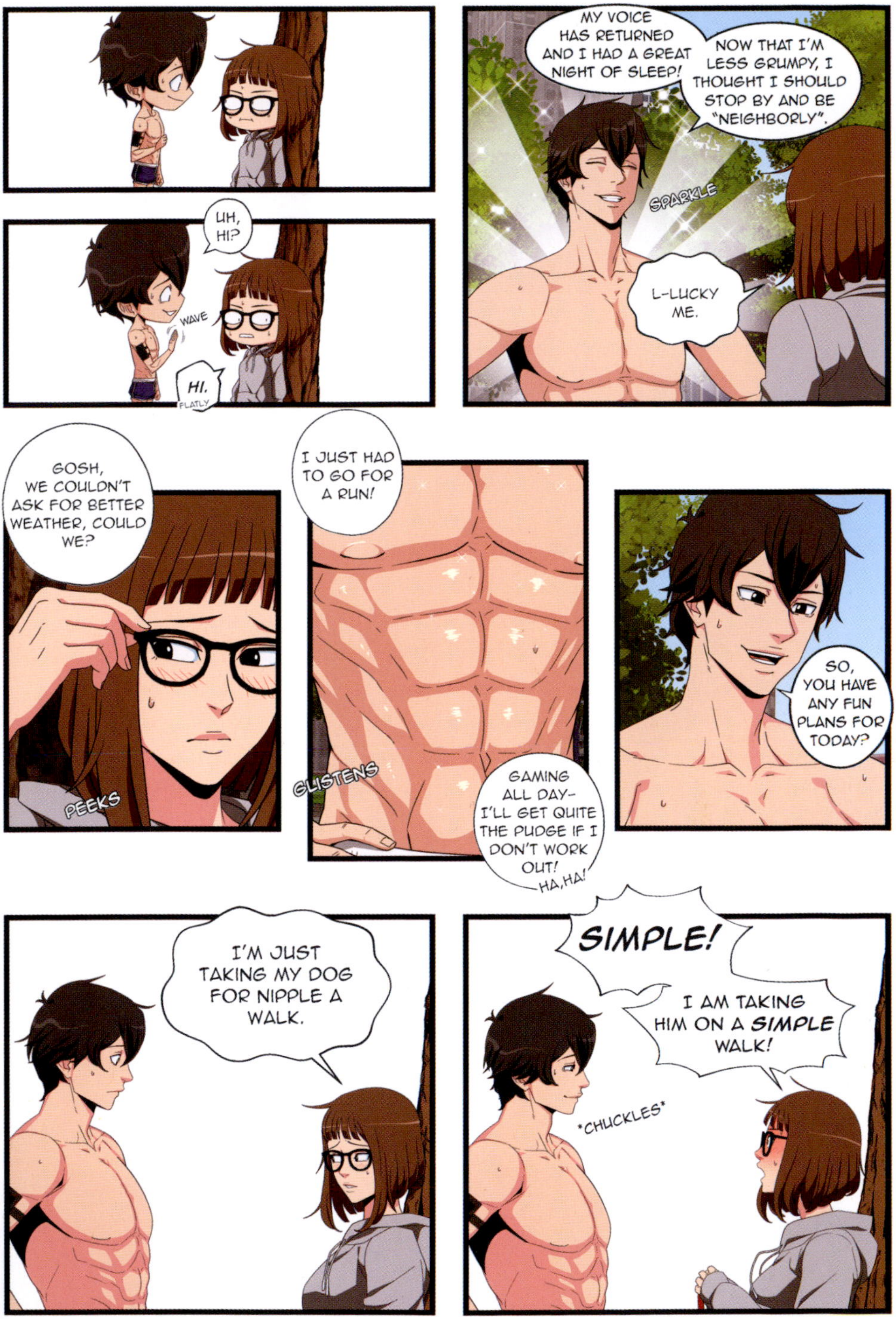
UH, HI?
WAVE
HI.
FLATLY
MY VOICE HAS RETURNED AND I HAD A GREAT NIGHT OF SLEEP!
NOW THAT I'M LESS GRUMPY, I THOUGHT I SHOULD STOP BY AND BE "NEIGHBORLY".
SPARKLE
L-LUCKY ME.
GOSH, WE COULDN'T ASK FOR BETTER WEATHER, COULD WE?
PEEKS
I JUST HAD TO GO FOR A RUN!
GLISTENS
GAMING ALL DAY- I'LL GET QUITE THE PUDGE IF I DON'T WORK OUT!
HA,HA!
SO, YOU HAVE ANY FUN PLANS FOR TODAY?
I'M JUST TAKING MY DOG FOR NIPPLE A WALK.
SIMPLE!
I AM TAKING HIM ON A SIMPLE WALK!
CHUCKLES

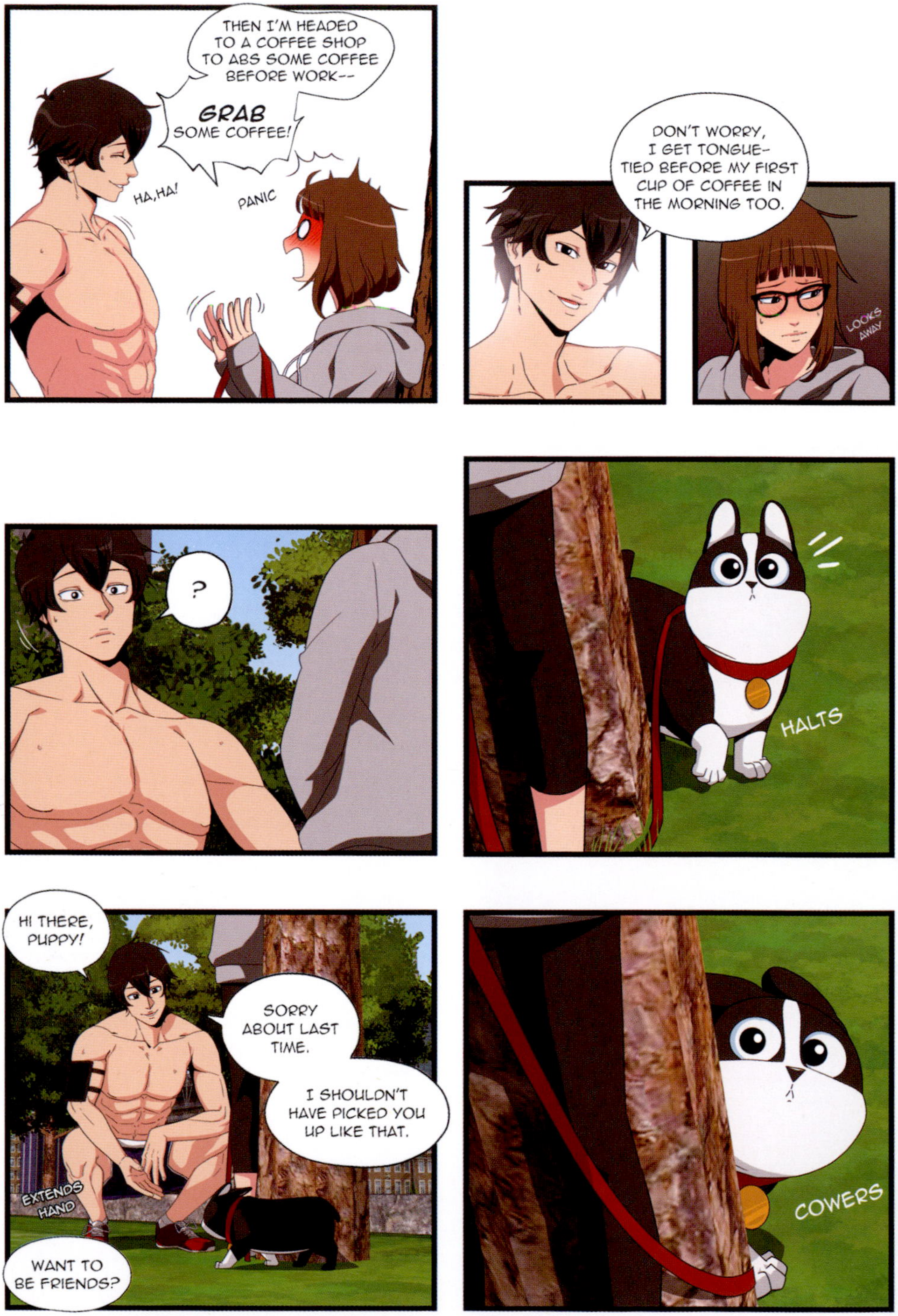
THEN I'M HEADED TO A COFFEE SHOP TO ABS SOME COFFEE BEFORE WORK--
GRAB SOME COFFEE!
HA,HA!
PANIC
DON'T WORRY, I GET TONGUE-TIED BEFORE MY FIRST CUP OF COFFEE IN THE MORNING TOO.
LOOKS AWAY
?
HALTS
HI THERE, PUPPY!
SORRY ABOUT LAST TIME.
I SHOULDN'T HAVE PICKED YOU UP LIKE THAT.
EXTENDS HAND
WANT TO BE FRIENDS?
COWERS

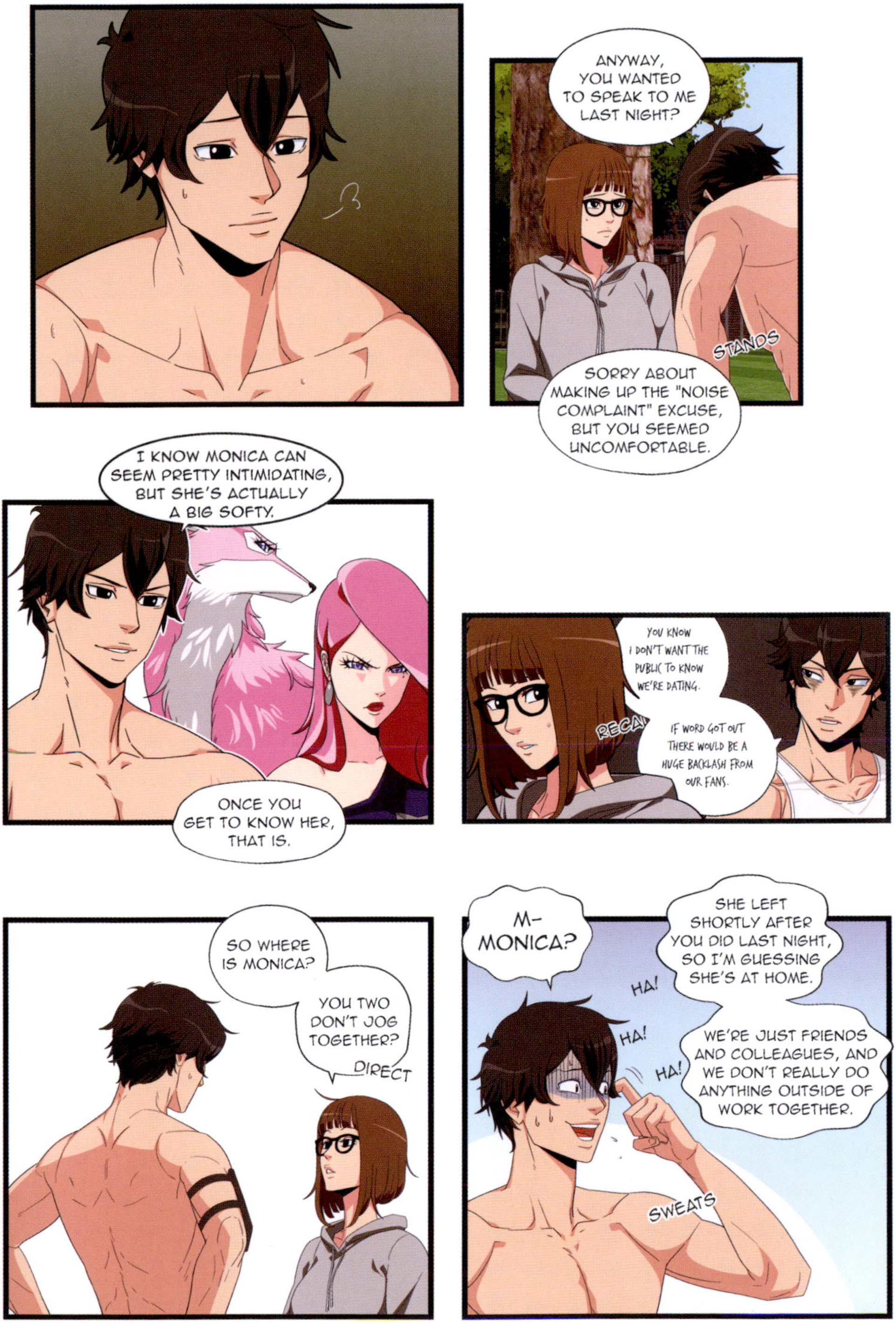
ANYWAY, YOU WANTED TO SPEAK TO ME LAST NIGHT?
STANDS
SORRY ABOUT MAKING UP THE "NOISE COMPLAINT" EXCUSE, BUT YOU SEEMED UNCOMFORTABLE.
I KNOW MONICA CAN SEEM PRETTY INTIMIDATING, BUT SHE'S ACTUALLY A BIG SOFTY.
ONCE YOU GET TO KNOW HER, THAT IS.
YOU KNOW I DON'T WANT THE PUBLIC TO KNOW WE'RE DATING.
IF WORD GOT OUT THERE WOULD BE A HUGE BACKLASH FROM OUR FANS.
SO WHERE IS MONICA?
YOU TWO DON'T JOG TOGETHER?
DIRECT
M-MONICA?
HA!
HA!
HA!
SHE LEFT SHORTLY AFTER YOU DID LAST NIGHT, SO I'M GUESSING SHE'S AT HOME.
WE'RE JUST FRIENDS AND COLLEAGUES, AND WE DON'T REALLY DO ANYTHING OUTSIDE OF WORK TOGETHER.
SWEATS

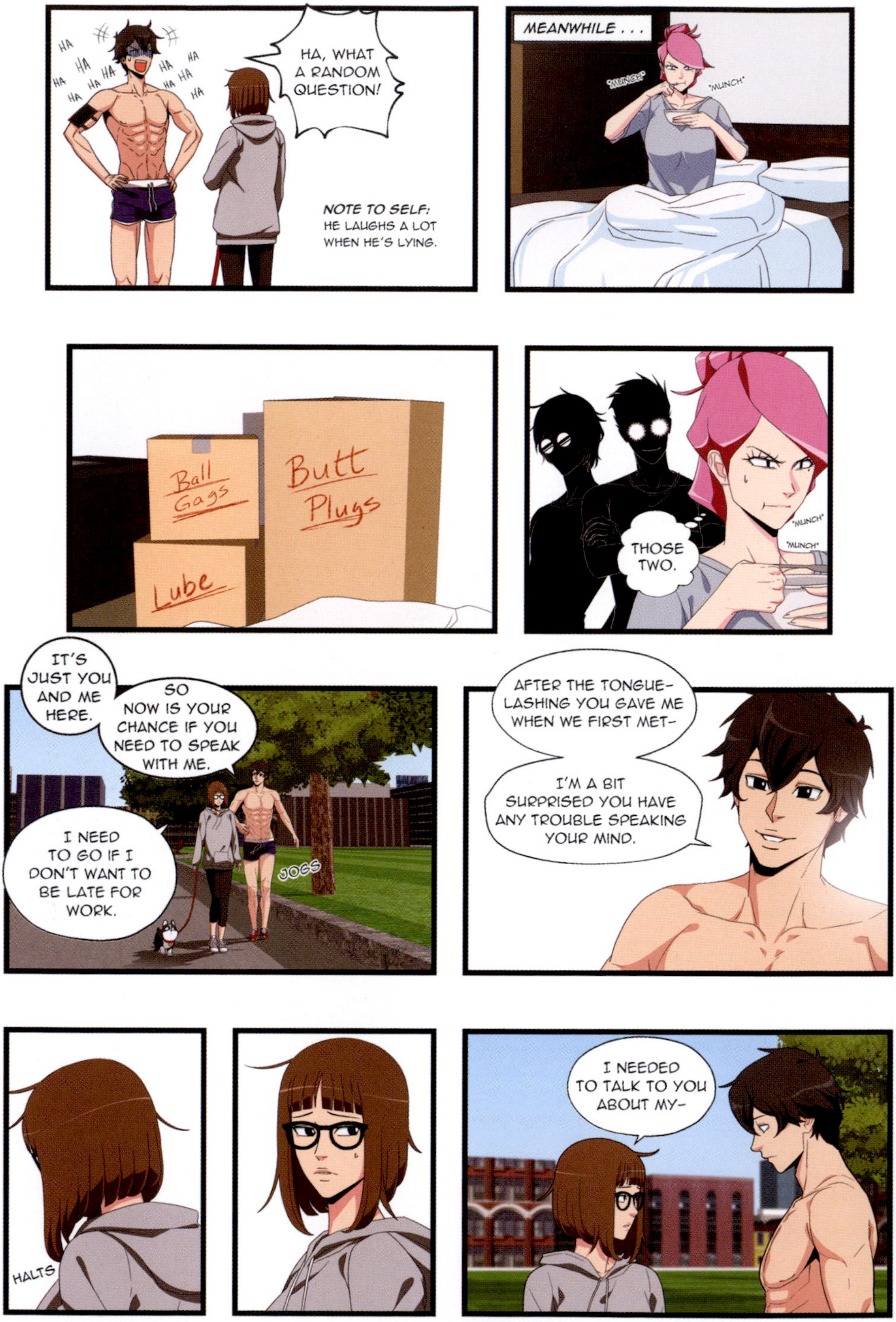
HA HA HA HA HA HA HA HA HA HA HA
HA, WHAT A RANDOM QUESTION!
NOTE TO SELF: HE LAUGHS A LOT WHEN HE'S LYING.
MEANWHILE . . .
"MUNCH"
"MUNCH"
Ball Gags
Butt Plugs
Lube
THOSE TWO.
"MUNCH"
"MUNCH"
IT'S JUST YOU AND ME HERE.
SO NOW IS YOUR CHANCE IF YOU NEED TO SPEAK WITH ME.
I NEED TO GO IF I DON'T WANT TO BE LATE FOR WORK.
JOGS
AFTER THE TONGUE-LASHING YOU GAVE ME WHEN WE FIRST MET-
I'M A BIT SURPRISED YOU HAVE ANY TROUBLE SPEAKING YOUR MIND.
HALTS
I NEEDED TO TALK TO YOU ABOUT MY-

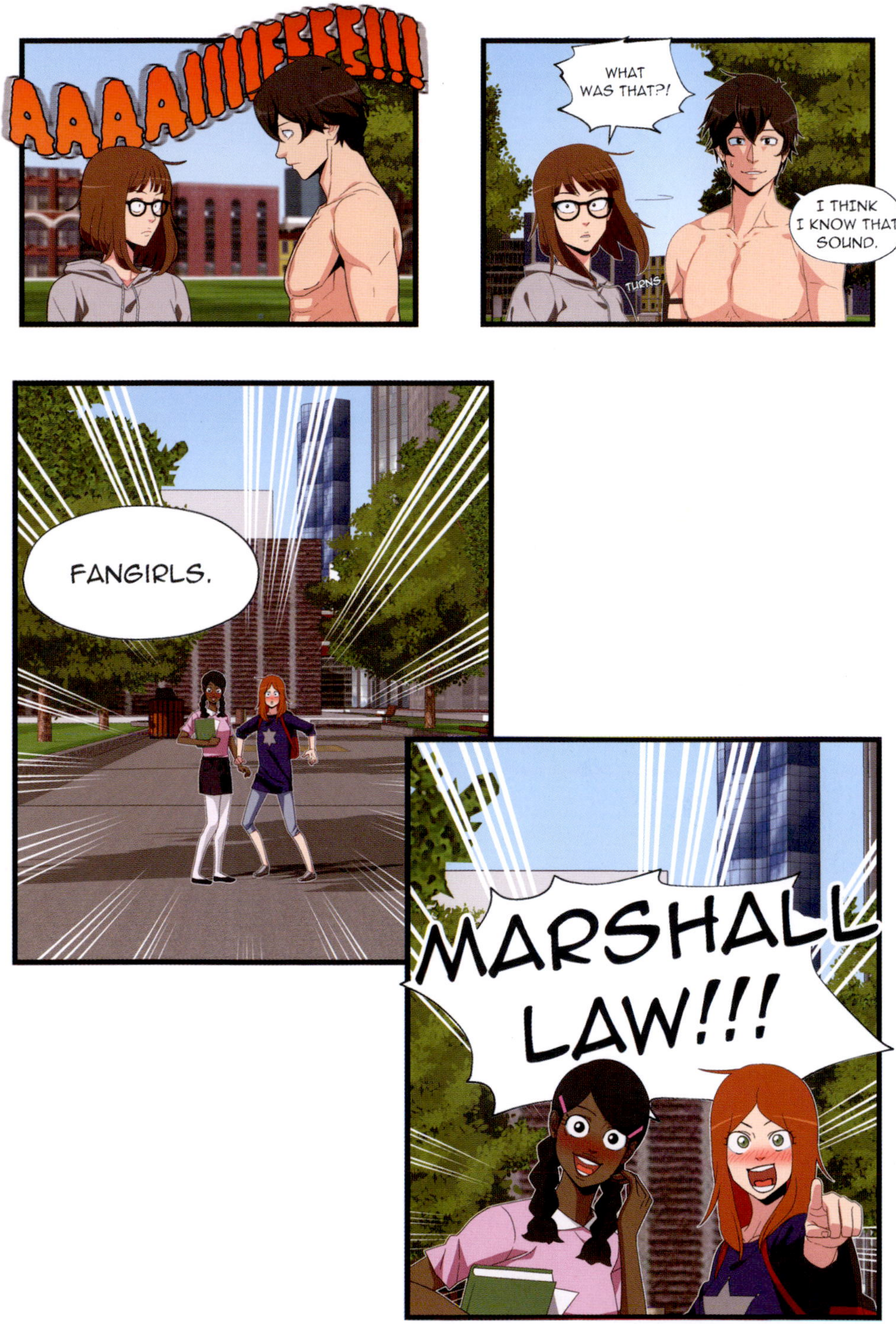
AAAAIIIIEEEE!!!
WHAT WAS THAT?!
TURNS
I THINK I KNOW THAT SOUND.
FANGIRLS.
MARSHALL LAW!!!

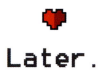

Later.

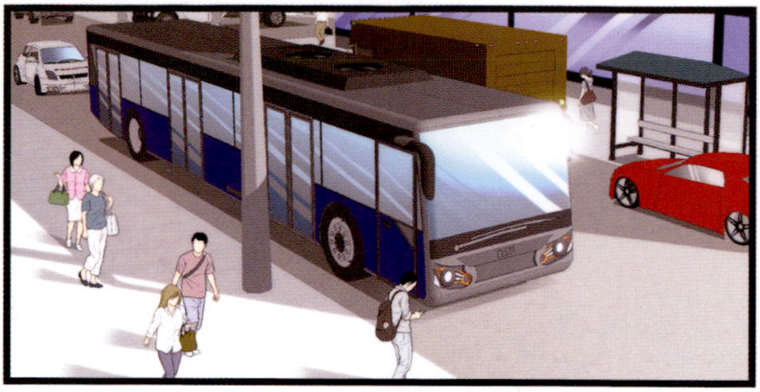

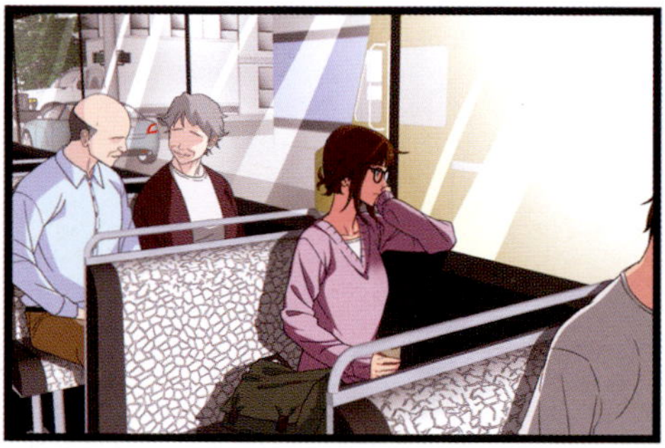

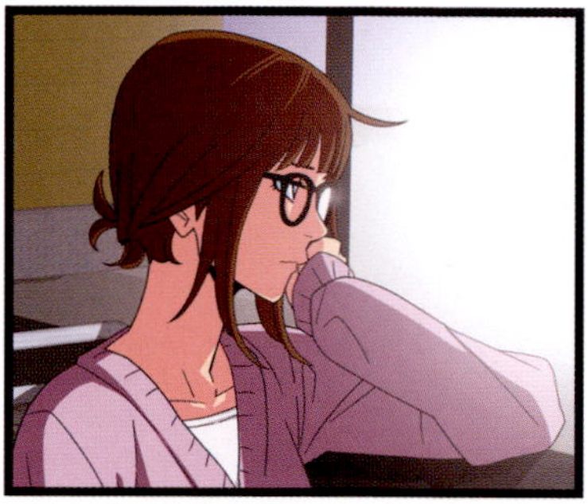

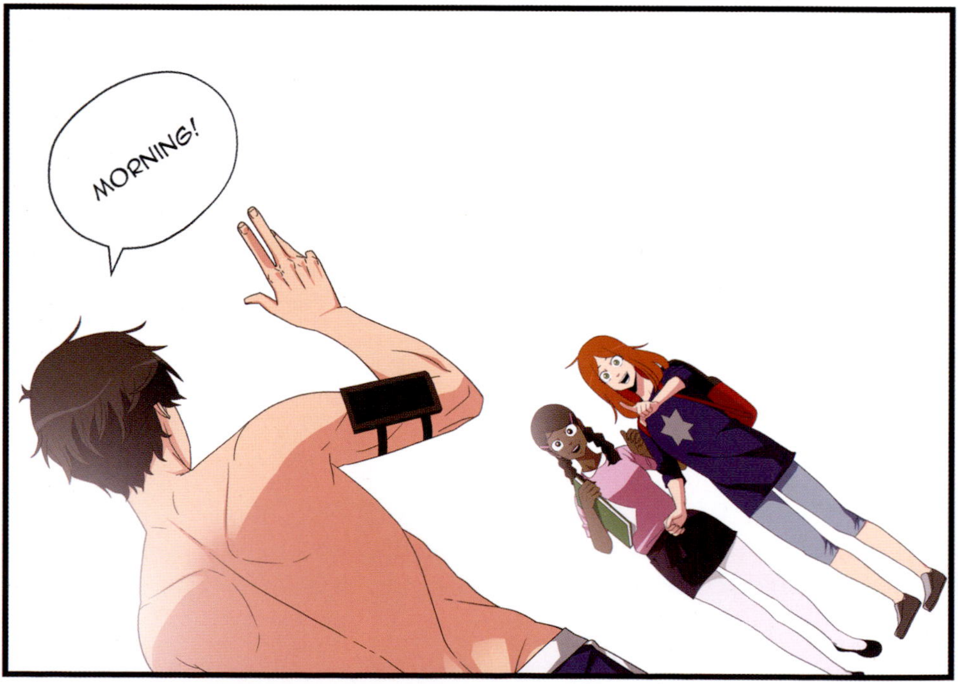
MORNING!

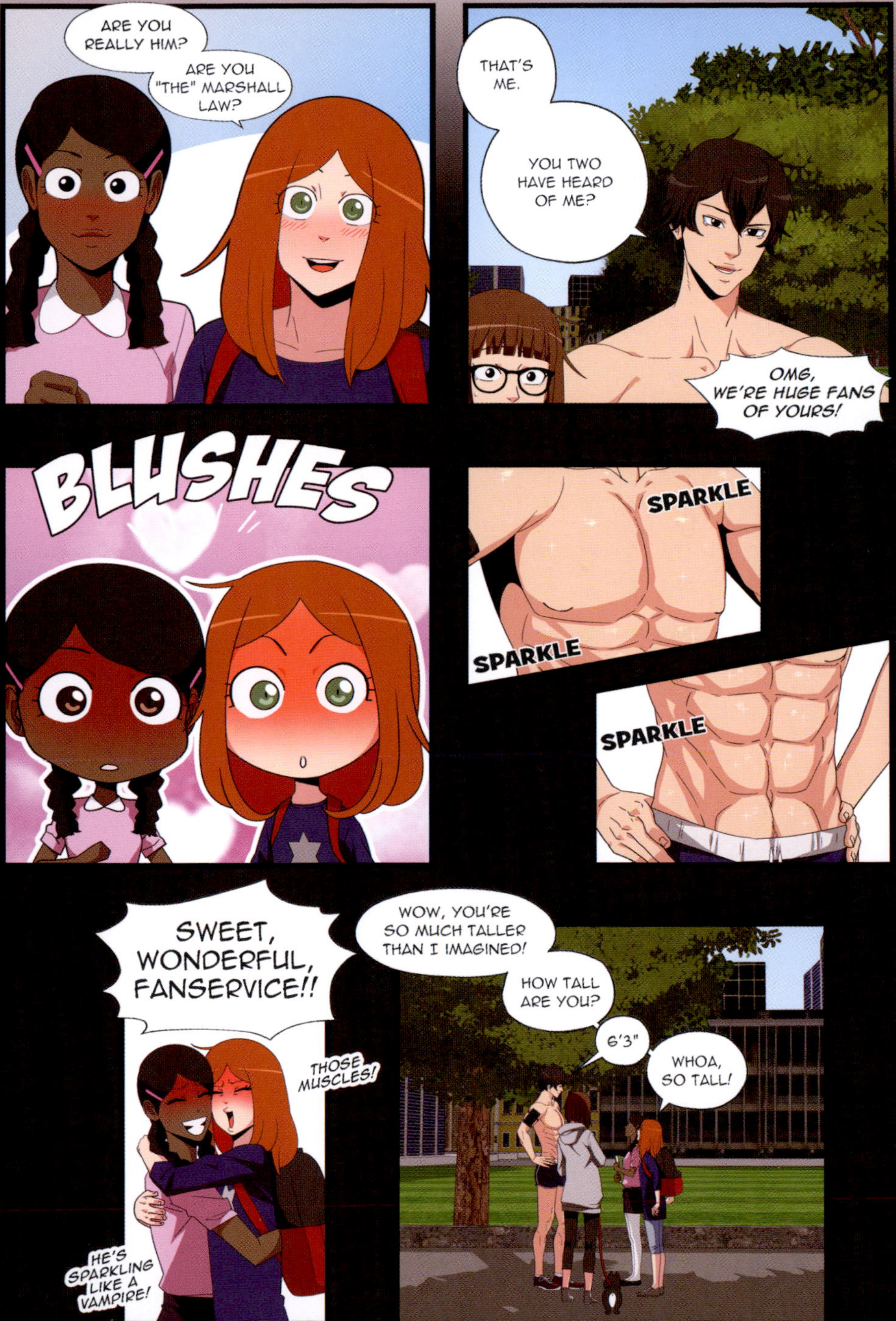
ARE YOU REALLY HIM?
ARE YOU "THE" MARSHALL LAW?
THAT'S ME.
YOU TWO HAVE HEARD OF ME?
OMG, WE'RE HUGE FANS OF YOURS!
BLUSHES
SPARKLE
SPARKLE
SPARKLE
SWEET, WONDERFUL, FANSERVICE!!
THOSE MUSCLES!
HE'S SPARKLING LIKE A VAMPIRE!
WOW, YOU'RE SO MUCH TALLER THAN I IMAGINED!
HOW TALL ARE YOU?
6'3"
WHOA, SO TALL!

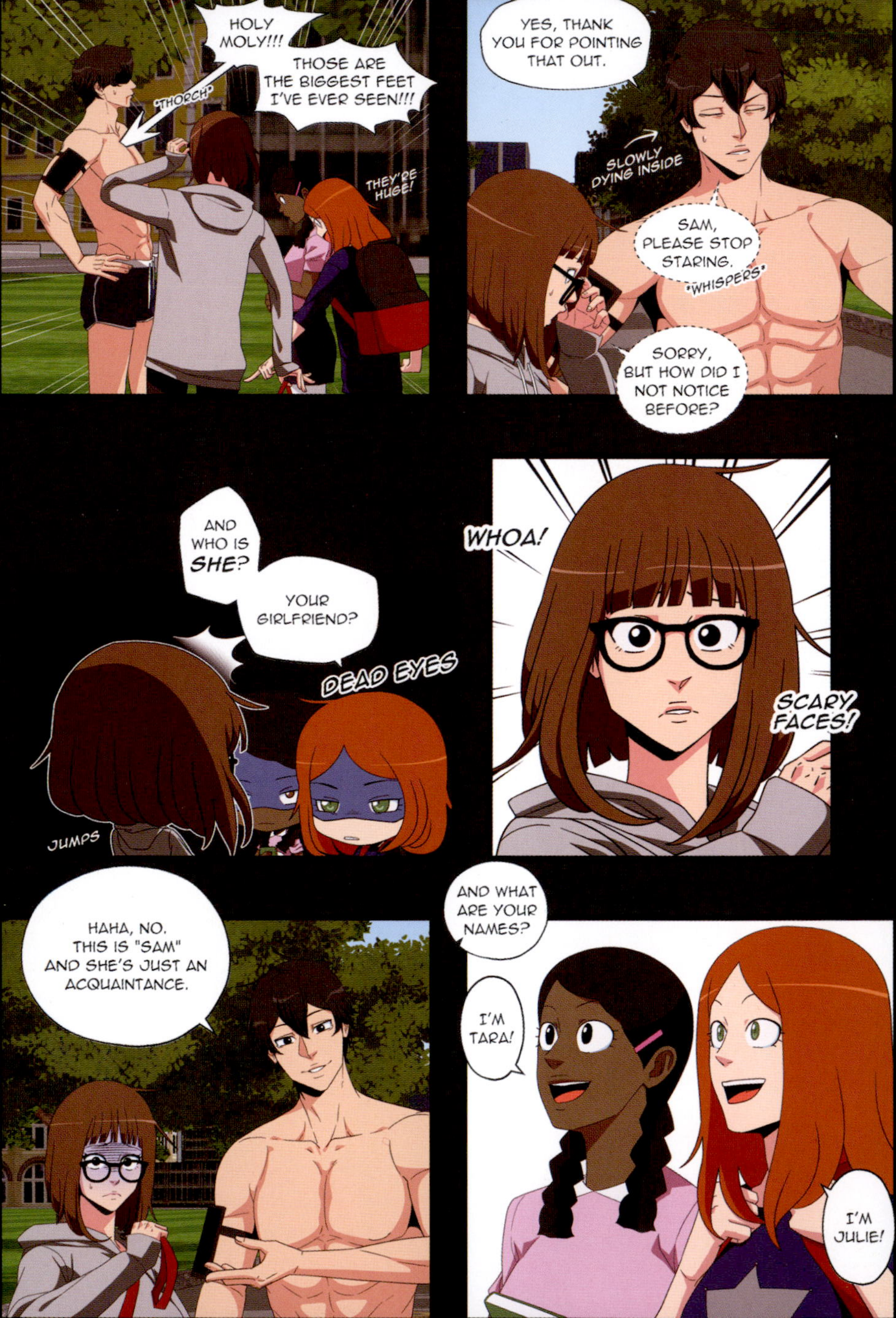
HOLY MOLY!!!
THOSE ARE THE BIGGEST FEET I'VE EVER SEEN!!!
THORCH
THEY'RE HUGE!
YES, THANK YOU FOR POINTING THAT OUT.
SLOWLY DYING INSIDE
SAM, PLEASE STOP STARING.
WHISPERS
SORRY, BUT HOW DID I NOT NOTICE BEFORE?
AND WHO IS SHE?
YOUR GIRLFRIEND?
DEAD EYES
JUMPS
WHOA!
SCARY FACES!
HAHA, NO. THIS IS "SAM" AND SHE'S JUST AN ACQUAINTANCE.
AND WHAT ARE YOUR NAMES?
I'M TARA!
I'M JULIE!

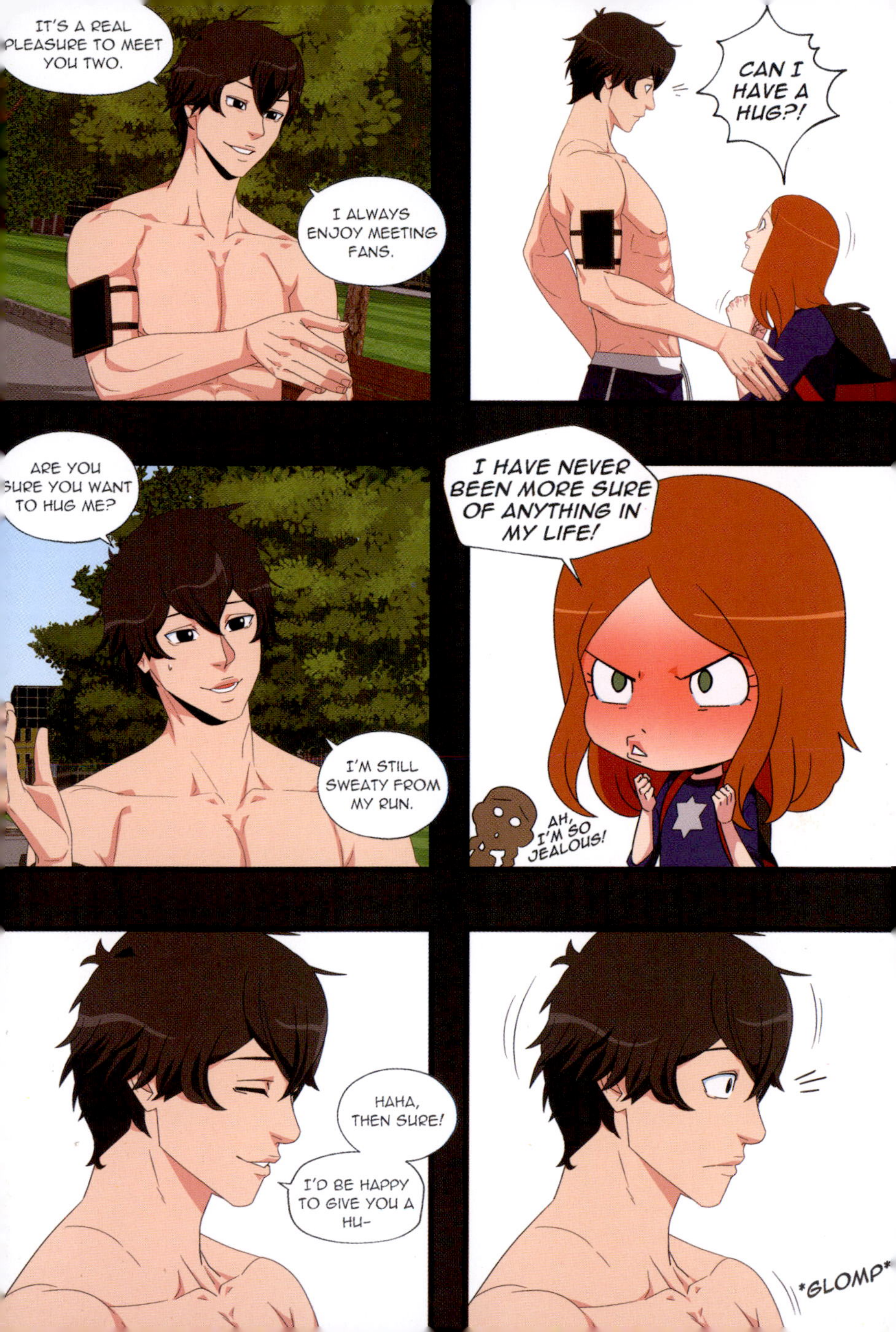
IT'S A REAL PLEASURE TO MEET YOU TWO.
I ALWAYS ENJOY MEETING FANS.
CAN I HAVE A HUG?!
ARE YOU SURE YOU WANT TO HUG ME?
I'M STILL SWEATY FROM MY RUN.
I HAVE NEVER BEEN MORE SURE OF ANYTHING IN MY LIFE!
AH, I'M SO JEALOUS!
HAHA, THEN SURE!
I'D BE HAPPY TO GIVE YOU A HU-
GLOMP

I'M NEVER WASHING THESE CLOTHES AGAIN.

OOF!

GLOMPS

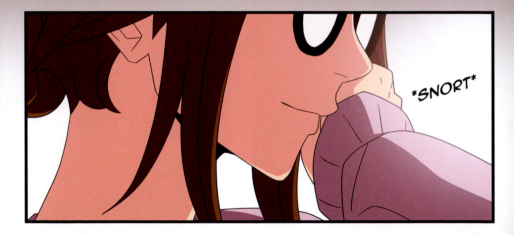

SNORT

E-EXCUSE ME.

CHUCKLE

SIGHS

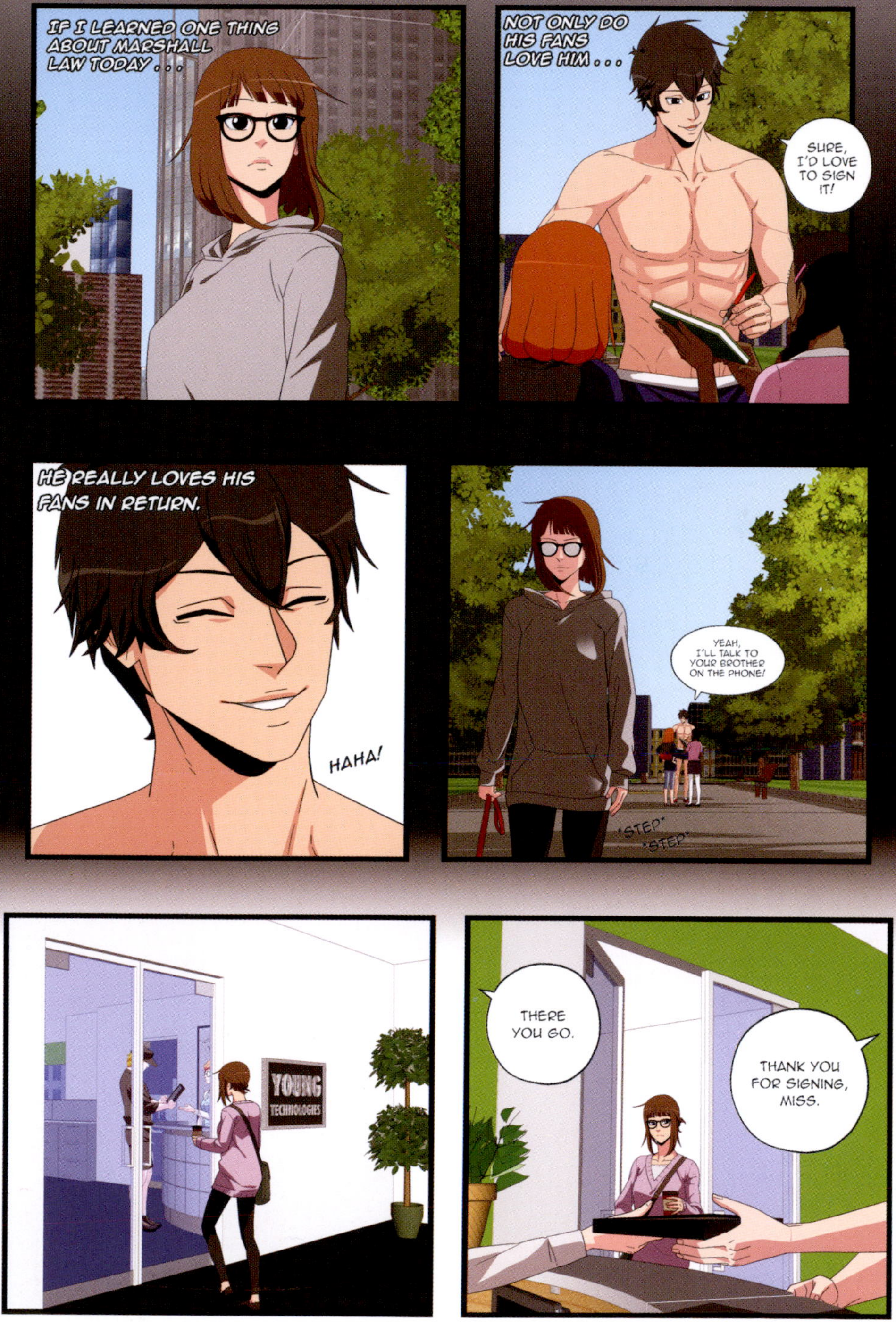
IF I LEARNED ONE THING ABOUT MARSHALL LAW TODAY . . .
NOT ONLY DO HIS FANS LOVE HIM . . .
SURE, I'D LOVE TO SIGN IT!
HE REALLY LOVES HIS FANS IN RETURN.
HAHA!
YEAH, I'LL TALK TO YOUR BROTHER ON THE PHONE!
STEP
STEP
YOUNG
TECHNOLOGIES
THERE YOU GO.
THANK YOU FOR SIGNING, MISS.

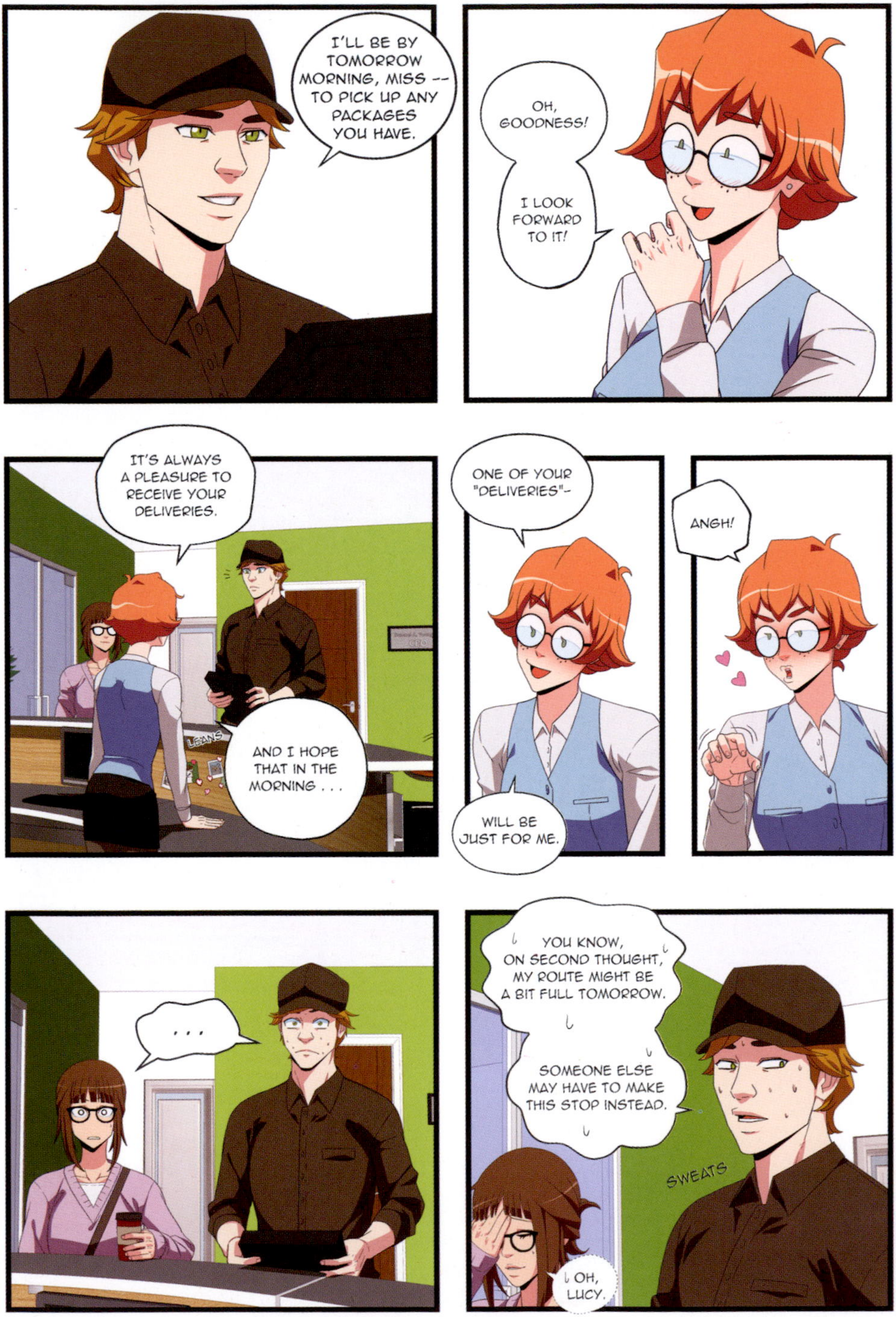
I'LL BE BY TOMORROW MORNING, MISS -- TO PICK UP ANY PACKAGES YOU HAVE.
OH, GOODNESS!
I LOOK FORWARD TO IT!
IT'S ALWAYS A PLEASURE TO RECEIVE YOUR DELIVERIES.
LEANS
AND I HOPE THAT IN THE MORNING . . .
ONE OF YOUR "DELIVERIES"-
WILL BE JUST FOR ME.
ANGH!
. . .
YOU KNOW, ON SECOND THOUGHT, MY ROUTE MIGHT BE A BIT FULL TOMORROW.
SOMEONE ELSE MAY HAVE TO MAKE THIS STOP INSTEAD.
SWEATS
OH, LUCY.

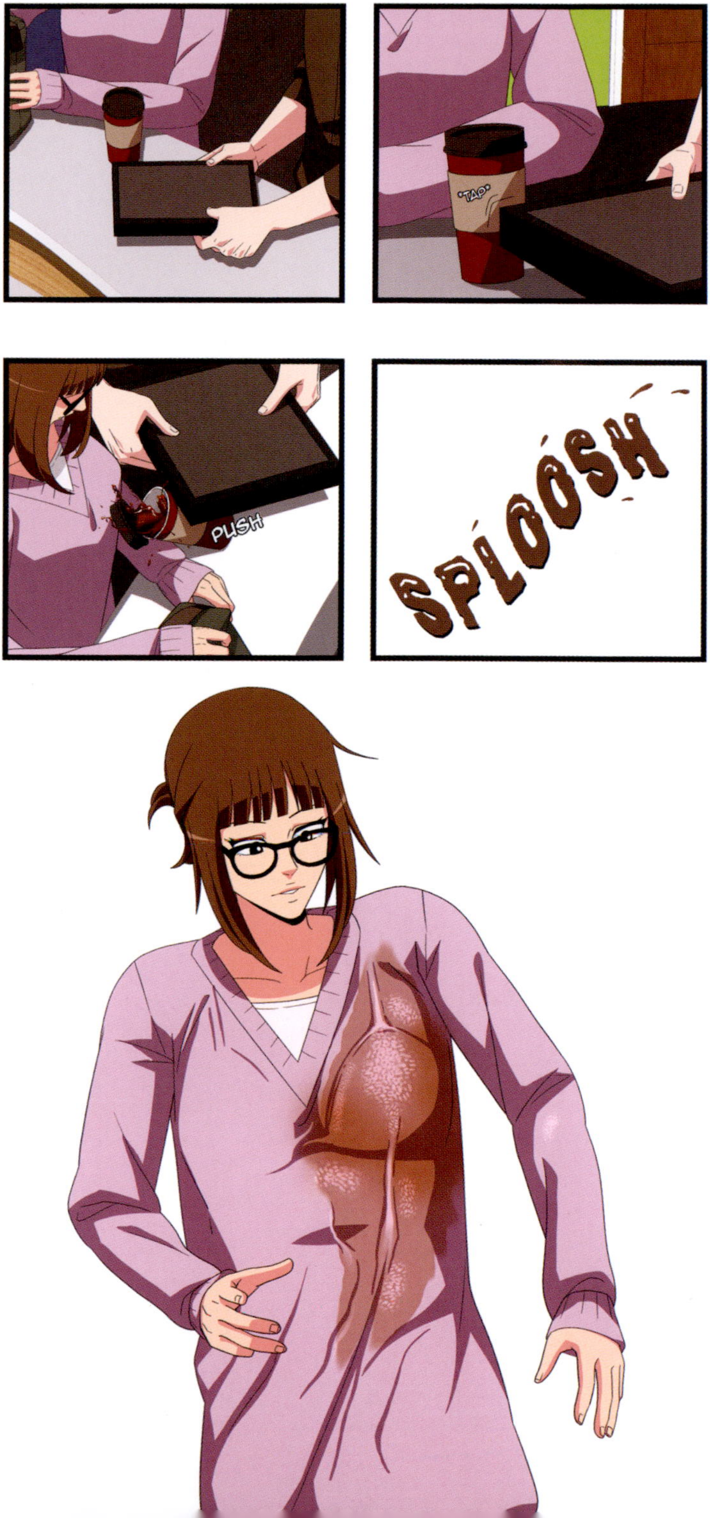
TAP
PUSH
SPLOOSH

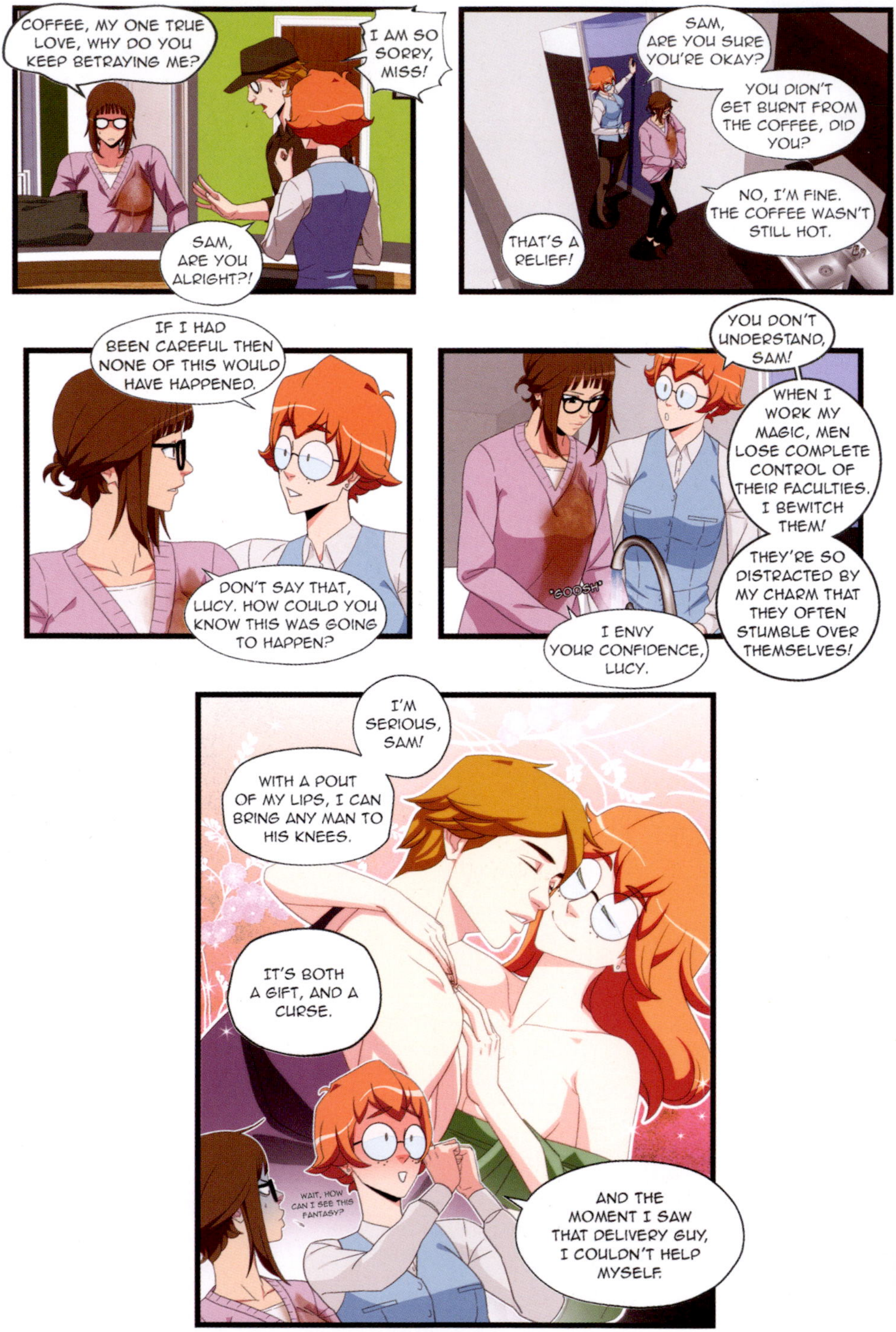
COFFEE, MY ONE TRUE LOVE, WHY DO YOU KEEP BETRAYING ME?
I AM SO SORRY, MISS!
SAM, ARE YOU ALRIGHT?!
SAM, ARE YOU SURE YOU'RE OKAY?
YOU DIDN'T GET BURNT FROM THE COFFEE, DID YOU?
NO, I'M FINE. THE COFFEE WASN'T STILL HOT.
THAT'S A RELIEF!
IF I HAD BEEN CAREFUL THEN NONE OF THIS WOULD HAVE HAPPENED.
DON'T SAY THAT, LUCY. HOW COULD YOU KNOW THIS WAS GOING TO HAPPEN?
YOU DON'T UNDERSTAND, SAM!
WHEN I WORK MY MAGIC, MEN LOSE COMPLETE CONTROL OF THEIR FACULTIES. I BEWITCH THEM!
THEY'RE SO DISTRACTED BY MY CHARM THAT THEY OFTEN STUMBLE OVER THEMSELVES!
GOOSH
I ENVY YOUR CONFIDENCE, LUCY.
I'M SERIOUS, SAM!
WITH A POUT OF MY LIPS, I CAN BRING ANY MAN TO HIS KNEES.
IT'S BOTH A GIFT, AND A CURSE.
WAIT, HOW CAN I SEE THIS FANTASY?
AND THE MOMENT I SAW THAT DELIVERY GUY, I COULDN'T HELP MYSELF.

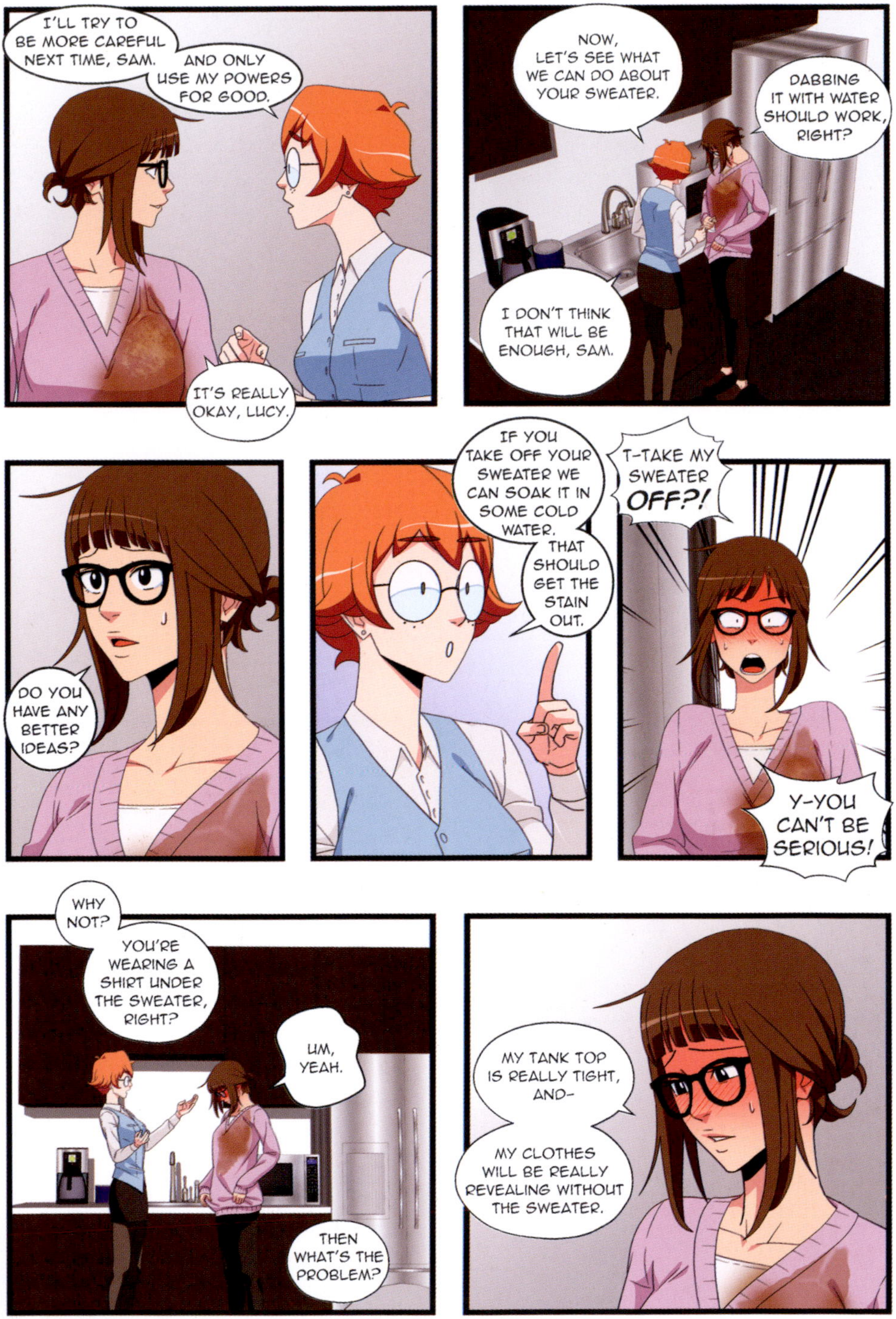
I'LL TRY TO BE MORE CAREFUL NEXT TIME, SAM.
AND ONLY USE MY POWERS FOR GOOD.
IT'S REALLY OKAY, LUCY.
NOW, LET'S SEE WHAT WE CAN DO ABOUT YOUR SWEATER.
DABBING IT WITH WATER SHOULD WORK, RIGHT?
I DON'T THINK THAT WILL BE ENOUGH, SAM.
DO YOU HAVE ANY BETTER IDEAS?
IF YOU TAKE OFF YOUR SWEATER WE CAN SOAK IT IN SOME COLD WATER.
THAT SHOULD GET THE STAIN OUT.
T-TAKE MY SWEATER OFF?!
Y-YOU CAN'T BE SERIOUS!
WHY NOT?
YOU'RE WEARING A SHIRT UNDER THE SWEATER, RIGHT?
UM, YEAH.
THEN WHAT'S THE PROBLEM?
MY TANK TOP IS REALLY TIGHT, AND-
MY CLOTHES WILL BE REALLY REVEALING WITHOUT THE SWEATER.

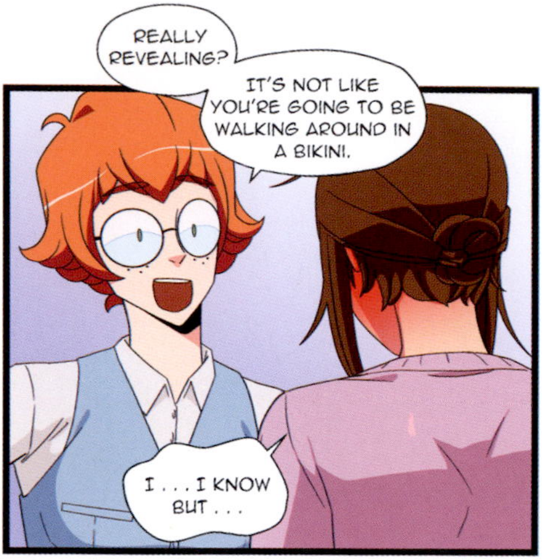
REALLY REVEALING?
IT'S NOT LIKE YOU'RE GOING TO BE WALKING AROUND IN A BIKINI.
I . . . I KNOW BUT . . .

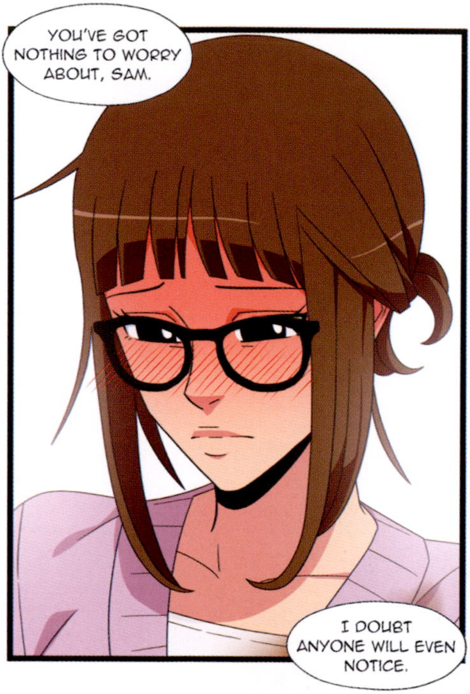
YOU'VE GOT NOTHING TO WORRY ABOUT, SAM.
I DOUBT ANYONE WILL EVEN NOTICE.

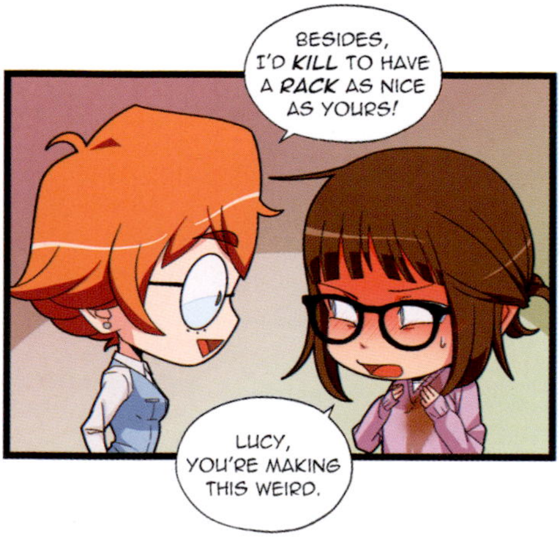
BESIDES, I'D **KILL** TO HAVE A **RACK** AS NICE AS YOURS!
LUCY, YOU'RE MAKING THIS WEIRD.

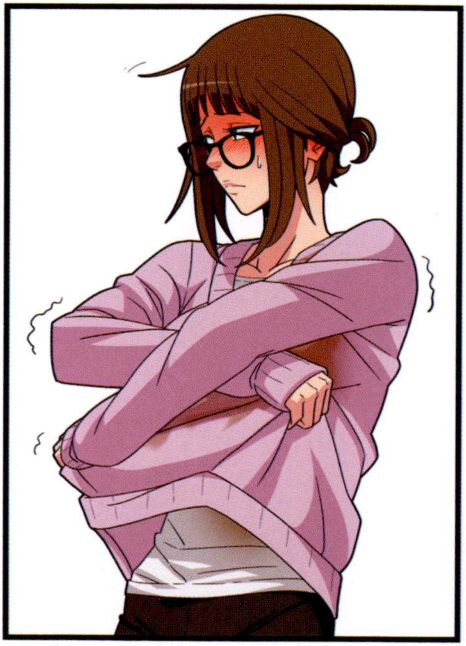

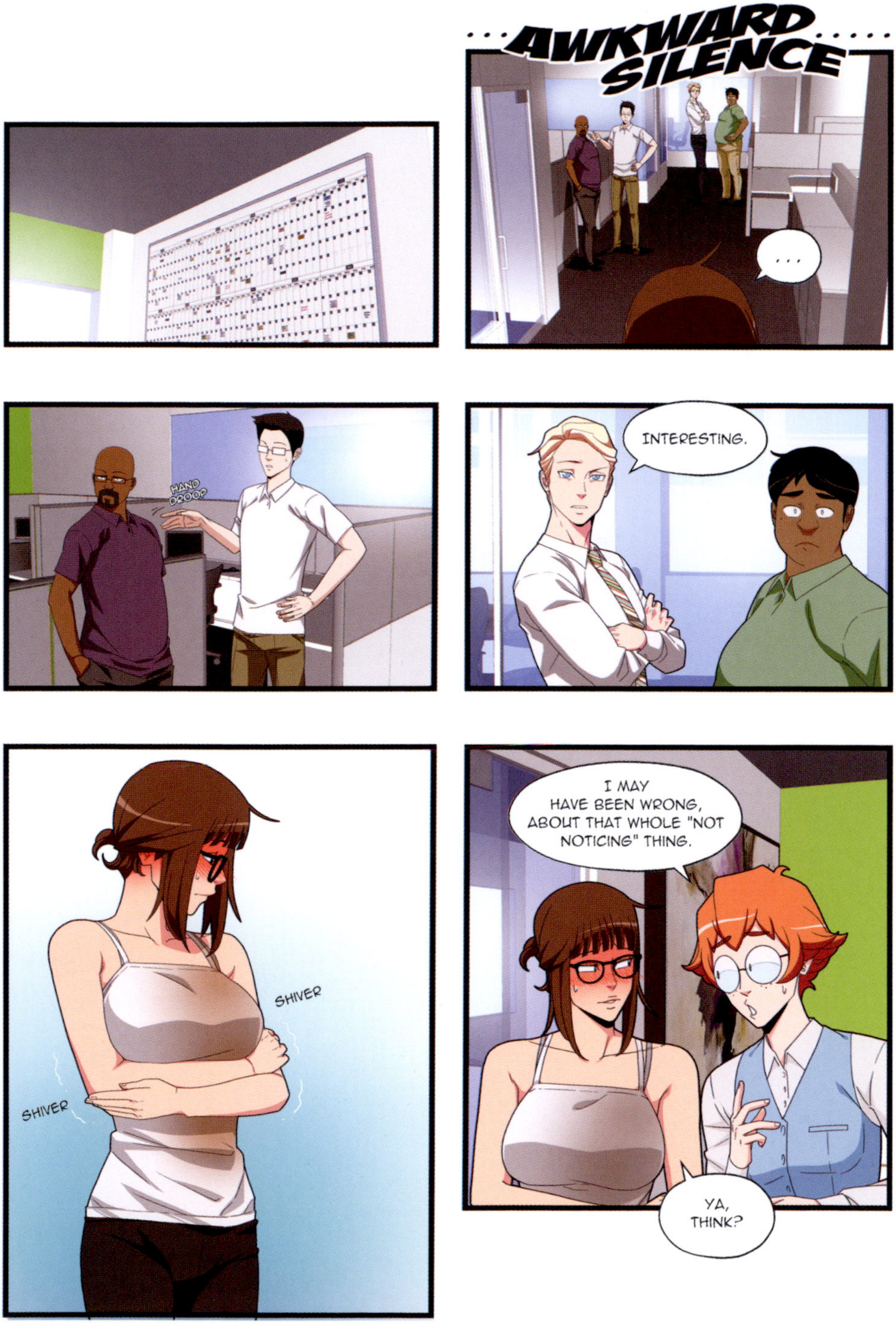
...AWKWARD SILENCE...
...
HAND DROOP
INTERESTING.
SHIVER
SHIVER
I MAY HAVE BEEN WRONG, ABOUT THAT WHOLE "NOT NOTICING" THING.
YA, THINK?

THIS IS SO EMBARRASSING – I CAN FEEL THEIR STARES.

I HATE WEARING TIGHT CLOTHES, THEY MAKE ME FEEL SO EXPOSED AND VULNERABLE.

I'VE WORN OVERSIZED CLOTHES SINCE I WAS A KID, AND HAVING TO WEAR TIGHT CLOTHES NOW AT WORK IS TORTURE.

TAP, TAP

I CAN'T UNDERSTAND HOW SOME PEOPLE . . .

CAN FEEL COMFORTABLE ENOUGH TO SHOW A LOT OF SKIN.

IF MY XXXL SWEATER WASN'T SOAKING IN THE SINK RIGHT NOW . . .

I'D CRAWL INSIDE OF IT AND DIE OF EMBARRASSMENT.

GOOD MORNING, SAM.

DID YOU HAVE SOME KIND OF "WARDROBE MALFUNCTION" TODAY?

JUMP

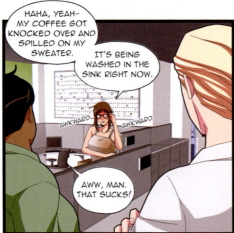

HAHA, YEAH– MY COFFEE GOT KNOCKED OVER AND SPILLED ON MY SWEATER.

IT'S BEING WASHED IN THE SINK RIGHT NOW.

AWKWARD   AWKWARD

AWW, MAN. THAT SUCKS!

YOU GOING TO HEAD HOME TO CHANGE?

AH, NO. I TOOK THE BUS.

DO YOU FEEL SELF-CONSCIOUS DRESSED LIKE THAT?

EXTREMELY.

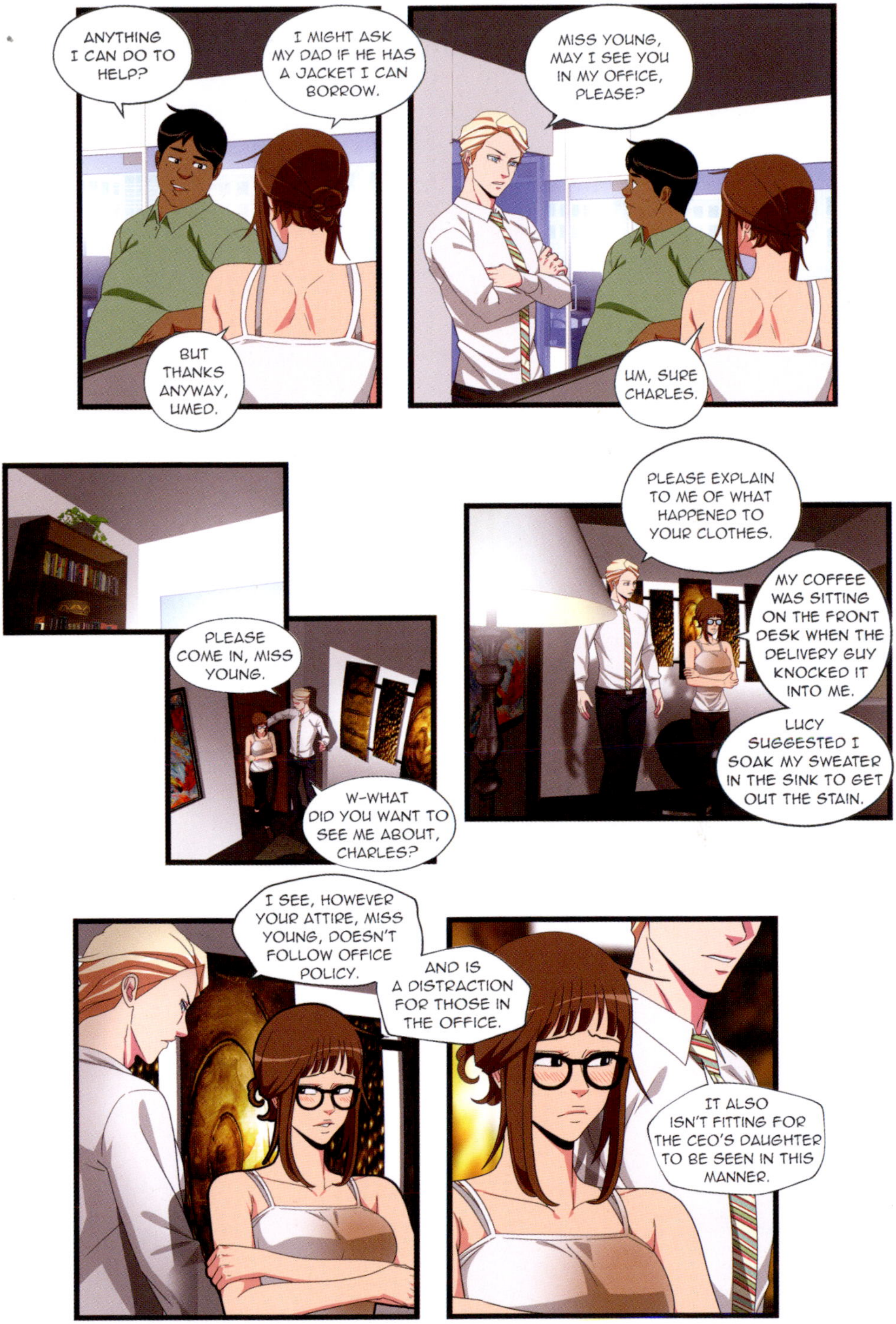
ANYTHING I CAN DO TO HELP?
I MIGHT ASK MY DAD IF HE HAS A JACKET I CAN BORROW.
BUT THANKS ANYWAY, UMED.
MISS YOUNG, MAY I SEE YOU IN MY OFFICE, PLEASE?
UM, SURE CHARLES.
PLEASE COME IN, MISS YOUNG.
W-WHAT DID YOU WANT TO SEE ME ABOUT, CHARLES?
PLEASE EXPLAIN TO ME OF WHAT HAPPENED TO YOUR CLOTHES.
MY COFFEE WAS SITTING ON THE FRONT DESK WHEN THE DELIVERY GUY KNOCKED IT INTO ME.
LUCY SUGGESTED I SOAK MY SWEATER IN THE SINK TO GET OUT THE STAIN.
I SEE, HOWEVER YOUR ATTIRE, MISS YOUNG, DOESN'T FOLLOW OFFICE POLICY.
AND IS A DISTRACTION FOR THOSE IN THE OFFICE.
IT ALSO ISN'T FITTING FOR THE CEO'S DAUGHTER TO BE SEEN IN THIS MANNER.

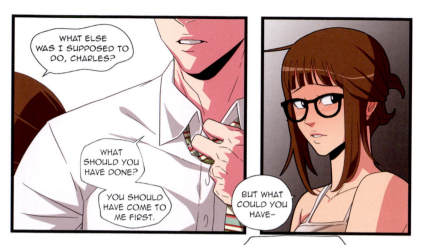

WHAT ELSE WAS I SUPPOSED TO DO, CHARLES?

WHAT SHOULD YOU HAVE DONE?

YOU SHOULD HAVE COME TO ME FIRST.

BUT WHAT COULD YOU HAVE—

YOU REPRESENT THE FUTURE OF THIS COMPANY, MISS YOUNG.

IT'S IMPORTANT YOU ARE THE PICTURE OF PROFESSIONALISM WHEN YOU ARE HERE.

LEANS

FWIP

bob

FWIP

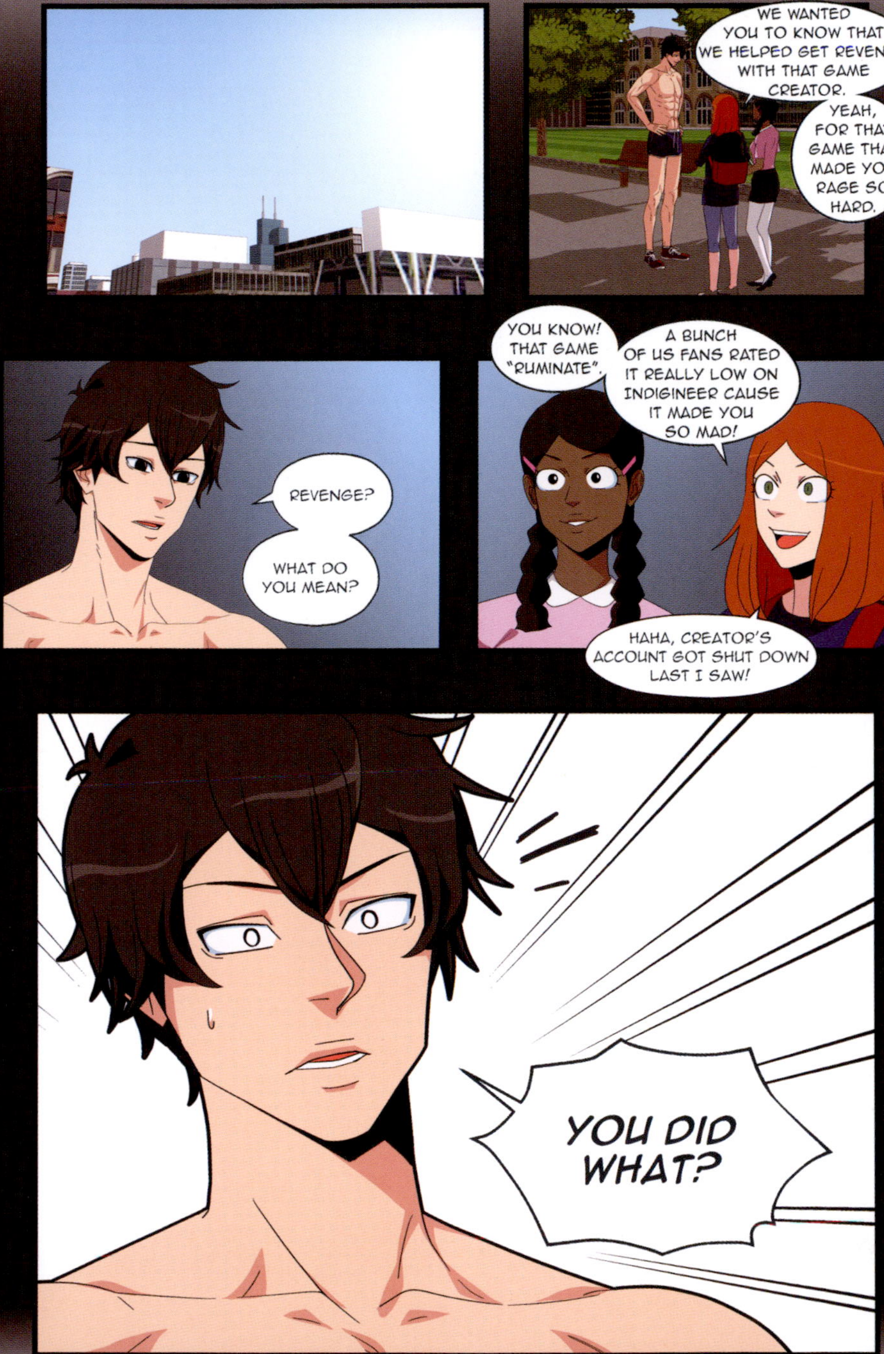
WE WANTED YOU TO KNOW THAT WE HELPED GET REVENGE WITH THAT GAME CREATOR.
YEAH, FOR THAT GAME THAT MADE YOU RAGE SO HARD.
REVENGE?
WHAT DO YOU MEAN?
YOU KNOW! THAT GAME "RUMINATE".
A BUNCH OF US FANS RATED IT REALLY LOW ON INDIGINEER CAUSE IT MADE YOU SO MAD!
HAHA, CREATOR'S ACCOUNT GOT SHUT DOWN LAST I SAW!
YOU DID WHAT?

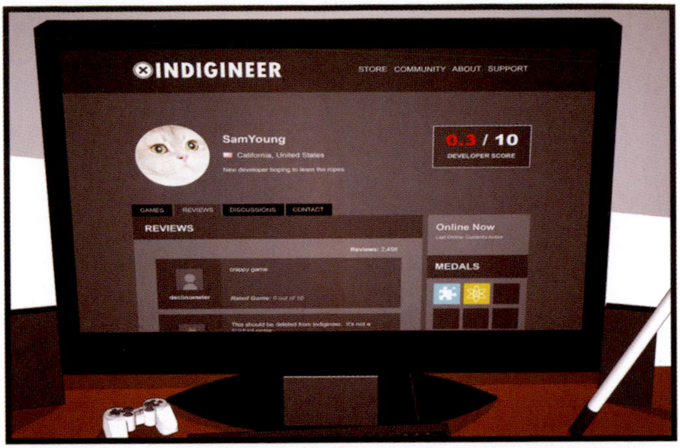
INDIGINEER
STORE COMMUNITY ABOUT SUPPORT
SamYoung
California, United States
New developer hoping to learn the ropes
0.3 / 10
DEVELOPER SCORE
GAMES REVIEWS DISCUSSIONS CONTACT
REVIEWS
Online Now
MEDALS
crappy game
declinometer

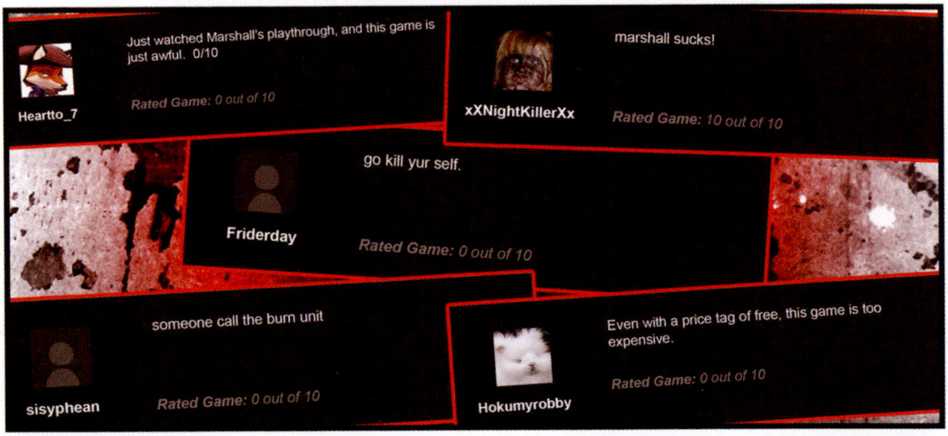
Heartto_7
Just watched Marshall's playthrough, and this game is just awful. 0/10
Rated Game: 0 out of 10
xXNightKillerXx
marshall sucks!
Rated Game: 10 out of 10
Friderday
go kill yur self.
Rated Game: 0 out of 10
sisyphean
someone call the burn unit
Rated Game: 0 out of 10
Hokumyrobby
Even with a price tag of free, this game is too expensive.
Rated Game: 0 out of 10

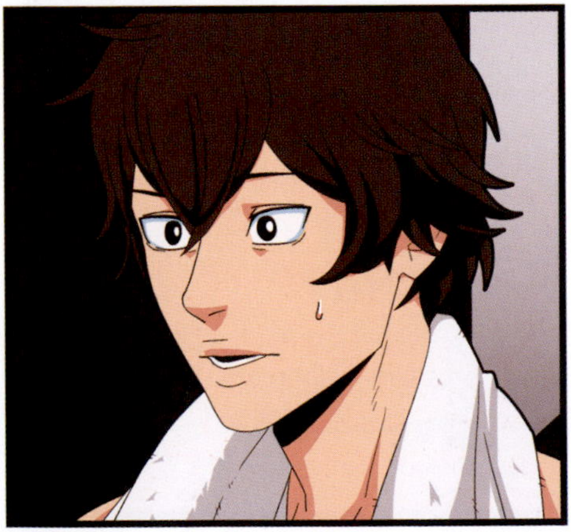

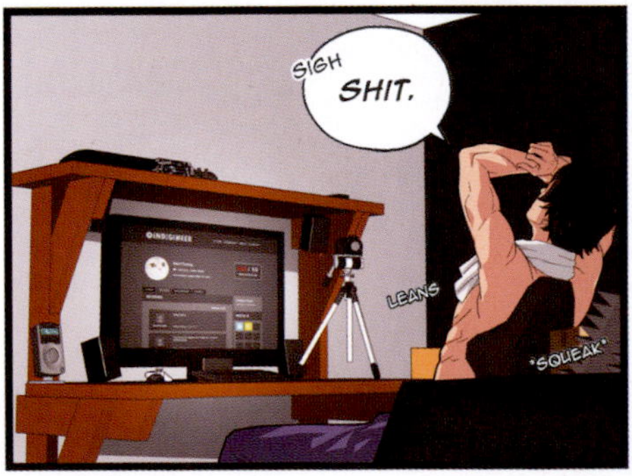
SIGH
SHIT.
LEANS
SQUEAK

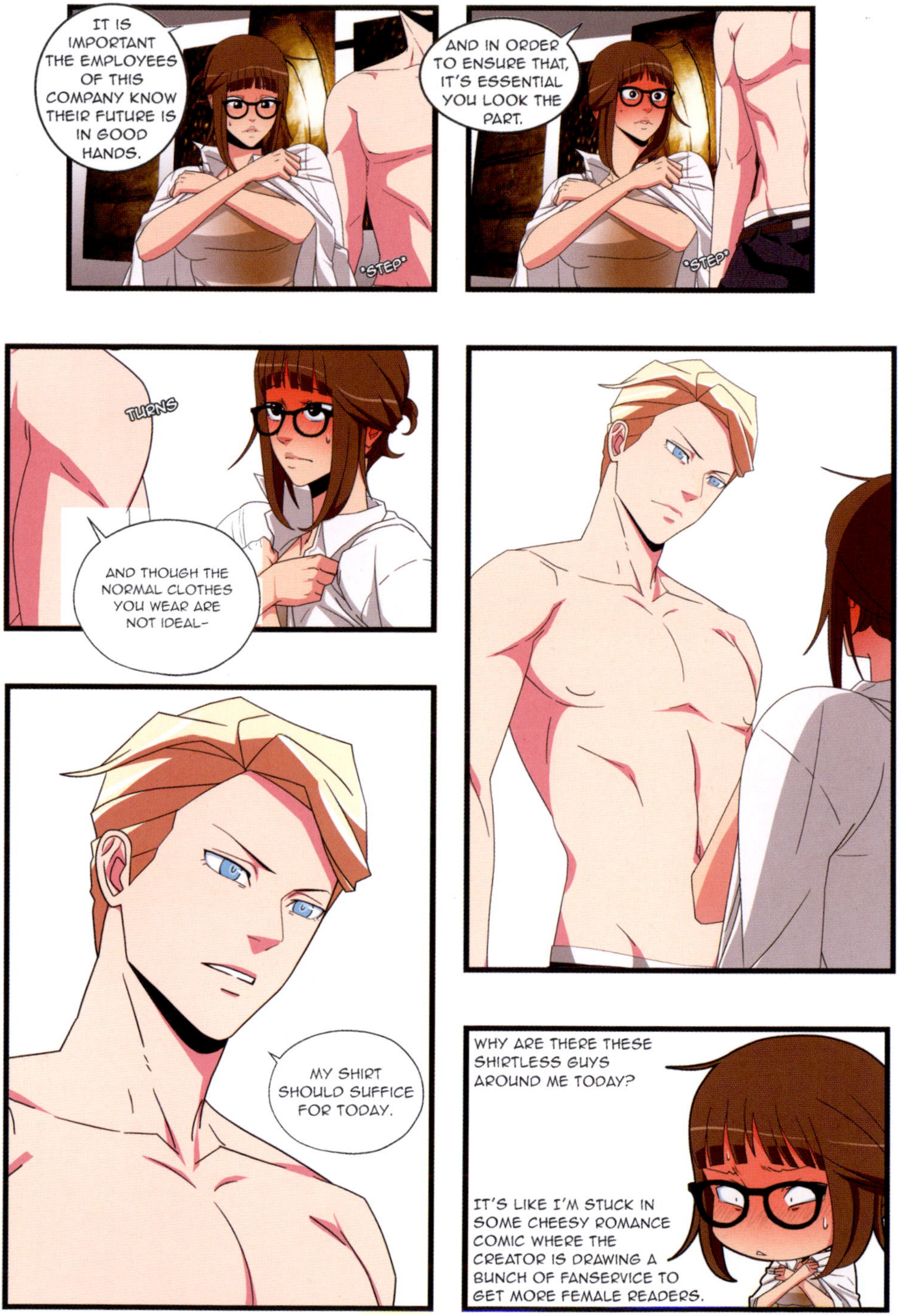
IT IS IMPORTANT THE EMPLOYEES OF THIS COMPANY KNOW THEIR FUTURE IS IN GOOD HANDS.
STEP
AND IN ORDER TO ENSURE THAT, IT'S ESSENTIAL YOU LOOK THE PART.
STEP
TURNS
AND THOUGH THE NORMAL CLOTHES YOU WEAR ARE NOT IDEAL-
MY SHIRT SHOULD SUFFICE FOR TODAY.
WHY ARE THERE THESE SHIRTLESS GUYS AROUND ME TODAY?
IT'S LIKE I'M STUCK IN SOME CHEESY ROMANCE COMIC WHERE THE CREATOR IS DRAWING A BUNCH OF FANSERVICE TO GET MORE FEMALE READERS.

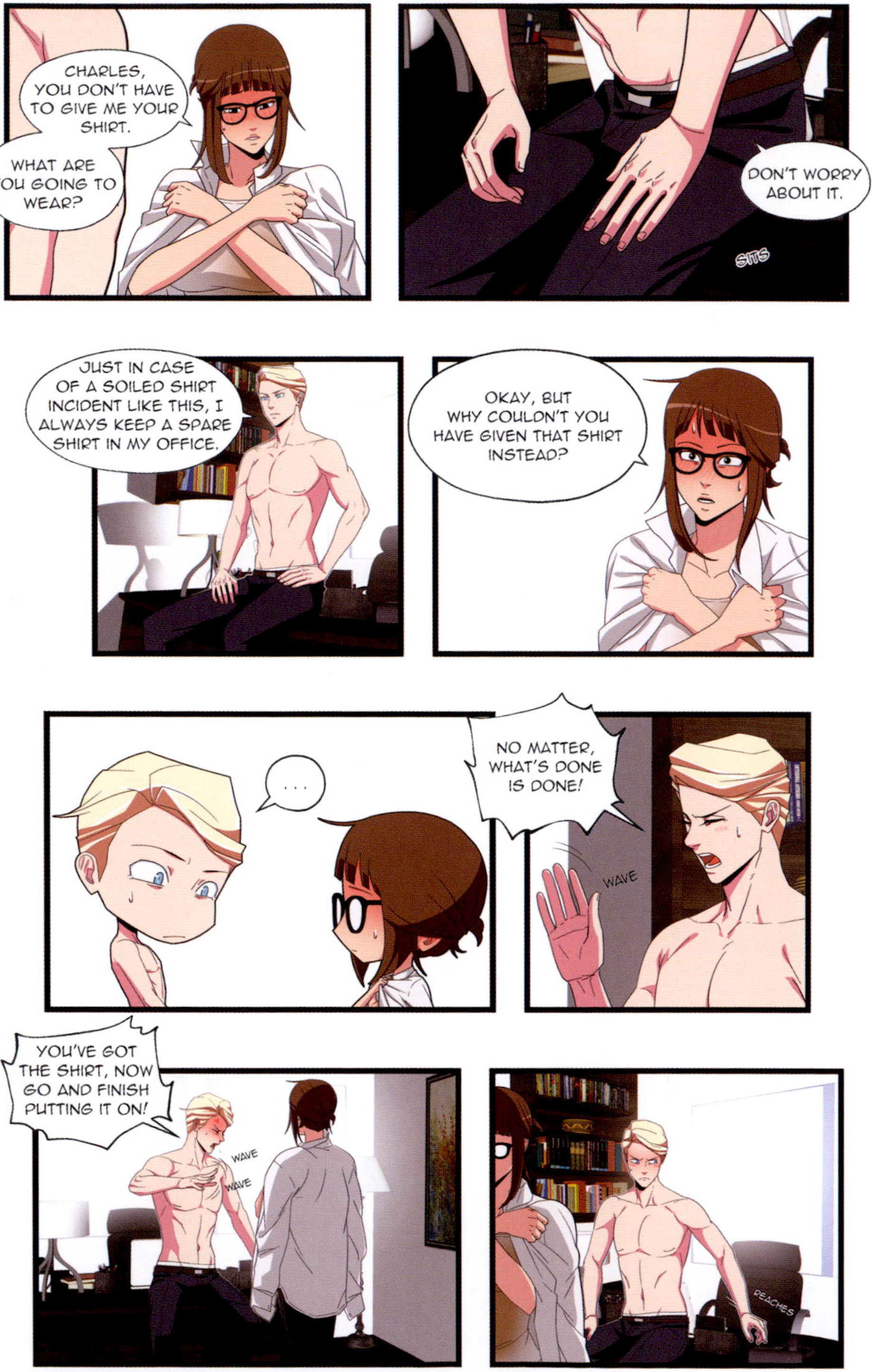
CHARLES, YOU DON'T HAVE TO GIVE ME YOUR SHIRT.
WHAT ARE YOU GOING TO WEAR?
DON'T WORRY ABOUT IT.
SITS
JUST IN CASE OF A SOILED SHIRT INCIDENT LIKE THIS, I ALWAYS KEEP A SPARE SHIRT IN MY OFFICE.
OKAY, BUT WHY COULDN'T YOU HAVE GIVEN THAT SHIRT INSTEAD?
. . .
NO MATTER, WHAT'S DONE IS DONE!
WAVE
YOU'VE GOT THE SHIRT, NOW GO AND FINISH PUTTING IT ON!
WAVE
WAVE
REACHES

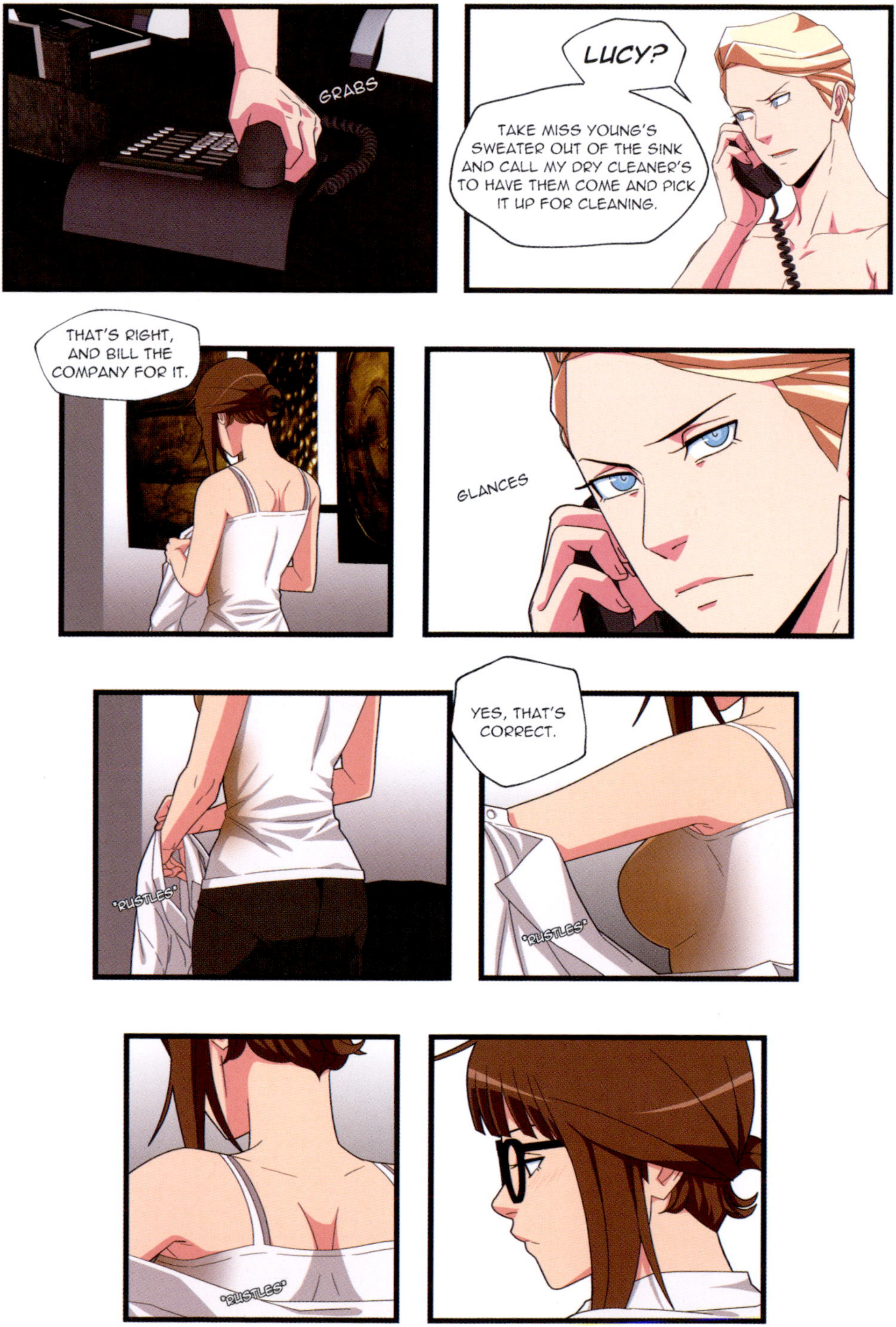
GRABS
LUCY?
TAKE MISS YOUNG'S SWEATER OUT OF THE SINK AND CALL MY DRY CLEANER'S TO HAVE THEM COME AND PICK IT UP FOR CLEANING.
THAT'S RIGHT, AND BILL THE COMPANY FOR IT.
GLANCES
RUSTLES
YES, THAT'S CORRECT.
RUSTLES
RUSTLES

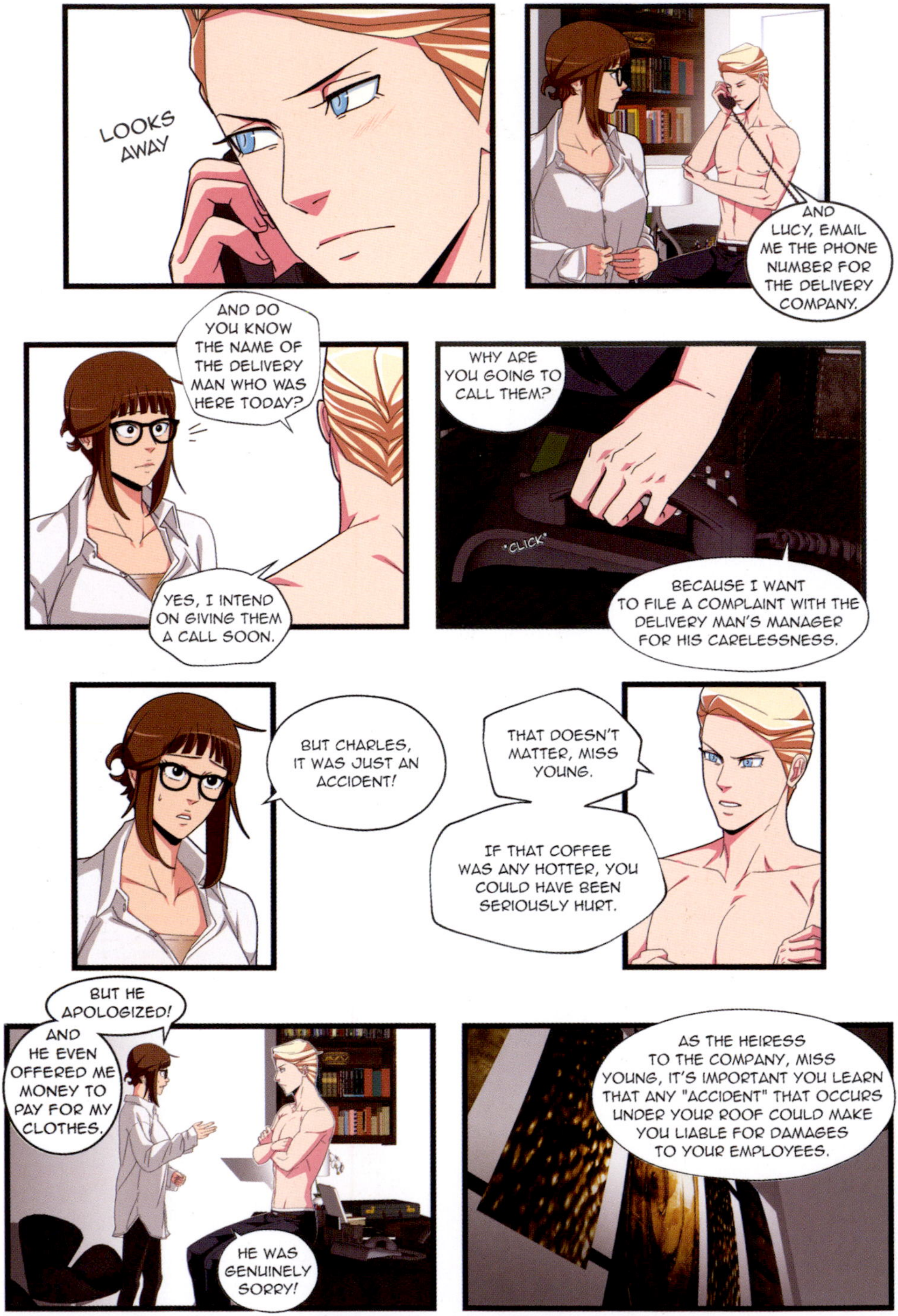
LOOKS AWAY
AND LUCY, EMAIL ME THE PHONE NUMBER FOR THE DELIVERY COMPANY.
AND DO YOU KNOW THE NAME OF THE DELIVERY MAN WHO WAS HERE TODAY?
YES, I INTEND ON GIVING THEM A CALL SOON.
WHY ARE YOU GOING TO CALL THEM?
CLICK
BECAUSE I WANT TO FILE A COMPLAINT WITH THE DELIVERY MAN'S MANAGER FOR HIS CARELESSNESS.
BUT CHARLES, IT WAS JUST AN ACCIDENT!
THAT DOESN'T MATTER, MISS YOUNG.
IF THAT COFFEE WAS ANY HOTTER, YOU COULD HAVE BEEN SERIOUSLY HURT.
BUT HE APOLOGIZED!
AND HE EVEN OFFERED ME MONEY TO PAY FOR MY CLOTHES.
HE WAS GENUINELY SORRY!
AS THE HEIRESS TO THE COMPANY, MISS YOUNG, IT'S IMPORTANT YOU LEARN THAT ANY "ACCIDENT" THAT OCCURS UNDER YOUR ROOF COULD MAKE YOU LIABLE FOR DAMAGES TO YOUR EMPLOYEES.

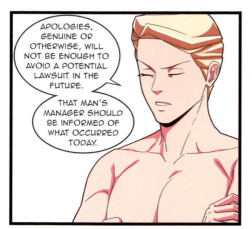

APOLOGIES, GENUINE OR OTHERWISE, WILL NOT BE ENOUGH TO AVOID A POTENTIAL LAWSUIT IN THE FUTURE.

THAT MAN'S MANAGER SHOULD BE INFORMED OF WHAT OCCURRED TODAY.

THAT SEEMS PRETTY HARSH.

I MEAN, MAYBE IT WOULDN'T HAVE HAPPENED IF HE WASN'T DISTRACTED WITH LUCY.

OR PERHAPS I SHOULDN'T HAVE PUT MY CUP THERE—

WAIT, WHAT DO YOU MEAN, "DISTRACTED WITH LUCY"?

SHE WAS JUST FLIRTING WITH HIM.

IT WAS ADORABLE. BUT I THINK IT ALSO CAUGHT HIM OFF GUARD.

LUCY, WAS FLIRTING . . . WITH HIM?

REACHES

YOU'RE NOT CALLING LUCY, ARE YOU?

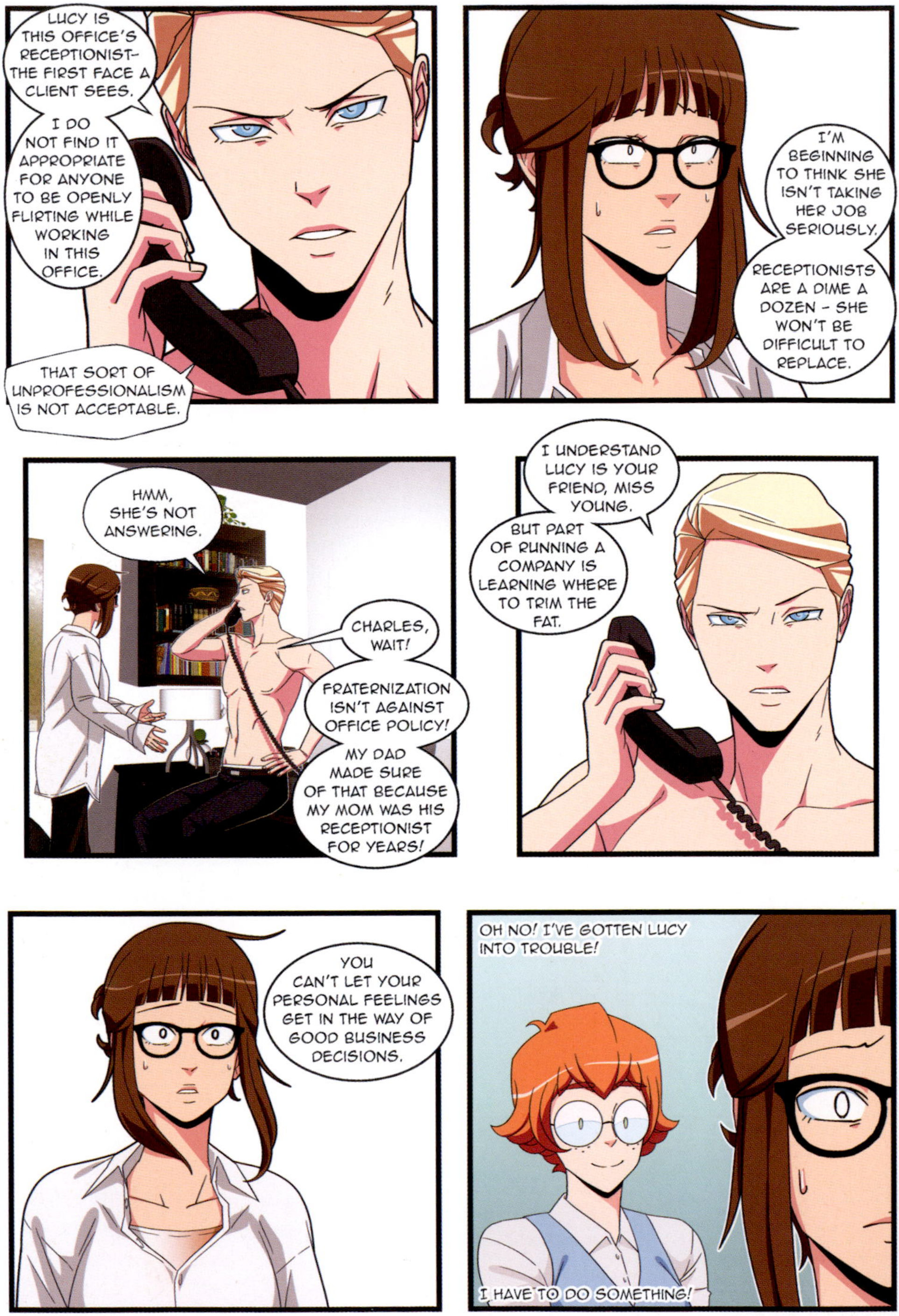
LUCY IS THIS OFFICE'S RECEPTIONIST- THE FIRST FACE A CLIENT SEES.
I DO NOT FIND IT APPROPRIATE FOR ANYONE TO BE OPENLY FLIRTING WHILE WORKING IN THIS OFFICE.
THAT SORT OF UNPROFESSIONALISM IS NOT ACCEPTABLE.
I'M BEGINNING TO THINK SHE ISN'T TAKING HER JOB SERIOUSLY.
RECEPTIONISTS ARE A DIME A DOZEN - SHE WON'T BE DIFFICULT TO REPLACE.
HMM, SHE'S NOT ANSWERING.
CHARLES, WAIT!
FRATERNIZATION ISN'T AGAINST OFFICE POLICY!
MY DAD MADE SURE OF THAT BECAUSE MY MOM WAS HIS RECEPTIONIST FOR YEARS!
I UNDERSTAND LUCY IS YOUR FRIEND, MISS YOUNG.
BUT PART OF RUNNING A COMPANY IS LEARNING WHERE TO TRIM THE FAT.
YOU CAN'T LET YOUR PERSONAL FEELINGS GET IN THE WAY OF GOOD BUSINESS DECISIONS.
OH NO! I'VE GOTTEN LUCY INTO TROUBLE!
I HAVE TO DO SOMETHING!

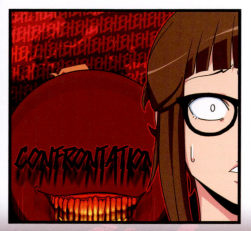

CONFRONTATION

HMM, SHE STILL ISN'T ANSWERING.

SHE MUST BE ON THE OTHER LINE.

GASP

GASP

W-WAIT . . .

GASP

GASP

GASP

GASP

CONFRONTATION

GASP

GASP

GASP

LUCY

. . .

MY FRIEND.

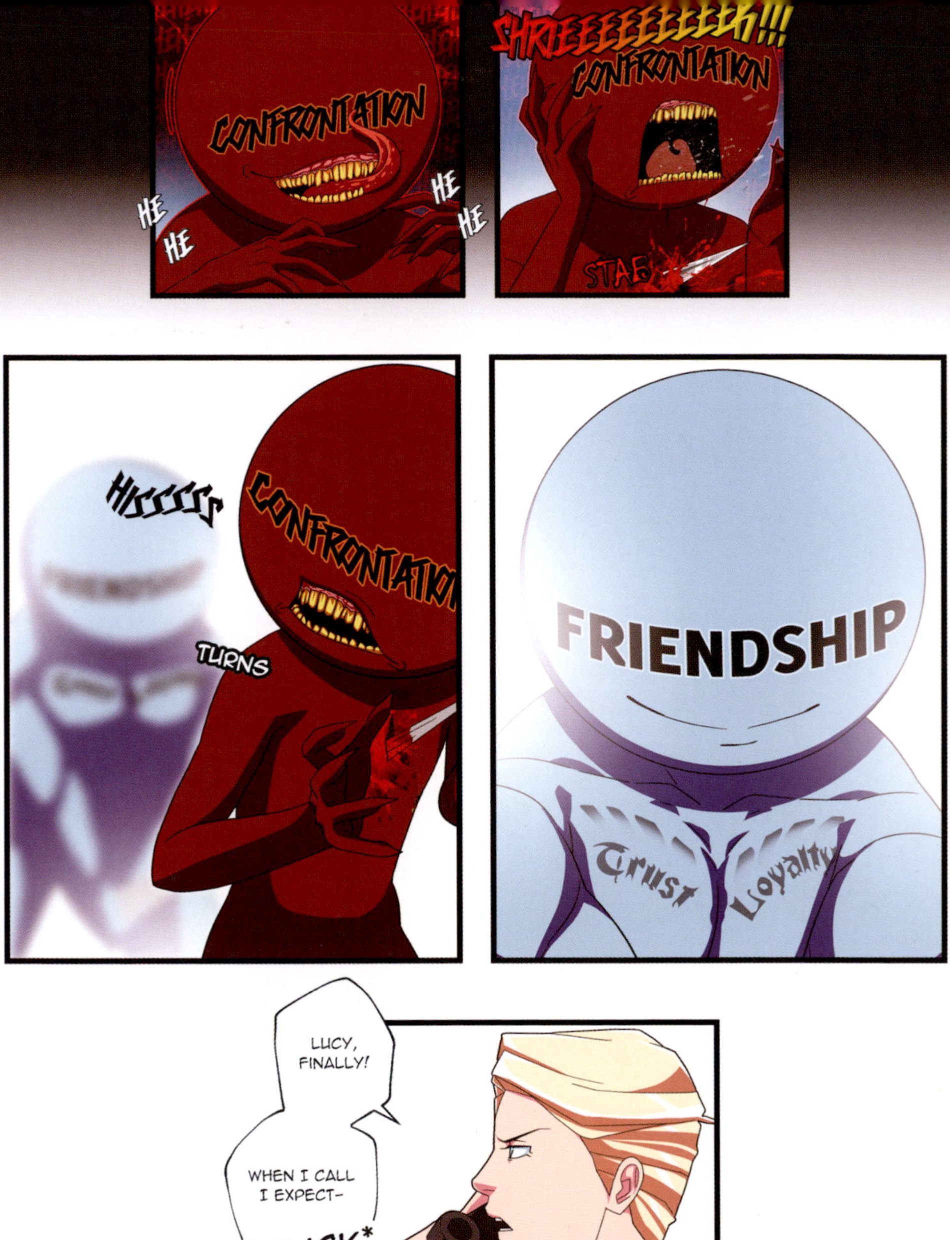
CONFRONTATION
HE
HE
HE
HE
SHRIEEEEEEEEEK!!!
CONFRONTATION
STAB
HISSSSS
CONFRONTATION
TURNS
FRIENDSHIP
Trust
Loyalty
LUCY, FINALLY!
WHEN I CALL I EXPECT-
CLICK

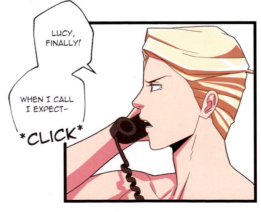

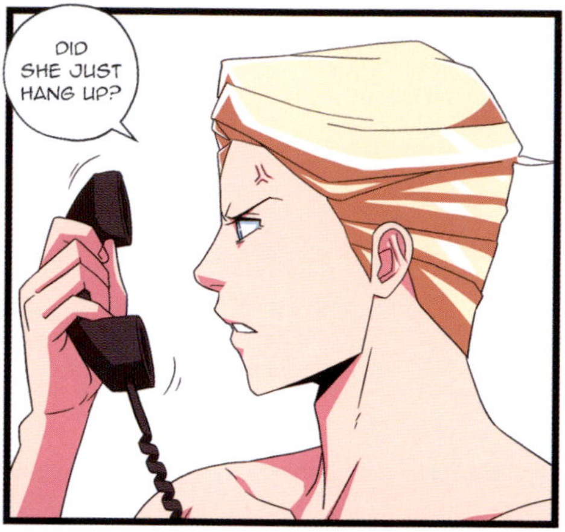
DID SHE JUST HANG UP?

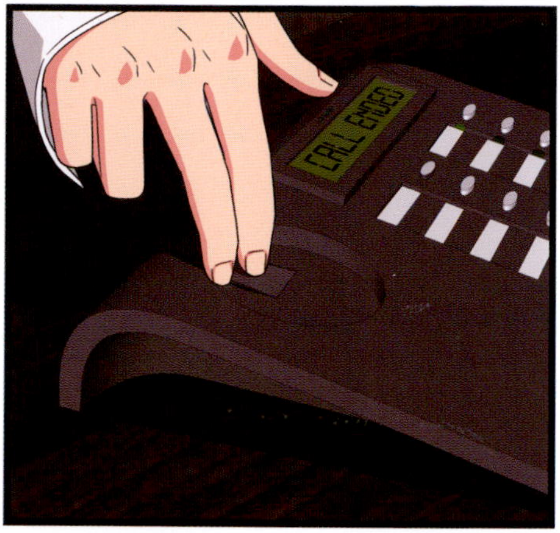
CALL ENDED

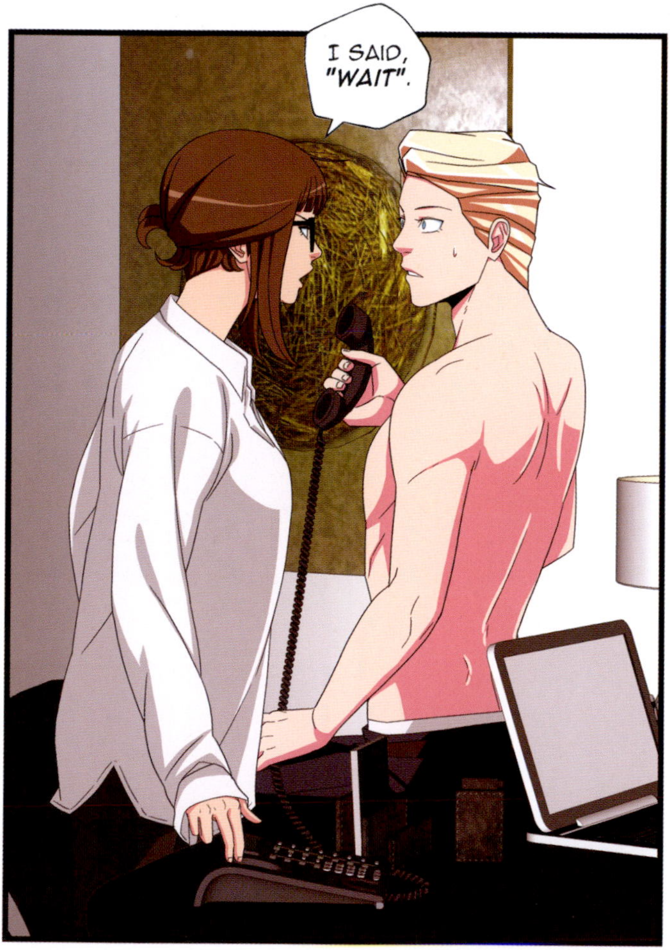
I SAID, "WAIT".

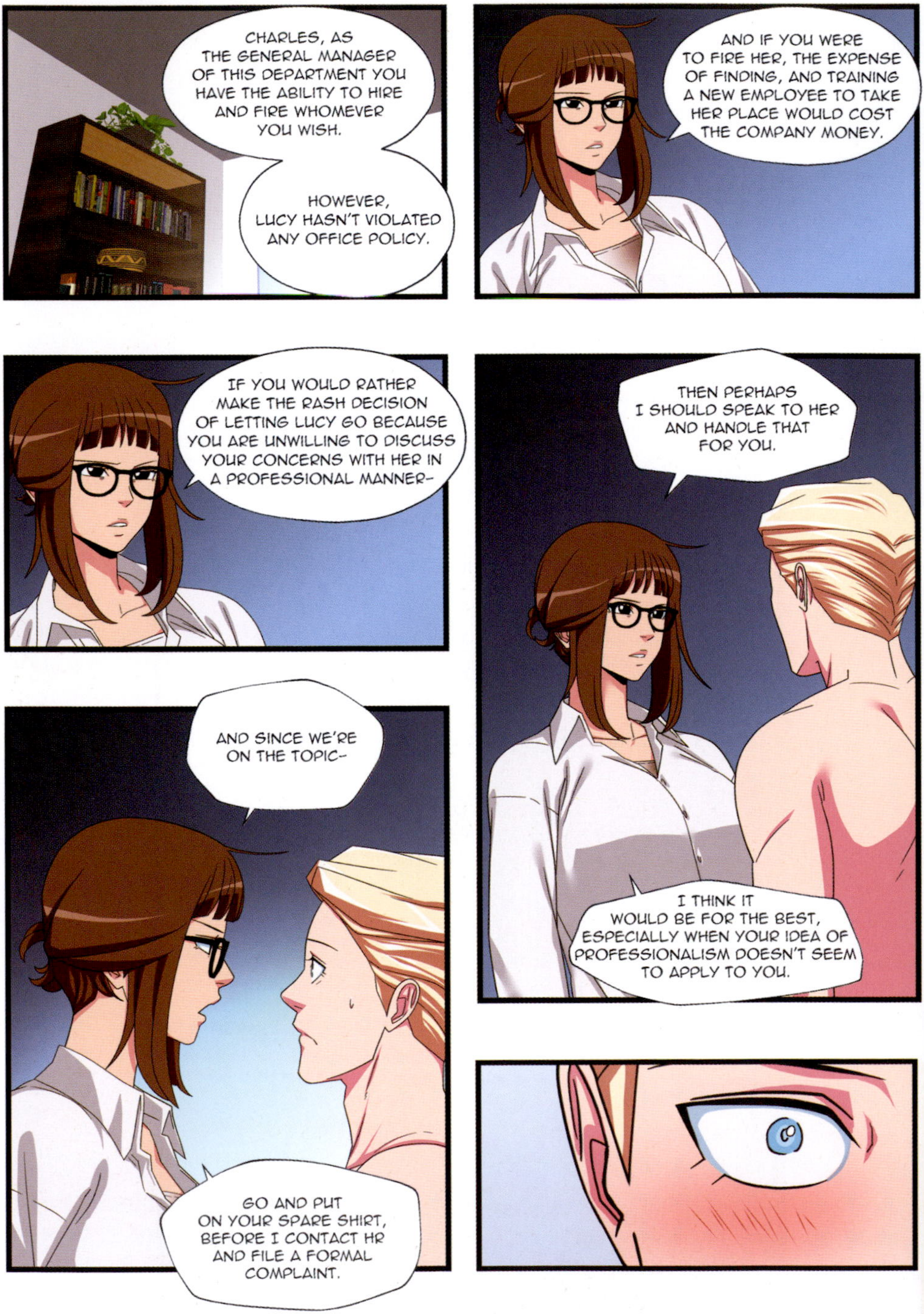
CHARLES, AS THE GENERAL MANAGER OF THIS DEPARTMENT YOU HAVE THE ABILITY TO HIRE AND FIRE WHOMEVER YOU WISH.
HOWEVER, LUCY HASN'T VIOLATED ANY OFFICE POLICY.
AND IF YOU WERE TO FIRE HER, THE EXPENSE OF FINDING, AND TRAINING A NEW EMPLOYEE TO TAKE HER PLACE WOULD COST THE COMPANY MONEY.
IF YOU WOULD RATHER MAKE THE RASH DECISION OF LETTING LUCY GO BECAUSE YOU ARE UNWILLING TO DISCUSS YOUR CONCERNS WITH HER IN A PROFESSIONAL MANNER-
THEN PERHAPS I SHOULD SPEAK TO HER AND HANDLE THAT FOR YOU.
I THINK IT WOULD BE FOR THE BEST, ESPECIALLY WHEN YOUR IDEA OF PROFESSIONALISM DOESN'T SEEM TO APPLY TO YOU.
AND SINCE WE'RE ON THE TOPIC-
GO AND PUT ON YOUR SPARE SHIRT, BEFORE I CONTACT HR AND FILE A FORMAL COMPLAINT.

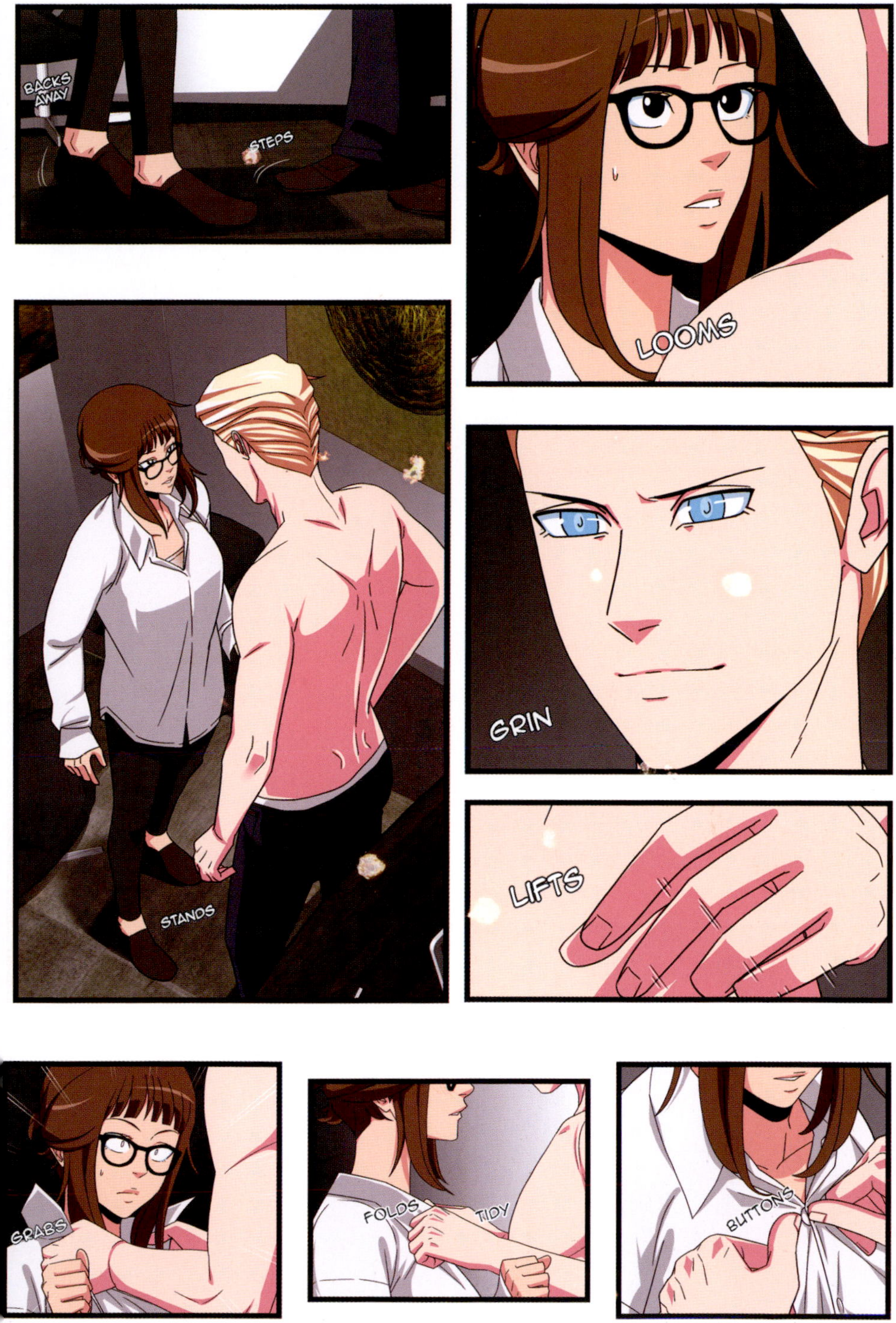
BACKS AWAY
STEPS
LOOMS
STANDS
GRIN
LIFTS
GRABS
FOLDS
TIDY
BUTTONS

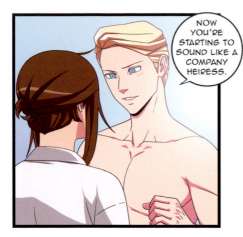

NOW YOU'RE STARTING TO SOUND LIKE A COMPANY HEIRESS.

ALLOW ME TO GET THE DOOR FOR YOU, MISS YOUNG.

T-THANKS.

FROZEN

OPENS

MR. YOUNG?

DAD?

ARE YOU ALRIGHT?

DAUGHTER

NOT DAUGHTER'S SHIRT

NERVOUS STANCE

GUILTY SWEATDROPP?!
SINGLE MALE
SHIRT AND TIE ARE OPEN
DAUGHTER AND SINGLE MALE IN ROOM ALONE?!
DAD?
NO PARENTAL SUPER-VISION
THIS IS TANYA CORTES REPORTING LIVE AT CORPORATE HILL, WHERE A MAN BY THE NAME OF SAMUEL YOUNG HAS BEEN ARRESTED FOR ALLEGEDLY STRANGLING HIS DEPARTMENT MANAGER TO DEATH WITH HIS BARE HANDS.
LIVE
24 NEWS
CORPORATE HI
NEWS
WITNESSES STATED MR. YOUNG WAS HEARD SCREAMING, "I MUST PROTECT THE VIRTUE OF MY PEACHY -PUMPKIN-POOH."
IT IS UNCLEAR WHAT PROVOKED THE ATTACK, BUT IT IS SUSPECTED IT WAS DUE TO MR. YOUNG'S DAUGHTER BEING IN A ROOM ALONE WITH A BOY.
SUCH A TRAGEDY.
24 NEWS
DAD?

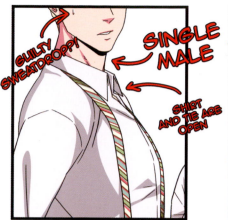

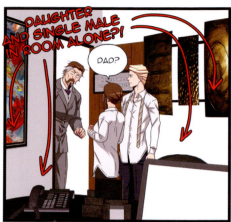

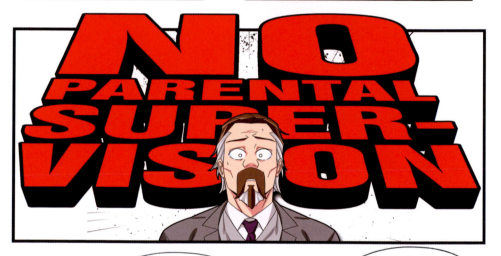

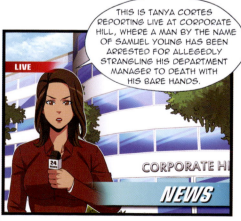

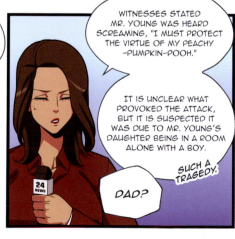

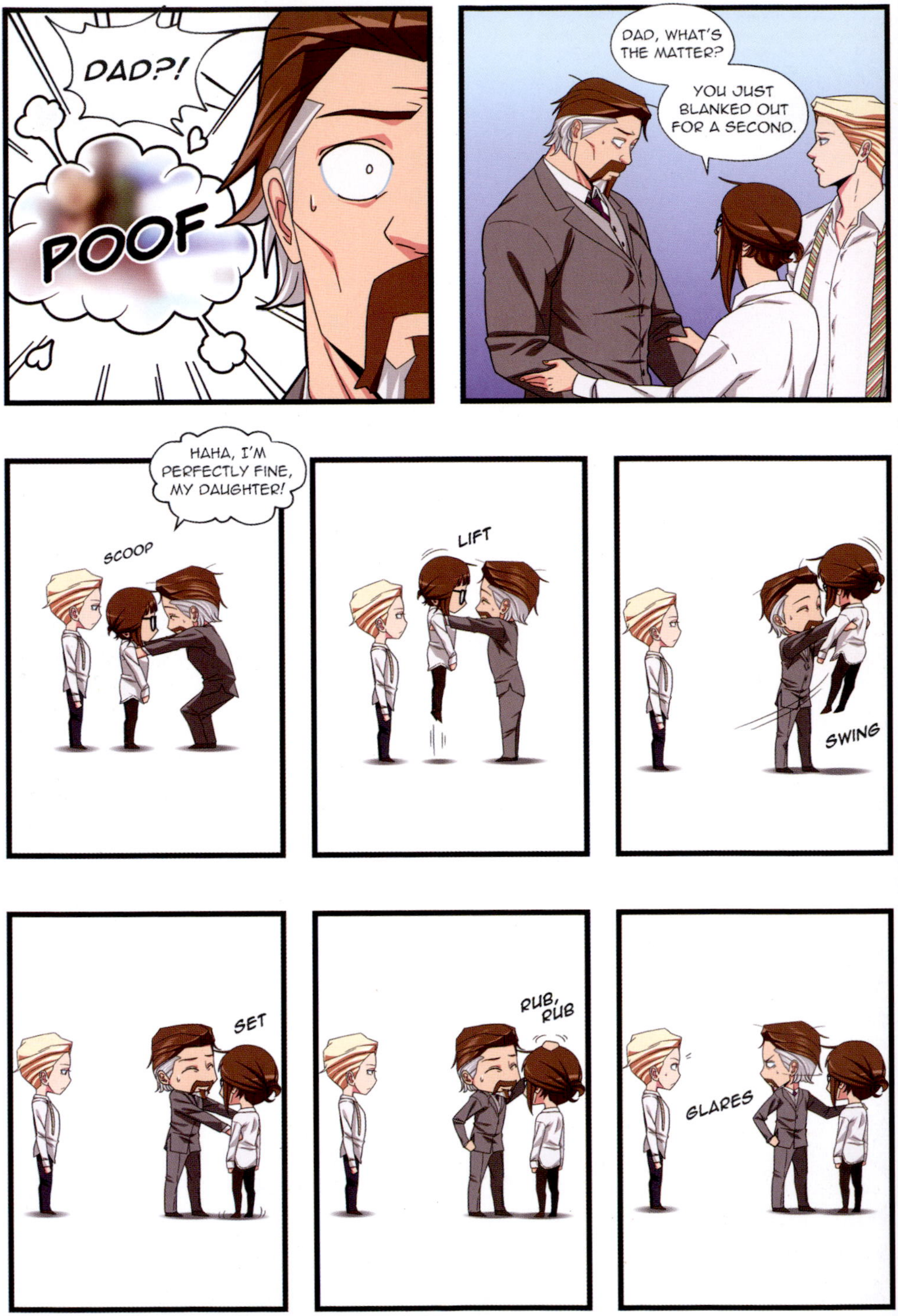
DAD?!
POOF
DAD, WHAT'S THE MATTER?
YOU JUST BLANKED OUT FOR A SECOND.
HAHA, I'M PERFECTLY FINE, MY DAUGHTER!
SCOOP
LIFT
SWING
SET
RUB, RUB
GLARES

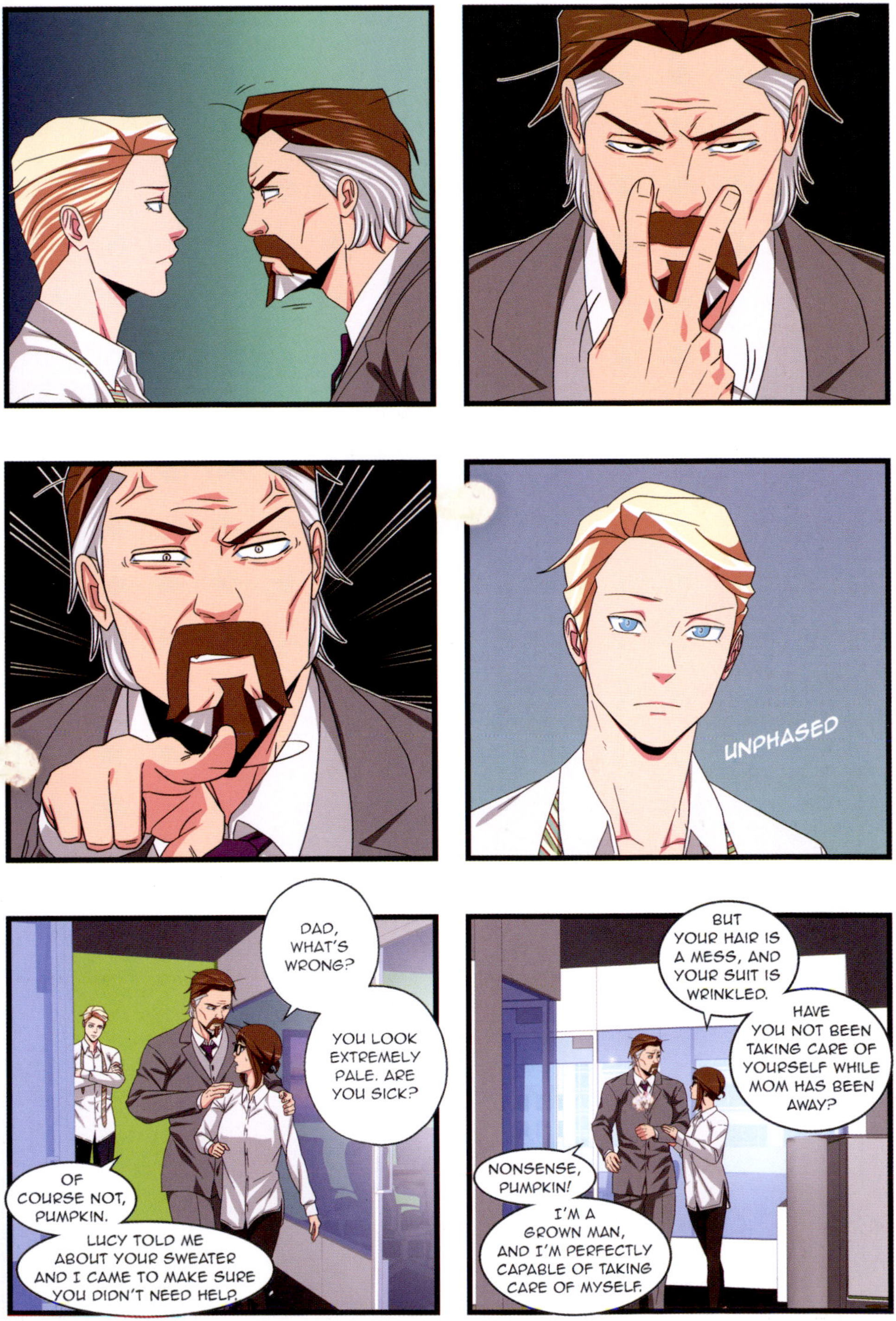
UNPHASED
DAD, WHAT'S WRONG?
YOU LOOK EXTREMELY PALE. ARE YOU SICK?
OF COURSE NOT, PUMPKIN.
LUCY TOLD ME ABOUT YOUR SWEATER AND I CAME TO MAKE SURE YOU DIDN'T NEED HELP.
BUT YOUR HAIR IS A MESS, AND YOUR SUIT IS WRINKLED.
HAVE YOU NOT BEEN TAKING CARE OF YOURSELF WHILE MOM HAS BEEN AWAY?
NONSENSE, PUMPKIN!
I'M A GROWN MAN, AND I'M PERFECTLY CAPABLE OF TAKING CARE OF MYSELF.

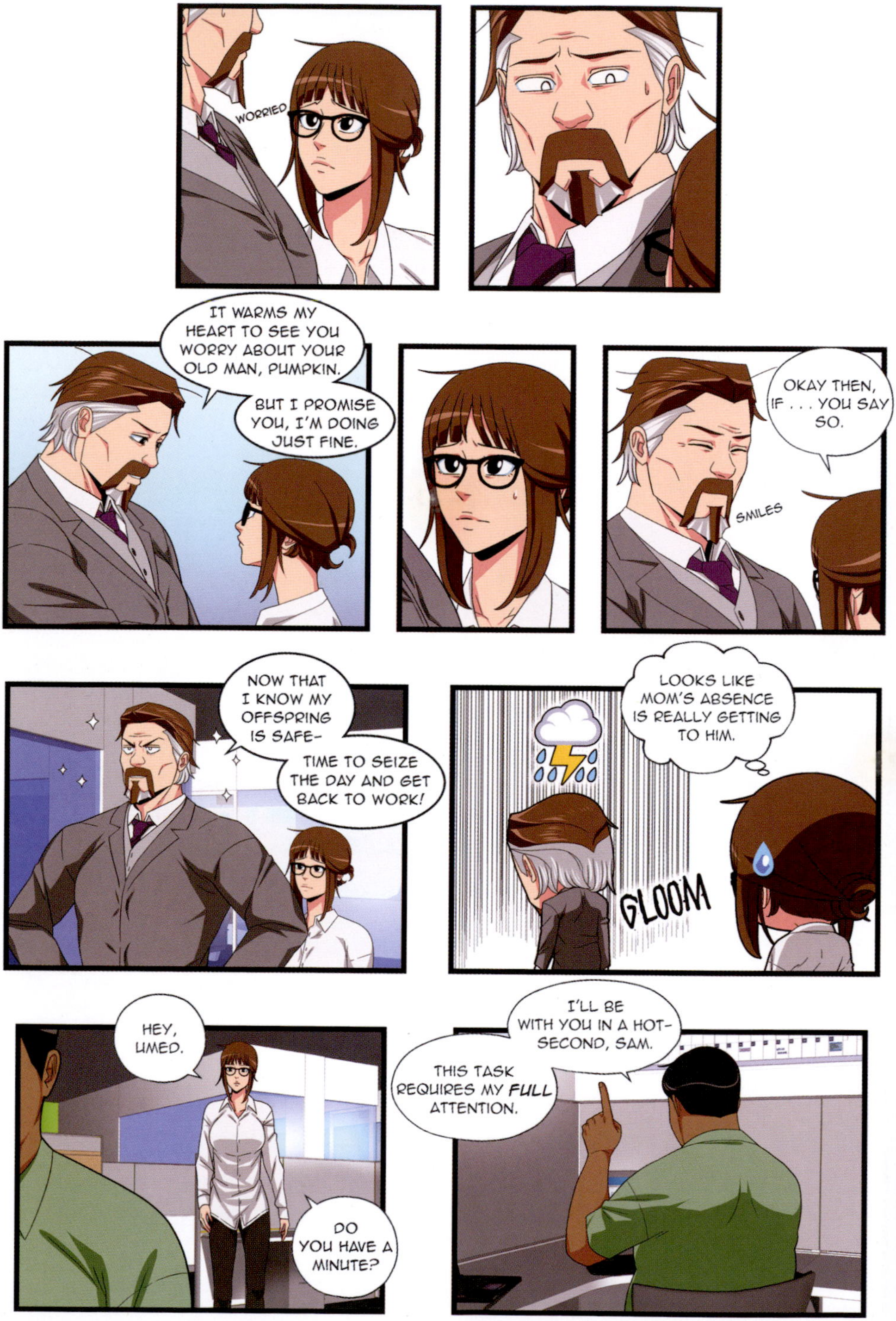
WORRIED
IT WARMS MY HEART TO SEE YOU WORRY ABOUT YOUR OLD MAN, PUMPKIN.
BUT I PROMISE YOU, I'M DOING JUST FINE.
OKAY THEN, IF . . . YOU SAY SO.
SMILES
NOW THAT I KNOW MY OFFSPRING IS SAFE-
TIME TO SEIZE THE DAY AND GET BACK TO WORK!
LOOKS LIKE MOM'S ABSENCE IS REALLY GETTING TO HIM.
GLOOM
HEY, UMED.
DO YOU HAVE A MINUTE?
I'LL BE WITH YOU IN A HOT-SECOND, SAM.
THIS TASK REQUIRES MY *FULL* ATTENTION.

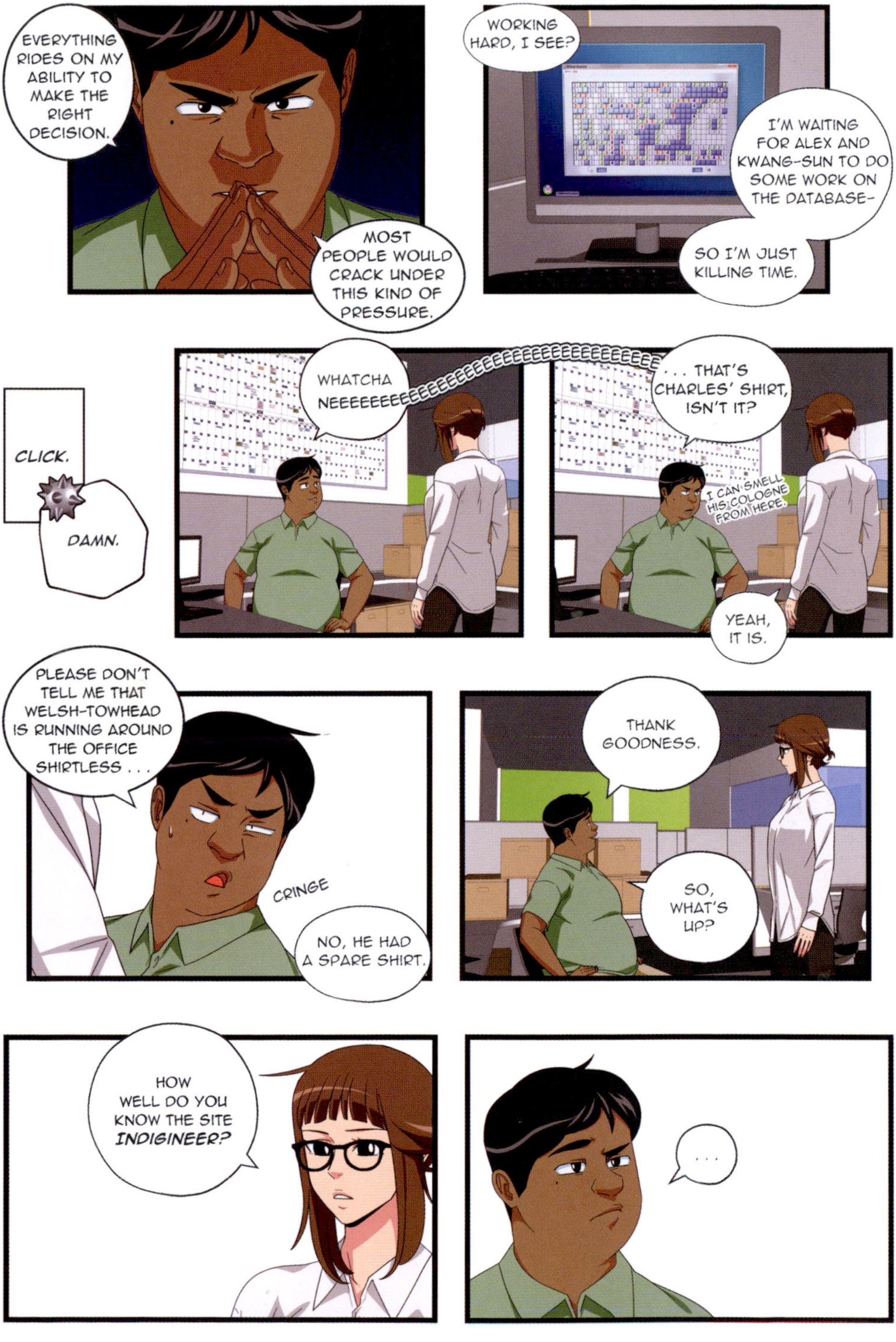
EVERYTHING RIDES ON MY ABILITY TO MAKE THE RIGHT DECISION.
MOST PEOPLE WOULD CRACK UNDER THIS KIND OF PRESSURE.
WORKING HARD, I SEE?
I'M WAITING FOR ALEX AND KWANG-SUN TO DO SOME WORK ON THE DATABASE-
SO I'M JUST KILLING TIME.
CLICK.
DAMN.
WHATCHA NEEEEEEEEEEEEEEEEEEEEEEEEEEEEEEEEEEEEEEEEEEEEEEEEEEEEE
. . . THAT'S CHARLES' SHIRT, ISN'T IT?
I CAN SMELL HIS COLOGNE FROM HERE.
YEAH, IT IS.
PLEASE DON'T TELL ME THAT WELSH-TOWHEAD IS RUNNING AROUND THE OFFICE SHIRTLESS . . .
CRINGE
NO, HE HAD A SPARE SHIRT.
THANK GOODNESS.
SO, WHAT'S UP?
HOW WELL DO YOU KNOW THE SITE *INDIGINEER*?
. . .

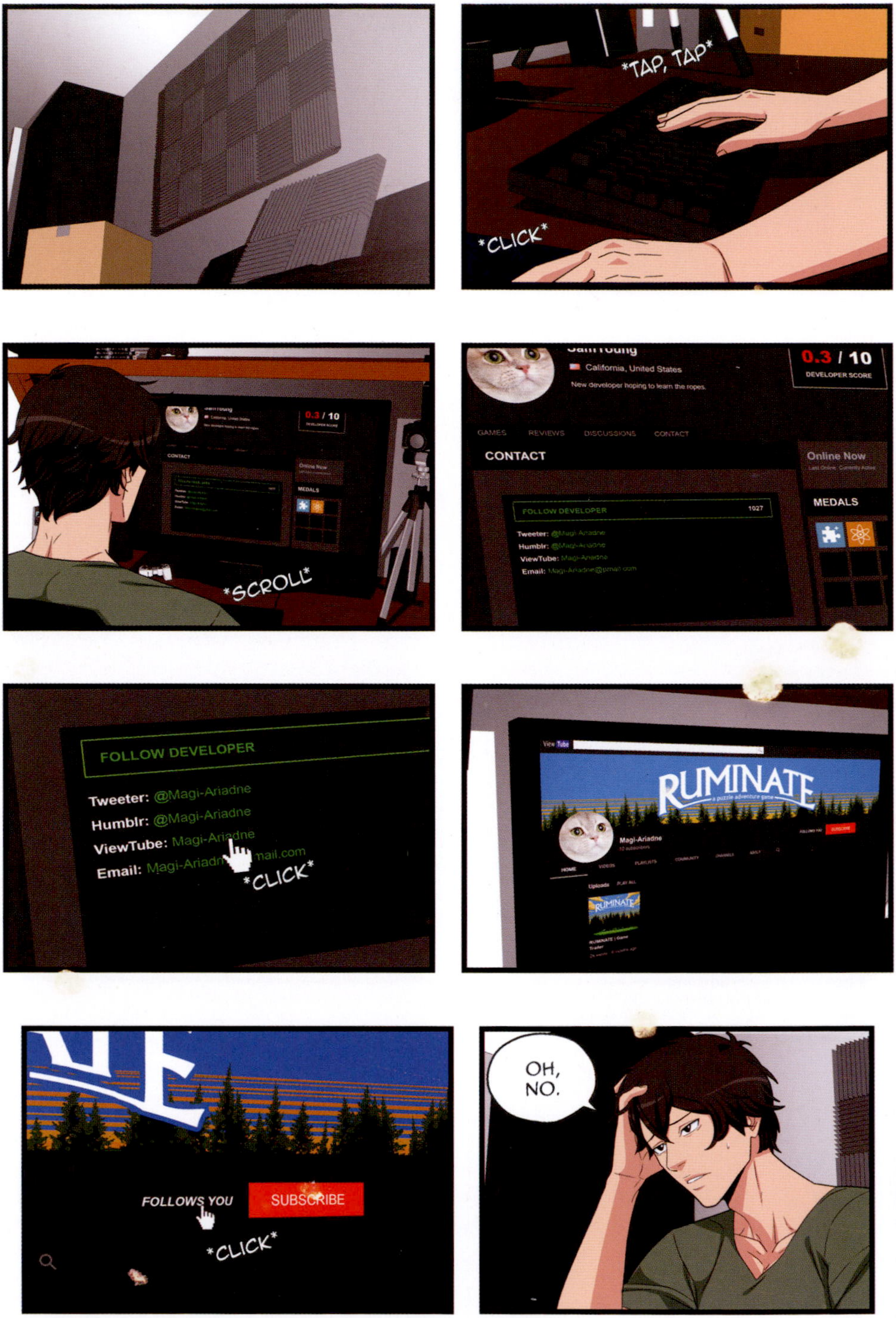
TAP, TAP
CLICK
SCROLL
0.3 / 10
DEVELOPER SCORE
California, United States
New developer hoping to learn the ropes.
GAMES REVIEWS DISCUSSIONS CONTACT
CONTACT
Online Now
MEDALS
FOLLOW DEVELOPER 1027
Tweeter: @Magi-Ariadne
Humblr: @Magi-Ariadne
ViewTube: Magi-Ariadne
FOLLOW DEVELOPER
Tweeter: @Magi-Ariadne
Humblr: @Magi-Ariadne
ViewTube: Magi-Ariadne
Email: Magi-Ariadn mail.com
CLICK
View Tube
RUMINATE
Magi-Ariadne
FOLLOWS YOU
SUBSCRIBE
CLICK
OH, NO.

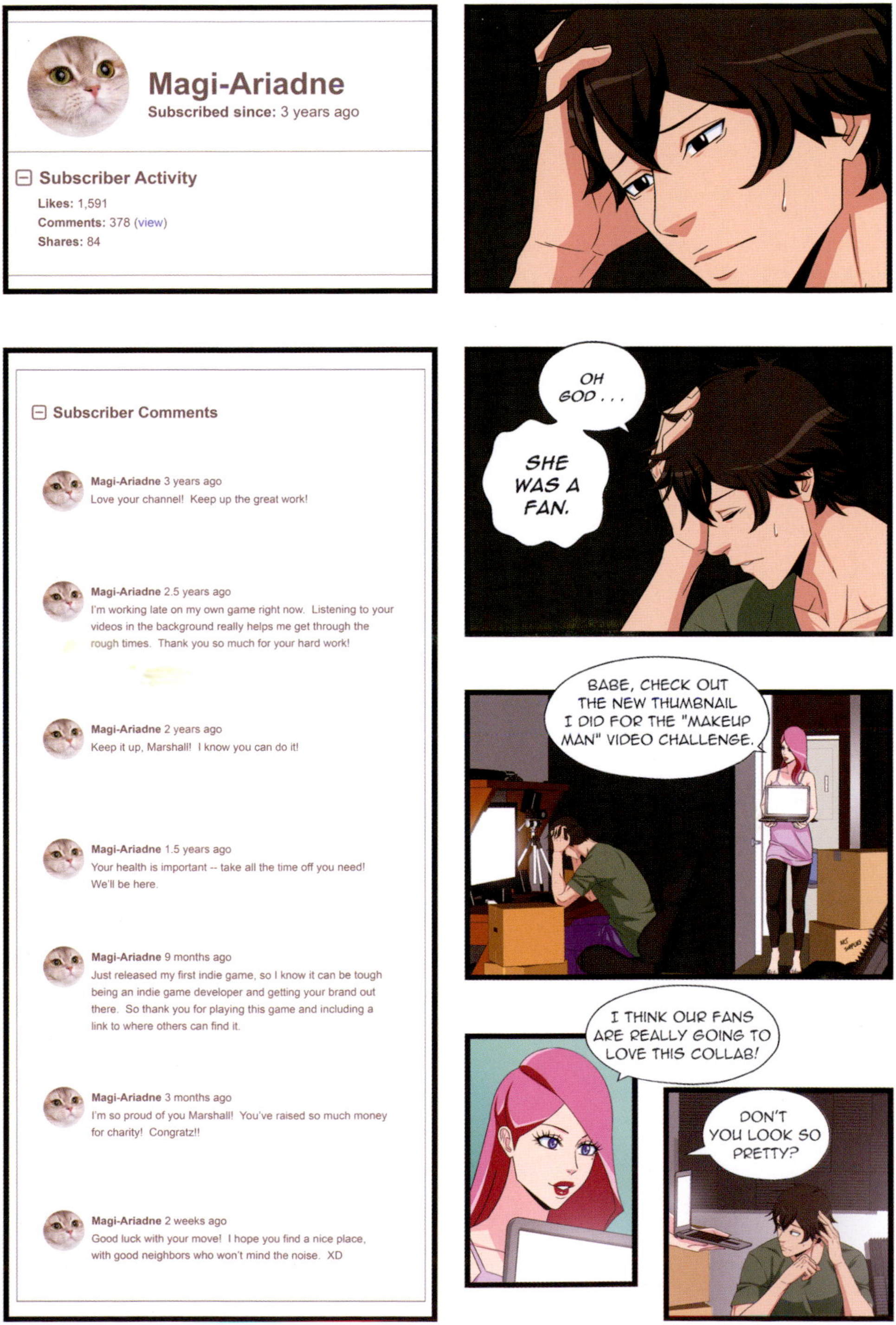
Magi-Ariadne
Subscribed since: 3 years ago
Subscriber Activity
Likes: 1,591
Comments: 378 (view)
Shares: 84
Subscriber Comments
Magi-Ariadne 3 years ago
Love your channel! Keep up the great work!
Magi-Ariadne 2.5 years ago
I'm working late on my own game right now. Listening to your videos in the background really helps me get through the rough times. Thank you so much for your hard work!
Magi-Ariadne 2 years ago
Keep it up, Marshall! I know you can do it!
Magi-Ariadne 1.5 years ago
Your health is important -- take all the time off you need! We'll be here.
Magi-Ariadne 9 months ago
Just released my first indie game, so I know it can be tough being an indie game developer and getting your brand out there. So thank you for playing this game and including a link to where others can find it.
Magi-Ariadne 3 months ago
I'm so proud of you Marshall! You've raised so much money for charity! Congratz!!
Magi-Ariadne 2 weeks ago
Good luck with your move! I hope you find a nice place, with good neighbors who won't mind the noise. XD
OH GOD . . .
SHE WAS A FAN.
BABE, CHECK OUT THE NEW THUMBNAIL I DID FOR THE "MAKEUP MAN" VIDEO CHALLENGE.
I THINK OUR FANS ARE REALLY GOING TO LOVE THIS COLLAB!
DON'T YOU LOOK SO PRETTY?

IT WAS *TOTALLY* WORTH IT!

MARSHALL LAW MAKE-UP MAN

THIS VIDEO IS GOING TO GET SO MANY VIEWS!

MY MOM WILL BE PROUD.

SO WHAT'S BOTHERING YOU?

ARE YOU IN ONE OF YOUR "MOODS"?

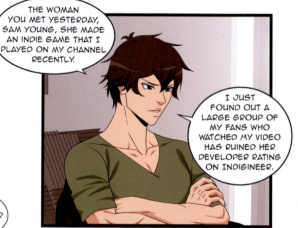

THE WOMAN YOU MET YESTERDAY, SAM YOUNG, SHE MADE AN INDIE GAME THAT I PLAYED ON MY CHANNEL RECENTLY.

I JUST FOUND OUT A LARGE GROUP OF MY FANS WHO WATCHED MY VIDEO HAS RUINED HER DEVELOPER RATING ON INDIGINEER.

INDIGINEER

STORE COMMUNITY ABOUT SUPPORT

SamYoung
California, United States
New developer hoping to learn the ropes.

0.3 / 10
DEVELOPER SCORE

GAMES   REVIEWS   DISCUSSIONS   CONTACT
CONTACT

FOLLOW DEVELOPER

Tweeter: @Magi-Ariadne
Humbilr: @Magi-Ariadne
ViewTube: Magi-Ariadne
Email: MagiAriadne@gmail.com

IT'S ESSENTIALLY BLACKLISTED HER AS A GAMES DEVELOPER.

I COULD TELL THAT SAM HAD A LOT OF ANIMOSITY TOWARDS ME, BUT I THOUGHT IT WAS BECAUSE SHE COULDN'T HANDLE CRITIQUE FOR HER GAME.

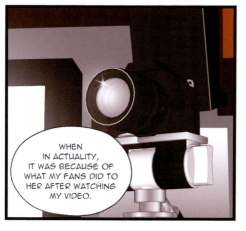

WHEN IN ACTUALITY, IT WAS BECAUSE OF WHAT MY FANS DID TO HER AFTER WATCHING MY VIDEO.

AND TO MAKE MATTERS WORSE, I ALSO JUST FOUND OUT SAM HAS BEEN A FAN OF MINE SINCE I STARTED ON VIEWTUBE.

I'VE . . . HURT ONE OF MY OLDEST FANS.

BUMMER.

SO WHAT ARE YOU GOING TO DO ABOUT IT?

I'M NOT SURE . . .

I THINK I SHOULD RECORD A VLOG ADDRESSING IT–

TELL MY FANS WHAT THEY DID WAS WRONG, AND THAT THEY SHOULD DELETE THEIR VOTES ON INDIGINEER.

THAT WAY SOME OF SAM'S RATING MIGHT BE SAVED.

GREAT IDEA.

THAT TOTALLY **WON'T BACKFIRE.**

WHAT DO YOU MEAN?

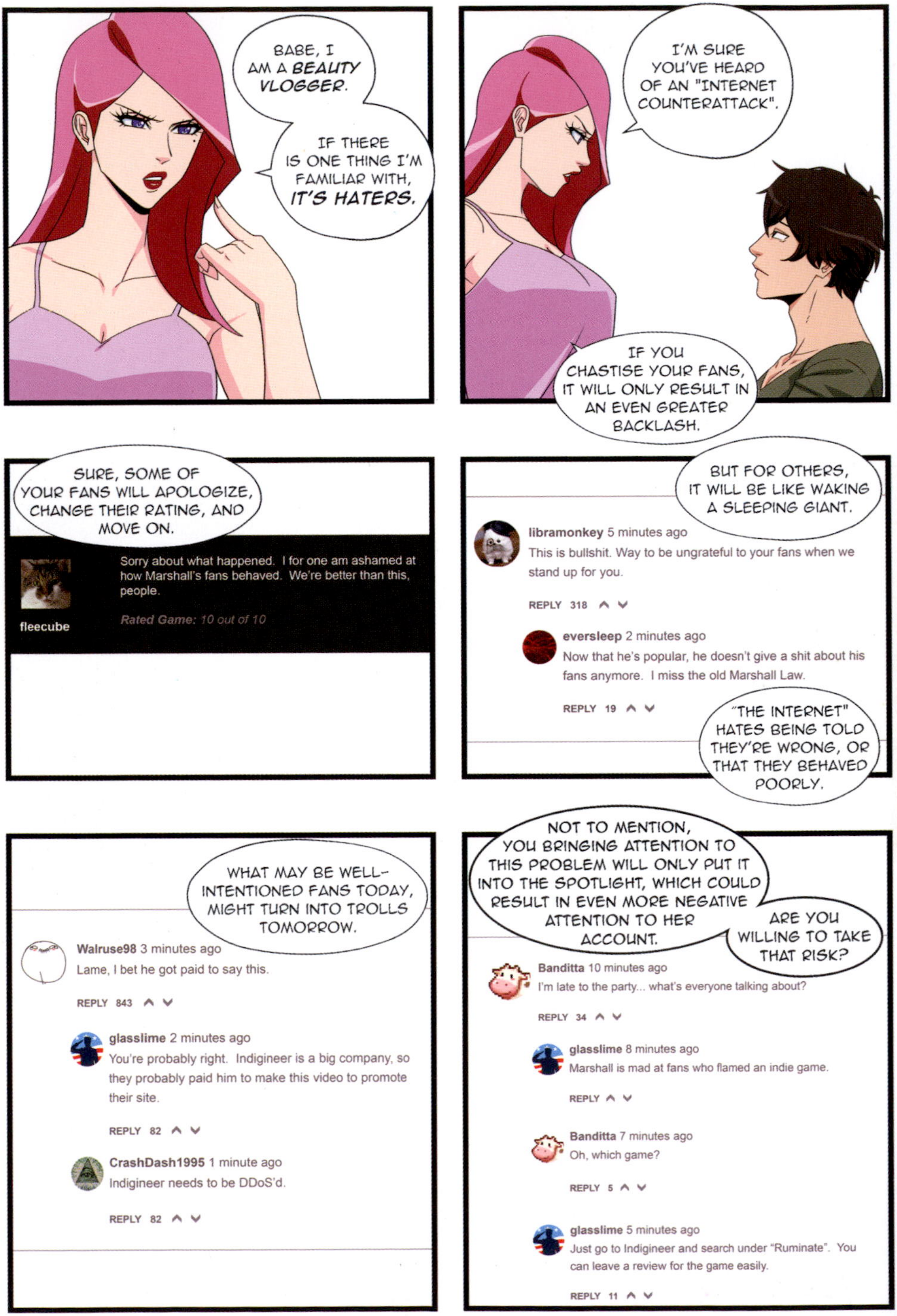
BABE, I AM A BEAUTY VLOGGER.
IF THERE IS ONE THING I'M FAMILIAR WITH, IT'S HATERS.
I'M SURE YOU'VE HEARD OF AN "INTERNET COUNTERATTACK".
IF YOU CHASTISE YOUR FANS, IT WILL ONLY RESULT IN AN EVEN GREATER BACKLASH.
SURE, SOME OF YOUR FANS WILL APOLOGIZE, CHANGE THEIR RATING, AND MOVE ON.
fleecube
Sorry about what happened. I for one am ashamed at how Marshall's fans behaved. We're better than this, people.
Rated Game: 10 out of 10
BUT FOR OTHERS, IT WILL BE LIKE WAKING A SLEEPING GIANT.
libramonkey 5 minutes ago
This is bullshit. Way to be ungrateful to your fans when we stand up for you.
REPLY 318
eversleep 2 minutes ago
Now that he's popular, he doesn't give a shit about his fans anymore. I miss the old Marshall Law.
REPLY 19
"THE INTERNET" HATES BEING TOLD THEY'RE WRONG, OR THAT THEY BEHAVED POORLY.
WHAT MAY BE WELL-INTENTIONED FANS TODAY, MIGHT TURN INTO TROLLS TOMORROW.
Walruse98 3 minutes ago
Lame, I bet he got paid to say this.
REPLY 843
glasslime 2 minutes ago
You're probably right. Indigineer is a big company, so they probably paid him to make this video to promote their site.
REPLY 82
CrashDash1995 1 minute ago
Indigineer needs to be DDoS'd.
REPLY 82
NOT TO MENTION, YOU BRINGING ATTENTION TO THIS PROBLEM WILL ONLY PUT IT INTO THE SPOTLIGHT, WHICH COULD RESULT IN EVEN MORE NEGATIVE ATTENTION TO HER ACCOUNT.
ARE YOU WILLING TO TAKE THAT RISK?
Banditta 10 minutes ago
I'm late to the party... what's everyone talking about?
REPLY 34
glasslime 8 minutes ago
Marshall is mad at fans who flamed an indie game.
REPLY
Banditta 7 minutes ago
Oh, which game?
REPLY 5
glasslime 5 minutes ago
Just go to Indigineer and search under "Ruminate". You can leave a review for the game easily.
REPLY 11

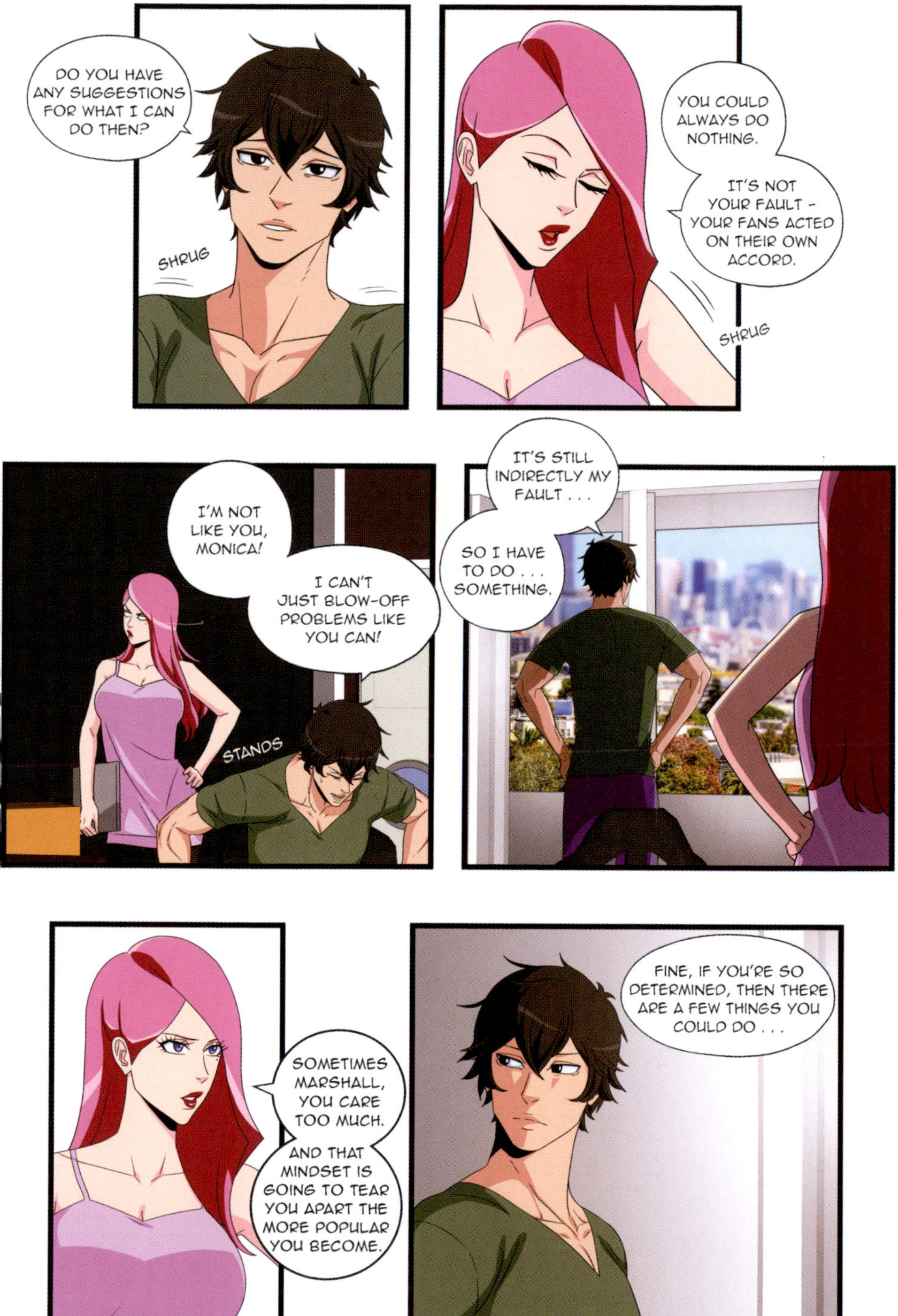
DO YOU HAVE ANY SUGGESTIONS FOR WHAT I CAN DO THEN?
SHRUG
YOU COULD ALWAYS DO NOTHING.
IT'S NOT YOUR FAULT - YOUR FANS ACTED ON THEIR OWN ACCORD.
SHRUG
I'M NOT LIKE YOU, MONICA!
I CAN'T JUST BLOW-OFF PROBLEMS LIKE YOU CAN!
STANDS
IT'S STILL INDIRECTLY MY FAULT . . .
SO I HAVE TO DO . . . SOMETHING.
SOMETIMES MARSHALL, YOU CARE TOO MUCH.
AND THAT MINDSET IS GOING TO TEAR YOU APART THE MORE POPULAR YOU BECOME.
FINE, IF YOU'RE SO DETERMINED, THEN THERE ARE A FEW THINGS YOU COULD DO . . .

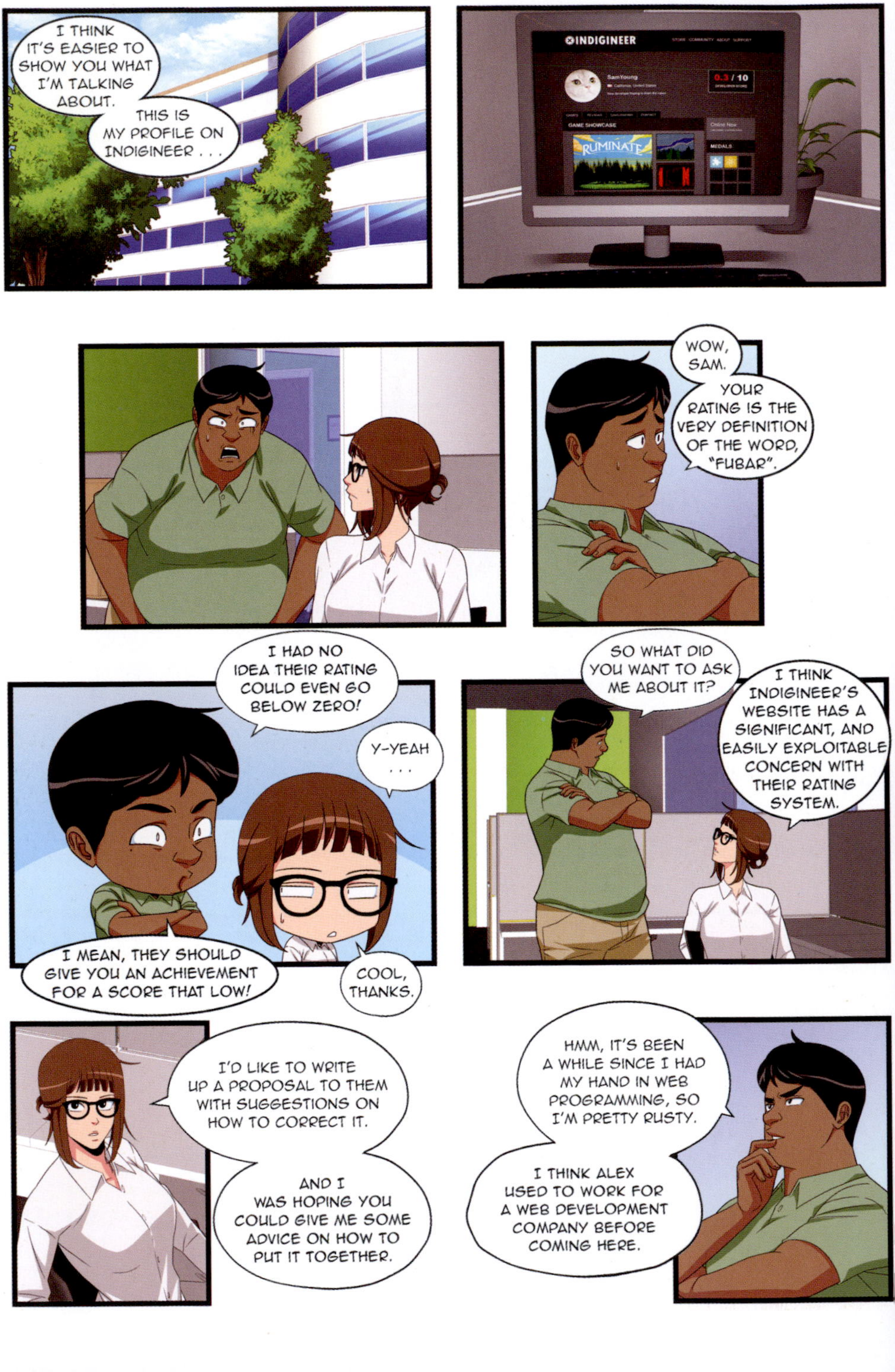

I THINK IT'S EASIER TO SHOW YOU WHAT I'M TALKING ABOUT.
THIS IS MY PROFILE ON INDIGINEER . . .
INDIGINEER
0.3 / 10
GAME SHOWCASE
RUMINATE
MEDALS
WOW, SAM.
YOUR RATING IS THE VERY DEFINITION OF THE WORD, "FUBAR".
I HAD NO IDEA THEIR RATING COULD EVEN GO BELOW ZERO!
Y-YEAH . . .
I MEAN, THEY SHOULD GIVE YOU AN ACHIEVEMENT FOR A SCORE THAT LOW!
COOL, THANKS.
SO WHAT DID YOU WANT TO ASK ME ABOUT IT?
I THINK INDIGINEER'S WEBSITE HAS A SIGNIFICANT, AND EASILY EXPLOITABLE CONCERN WITH THEIR RATING SYSTEM.
I'D LIKE TO WRITE UP A PROPOSAL TO THEM WITH SUGGESTIONS ON HOW TO CORRECT IT.
AND I WAS HOPING YOU COULD GIVE ME SOME ADVICE ON HOW TO PUT IT TOGETHER.
HMM, IT'S BEEN A WHILE SINCE I HAD MY HAND IN WEB PROGRAMMING, SO I'M PRETTY RUSTY.
I THINK ALEX USED TO WORK FOR A WEB DEVELOPMENT COMPANY BEFORE COMING HERE.

HEY, ALEX!

COME HERE FOR A SECOND— WE WANT TO ASK YOU SOMETHING.

PRAIRIE DOG

YOU USED TO BUILD WEBSITES BEFORE YOU WERE HIRED ON HERE, RIGHT?

MMHMM.

OKAY, HYPOTHETICAL QUESTION—

YOU'VE BUILT AN ONLINE STORE THAT USES A RATING SYSTEM FOR ITS PRODUCTS.

BUT ONE OF THE PRODUCTS GOES VIRAL, AND THOUSANDS OF PEOPLE COME TO THE SITE TO RATE THE PRODUCT POORLY FOR NO OTHER REASON THAN MOB MENTALITY.

HOW WOULD YOU, AS A PROGRAMMER, DEVELOP YOUR CODE TO KEEP THAT FROM HAPPENING?

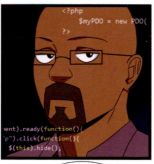

. . .

BRUH?

HEY, FREDDIE!

COME HERE FOR A SEC!

PRAIRIE DOG

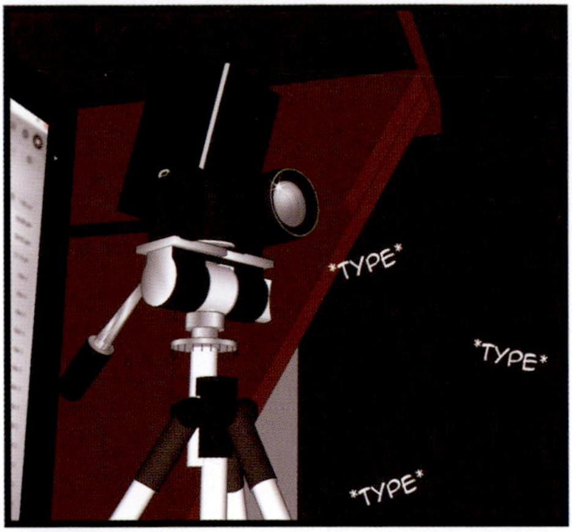
TYPE
TYPE
TYPE

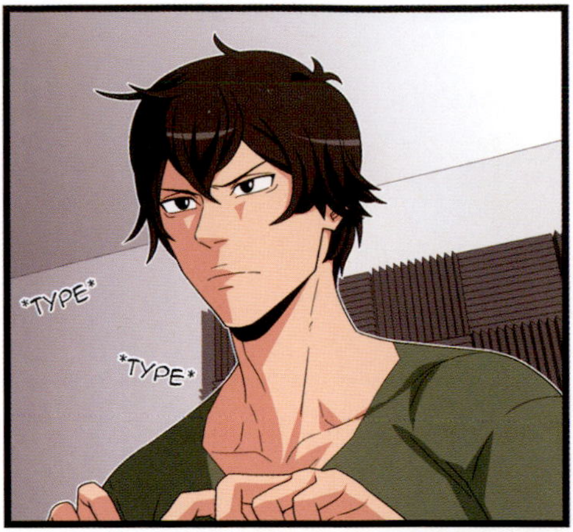
TYPE
TYPE

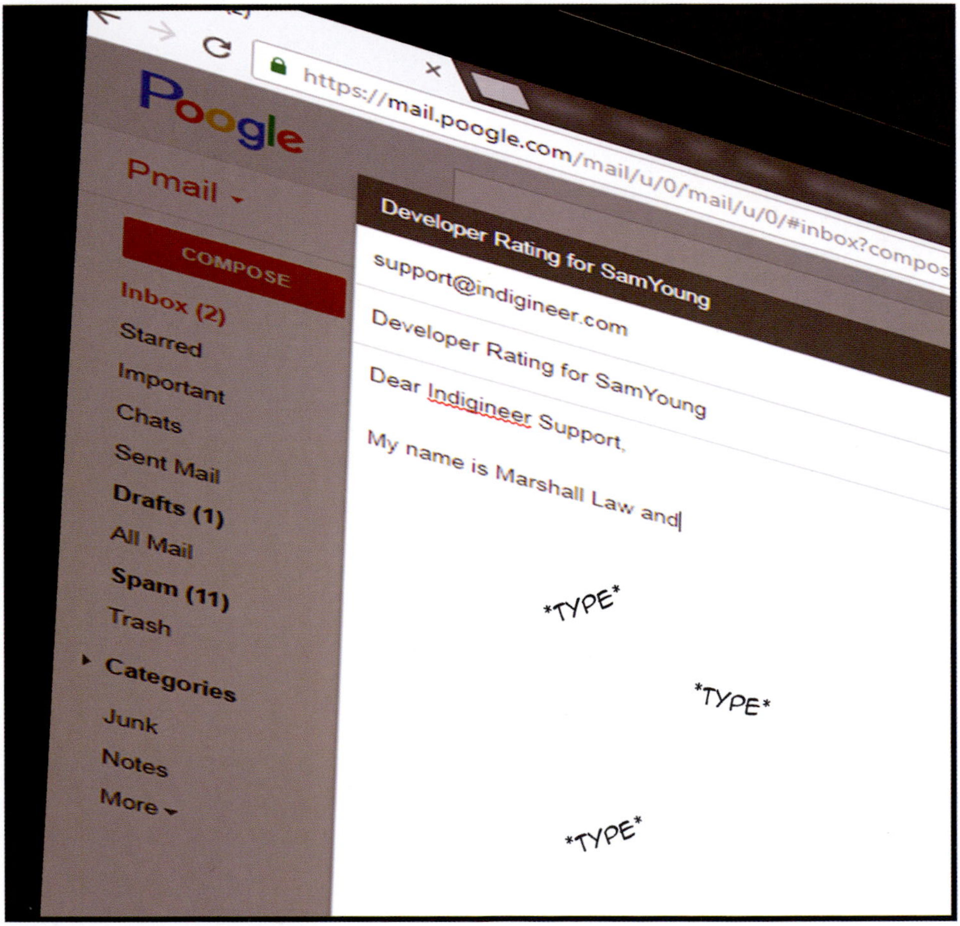
https://mail.poogle.com/mail/u/0/mail/u/0/#inbox?compos
Poogle
Pmail
COMPOSE
Inbox (2)
Starred
Important
Chats
Sent Mail
Drafts (1)
All Mail
Spam (11)
Trash
Categories
Junk
Notes
More
Developer Rating for SamYoung
support@indigineer.com
Developer Rating for SamYoung
Dear Indigineer Support,
My name is Marshall Law and
TYPE
TYPE
TYPE

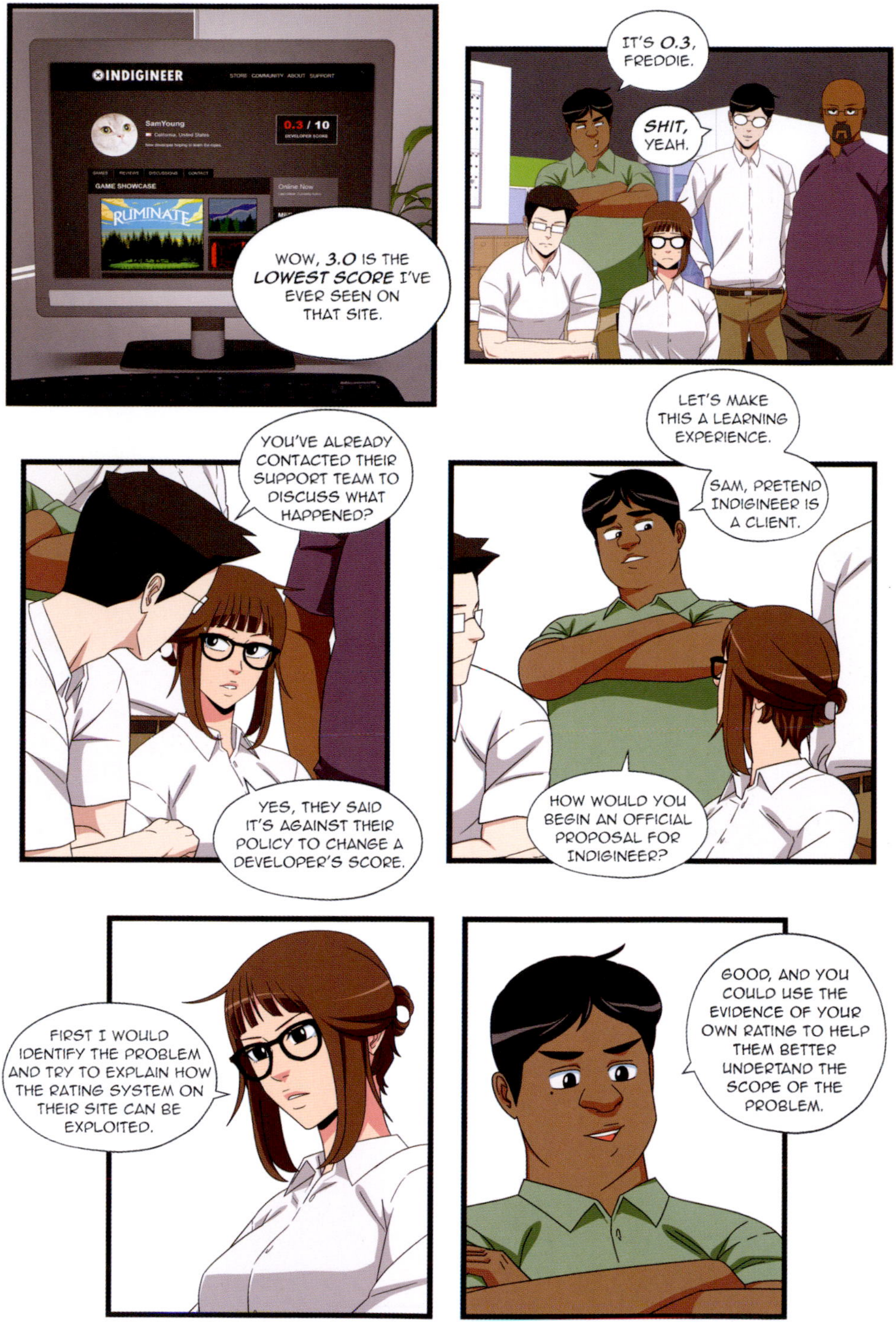
INDIGINEER
STORE COMMUNITY ABOUT SUPPORT
SamYoung
California, United States
0.3 / 10
DEVELOPER SCORE
GAMES REVIEWS DISCUSSIONS CONTACT
GAME SHOWCASE
RUMINATE
Online Now
WOW, *3.0* IS THE *LOWEST SCORE* I'VE EVER SEEN ON THAT SITE.
IT'S *0.3*, FREDDIE.
SHIT, YEAH.
YOU'VE ALREADY CONTACTED THEIR SUPPORT TEAM TO DISCUSS WHAT HAPPENED?
YES, THEY SAID IT'S AGAINST THEIR POLICY TO CHANGE A DEVELOPER'S SCORE.
LET'S MAKE THIS A LEARNING EXPERIENCE.
SAM, PRETEND INDIGINEER IS A CLIENT.
HOW WOULD YOU BEGIN AN OFFICIAL PROPOSAL FOR INDIGINEER?
FIRST I WOULD IDENTIFY THE PROBLEM AND TRY TO EXPLAIN HOW THE RATING SYSTEM ON THEIR SITE CAN BE EXPLOITED.
GOOD, AND YOU COULD USE THE EVIDENCE OF YOUR OWN RATING TO HELP THEM BETTER UNDERTAND THE SCOPE OF THE PROBLEM.

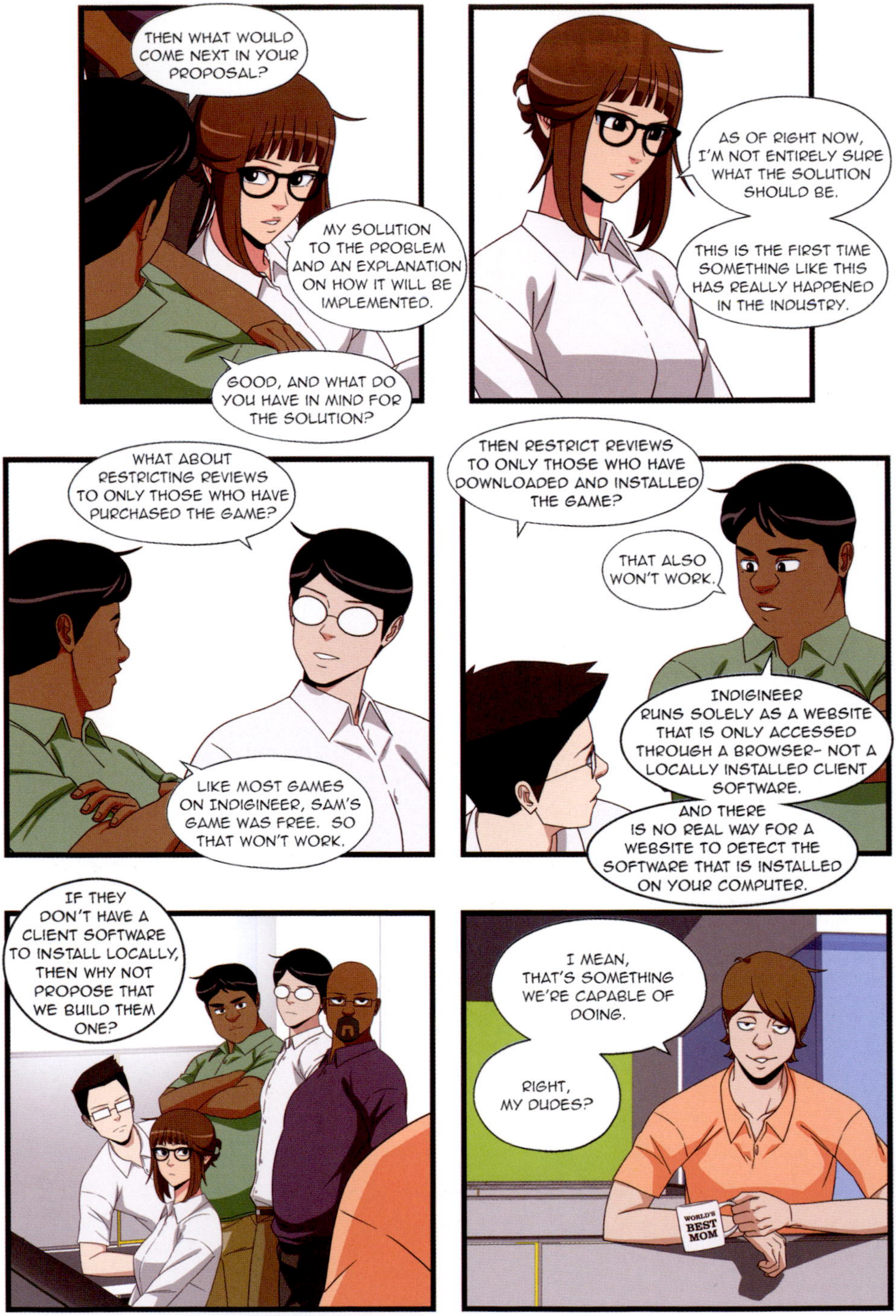
THEN WHAT WOULD COME NEXT IN YOUR PROPOSAL?
MY SOLUTION TO THE PROBLEM AND AN EXPLANATION ON HOW IT WILL BE IMPLEMENTED.
GOOD, AND WHAT DO YOU HAVE IN MIND FOR THE SOLUTION?
AS OF RIGHT NOW, I'M NOT ENTIRELY SURE WHAT THE SOLUTION SHOULD BE.
THIS IS THE FIRST TIME SOMETHING LIKE THIS HAS REALLY HAPPENED IN THE INDUSTRY.
WHAT ABOUT RESTRICTING REVIEWS TO ONLY THOSE WHO HAVE PURCHASED THE GAME?
LIKE MOST GAMES ON INDIGINEER, SAM'S GAME WAS FREE. SO THAT WON'T WORK.
THEN RESTRICT REVIEWS TO ONLY THOSE WHO HAVE DOWNLOADED AND INSTALLED THE GAME?
THAT ALSO WON'T WORK.
INDIGINEER RUNS SOLELY AS A WEBSITE THAT IS ONLY ACCESSED THROUGH A BROWSER- NOT A LOCALLY INSTALLED CLIENT SOFTWARE.
AND THERE IS NO REAL WAY FOR A WEBSITE TO DETECT THE SOFTWARE THAT IS INSTALLED ON YOUR COMPUTER.
IF THEY DON'T HAVE A CLIENT SOFTWARE TO INSTALL LOCALLY, THEN WHY NOT PROPOSE THAT WE BUILD THEM ONE?
I MEAN, THAT'S SOMETHING WE'RE CAPABLE OF DOING.
RIGHT, MY DUDES?
WORLD'S BEST MOM

INDIGINEER DOES SEEM TO HAVE OUTGROWN ITS WEBSITE-ONLY PLATFORM.

THAT'S NOT A HALF-BAD IDEA, JACOB.

THANK YOU FOR ACKNOWLEDGING, MY DUDE.

WORLD'S BEST MOM

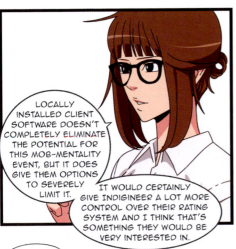

LOCALLY INSTALLED CLIENT SOFTWARE DOESN'T COMPLETELY ELIMINATE THE POTENTIAL FOR THIS MOB-MENTALITY EVENT, BUT IT DOES GIVE THEM OPTIONS TO SEVERELY LIMIT IT.

IT WOULD CERTAINLY GIVE INDIGINEER A LOT MORE CONTROL OVER THEIR RATING SYSTEM AND I THINK THAT'S SOMETHING THEY WOULD BE VERY INTERESTED IN.

I LIKE IT.

WRITE UP THE PROPOSAL, SAM.

AND THEN I'LL REVIEW IT, BEFORE WE SHOW IT TO YOUR DAD AND CHARLES FOR APPROVAL.

THIS COULD BE A GREAT OPPORTUNITY FOR OUR COMPANY.

YOU ACTUALLY WANT ME . . .

TO WRITE IT ON MY OWN?

HECK YEAH! THIS IS YOUR BABY, AND IT WOULD BE GOOD FOR YOU TO GET MORE EXPERIENCE OUTSIDE OF CODING AND DESIGN.

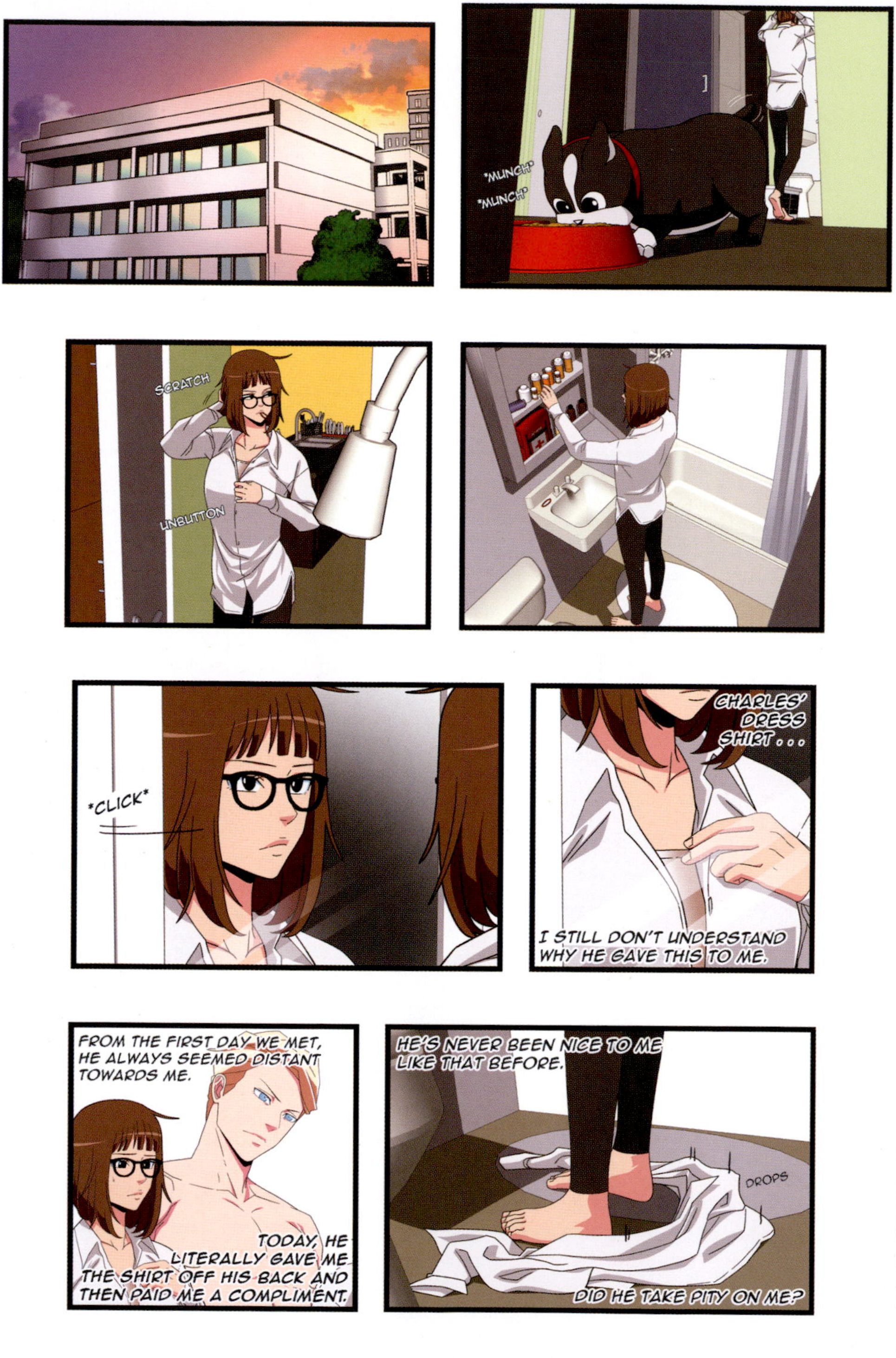
MUNCH
MUNCH
SCRATCH
UNBUTTON
CLICK
CHARLES' DRESS SHIRT . . .
I STILL DON'T UNDERSTAND WHY HE GAVE THIS TO ME.
FROM THE FIRST DAY WE MET, HE ALWAYS SEEMED DISTANT TOWARDS ME.
TODAY, HE LITERALLY GAVE ME THE SHIRT OFF HIS BACK AND THEN PAID ME A COMPLIMENT.
HE'S NEVER BEEN NICE TO ME LIKE THAT BEFORE.
DROPS
DID HE TAKE PITY ON ME?

AND WAS HE REALLY GOING TO FIRE LUCY?

SQUEAKS

CHARLES HAS ALWAYS BEEN A STICKLER FOR THE RULES, BUT EVEN HE DOESN'T NORMALLY ACT THAT RASH.

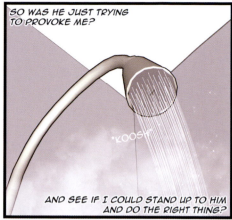

SO WAS HE JUST TRYING TO PROVOKE ME?

KOOSH

AND SEE IF I COULD STAND UP TO HIM AND DO THE RIGHT THING?

IF THAT'S THE CASE, I'M NOT SURE IF I LIKE THE IDEA OF BEING "TESTED".

KLINK

KLINK

I WAS ABLE TO CONFRONT HIM THAT TIME FOR LUCY'S SAKE, BUT I MAY NOT BE ABLE TO THE NEXT TIME.

SHOOOOSH

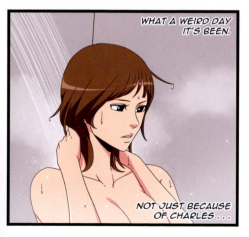

WHAT A WEIRD DAY IT'S BEEN.

NOT JUST BECAUSE OF CHARLES . . .

BUT RUNNING INTO MARSHALL LAW AND HIS FANS.

THANKS FOR WATCHING MY VLOG, GUYS!

AND THANKS AGAIN FOR 500 SUBSCRIBERS!

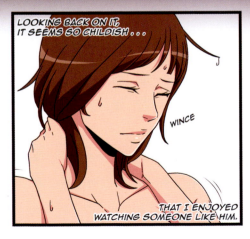

LOOKING BACK ON IT, IT SEEMS SO CHILDISH . . .

WINCE

THAT I ENJOYED WATCHING SOMEONE LIKE HIM.

"DRIP, DRIP"

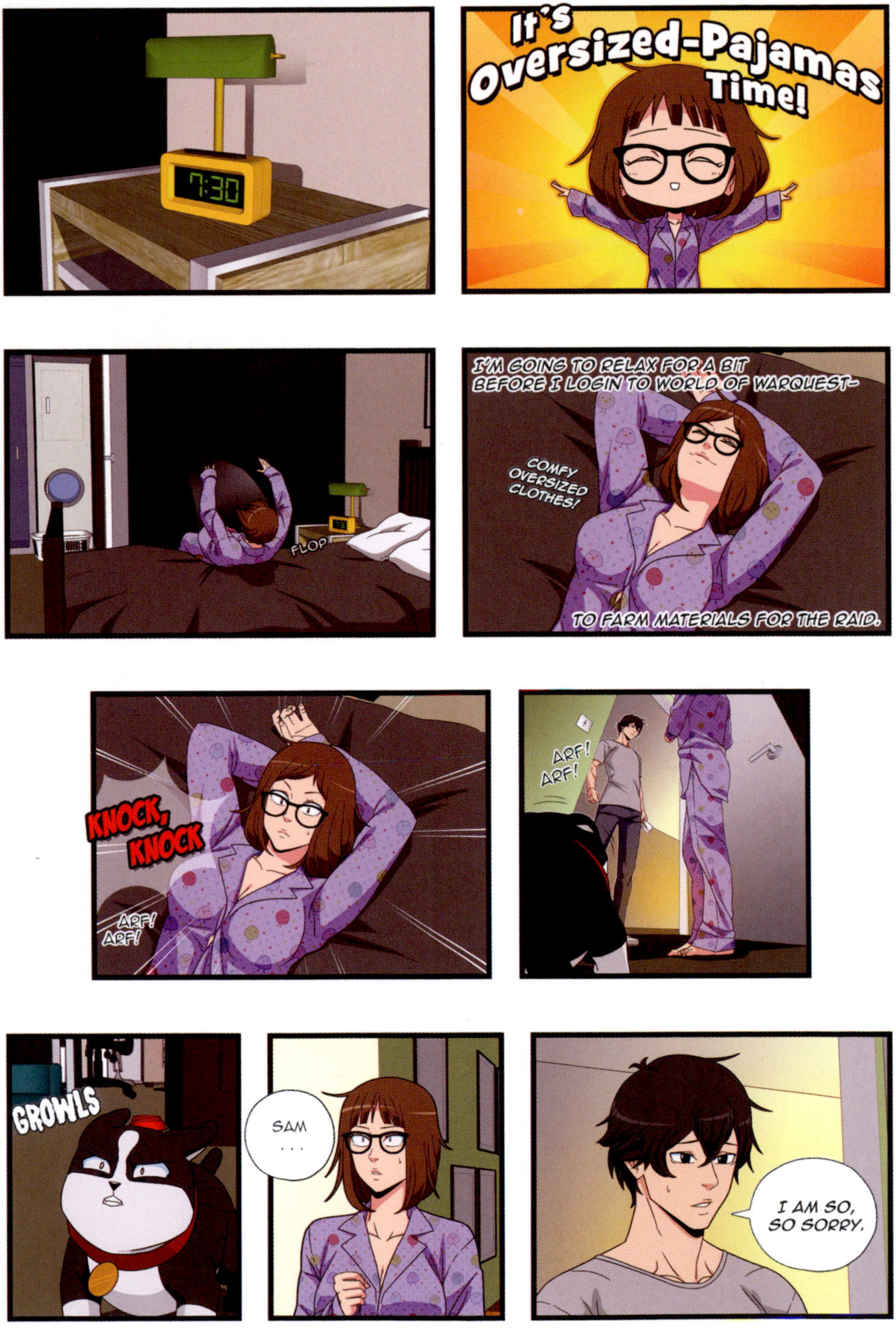
It's Oversized-Pajamas Time!
FLOP
I'M GOING TO RELAX FOR A BIT BEFORE I LOGIN TO WORLD OF WARQUEST-
COMFY OVERSIZED CLOTHES!
TO FARM MATERIALS FOR THE RAID.
KNOCK, KNOCK
ARF! ARF!
ARF! ARF!
GROWLS
SAM . . .
I AM SO, SO SORRY.

EASY BOWSER.

IT'S ALRIGHT.

WHAT . . . ARE YOU SORRY FOR?

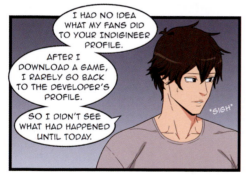

I HAD NO IDEA WHAT MY FANS DID TO YOUR INDIGINEER PROFILE.

AFTER I DOWNLOAD A GAME, I RARELY GO BACK TO THE DEVELOPER'S PROFILE.

SO I DIDN'T SEE WHAT HAD HAPPENED UNTIL TODAY.

SIGH

IT'S NO WONDER YOU WERE SO UPSET WITH ME WHEN WE FIRST MET.

I'VE CONTACTED INDIGINEER TO EXPLAIN TO THEM WHAT HAPPENED.

I ASKED THEM TO CHANGE YOUR SCORE BACK TO WHAT IT WAS BEFORE ALL OF THIS HAPPENED.

SCRATCH SCRATCH

I SEND A LOT OF TRAFFIC THEIR WAY, SO I SHOULD HAVE SOME CLOUT WITH THEM.

HOPEFULLY THEY'LL COMPLY.

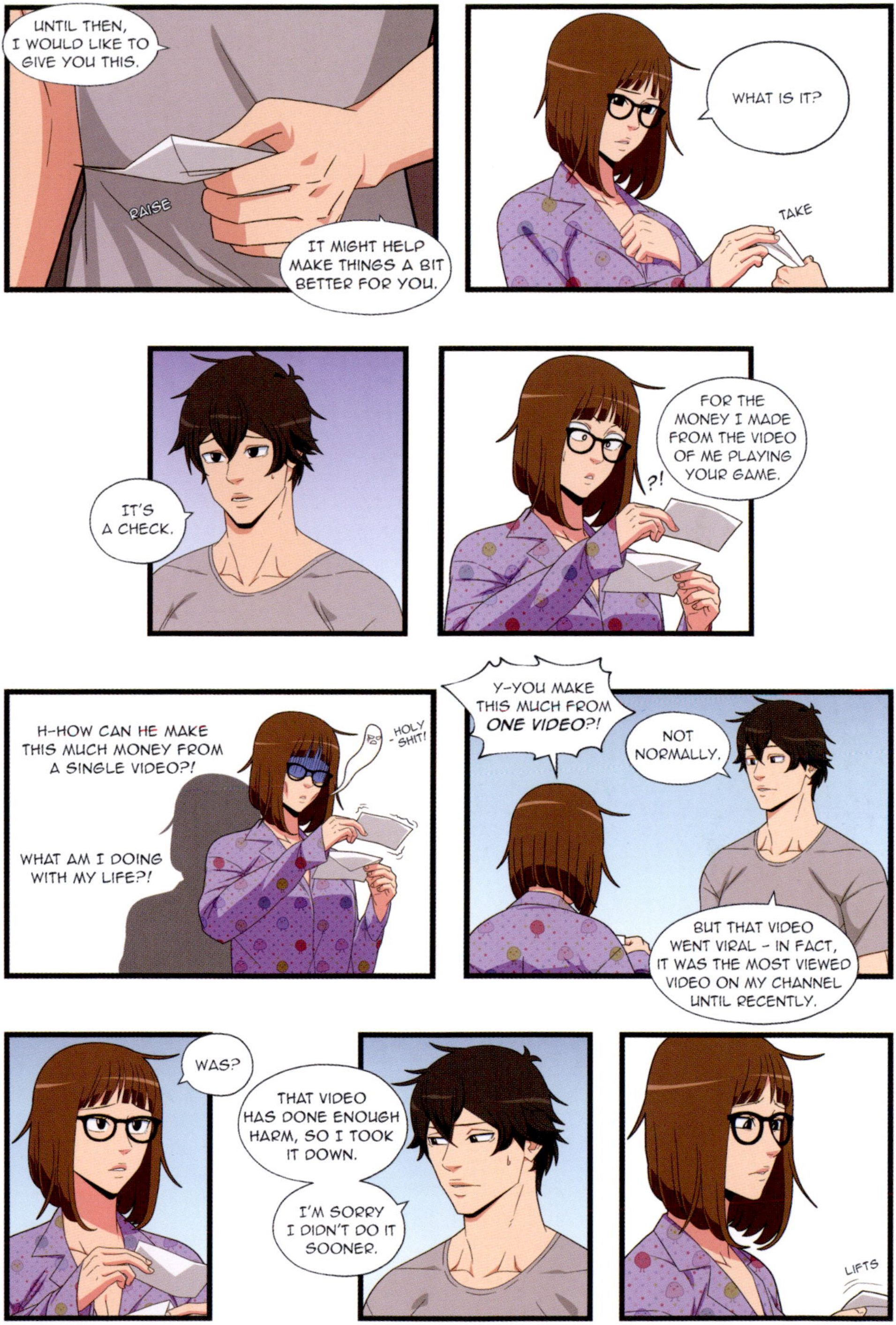
UNTIL THEN, I WOULD LIKE TO GIVE YOU THIS.
RAISE
IT MIGHT HELP MAKE THINGS A BIT BETTER FOR YOU.
WHAT IS IT?
TAKE
IT'S A CHECK.
?!
FOR THE MONEY I MADE FROM THE VIDEO OF ME PLAYING YOUR GAME.
H-HOW CAN HE MAKE THIS MUCH MONEY FROM A SINGLE VIDEO?!
HOLY - SHIT!
WHAT AM I DOING WITH MY LIFE?!
Y-YOU MAKE THIS MUCH FROM *ONE VIDEO*?!
NOT NORMALLY.
BUT THAT VIDEO WENT VIRAL - IN FACT, IT WAS THE MOST VIEWED VIDEO ON MY CHANNEL UNTIL RECENTLY.
WAS?
THAT VIDEO HAS DONE ENOUGH HARM, SO I TOOK IT DOWN.
I'M SORRY I DIDN'T DO IT SOONER.
LIFTS

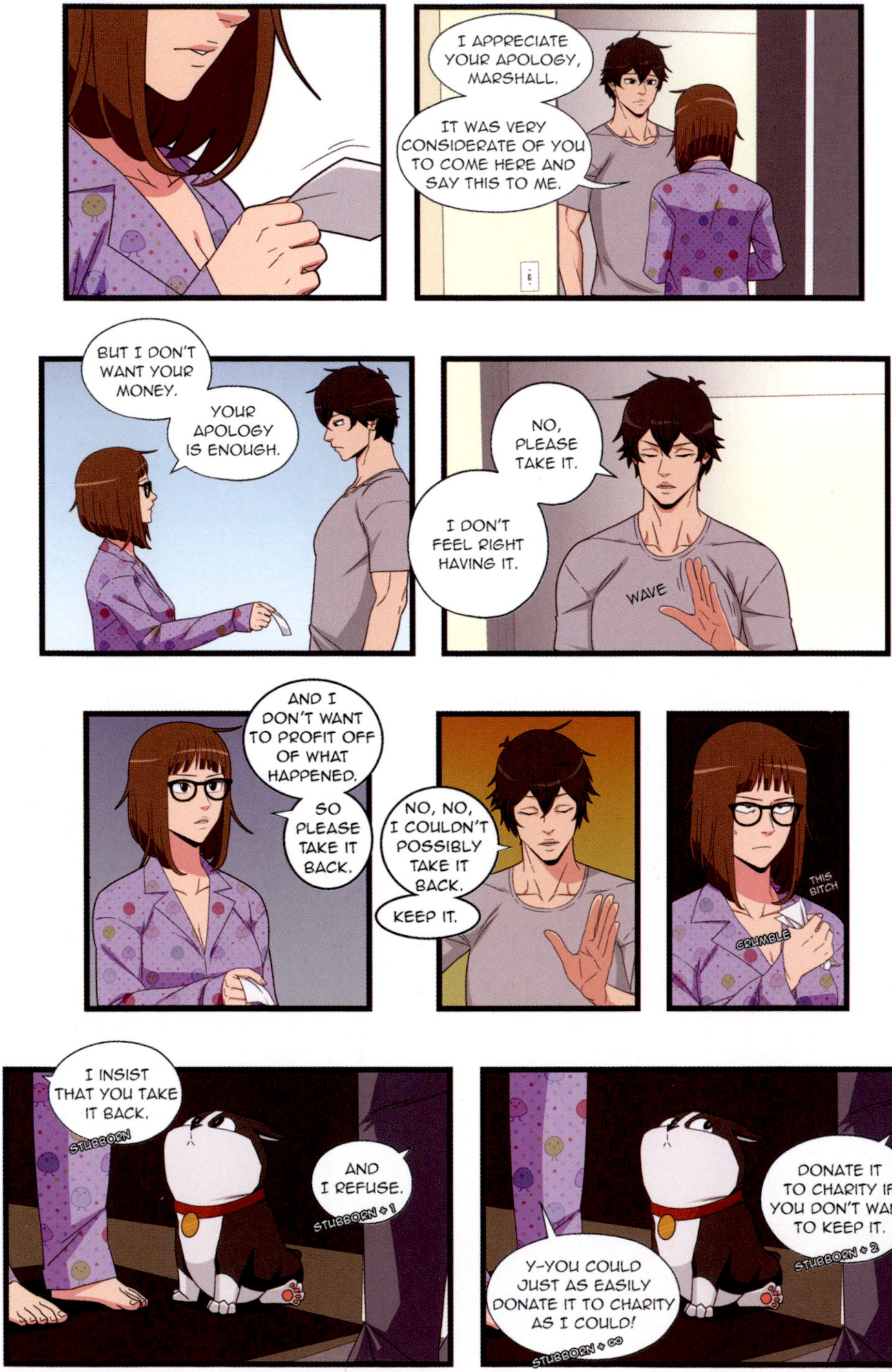
I APPRECIATE YOUR APOLOGY, MARSHALL.
IT WAS VERY CONSIDERATE OF YOU TO COME HERE AND SAY THIS TO ME.
BUT I DON'T WANT YOUR MONEY.
YOUR APOLOGY IS ENOUGH.
NO, PLEASE TAKE IT.
I DON'T FEEL RIGHT HAVING IT.
WAVE
AND I DON'T WANT TO PROFIT OFF OF WHAT HAPPENED.
SO PLEASE TAKE IT BACK.
NO, NO, I COULDN'T POSSIBLY TAKE IT BACK.
KEEP IT.
THIS BITCH
CRUMBLE
I INSIST THAT YOU TAKE IT BACK.
STUBBORN
AND I REFUSE.
STUBBORN + 1
Y-YOU COULD JUST AS EASILY DONATE IT TO CHARITY AS I COULD!
STUBBORN + ∞
DONATE IT TO CHARITY IF YOU DON'T WANT TO KEEP IT.
STUBBORN + 2

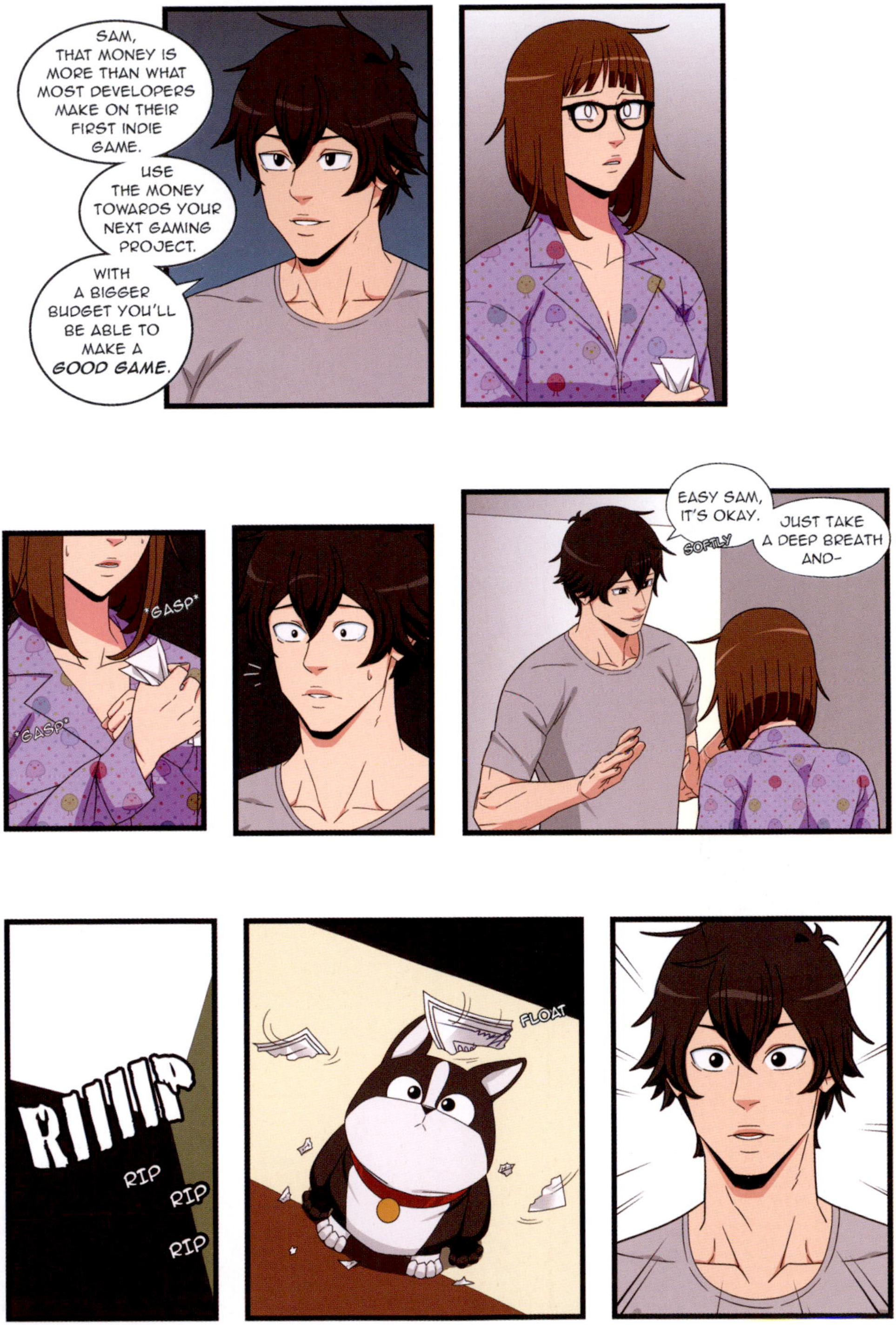
SAM, THAT MONEY IS MORE THAN WHAT MOST DEVELOPERS MAKE ON THEIR FIRST INDIE GAME.
USE THE MONEY TOWARDS YOUR NEXT GAMING PROJECT.
WITH A BIGGER BUDGET YOU'LL BE ABLE TO MAKE A GOOD GAME.
GASP
GASP
EASY SAM, IT'S OKAY.
SOFTLY
JUST TAKE A DEEP BREATH AND-
RIIIIP
RIP
RIP
RIP
FLOAT

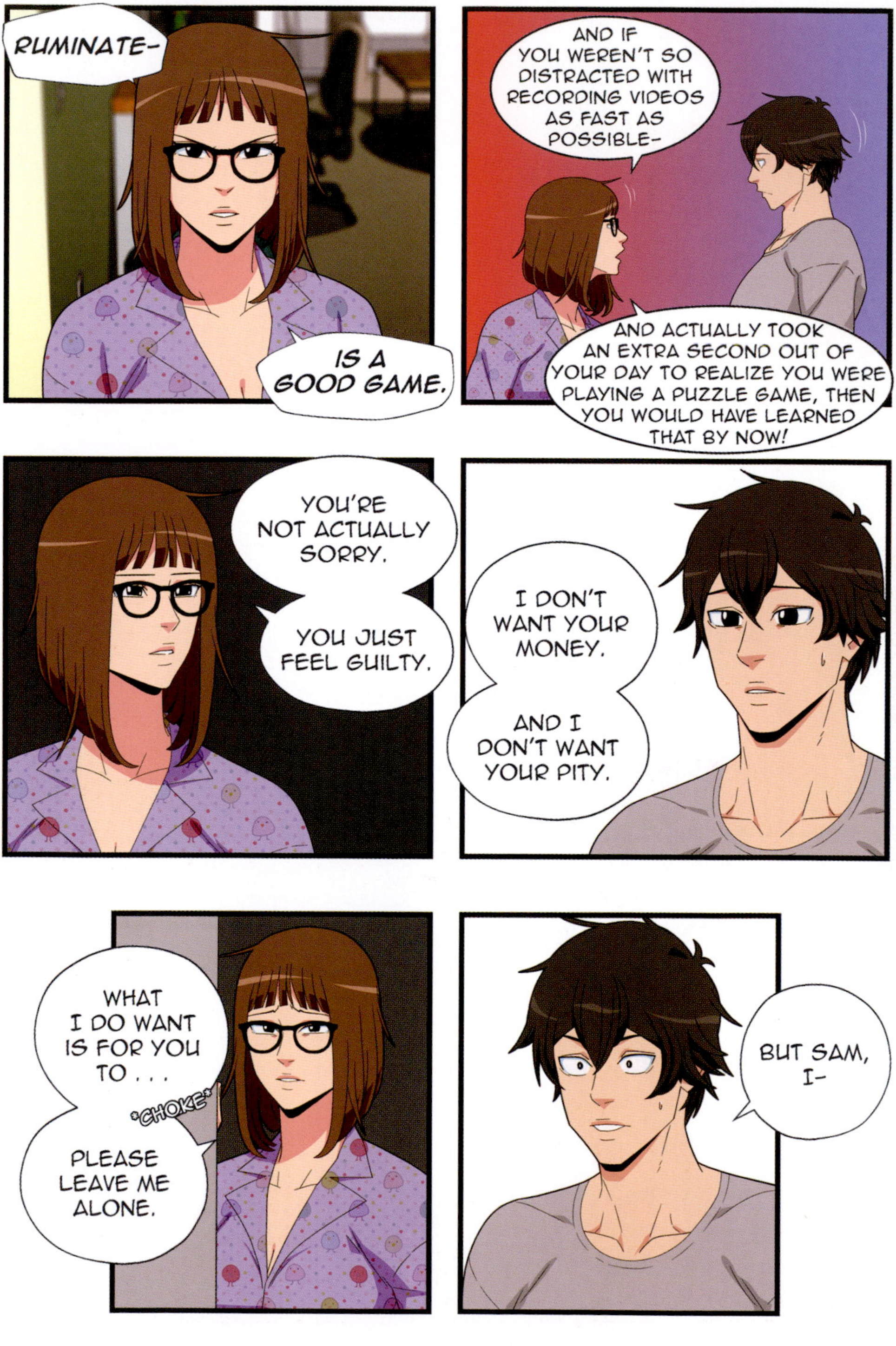
RUMINATE-
IS A GOOD GAME.
AND IF YOU WEREN'T SO DISTRACTED WITH RECORDING VIDEOS AS FAST AS POSSIBLE-
AND ACTUALLY TOOK AN EXTRA SECOND OUT OF YOUR DAY TO REALIZE YOU WERE PLAYING A PUZZLE GAME, THEN YOU WOULD HAVE LEARNED THAT BY NOW!
YOU'RE NOT ACTUALLY SORRY.
YOU JUST FEEL GUILTY.
I DON'T WANT YOUR MONEY.
AND I DON'T WANT YOUR PITY.
WHAT I DO WANT IS FOR YOU TO . . .
CHOKE
PLEASE LEAVE ME ALONE.
BUT SAM, I-

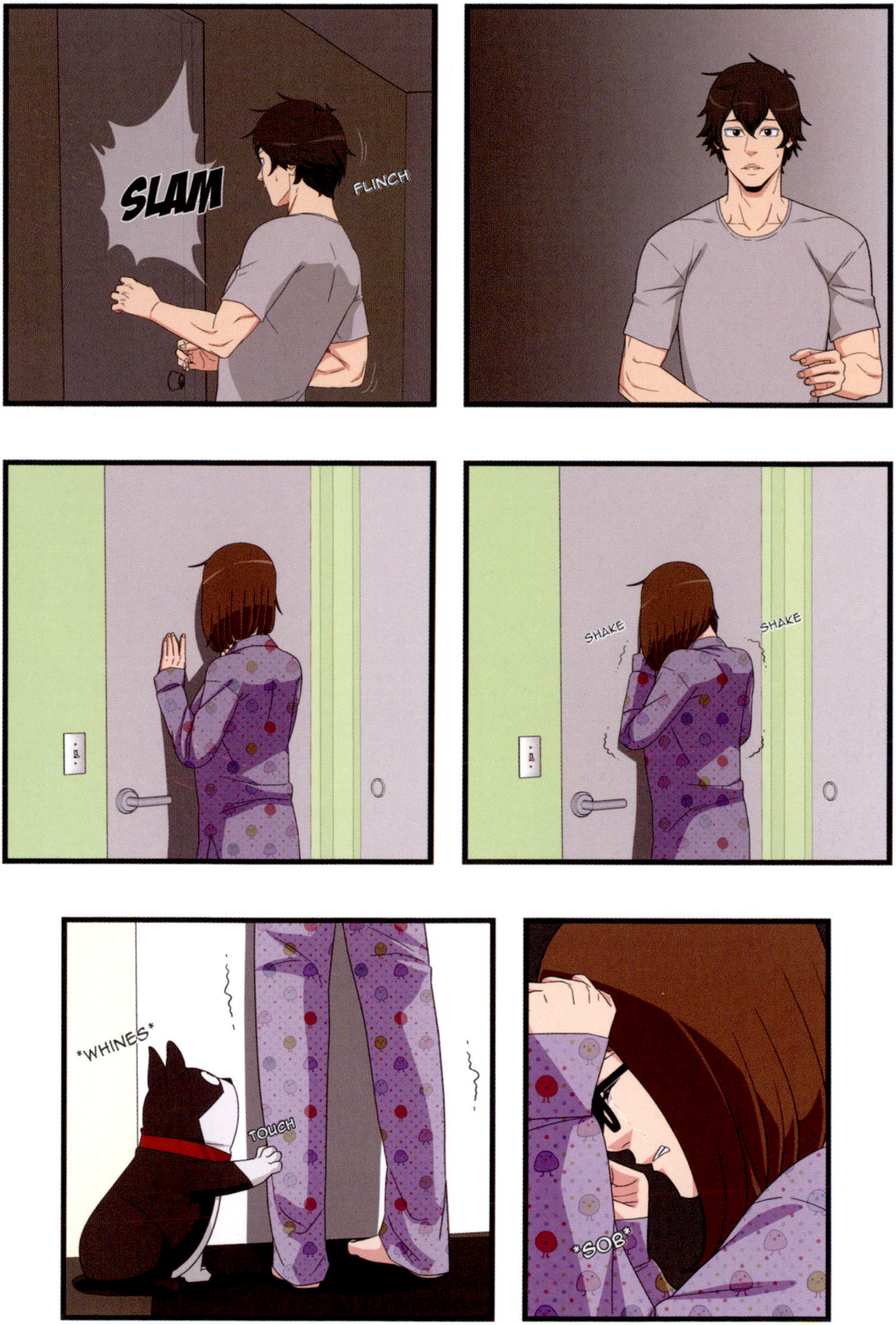
SLAM
FLINCH
SHAKE
SHAKE
WHINES
TOUCH
SOB

The next morning.

KNOCK
KNOCK
GOOD MORNING, SAM!
DO YOU HAVE A SECOND TO TALK-

SLAM
PONDER
HMM.
SCRUNCH
SCRUNCH

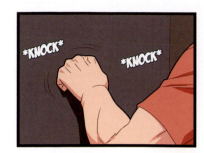

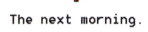

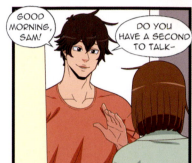

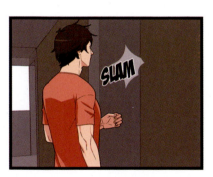

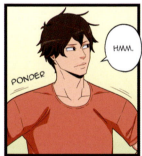

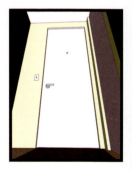

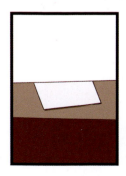

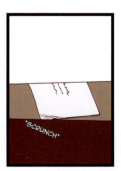

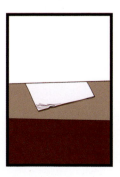

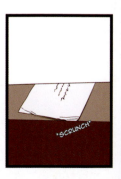

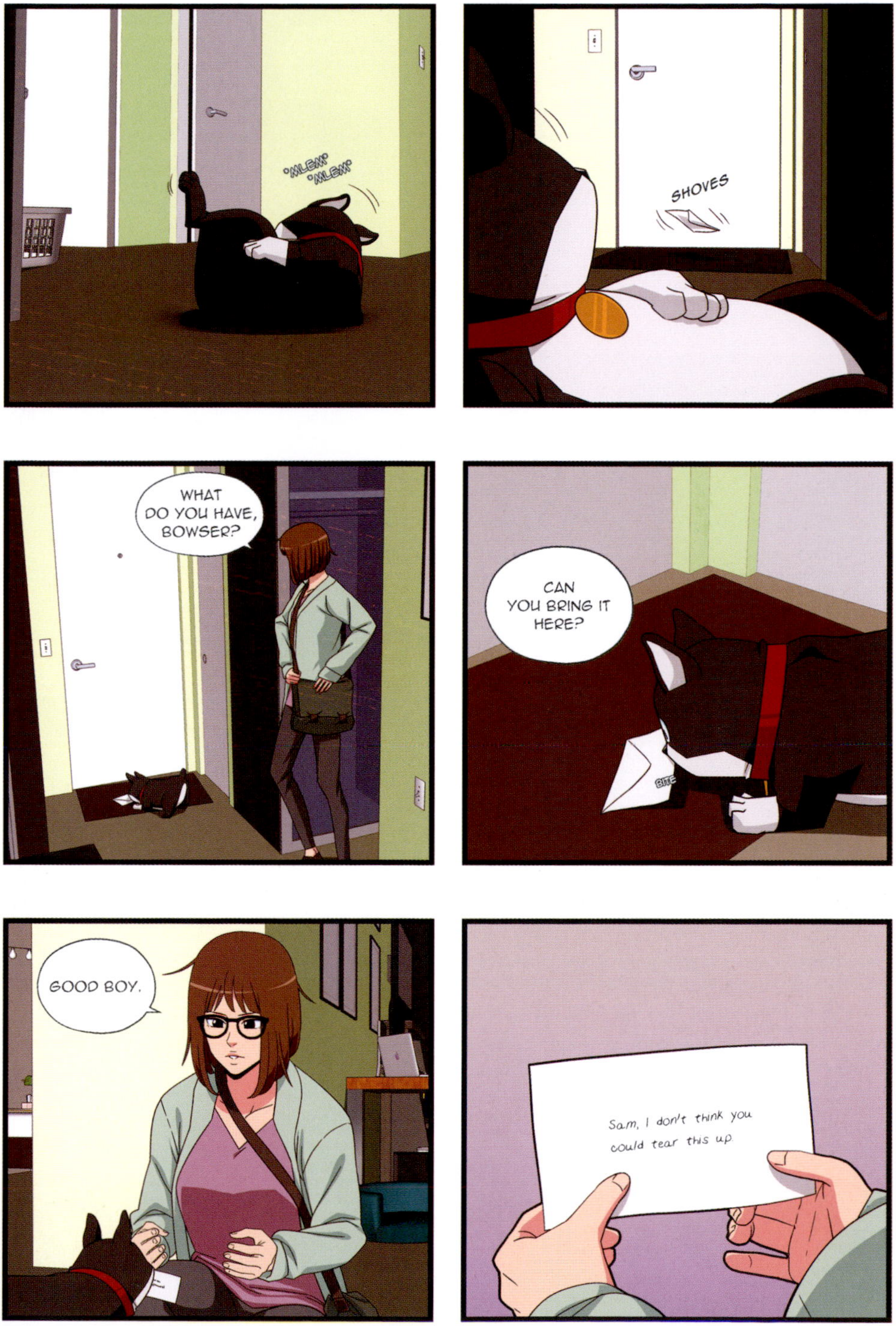
MLEM
MLEM
SHOVES
WHAT DO YOU HAVE, BOWSER?
CAN YOU BRING IT HERE?
BITE
GOOD BOY.
Sam, I don't think you could tear this up.

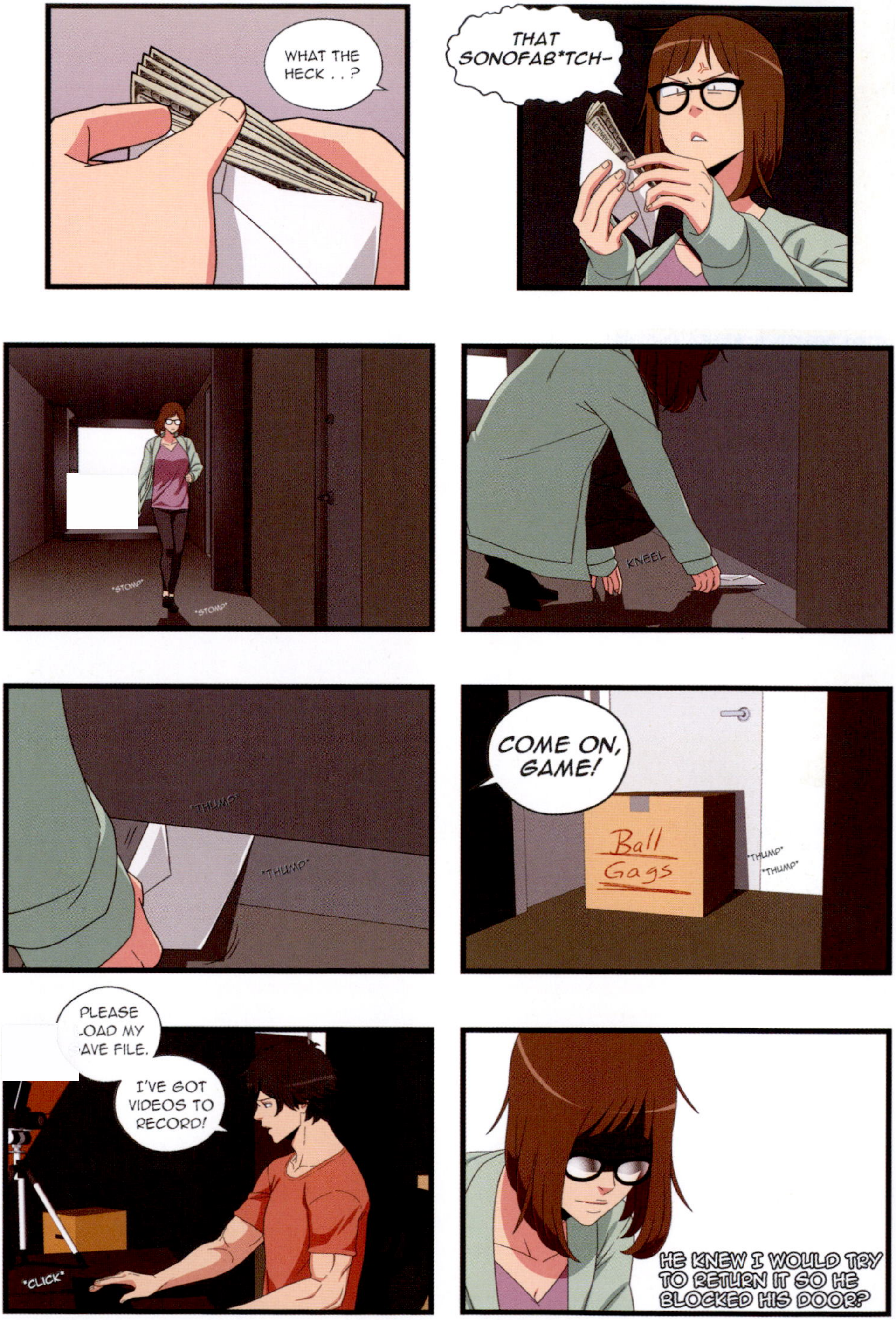
WHAT THE HECK . . ?
THAT SONOFAB*TCH-
STOMP
STOMP
KNEEL
THUMP
THUMP
COME ON, GAME!
Ball Gags
THUMP
THUMP
PLEASE OAD MY AVE FILE.
I'VE GOT VIDEOS TO RECORD!
CLICK
HE KNEW I WOULD TRY TO RETURN IT SO HE BLOCKED HIS DOOR?

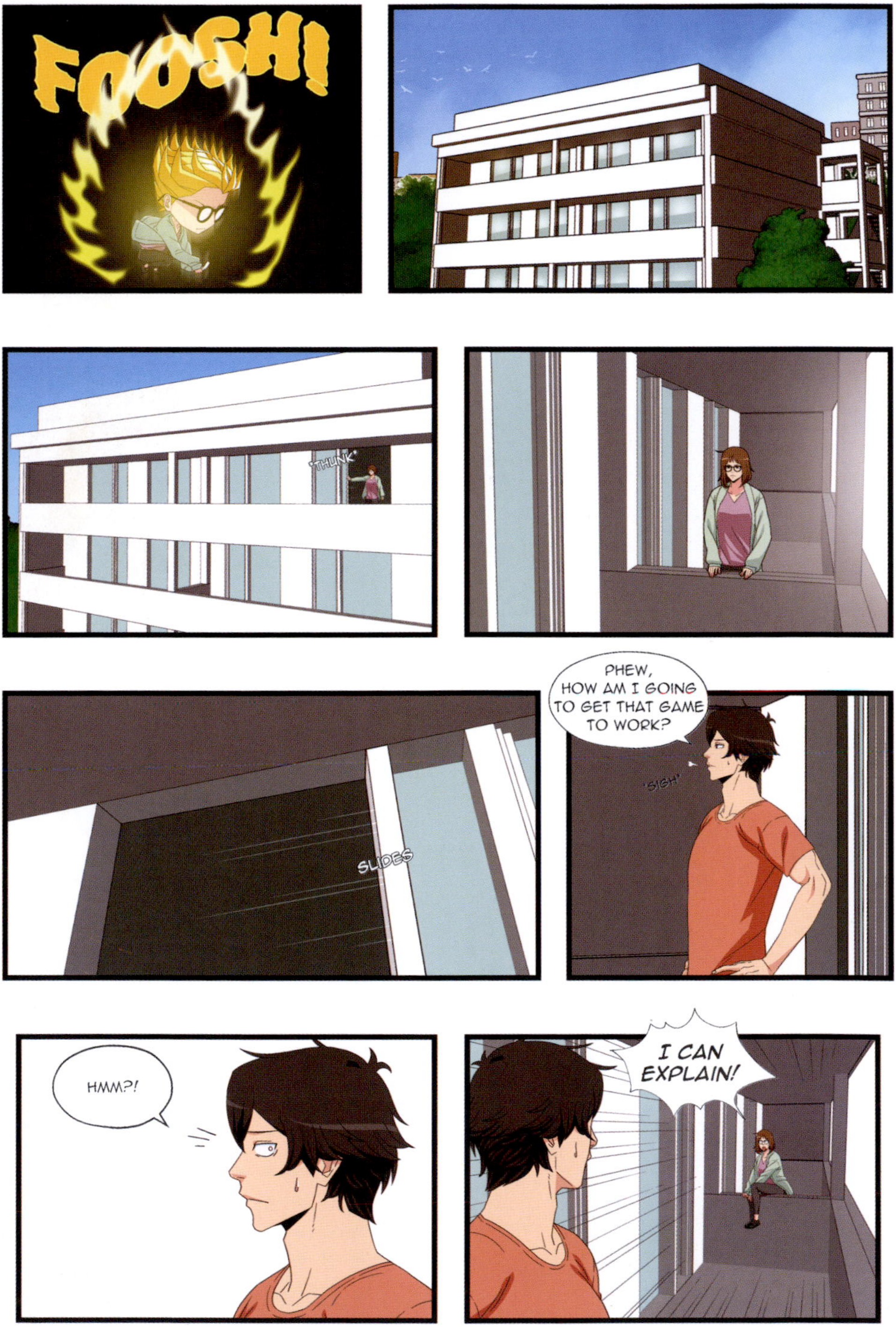
FOOSH!
THUNK
SLIDES
PHEW, HOW AM I GOING TO GET THAT GAME TO WORK?
SIGH
HMM?!
I CAN EXPLAIN!

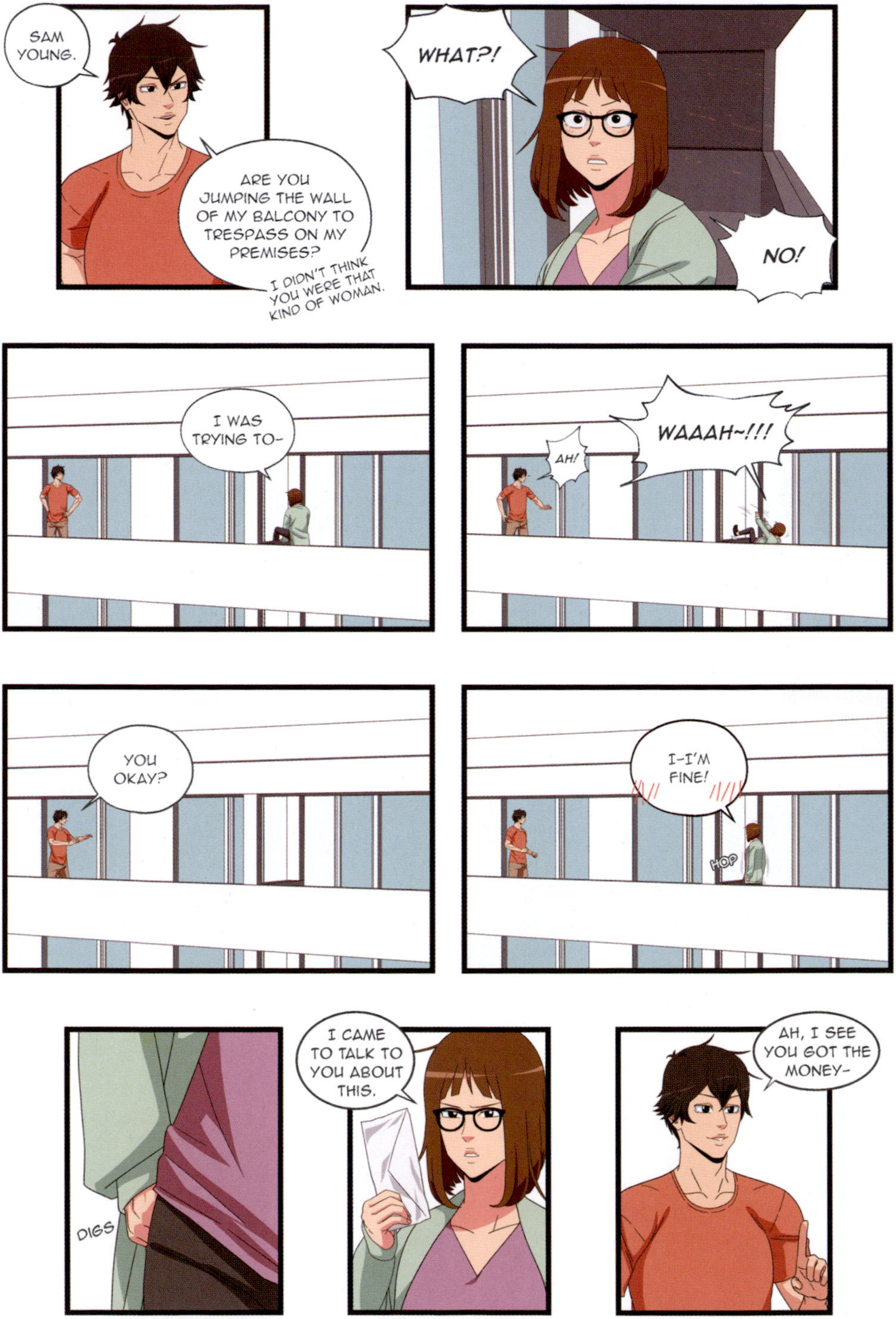
SAM YOUNG.
ARE YOU JUMPING THE WALL OF MY BALCONY TO TRESPASS ON MY PREMISES?
I DIDN'T THINK YOU WERE THAT KIND OF WOMAN.
WHAT?!
NO!
I WAS TRYING TO-
AH!
WAAAH~!!!
YOU OKAY?
I-I'M FINE!
HOP
DIGS
I CAME TO TALK TO YOU ABOUT THIS.
AH, I SEE YOU GOT THE MONEY-

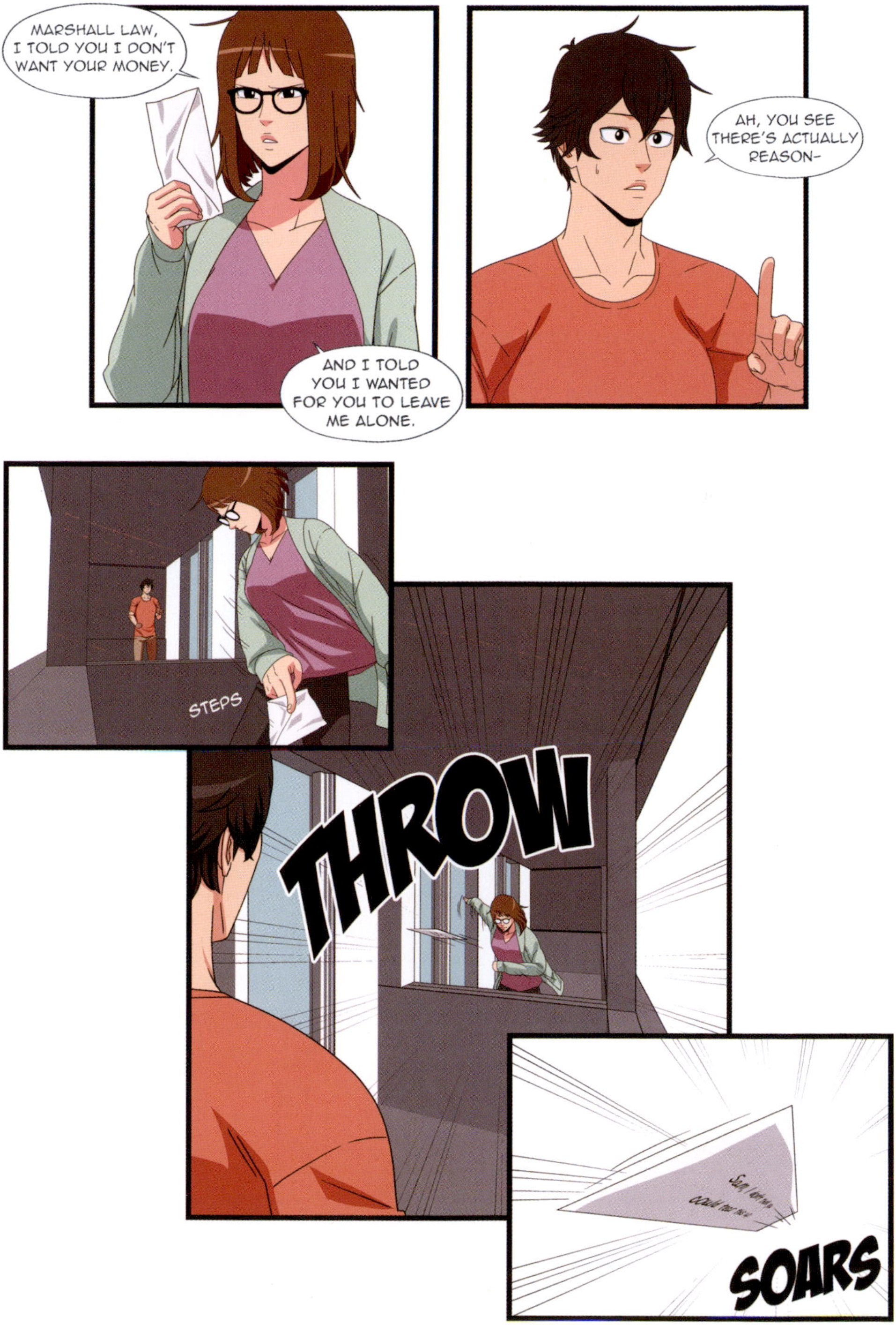
MARSHALL LAW, I TOLD YOU I DON'T WANT YOUR MONEY.
AND I TOLD YOU I WANTED FOR YOU TO LEAVE ME ALONE.
AH, YOU SEE THERE'S ACTUALLY REASON-
STEPS
THROW
SOARS

OOF!

wasted

DROP

OUCHIES, THAT SMARTS.

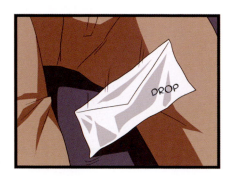

OH MY GOD, I'M SO SORRY!

I HAD NO IDEA THAT WOULD ACTUALLY HIT YOU!

NICE HEADSHOT.

FORTUNATELY I HAVE A PRETTY HARD HEAD.

DON'T TRY TO GIVE ME MONEY AGAIN!

AND IF YOU TRY PUTTING IT UNDER MY DOOR AGAIN, MY DOG WILL EAT IT!

BUT SAM, I WAS ONLY TRYING TO–

PLEASE, MARSHALL.

DON'T MAKE ME HAVE TO ASK YOU AGAIN.

. . .
ARE YOU SURE YOU'RE OKAY?
YOU DIDN'T GET HURT?
HEH, YEAH I'M FINE.
OKAY, GOOD.
. . . BYE.
TAP
TAP

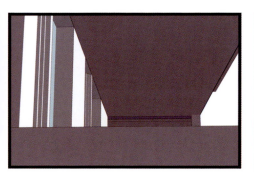

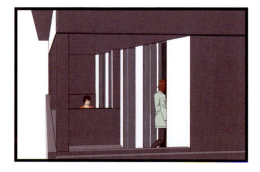

To be continued...

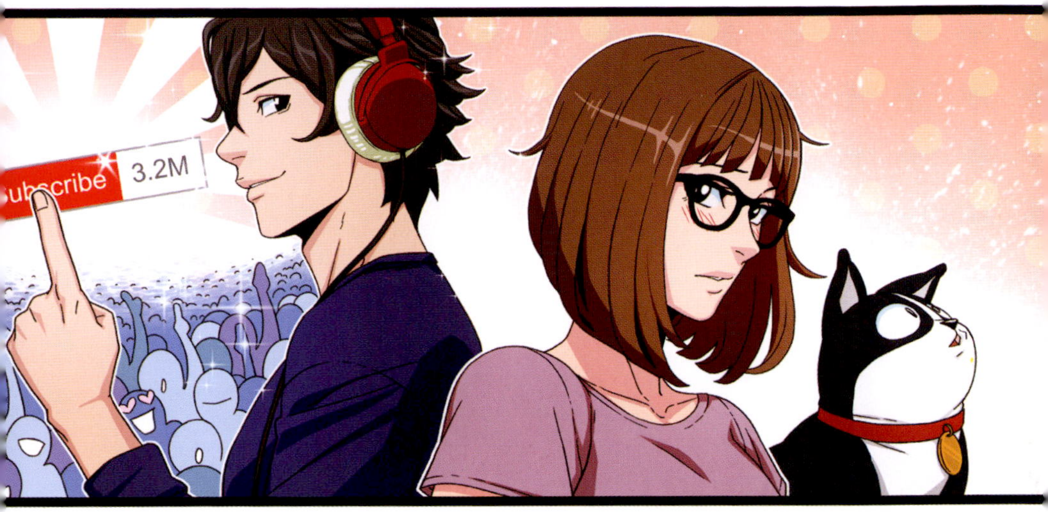

ubscribe
3.2M

INTERVIEW WITH

LEEANNE "MONGIE" KRECIC

by Jed Keith, *Editor-In-Chief, Freaksugar.com*

How do the reviews we post online—both positive and negative—affect real world people? For Sam, the protagonist of Leeanne "Mongie" Krecic's LINE Webtoon webcomic Let's Play, the consequences impact her in a hard way. After an internet gaming celebrity gives Sam's debut game an unkind review, her path to being an indie game developer looks to be a treacherous one. In the meantime, the reviewer moves next door to her, adding another kink in the works.

Mongie spoke with us recently about the conceit of Let's Play, how the idea behind the webcomic come to light and what she hopes readers get out of reading the webseries.

Jed Keith: What is the conceit of Let's Play Volume 1?

Leeanne "Mongie" Krecic: Volume 1 is the first 23 chapters of my webcomic Let's Play, which is about a young woman named Sam, who works as a software developer by day and an indie game developer by night. In the first chapter, we learn that Sam's first game, Ruminate, is reviewed by an internet gaming celebrity who goes by the name "Marshall Law." Unfortunately, Marshall gives Sam's game a negative review and posts the video online for his 3 million subscribers to see. As a result, Marshall's fans ruin Sam's online reputation, making her debut as an indie game dev a rocky one. By the end of the first chapter, we learn that Marshall is moving into the apartment next door.

The comic, which is a rom-com, focuses on gaming culture, working as a woman in a STEM field, life as an internet celebrity, and mental health.

JK: Following up on that, what was the genesis of the series?

LMK: I worked as a web developer for 11 years. While working, I often listened to "Let's Players" on YouTube who played and reviewed games. One day, I watched a video from one of those YouTubers who was playing a fan-made game. Halfway through the game, they got so frustrated with the game that they rage-quit, followed by a long, critical lecture addressed to the developer via the video recording. After watching that video, I felt awful for the developer; especially being a developer myself. It was true that the game was rough, and needed a lot of polish, but it was probably their first game, and I doubted they suspected this famous

YouTuber would even hear of their game, let alone play it. So I started to wonder what would happen if that developer met the YouTuber in person? Would the developer point out who they were? Would the YouTuber apologize? What would be the interaction? That was the genesis of Let's Play. A comic where those two people actually meet.

JK: The cast is diverse and incredibly fleshed-out. Can you tell us about the characters?

LMK: Sam is a young woman who suffered from poor health through most of her young life. As a result, she spent a great deal of her time playing video and computer games. As Sam grew older, she noticed how gaming was an excellent escape for others much like herself. As a result, she decided she wanted to become a game developer so she could create games for others to enjoy. Unfortunately, having lived such a sheltered life, Sam developed a lot of social anxiety and struggled with things like confrontation.

Marshall Law is a rising internet celebrity on a website called

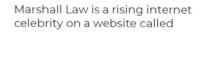

"Viewtube." He's high energy and loves sharing a good laugh. He adores his fans and will often push himself past limits that are healthy to maintain his video upload schedule. As the series has progressed, we've learned that there may be more to the celebrity than what we originally thought, and that "Marshall Law" may not be his real personality.

Bowser, who is Sam's pet dog, is a Corgi and Boston Terrier mix. He has a very close bond with Sam and will come to her aid when she's in need. He hates squirrels, loves his little stuffed princess doll, and enjoys walkies.

Other characters for Let's Play include a rock-climbing barista, Sam's coworkers, the motley crew that is Sam's MMO guild, and numerous other exciting characters.

JK: Following up on that, what are your influences behind the series?

LMK: My time as a web developer is a substantial influence behind the series. I was never a game developer, but I do have plenty of experience with computer logic and software development to have a conventional understanding of the process. Also working in a field that is a predominately male industry has sparked a lot of influence in the character Sam and what she experiences in her job. also grew up gaming — having learned how to read playing text-based games on the Commodore 64 back in 1985. Some of my fondest memories is playing SNES with my cousin, or beating Earthworm Jim on the Sega Genesis for the umpteenth time, or trying to get through Myst on the PC with my dad. I've also logged an embarrassing amount of time on MMOs that I'm afraid to run the check commands to learn the answer.

JK: Beyond being entertained, what do you hope readers take from Let's Play?

LMK: Let's Play touches a lot on mental health, and I hear from a lot of readers who are at a difficult place in their lives. They tell me that reading about my characters going through similar problems helps them understand that others are going through the same struggles. If anything, I hope my comic helps readers feel more comfortable talking about mental health and more open to the idea of asking for help when it's needed.

JK: What is next for Let's Play?

LMK: Since the Kickstarter went so well, we're planning on running the Kickstarter for Volume 2 soon. The fans of Let's Play have also been hounding me for games based on the series, whether it actually be Ruminate the game that Sam created, or a dating game that will allow you to date the characters of Let's Play. We're exploring a lot of options! In the meanwhile, Let's Play will continue to be updated weekly on Webtoon!

-Jed Keith

Two years earlier.

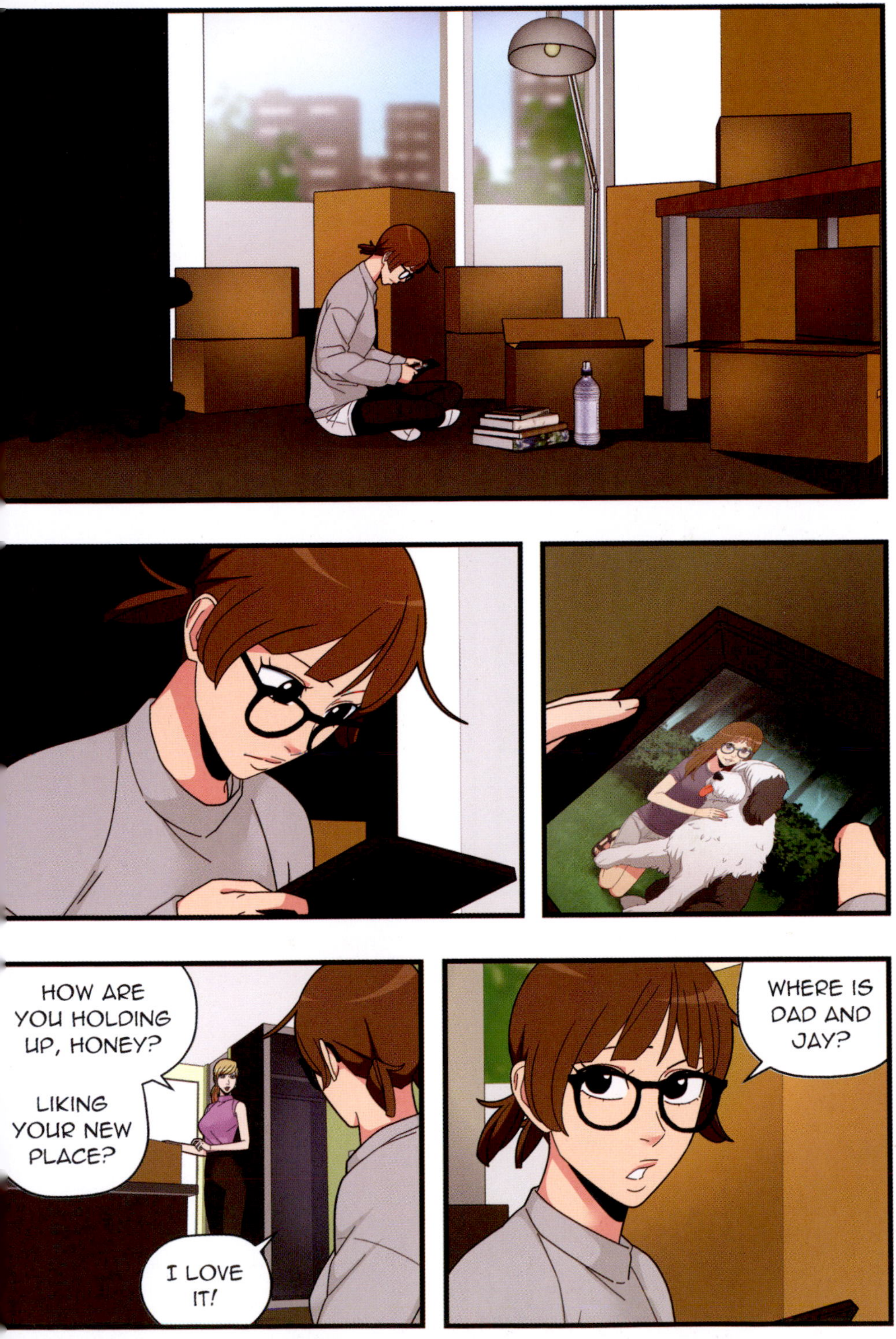
HOW ARE YOU HOLDING UP, HONEY?
LIKING YOUR NEW PLACE?
I LOVE IT!
WHERE IS DAD AND JAY?

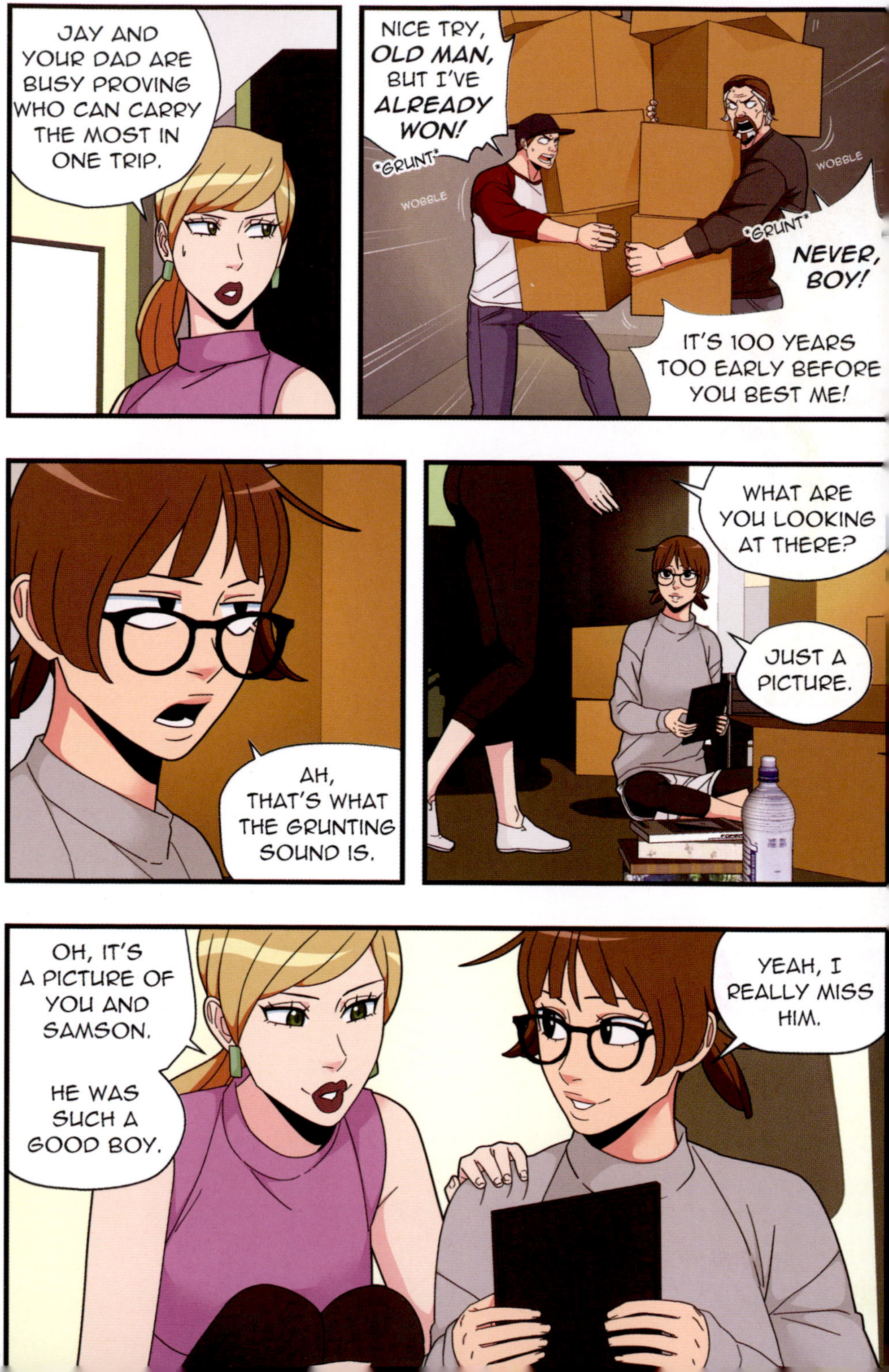
JAY AND YOUR DAD ARE BUSY PROVING WHO CAN CARRY THE MOST IN ONE TRIP.
NICE TRY, OLD MAN, BUT I'VE ALREADY WON!
GRUNT
WOBBLE
WOBBLE
GRUNT
NEVER, BOY!
IT'S 100 YEARS TOO EARLY BEFORE YOU BEST ME!
AH, THAT'S WHAT THE GRUNTING SOUND IS.
WHAT ARE YOU LOOKING AT THERE?
JUST A PICTURE.
OH, IT'S A PICTURE OF YOU AND SAMSON.
HE WAS SUCH A GOOD BOY.
YEAH, I REALLY MISS HIM.

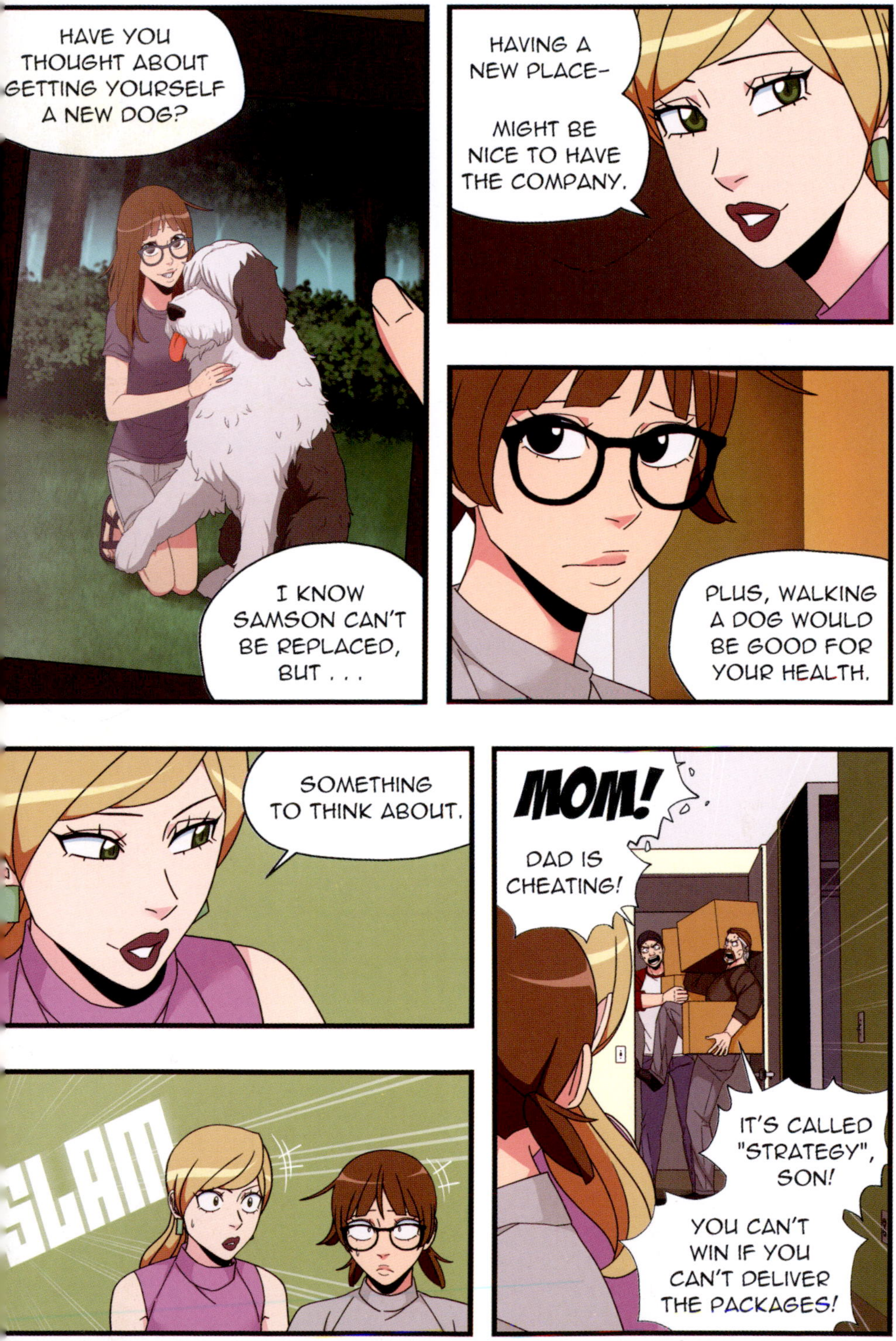
HAVE YOU THOUGHT ABOUT GETTING YOURSELF A NEW DOG?
I KNOW SAMSON CAN'T BE REPLACED, BUT . . .
HAVING A NEW PLACE-
MIGHT BE NICE TO HAVE THE COMPANY.
PLUS, WALKING A DOG WOULD BE GOOD FOR YOUR HEALTH.
SOMETHING TO THINK ABOUT.
MOM!
DAD IS CHEATING!
IT'S CALLED "STRATEGY", SON!
YOU CAN'T WIN IF YOU CAN'T DELIVER THE PACKAGES!
SLAM

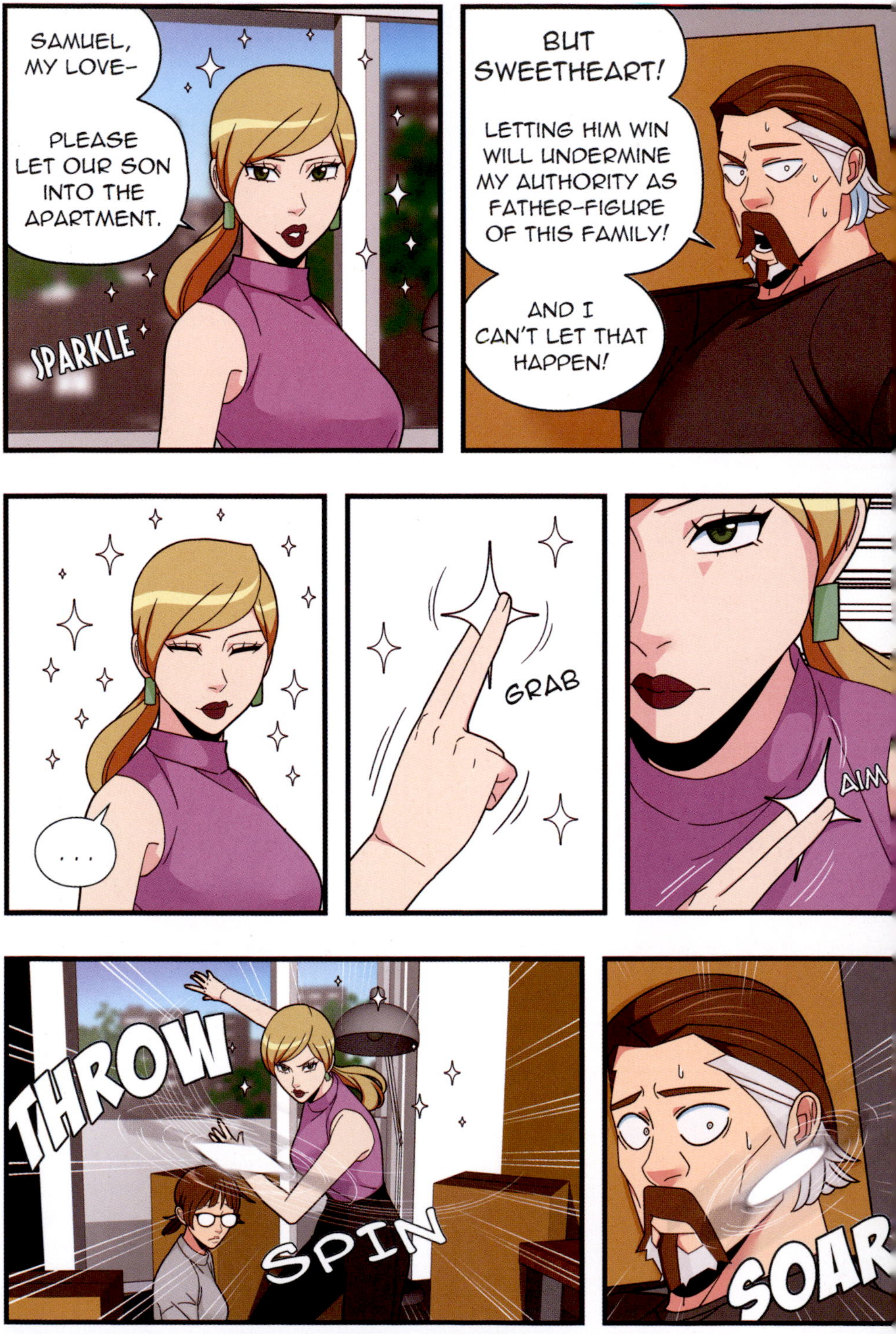
SAMUEL, MY LOVE-
PLEASE LET OUR SON INTO THE APARTMENT.
SPARKLE
BUT SWEETHEART!
LETTING HIM WIN WILL UNDERMINE MY AUTHORITY AS FATHER-FIGURE OF THIS FAMILY!
AND I CAN'T LET THAT HAPPEN!
. . .
GRAB
AIM
THROW
SPIN
SOAR

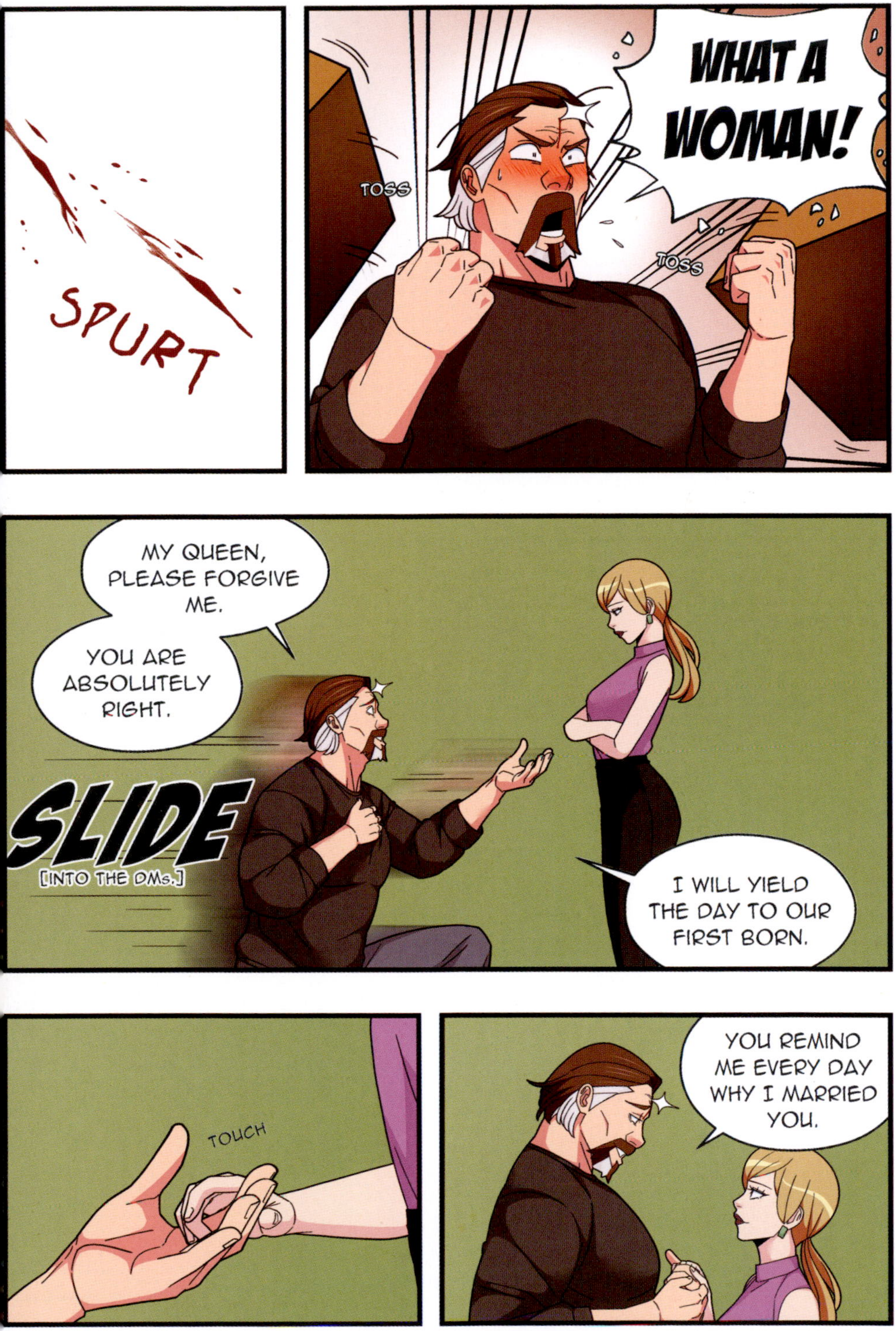
SPURT
TOSS
TOSS
WHAT A WOMAN!
MY QUEEN, PLEASE FORGIVE ME.
YOU ARE ABSOLUTELY RIGHT.
SLIDE
[INTO THE DMs.]
I WILL YIELD THE DAY TO OUR FIRST BORN.
TOUCH
YOU REMIND ME EVERY DAY WHY I MARRIED YOU.

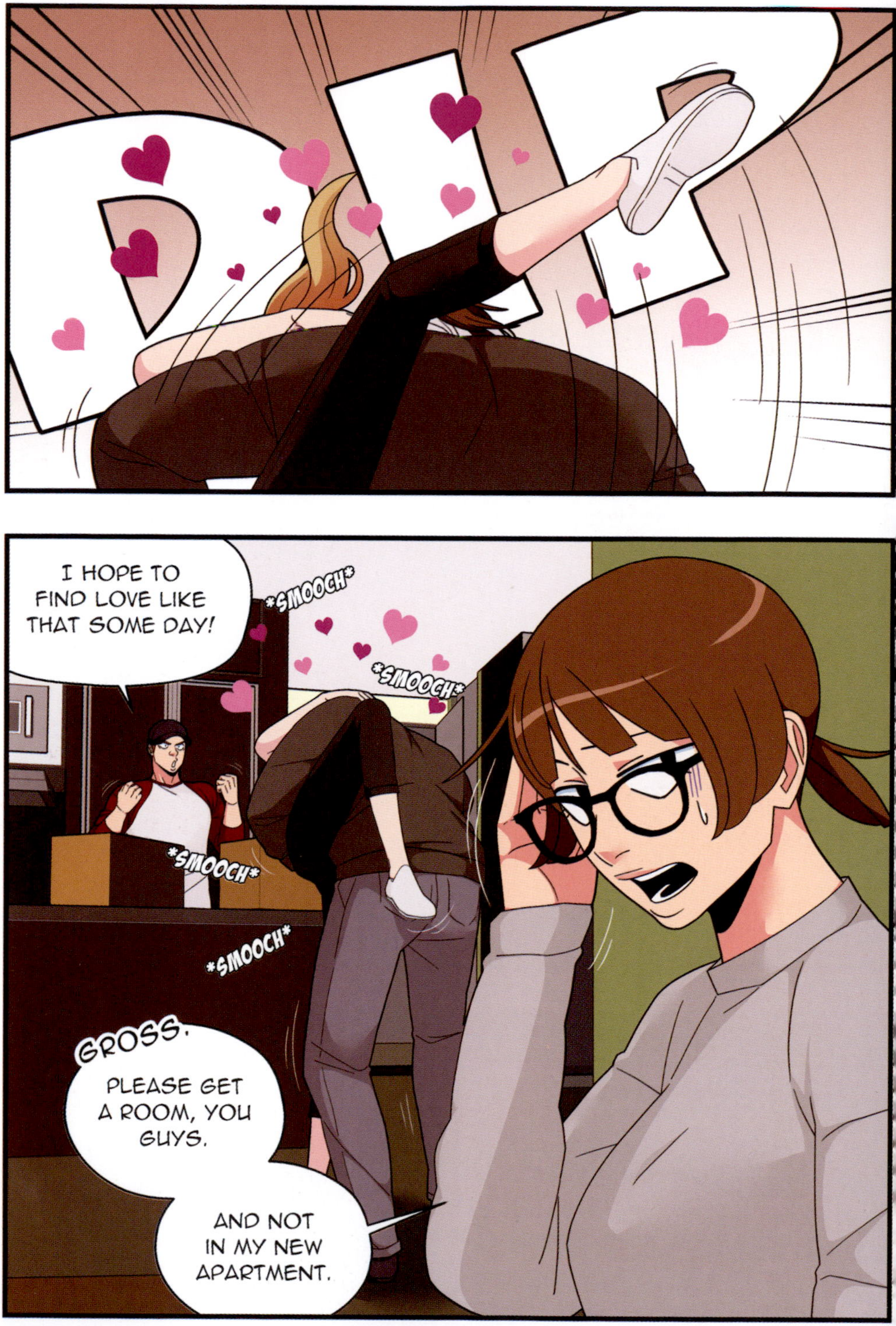
DIP
I HOPE TO FIND LOVE LIKE THAT SOME DAY!
SMOOCH
SMOOCH
SMOOCH
SMOOCH
GROSS.
PLEASE GET A ROOM, YOU GUYS.
AND NOT IN MY NEW APARTMENT.

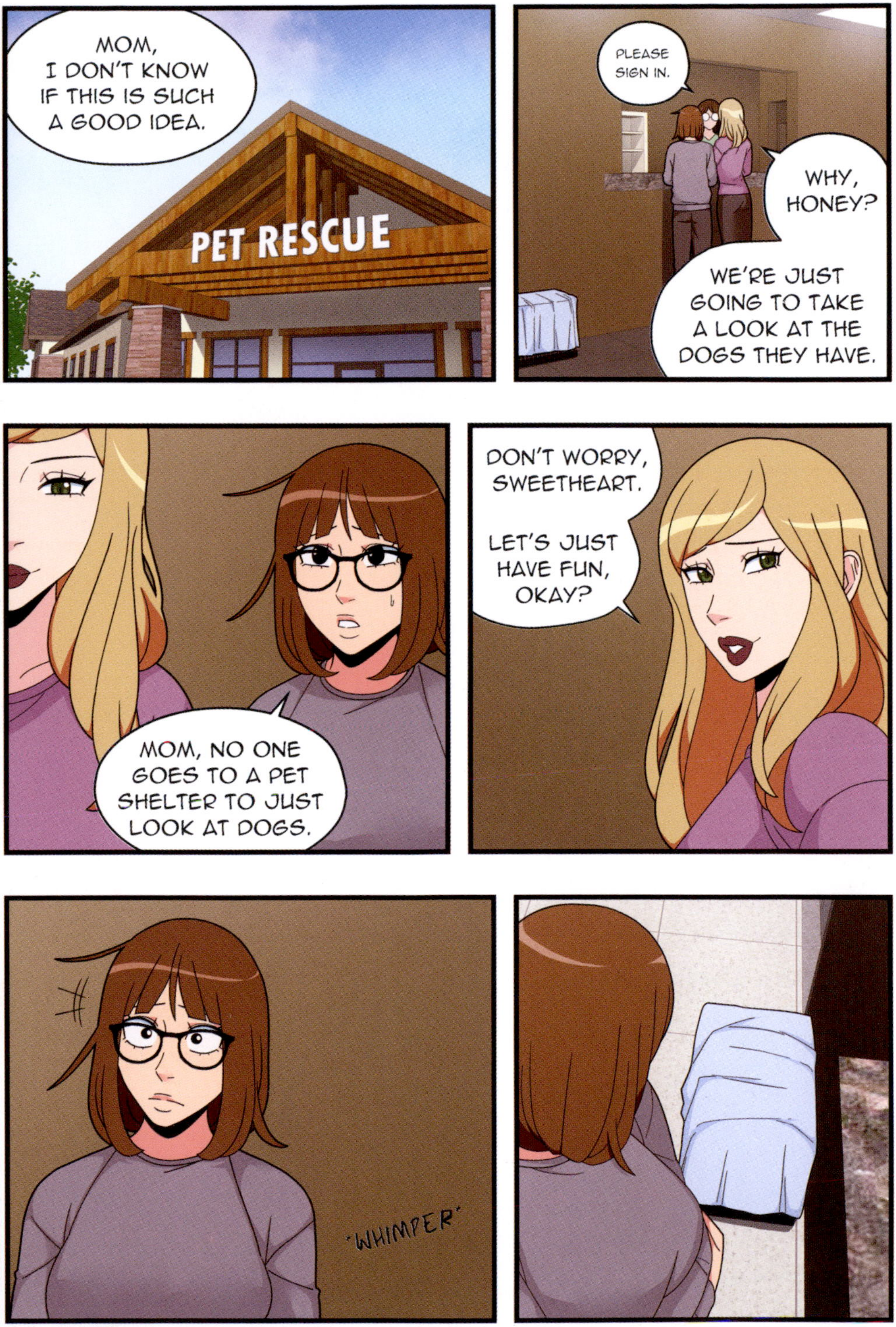
MOM, I DON'T KNOW IF THIS IS SUCH A GOOD IDEA.
PET RESCUE
PLEASE SIGN IN.
WHY, HONEY?
WE'RE JUST GOING TO TAKE A LOOK AT THE DOGS THEY HAVE.
MOM, NO ONE GOES TO A PET SHELTER TO JUST LOOK AT DOGS.
DON'T WORRY, SWEETHEART.
LET'S JUST HAVE FUN, OKAY?
WHIMPER

WHAT'S THIS?

LIFT

'WHIMPER'

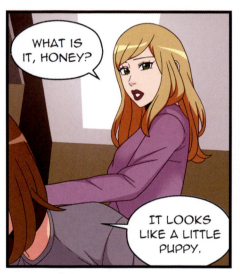

WHAT IS IT, HONEY?

IT LOOKS LIKE A LITTLE PUPPY.

I'M SORRY, BUT THAT PUPPY ISN'T UP FOR ADOPTION.

AHEM.

HE'S GOING TO BE TAKEN TO THE VET TO BE . . . HUMANELY DEALT WITH.

I DON'T UNDERSTAND.

I THOUGHT THIS WAS A "NO KILL" SHELTER.

IT IS, BUT WHEN A DOG HAS A SERIOUS ILLNESS, WE DON'T HAVE THE FUNDS TO TREAT THEM.

THE MOST HUMANE THING IS TO TAKE CARE OF THEM BEFORE THEY HAVE TO SUFFER.

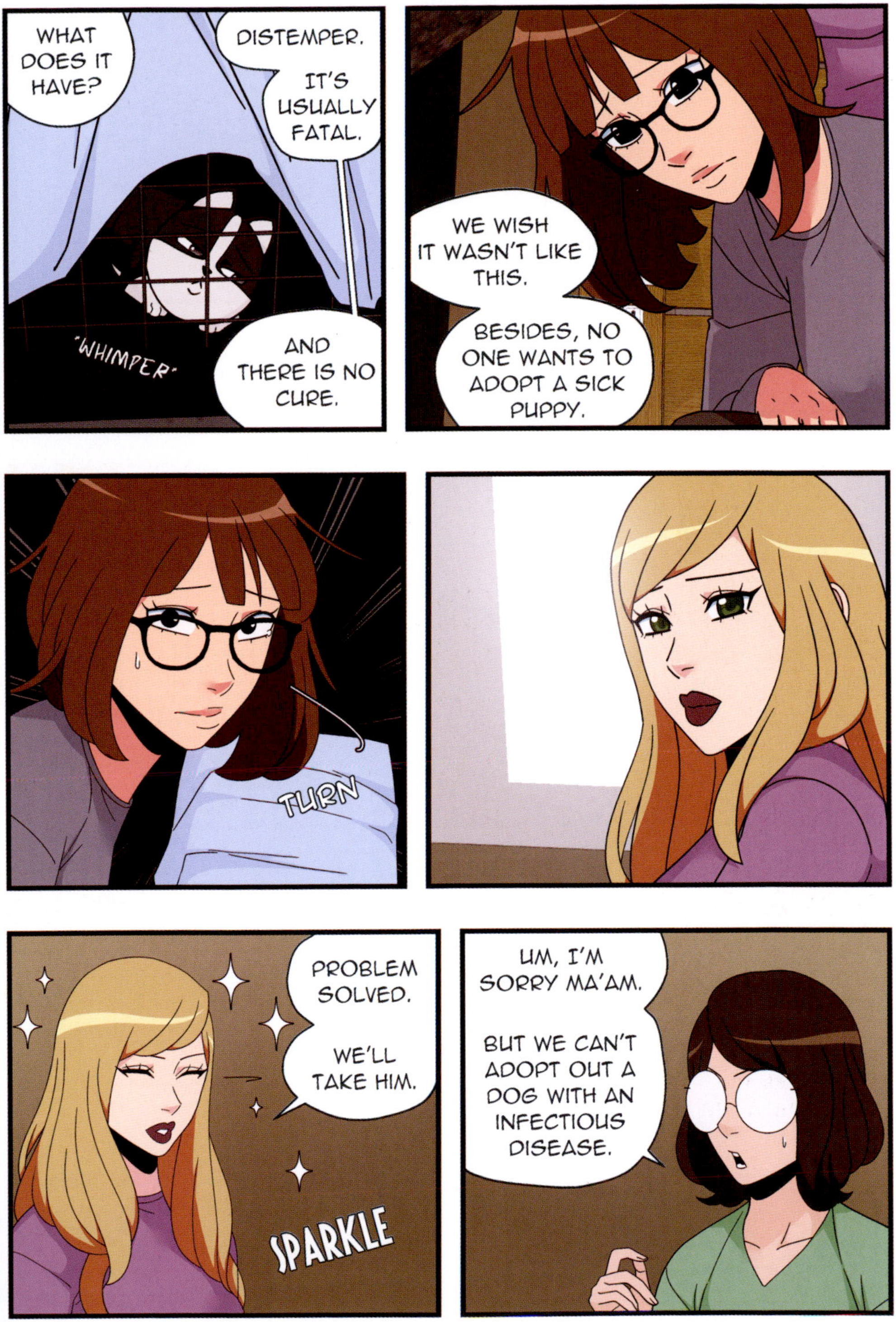
WHAT DOES IT HAVE?
DISTEMPER.
IT'S USUALLY FATAL.
"WHIMPER"
AND THERE IS NO CURE.
WE WISH IT WASN'T LIKE THIS.
BESIDES, NO ONE WANTS TO ADOPT A SICK PUPPY.
TURN
PROBLEM SOLVED.
WE'LL TAKE HIM.
SPARKLE
UM, I'M SORRY MA'AM.
BUT WE CAN'T ADOPT OUT A DOG WITH AN INFECTIOUS DISEASE.

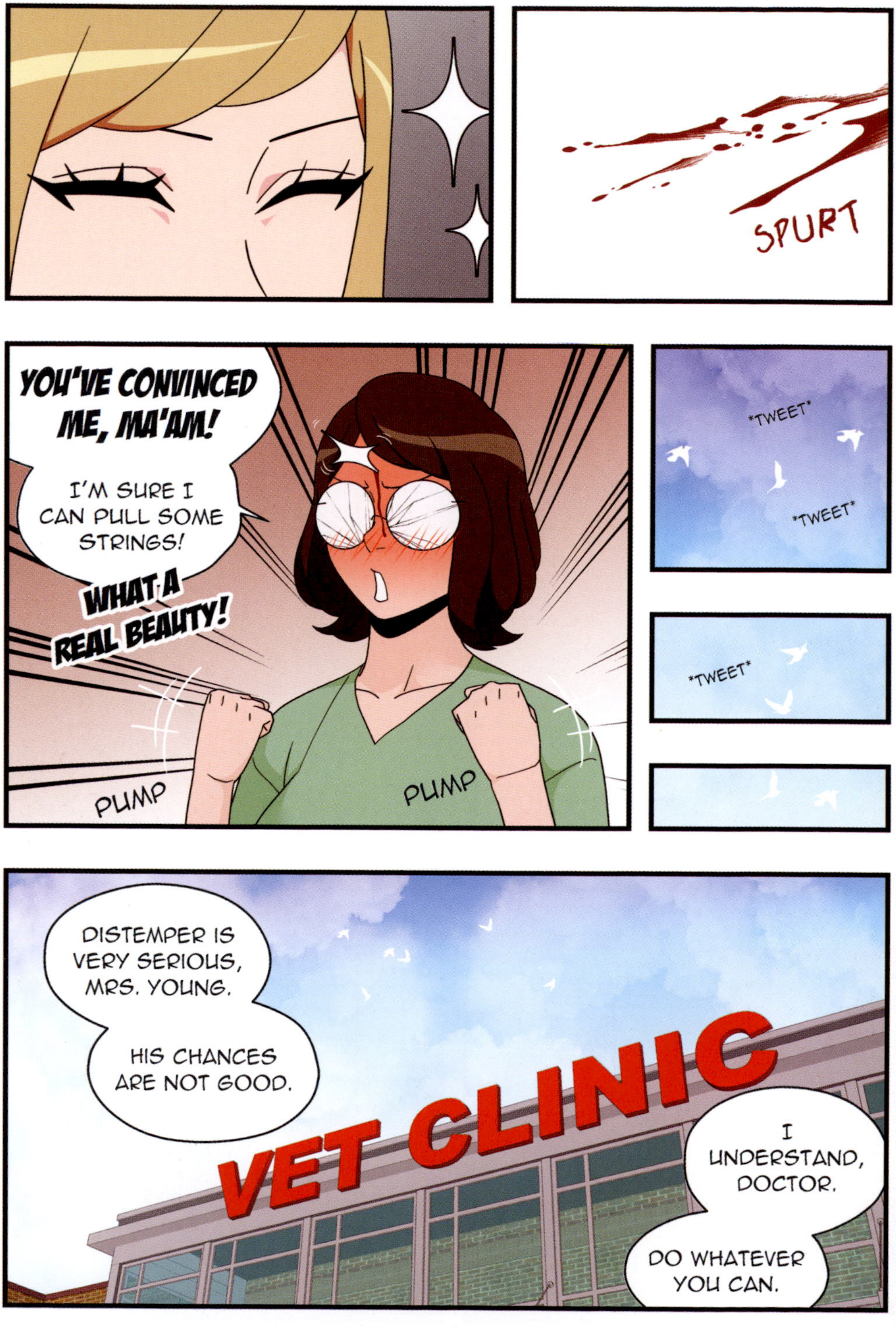
SPURT
YOU'VE CONVINCED ME, MA'AM!
I'M SURE I CAN PULL SOME STRINGS!
WHAT A REAL BEAUTY!
PUMP
PUMP
TWEET
TWEET
TWEET
DISTEMPER IS VERY SERIOUS, MRS. YOUNG.
HIS CHANCES ARE NOT GOOD.
VET CLINIC
I UNDERSTAND, DOCTOR.
DO WHATEVER YOU CAN.

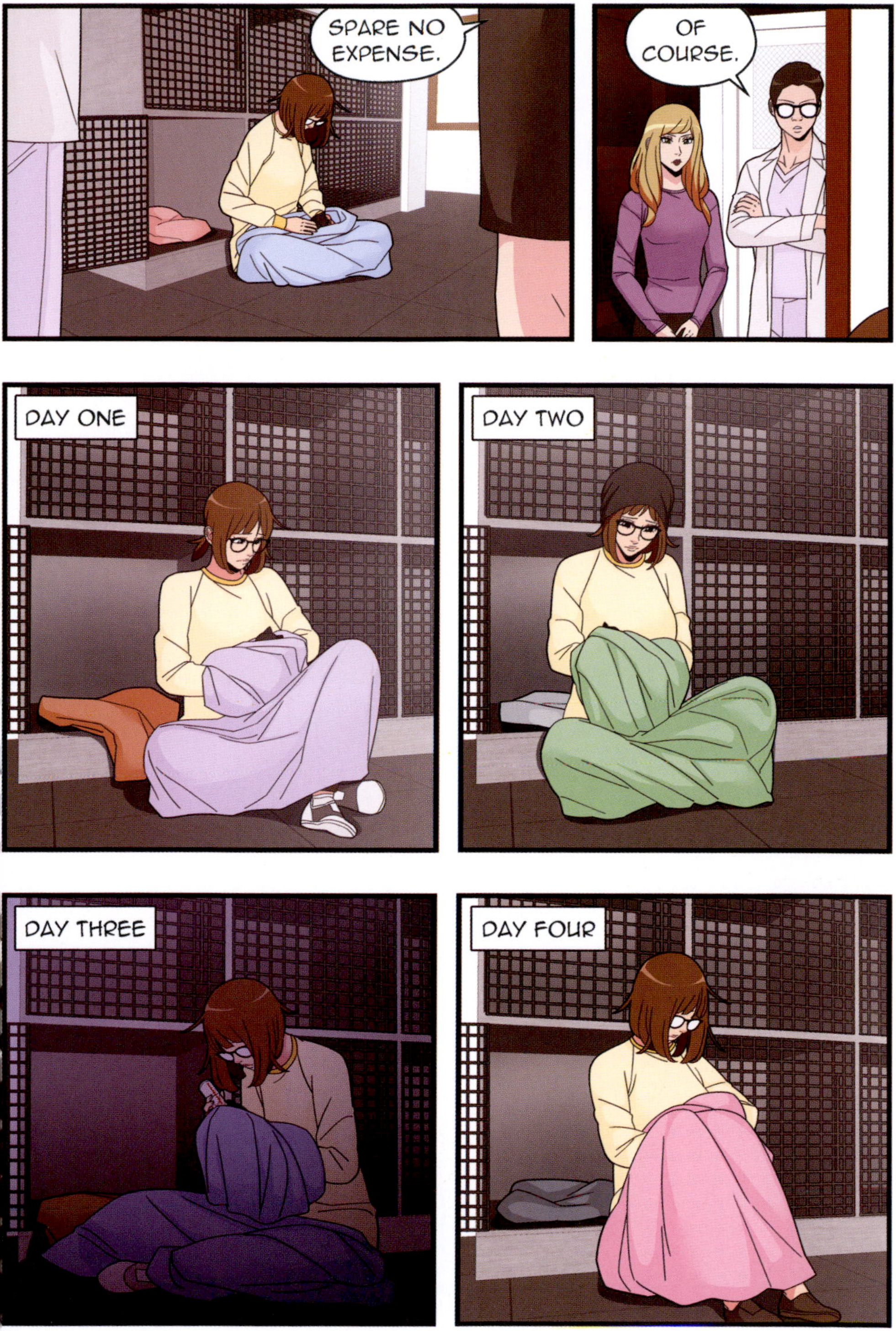
SPARE NO EXPENSE.
OF COURSE.
DAY ONE
DAY TWO
DAY THREE
DAY FOUR

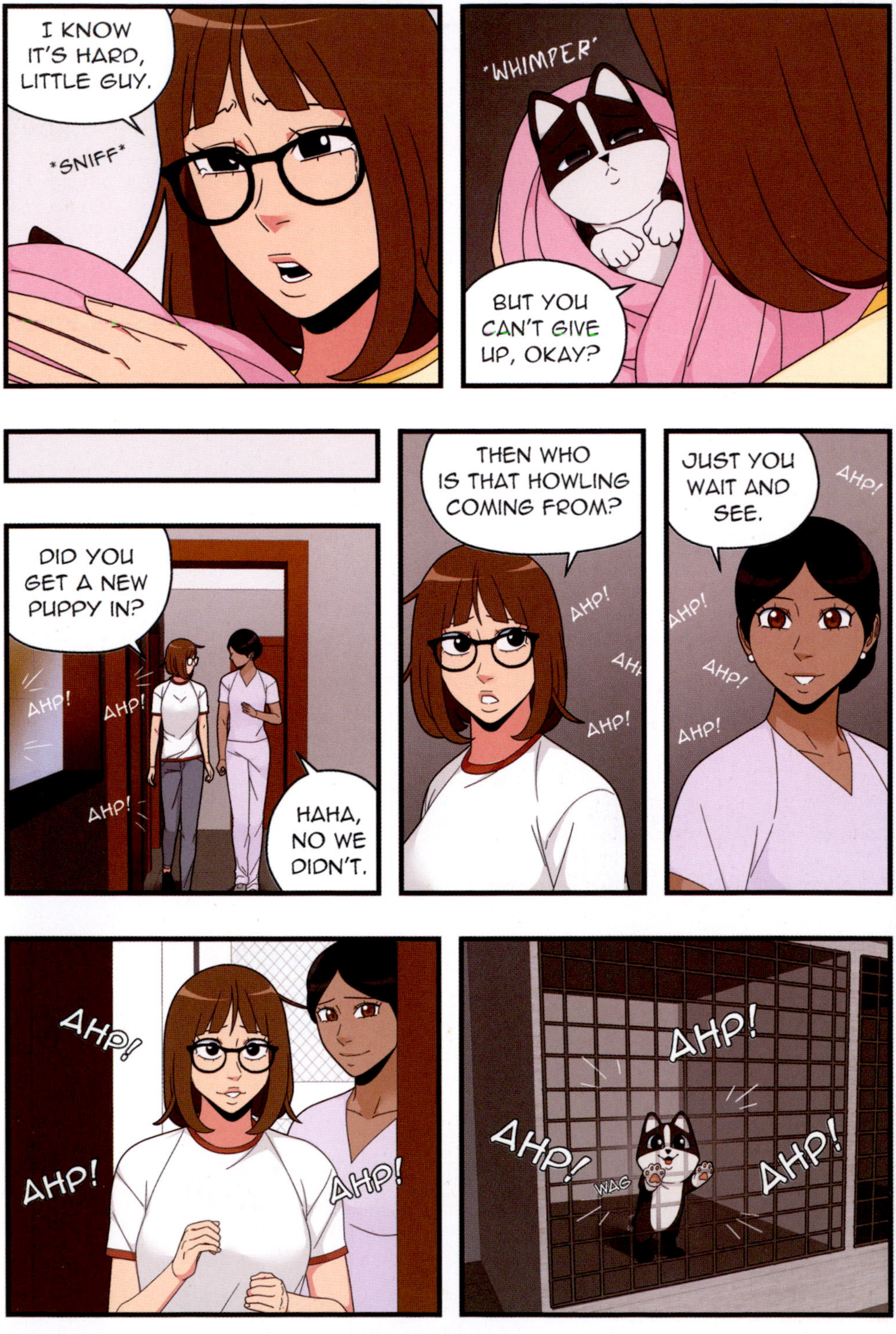
I KNOW IT'S HARD, LITTLE GUY.
SNIFF
WHIMPER
BUT YOU CAN'T GIVE UP, OKAY?
DID YOU GET A NEW PUPPY IN?
AHP!
AHP!
AHP!
HAHA, NO WE DIDN'T.
THEN WHO IS THAT HOWLING COMING FROM?
AHP!
AHP!
JUST YOU WAIT AND SEE.
AHP!
AHP!
AHP!
AHP!
AHP!
AHP!
AHP!
AHP!
AHP!
WAG
AHP!

BOWSER, AS A "WELCOME HOME" PRESENT, GRANDMA GOT YOU A LITTLE GIFT!

PANT *PANT*

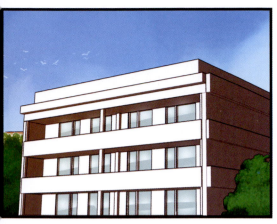

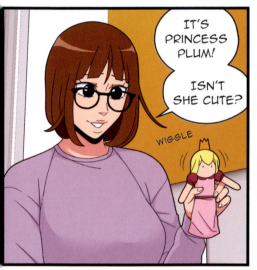

IT'S PRINCESS PLUM!

ISN'T SHE CUTE?

WIGGLE

GRANDMA GOT THIS BECAUSE IT LOOKS LIKE HER.

BUT I THINK IT'S PERFECT!

AHP!

WAG

AHP!
AHP!
AHP!
WAG
JIGGLE

AHP!

AHP!